CITY *of* DARK
H...

Now writing as James Conan, William Horwood and Helen Rappaport are both established authors.

William Horwood was a city and feature editor with the *Daily Mail* until, in 1978, he wrote the first of his now classic *Duncton Chronicles*, which became instant international bestsellers. His wide-ranging books since then have included the critically acclaimed memoir *The Boy with No Shoes*. William has been married three times, has six children and now lives in Oxford.

Helen Rappaport studied Russian at university and for many years worked as an actress in TV and films before turning to historical writing in the early 1990s. She is the author of books on Joseph Stalin, Queen Victoria and women social reformers. Her most recent titles are *No Place for Ladies: The Untold Story of Women in the Crimean War* (2007) and *Ekaterinburg: The Last Days of the Romanovs* (2008).

CITY *of* DARK HEARTS

HEARTS

JAMES CONAN

arrow books

This is a shortened and revised edition of a novel first published under the title *Dark Hearts of Chicago* by William Horwood and Helen Rappaport

Published by Arrow 2008
6 8 10 9 7 5

First published under the title *Dark Hearts of Chicago*
in Great Britain in 2007 by
Hutchinson
Random House, 20 Vauxhall Bridge Road,
London SW1V 2SA

www.rbooks.co.uk

Addresses for companies within The Random House Group Limited can be found at: www.randomhouse.co.uk/offices.htm

The Random House Group Limited Reg. No. 954009

A CIP catalogue record for this book
is available from the British Library

ISBN 9780099502173

The Random House Group Limited supports The Forest Stewardship Council (FSC), the leading international forest certification organisation. All our titles that are printed on Greenpeace approved FSC certified paper carry the FSC logo. Our paper procurement policy can be found at:
www.rbooks.co.uk/environment

Typeset by SX Composing DTP, Rayleigh, Essex
Printed and bound in Great Britain by CPI Bookmarque, Croydon, CR0 4TD

DAY ONE

Thursday October 19, 1893

I

Bubbly Creek

There are good times and bad times to dump a body in Bubbly Creek, as locals call the south fork of the Chicago River.

Winter's not much good because the Creek freezes over, so the evidence of your crime stays right where it falls. Summer's no better because the flow slows right up, the place smells bad and you don't want to go anywhere near it. If you do you'll soon work out why it's called Bubbly – the water's so polluted with bones and offal from the Union Stock Yard that it's busy fermenting with the rottenness beneath the surface.

Spring and Fall are best because that's when it flows, especially after rain, which ensures that the evidence of your crime drifts slowly away, out of sight and out of mind.

You hope.

One misty morning in October 1893, a body came to rest at Benson Street, opposite Mr Armour's glue factory and a couple of hundred yards from where the Creek comes to an end as it flows into the Chicago River proper. It lay there as soot descended gently on it from the furnaces of the Illinois Steel Company on the far side of the Creek.

An immigrant heading for the Union Stock Yard in

3

search of a day's hire noticed it at six, shook his head wearily and walked on by. Finding work was more important.

Finally, a barefoot boy, clambering over the mud looking for something to salvage among the washed up detritus along the shoreline, touched its bare back with his foot and then its face.

Then he peered a bit closer, holding his breath; and closer still, looking for any valuables, when suddenly it half opened an eye and let out a watery moan.

'Jesus, it's alive!' he screamed, toppling back into the mud.

Men came running over and pulled the body up onto the street but the women took over after that, shooing the men and boys away. The girls could stay if they liked, but at a distance.

She was female and wearing a torn and filthy dress that was thick with slime. The stocking on one leg was torn and round her ankle. The other leg was bare. Her dark hair was a mess made slimy with mud.

You didn't need to be a doctor to tell she was nearer dead than alive and you needn't have lived by the Creek for long to guess that she'd been right in it, and the water had got into her, in which case she'd be sure to fall sick and die later if not right away.

There was nothing about her that told who she was, why she was there, or why she was still alive. Nor could the women now gathered round the woman get any sense out of her with their questions: the gibberish she spoke was a madwoman's talk.

So they sent a boy to find a patrolman on 31st Street. When he arrived, he took one look at the woman and went and telegraphed Harrison Street Police Station for the wagon.

Eventually, at around 8.15, a square, high-sided

4

black wagon on four sturdy wheels arrived. It looked like a paddy wagon but everyone knew it was worse than that. A few mothers pushed their kids indoors, telling them it was unlucky to see the wagon standing there.

A uniformed man climbed out of the vehicle while the driver, the boss, got down and looked the woman over. Most people knew him in those parts. He was Padraic 'Donko' O'Banion and driving this vehicle was his day job. At nights he worked in a brothel on the Levee.

'She's twenty or so,' said Donko, adding, 'and she's been beat real bad.'

'Been for a swim,' said the other laconically.

'Client tried to kill her more likely,' said Donko.

He backed the wagon expertly round and then headed up to 31st and Throop Street for the run downtown. Folk looked away and got on with their business, but the boy who found the woman who had been a body stood there staring at the wagon and at the scratched and faded lettering on it.

He couldn't read but he knew what it said: *Cook County Insane Asylum.*

'Is that where they are taking her?' said the man who had first seen the woman earlier that morning, now returning the way he had come. He was new round here. He had the shaggy beard, the clothes and the accent of an immigrant from Eastern Europe. Now his eyes carried the despair of someone who had failed to get the day's work he so desperately needed.

'Not straight away,' said Donko. 'First they have to take her to the Detention Hospital and then, if it's a suicide attempt – and more'n likely it is – to the Insane Court,' said one of the women.

'Yeah, and then she'll go to Dunning,' added the

boy, spitting tobacco juice right on the sidewalk where she had been laid, 'so she ain't *never* coming back.'

They stood in silence staring after the black wagon for a minute or so. Everyone round here knew what being sent to the Insane Asylum out at Dunning meant. Then the man went one way and the boy another. Where the anonymous woman had washed up at the edge of the Creek nothing remained but a stain of red blood turning brown in the mud.

DAY TWO

Friday October 20, 1893

2

The Baker

Anna Jelena Zemeckis, only child of Janis Zemeckis, a Latvian baker on New York's Lower East Side, went missing in Chicago some time between 1.35 p.m. September 7, 1893, and 3.00 p.m. the same day. That was between the time she left Mrs Clark's Lunch Room at 145 Wabash Avenue and the time she was due to meet a friend at the World's Columbian Exposition at Jackson Park seven miles away on the city's South Side. An appointment she did not keep.

Anna was a modest girl, just twenty-one. She was gregarious, attractive and intelligent. Until only four months before she had been her father's mainstay in his small but well-respected and profitable bakery, responsible for keeping the accounts, as well as having a part-time job in the Aguilar Free Library on East Fifth Street.

Anna's departure for Chicago had come as a surprise; nobody in their little circle would have believed it possible that so loving and protective a father could let his daughter go to that monstrous city, of all places. Anna herself had often voiced her dislike of big city life and her desire to go and spend time on her Aunt Inga's farm up beyond Winnipeg on Lac du Bonnet in Canada. But this Zemeckis had refused; the hardship of rural life endured by his dead wife's family in Latvia, and now in Canada, were what he had wanted to leave behind when he emigrated. He had repeatedly refused his sister-in-law's request to send Anna to stay with them. For he was a man mindful of the future, of business and enterprise and what the World's Fair might offer by way of modernizing his own modest, but growing business. Anna must go as his representative.

So it was that, on Anna's twenty-first birthday in April 1893, Janis Zemeckis made an announcement to their Lutheran friends at church:

'I am sending Anna to Chicago,' he declared, with a look of pride and pleasure on his face. 'My brother-in-law Hendriks has written confirming that she can stay as long as she likes with him and his family and see everything there is at this great Fair. She will have time to discover new things and learn all she can, as well as working part-time for the Chicago Public Library, which has been arranged for her.

'Someone from every family in America should go to this great event and as I cannot be spared from our business Anna must go in my place!'

Anna was as astonished as she was overjoyed. She burst into tears and she and Janis held each other tight. Janis was a hard worker and a good man but it was rare for him to make displays of affection and generosity in front of others.

Anna's uncle, Hendriks Markulis, was her mother's brother. While her aunt, Inga, had married into good stolid farming stock and gone to Canada, Hendriks had been more ambitious and found a wife from an enterprising German family on Chicago's North Side with whom he now ran their hardware store. He and his wife had visited the Zemeckises twice in New York and were good, prosperous people. Liesel Markulis was active in the woman's temperance movement and Janis was certain they would offer Anna a home from home and ensure that she would be chaperoned at all times.

'It's not a holiday,' warned Janis later, 'but *work*. This great Exposition will have much that is new which we should know about; many technical and educational things. You will go; I can manage without you for two or three months. Your job at the library in Chicago will pay your way; but most of all you will learn, learn, learn.'

If Anna wept as she hugged her father, it was for joy; if he smiled with pride, it was because, after holding on to her so protectively for so long – too long perhaps – he felt he was doing the right thing in letting her go.

So it was that Anna Zemeckis, after being accompanied across to Jersey City on the ferry by her father, set off on the Columbian Express for Chicago one day in early May, preceded by a thousand instructions from Janis Zemeckis to the Markulises about when and where they were to meet her when she arrived at the Union Depot on Canal Street, twenty-six hours after leaving the East Coast.

All of which went perfectly, as did Anna's stay with the Markulises during the seventeen weeks that followed until, on September 8, Janis received a stark, heart-stopping telegraph from his brother-in-law:

'*Anna went missing yesterday. Have you heard from her?*'

Two days after that, September 10, Janis Zemeckis closed the doors of his bakery and took the first train to Chicago on which he had been able to get a seat. What he found when he got there and in the grim

11

weeks that followed gave him every reason to believe she must be dead.

On arrival he began searching the city for Anna. He placed advertisements in the papers, and he talked to the police who advised him to visit the morgue; he did so, daily, and saw terrible things there, but he did not find his daughter. He called on City Hall officials who advised him to check out the patients at the city hospitals. He did that too, and saw yet more terrible things, but he never found Anna.

He took the new Elevated Railroad from Congress Street to the site of the World's Fair at Jackson Park, his desperate eyes searching the crowds wherever he went. He never found her. Everywhere he went, he talked to people, and then more people, showing them Anna's picture. But all they could tell him was that people go missing in big cities, it happens every day, to young women especially.

Some disappear because they want to; some because they need to; some are abducted against their will, taken by men. It was terrible, truly terrible. But Janis Zemeckis refused to believe any of this of his Anna.

Nevertheless, he walked the red-light districts around the Levee asking questions. He got threatened every time, mugged twice and hospitalized once.

And then, two weeks later on September 26 and running out of funds, he reluctantly went back to New York.

He returned a week later, his business left in temporary hands. But when problems arose he was obliged to return once more to New York. He knew his business was beginning to die. He knew ten years of savings would run out. But he also knew that without Anna he had nothing, nothing at all.

The search came to its final and perhaps inevitable end in the second week of October with a telegraph from a Mr Freeman of the Cook County Hospital Morgue. It was the kind of message every parent dreads and none ever wants to receive.

A body had been brought in that appeared to match the physical description Zemeckis had left of his daughter. Could he arrange to put through a telephone call and help with the identification?

He did so.

Mr Freeman was kindly and diplomatic but the job had to be done. Was there anyone in Chicago who had known his daughter and might be willing to identify her?

Zemeckis named the Markulises.

Meanwhile . . . did Anna have any distinguishing features?

Zemeckis could barely speak. His hand trembled as he held the telephone which crackled and hummed at his ear and he could hardly bring himself to murmur into the mouth piece.

'How did she die?' he asked.

'A streetcar accident. Now . . .'

'She has . . . She always wore a crucifix but no other jewelry. . . . I wouldn't allow it.'

'Mr Zemeckis, I know this is hard. But could you describe the crucifix.'

'It was special to her. Nothing much. Grey metal, not real silver. It was her mother's and she . . .'

Zemeckis broke down.

'Sir, I need a better description. Its size, any particular decoration . . .'

Zemeckis did his best.

The silence that followed was the longest he had ever endured.

Then Mr Freeman came back on the line: 'I'm sorry, sir, but what you've described is pretty much the same as the crucifix this girl was wearing. But . . . we better wait for Mrs Markulis to come. Maybe . . .'

'If she's wearing that crucifix it's Anna,' said Zemeckis, his voice thin and bleak. 'I've never seen another one like it.'

They arranged for another call that evening.

When the connection came through it was Liesel Markulis. She was weeping.

'It's Anna, Janis, I'm sure of it,' she said, and that was all she needed to say.

Janis Zemeckis travelled to Chicago a final, desolate time on October 14, exhausted and heartbroken.

Liesel Markulis accompanied him to the potter's field outside the city where Anna had had to be temporarily buried. They put a few flowers on the grave marked with a temporary wooden cross and a number, and said a prayer.

They were not the only ones in that grim place and others arrived as they left, searching for Chicago's lost, forgotten and unidentified dead.

They went next to the morgue and met Mr Freeman. The first thing they were shown was the dress the body had been wearing. Any lingering doubts Zemeckis might have had evaporated. Though it was torn and blood-stained he recognized it at once, just as Mrs Markulis had done. It had been made by Anna herself.

Holding it in his hands, Zemeckis wept. But when he was shown the crucifix he fell silent, head slumped. It had been bought as a gift for Anna's Catholic mother during a religious pilgrimage in Latvia when she was a girl; Janis had handed it down to Anna on her mother's death.

No further confirmation was needed for Janis Zemeckis but when the morgue asked that he formally identify his daughter from photographs of the corpse he numbly agreed, words failing him.

He said nothing then, or for hours afterwards. Nor did he discuss with his sister-in-law the obvious question – what Anna might have been doing during the five weeks between her disappearance from their home and her tragic death on Michigan Avenue. He retreated into silence and asked for only one thing more – that Anna's body be exhumed so she might have a proper burial back home in New York.

This was arranged for two weeks' time. Janis Zemeckis finally returned home on October 17, his search over. He felt and looked a broken man. Anna was never coming back and he knew that he had failed her. Almost overnight it seemed he had lost his reason for living.

For two days he did not sleep. Nor did he open up his shop. He felt he never would again. What made it all the worse for him was the fact that it now seemed certain that Anna's disappearance had been of her own volition. It was bad enough that she had left the Markulis household without an explanation, but to make no attempt to contact him was both selfish and cruel.

Very soon, however, his inward grief gave way to outward anger – at Anna and at Chicago, a city which had failed to protect her. His anger deepened and for a few hours he was incoherent with rage.

Then it gave way to a different emotion: pity, forgiveness of a kind and a desire to warn other parents of the perils of allowing their daughters to venture forth to distant cities.

On October 19, having had a notice placed in the Chicago newspapers announcing Anna's death, Janis found himself in the Aguilar Free Library at 206 East Fifth Street, sitting, staring sightlessly at that day's copy of the New York *World*, doing nothing. He could not remember how he had got there and he saw he was not alone. Cities have many casualties.

Unable to suffer his loss and pain, anger and shame any longer and hoping to forget it for a little while through activity, he impulsively wrote a letter and put it in the mailbox.

The letter was addressed to the proprietor of the New York *World*, Mr Joseph Pulitzer, the greatest newspaper man of the age.

What Janis Zemeckis sent was rather more than a letter. It was a prayer, an agonized cry to other parents and a warning: *don't let your daughters out of your sight*. But if you must, *never* let them go to Chicago.

Naturally he had no hope his letter would ever be read or taken notice of. This was America and, angry and disillusioned as he had now become, he thought he knew what that meant: no-one would help, no-one would listen, no-one would offer comfort.

But Janis Zemeckis was wrong.

Someone did listen and someone did act.

DAY THREE

Saturday October 21, 1893

3

Emily Strauss

'Mr Pulitzer, sir, you have a visitor. A very insistent one. And she's female.'

It was just after twelve and Joseph Pulitzer was taking a break, in anticipation of his lunch and afternoon nap.

Seated in a vast wicker chair in his conservatory, a glass of water before him, neat piles of books and papers on a table nearby, he turned toward his secretary. His left eye was dull and half closed, his right was bright blue and seemed to see, though in fact it did not.

'What does she want, Mr Butes?' he said.

Arthur Butes was one of Pulitzer's four male secretaries. He was English, discreet and well-spoken with just that combination of learning, quickness and subservience that the great man liked. He hesitated briefly and then said, 'Well she hasn't much English, but as I understand it she insists she is a relative of the distant sort . . . the daughter of Mrs Pulitzer's niece . . .'

'Let Mrs Pulitzer see her then,' his employer said, turning away.

Butes was unruffled. 'She has specifically requested to see *you*, sir,' he continued with calm assurance. 'Indeed, she refuses to budge without doing so.'

The afternoon was a bright one after several days

19

of rain and though it was cold outside the sun made the conservatory pleasantly warm. Joseph Pulitzer sat thinking awhile, the light emphasizing the striking contrast between his thick brown hair and the red of his beard.

'Chatwold', his rented home at Bar Harbor, had fine views over the sea where his yacht, *Liberty*, was anchored. Joseph Pulitzer could see neither, but close up things were easier. The touch and aroma of his plants pleased him and the fresh sea breeze at open doors and windows helped if his throat and lungs were troubling him, which they often were.

He liked nothing worse than idleness. His great wealth had brought him no contentment, no peace: he was as he looked – restless, hungry to be doing, always imminently bored, permanently dissatisfied.

Butes had judged his employer's mood right that afternoon but it was no surprise that before proceeding any further Mr Pulitzer wanted some hard facts.

'So, Mr Butes, what exactly does her card say?'

'It says she's a Fraulein . . . Eva Berger, of . . .'

'Repeat that, Mr Butes. You're mumbling.'

'*Berger*, sir. Of Mulheim.'

'Address?'

'Ponitz Strasse, number 10.'

Pulitzer frowned.

'I don't believe it,' he said matter of factly.

'I'm inclined to agree, sir. She says she's just arrived from Europe, but she doesn't look like she has to me.'

'What's she look like?'

'Tall, fair-haired, handsome I would say. Perhaps twenty-two or three.'

'Intelligent?'

'Possibly. Bold certainly. She's not the kind of lady who will go *easily,* sir.'

'But she speaks real German?'

'Well, I'm no judge of the German tongue, Mr Pulitzer, but it strikes me there's a certain oddity about her accent . . .'

'You'd better show her in then. But if she looks as if she's going to cause trouble, remove her immediately!'

Out-of-work journalist Emily Strauss had spent the last six fruitless days learning the ways of New York journalism fast. It was harder, meaner and a deal more ruthless than anything she had ever experienced on the Pittsburgh *Daily Echo* in her past twelve unhappy months as a cub reporter – a job from which she had been fired a month before. New York promised much more – or had seemed to until she started tramping Newspaper Row in search of a reporter's job and had received nothing but a score of rejections.

So she stopped, right there on the sidewalk, and asked herself a simple question: what would Mr Joseph Pulitzer, the top newspaperman in the world, have done in her situation when he was first starting out as a news reporter?

The answer was obvious: beard the lion in his den. In fact it's precisely what he *did* do if she remembered right. So she would do the same. Heading straight for the rail depot, she spent her last few dollars on getting from Manhattan to Ellsworth and then a hack out to Bar Harbor and Mr Pulitzer's house. Time enough to work out how to con her way past the gateman.

Butes came back through the door with Emily.

Joseph Pulitzer stood up to offer her his right hand, and then, after a brief exchange in English, they both sat down.

Emily eyed him nervously, wondering how long she would be able to keep the game up. Joseph Pulitzer was altogether more intimidating than she had expected: he was taller, his presence was powerful, his supposedly blind gaze was – or seemed – penetrating and his face bristled with intelligence.

She decided to let him take the lead.

'Von *Mulheim?*' he said, his emphasis conveying general skepticism about her story.

Since he spoke in German she replied in it. It was, she guessed, about her only trump card. The rest were all poor ones rubbed up to look good.

'Ja, Herr Pulitzer, ich . . .'

'Von Ponitz Strasse, im nord der stadt?'

'Jahrwohl, ich bin . . .'

She stopped, taken unawares at her own sudden inability to keep the pretense going. Not that she couldn't speak fluent German; no, her father had insisted she always speak it at home. It was just that now she had finally made it into the great Joseph Pulitzer's presence, her nerve was failing her. Her stunt felt cheap and tawdry. There was nothing for it but to come clean and hope he was indeed the man his own newspapers said he was, that he would listen to what she had to say, weigh it on its merits and give her the assignment she craved.

Pulitzer immediately picked up on her hesitation.

'Let's talk English, Miss Berger. Only that isn't your real name, is it? And you're no relative of my wife's, newly arrived from Germany either, are you?

Your German's good but it has an American twang. Even Mr Butes here, and he's English, picked that up. How long have you lived in America?'

'I was born here, sir,' she admitted after a pause, looking at the floor, 'in Pittsburgh. My father was a steelworker.'

'Was?'

'Died last year.'

'In the Homestead strike?'

'Yes, sir.'

She studied his face, but expressive though it was, it looked inscrutable now.

After a pause he said, 'I reckon I'm a pretty good judge of character.'

'I expect you must be, Mr Pulitzer.'

'And I would say, on the strength of this brief acquaintance, which is not going to last much longer, that you're a willing liar when you need to be, as stubborn as a mule and you don't give up on anything, which must be trying for those who know you. Am I right?'

'Pretty much, sir. But from the descriptions I've read of you in your own newspapers, sounds to me as though you've just described yourself.'

He looked surprised at her audacity rather than amused, eyeing her in that strange, disconnected way of his and reached out unerringly for his glass of water, from which he slowly took a sip or two.

She waited, judging he was a man who liked to set the pace. She would have liked to put on her most charming of expressions for his benefit but knew it would have no effect.

'So why are you *really* here?' said Pulitzer, beginning to sound bored.

'I wrote to you, I . . .'

'Lots of folk write to me, *lots*.'

'I telegraphed . . .'

'Folk do that too. Lots of them.'

'I visited the offices of the *World* and . . .'

'How far did you get?'

'Not very.'

Pulitzer nodded and smiled.

Emily paused and decided to take a different, more direct, tack. Her time was running out and she'd better get to the point fast.

'I just wanted a tryout,' she said simply.

Pulitzer let out a groan and turned toward Butes.

'If she's what I'm beginning to fear she is, Mr Butes – a cub reporter from out of town – you're going to get fired.'

He turned back to Emily.

'Well?'

'I *am* from out of town but I'm no cub. I've done twelve months on the Pittsburgh *Echo* and I've just finished a stint in Chicago, working women's angles at the World's Fair. I resigned. Mr Coombs wouldn't give me a raise or a byline.'

It was her turn to pause. Then she added, a smile in her voice, 'I reckon that all adds up to Mr Butes here maybe having his pay cut but keeping his job.'

Pulitzer laughed aloud. Then he leaned forward and his expression turned mean.

'You know that one word from me can ruin your journalistic career forever?'

'I do. But I also know that one word from you can give it the kind of leg-up no-one else can,' Emily replied coolly. 'I thought it a risk worth taking and that if you heard me out you might agree!'

Pulitzer settled back in his chair, scowling.

Emily's heart thumped. She knew she was about to be either given her chance or thrown out but she couldn't guess which.

'You better make it good,' he said with a scowl.

She tried but she could see he wasn't listening, not really. He nodded, scowled, put the tips of his fingers together and sighed. She poured out her ideas to him but he reacted like any editor on any paper.

'You know what?' she said finally.

He sat up, paying attention.

'This is a waste of my time and it's a waste of yours. What I say won't convince you. But what I *write*, and how I write it, will. I know it.'

'So what do you suggest?'

'Give me a tryout. Right here and now. Choose a subject and I'll write about it . . .'

Pulitzer raised a hand and turned to Butes.

'Where's the latest post from readers?'

'Right here, sir.'

'Give it to the lady.'

Butes handed Emily a pile of twenty or so letters from the table nearby.

'I like to stay in touch with what my readers have to say and they like to stay in touch with me,' growled Pulitzer. 'Here's the latest batch. I'm going to take a little walk around my garden for about a quarter of an hour or so. That's the time you've got to go through these letters and come up with something worth writing. Let's see if you're as good as you think you are.'

As he got up and headed for the door into the garden on Butes's arm, Pulitzer called back at her:

'A quarter of an hour. After that I expect you to leave.'

'Thank you, sir,' she responded demurely.

'By the way,' he added, 'you never told me your real name.'

'Emily Strauss,' she said.

4
Far Side

Cook County Insane Asylum, or Dunning as Chicagoans called it, after the farmer who had owned the land on which it was built after the Civil War, lay across the prairie eleven miles northwest of the city center.

It was a vast, forbidding establishment newly rebuilt in gothic style, complete with a nicely turreted gatehouse, to make it look solid and respectable.

Close up, it was anything but. Not that it mattered if you were an inmate; once in you didn't need to come out again because Dunning was entirely self-sufficient and had everything, from its own bakery to a separate burial ground.

It was originally built in the spirit of public philanthropy to house the poor on one side and the mad on the other. Over the years they got all mixed up. The poor got to look after the mad and when the poor fell sick it sometimes went the other way about.

No wonder that kids in Chicago who didn't do what their parents told them were warned, 'Be careful, or you're going to Dunning.'

It gave them nightmares; nightmares that reminded them of the virtues of obedience and the fact that

26

those who do wrong on this earth may find themselves in hell sooner than they think.

'Jane Doe' – as they had named the woman from Bubbly Creek on arrival, not knowing her real name – realized she was in hell the moment she arrived at Dunning. Hell in the shape of Maureen Riley was there to greet her.

Riley was in charge of what they called 'Far Side', the grimmest, oldest and most run-down part of Dunning. Stone-built, damp, broken-windowed and freezing cold most of the time, Far Side was the part visitors, even governors, never got to see. In her own way Riley was as skilled as any alienist and as clever as any surgeon. Certainly the results she got were cheaper and far more dependable. This was because she ruled Far Side by fear.

It had big wards and small wards, iron doors and wooden ones, nicely studded with metal rivets. It had a first floor reception that conveyed a congenial enough atmosphere, but for the rest – upstairs and down – it was medieval in feel, condition and appearance and in the basement there were cells so far back, so thick-walled, so secluded and lost in a maze of corridors and walkways that the most agonized groan or loudest scream would never have been heard.

As for the pitiable cries of the abandoned mad and the pauper sick, upstairs or down, they were lost in the drip drip drip of the fetid drains and the creaking of hinges and boards and spy-holes that few knew were even there.

This was Riley's domain as it had been her father's before her, and his father's before that.

Far Side was imbued with the vile odor of an evil

family whose pleasure was control and whose middle name was callousness.

Maureen Riley was tall, like her father, a shade under six feet. Her arms were a man's, her hands too. And her face was a granite block with pig eyes.

Her upper lip was stubbly with hair.

Her teeth were stained with tobacco.

Her breath stank of liquor.

She knew how to put fear into the most difficult of inmates, and to control them physically and mentally.

When the woman from Bubbly Creek (as Riley thought of her) had arrived two days before she grabbed her by the hair and arm by way of welcome and, on the principle that all new inmates were potential troublemakers, crashed her into the stone upright of the door into the building and then dragged her up some steps, two at a time, before hauling her bodily through a ward of eighty women, who stared and laughed and dribbled and spat.

They watched the woman's humiliation with the smug looks of those who know that they are not about to be punished but who know what lies in store for the one who is. Riley reached an isolation room, opened the door and threw the woman in. She left her there a few hours.

It was a procedure that had a marvelous subduing effect on everybody, lunatic, pauper, hysteric and wanton alike. They all emerged from the experience quieter than when they began it.

Two days had passed and the woman was subdued.

She was already scheming to get out.

But she knew it would help if she could remember what had happened and stop feeling sick from the poisoned water of the Creek and remember her own name.

Nothing was designed to make her feel good.

The wake-up call was the rap of a nightstick on the metal bars of the window and the women got up fast for fear of being beaten.

Breakfast was no more than grits, stale bread and bad coffee. Now . . .

'*Jane!*' yelled Riley, grabbing the arm of the woman from Bubbly Creek, 'Jane, you're goin' to the doctor. Put this shift on and come with me.'

For some reason Riley had taken against 'Jane'. There was a look in her eyes that came close, she declared, to insubordination. So she had hit her every time she passed her and that morning made her do jobs like cleaning up the vomit and emptying the slops and de-lousing the bolsters just to show her who was boss.

Jane didn't complain. Her memory was beginning to come back to her, even if the events leading up to her falling in the Creek were still a blank.

As Riley led her out of Far Side, she grasped the opportunity of trying to work out the hospital's layout, not easy in such a huge establishment. But she had caught a glimpse of the prairie from the windows and from that and what the women on her ward had said she had an idea of where she was relative to the outside world and the direction in which Chicago lay. She made a mental note too of the fact that somewhere near, though out of sight, she heard the chuff-chuff and whistle of a locomotive and the shouts of men.

Then Riley slammed open a door right in front of her and she was inside again, this time in what they called 'Main Building'. She was told to climb a flight of stairs. She did so obediently, aware of Riley's wheezing, aware of the smell of antiseptic, polish and urine all at one go. Better than the malodorous air of Far Side.

After a ten-minute wait in a freezing corridor Riley shoved her into the doctor's examination room. Anna stumbled, then righted herself. The moment she looked up and saw the doctor standing there in the middle of the room a shiver went through her.

He was of medium height and thin, with eyes so dark and expressionless behind his spectacles that it was hard to tell where the pupils ended and the rest began. They had a nasty glitter to them.

His mouth was a scissor-snip in pinched pale skin, his face clean-shaven, his nose pointed. His thin, dark, neatly trimmed hair was lightly greased with a lotion that gave out the scent of lemons.

He wore a jacket, waistcoat and pants in the style of an East Coast medical consultant. His shoes were all polished and squeaky. He wasn't more than twenty-nine or thirty but he looked like a man for whom the financial rewards of a successful medical career were already coming his way.

'I am Dr Morgan Eels,' he said, 'and I'm going to make you better. This is my assistant, Mr Mould.'

Eels's voice had the edge of oiled steel to it, his brief smile was like a momentary break in bleak midwinter.

Dr Eels, who had only recently been appointed as the Insane Asylum's Deputy Medical Superintendent, stood silently, observing his latest patient. From her physiognomy, on which subject he had made himself a diagnostic expert, he was certain she was of low immigrant stock. Probably Bohemian or something like it.

'What is her name?'

Eels addressed this to Riley and his voice was sharp and unpleasant, its affected accent more English than American.

Riley explained that no-one knew her name including even the patient.

'Forgot 'erself,' said Riley, 'or won't say. The Court sent her over without one. Hoped you'd find it out, I expect.'

Still not moving, Eels examined the woman for a full minute more from where he stood.

'Where did they find her?'

'She was the one they fished out of Bubbly Creek two days ago.'

Eels eyed his patient some more.

'Turn round,' he commanded her.

'Jane' seemed slow to move so Riley gave her a shove.

'By herself, if you please,' said Eels sternly.

His examinations had method and purpose. He liked to see how patients responded to his instructions.

'Turn round again,' he said finally.

The woman did so, aware of the doctor and the orderly staring and of Riley looming behind her. She had been uneasy from the first but she felt even more so now. She tried to pull the ill-fitting shift closer to her.

'Remove it,' said Eels.

His examination was thorough but she stayed quiet.

Only when he pulled back a curtain to reveal a camera on a tripod did she react.

'Please, no,' she said, covering her modesty with her hands.

'Don't be silly,' he snapped.

His camera was Dr Eels's pride and joy, a valuable tool in furthering his study of the physiognomy of the mentally ill. Convinced that the cause of madness was physical, what better way of finding a cure than by understanding the mad through a study of their physical shape?

Ignoring the woman's further protests he and Mr Mould took photographs from all angles, especially of her head.

'Good,' said Eels finally. 'Now put your shift back on. Take her back to her ward, Riley. I will not need her again today.

As he said this he was watching the woman closely. He saw her relax, he saw her breathe more easily. He watched as she headed with Riley for the door.

'Stop!' he called out at the last moment.

'*Do you remember your name?*' he said, as the woman turned, his voice sharp and commanding once more. He took up his clipboard and silver propelling pencil. 'Eh?'

He looked hard as if he could read her thoughts.

'I . . .'

Even had she been able to remember it, she knew she must not say it. 'I . . .'

But she did not know why.

'Well?' he said softly, the silver pencil glinting in his hand, the lens of his spectacles flashing too.

'I . . . can't remember.'

'Oh, but I think you do,' said Dr Eels coming closer.

I don't know it, mustn't say it, I mustn't, I . . .

'Well?' he purred.

His eyes were silvery pits behind the lenses of his spectacles.

It was then she finally remembered her name.

Anna Zemeckis, the baker's daughter screamed inside herself in relief and terror, *but I mustn't say it.*

'I can't remember my name,' she said, flushing at the lie.

'I think you can and that you will,' said Eels, studying her. He was frowning. 'Eh?'

'I don't know my name,' said Anna Zemeckis stubbornly.

'Take her away, Riley,' said Eels with a look of distaste. 'We will continue tomorrow.' He would get her name out of her if he had to cut it out with a scalpel.

Eels smiled thinly at the thought. Preeminence as a brain surgeon was his ultimate aspiration. Dr Gottleib Burckhardt had already shown in Berlin how effective surgical intervention in the lobes of the brain could be. Not in all cases, it was true, but pioneers must take risks.

Eels did not like it when a patient refused to yield to his demands but he felt himself to be too much of an objective scientist to let personal feelings get in the way, especially in challenging cases like that of the woman from Bubbly Creek.

The simple fact was that the unreasonable obduracy exhibited by some patients was, in his view, a certain sign of willful madness. This made the search for a cure at once so difficult and so urgent, given the rising numbers of patients in insane asylums across America, especially in cities such as Chicago with a high intake of immigrants.

For this reason it was Dr Eels's intention in the coming days to operate on twenty or so patients using Burckhardt's Procedure. He could wish for a better, more sophisticated approach, but needs must . . .

He took out his propelling pencil and twisted it slightly to get a fresh bit of lead. Then he surveyed the clipboard of forms and lists on his desk, pulling out one from the bottom and clipping it to the top.

Trouble was, he still did not have the name of the woman from Bubbly Creek, and Eels was meticulous about keeping records, especially for important experiments of the kind he had now decided she should be part of. He did not like gaps and he did not take kindly to being bested.

'I *will* have her name,' he whispered as he put the clipboard back in place on his desk.

5

Assignment

BAR HARBOR, MAINE Saturday October 21, 1893   12.40 PM

It was the very first letter Emily read that had spoken to her, though she skimmed the others through just to be sure, before coming right back to that one.

It was short and stark and sad.

It was from a Mr Janis Zemeckis, a Latvian baker on the Lower East Side. He'd been in America ten years. His only daughter had disappeared in Chicago six weeks previously and had only now turned up again – apparently killed in a streetcar accident. He had written begging Mr Pulitzer to warn his readers not to make the mistake he had made of letting his child go off to the World's Fair in that terrible place, a city that was no better than the wild frontier, where bad things happened.

'What's the story, Miss Strauss?' asked Joseph Pulitzer when he returned.

'The dangers of the big city for single women,' she said simply.

Pulitzer looked dubious. 'Women in cities have been vulnerable since time immemorial. That's what *happens* to them. It's an old story.'

'But it hasn't been done through the eyes of those left behind, not through the eyes of a man like Mr Zemeckis,' said Emily, holding up his letter. 'Nor through the eyes of others like him who've lost their loved ones. There's been a cover up about this in Chicago. Mayor Harrison doesn't want bad news ruining things for the World's Fair. Crime's gone up since long before it kicked off in May but you wouldn't know it from what you read in the papers. All the papers want to print is how big and great and modern Chicago is and how revolutionary all that stuff is that they have on display at Jackson Park. I may not be a Chicagoan but I've walked its streets and I can tell you it's not all pretty and modern and going places by any means.'

'But it's all been done before,' repeated Pulitzer, stubbornly. 'You can warn all you like but girls are still going to head off to the city and predators of all kinds – good and bad, wicked and worse – will still be there waiting for them.'

'Yes, and they're mainly men! No wonder your editors don't run stories like this. They're men too!'

'All in all, you don't have a very cheerful view of the male of the species, do you, Miss Strauss?'

'I have a more cheerful view of the female, Mr Pulitzer. Otherwise I wouldn't be standing here right now asking you to send me to Chicago. Let me chase this story and come up with something that the gripman on a New York streetcar and his wife want to read because they both understand it and it grabs their hearts. Let me get to the truth of this girl's story and others like it and you'll have a story that's worth printing. Send me to Chicago.'

Pulitzer said nothing, he was thinking.

'The Fair ends when precisely?' he finally asked.

'Thirtieth of this month,' said Emily. 'Nine days' time.'

He thought some more; Emily held her breath and stayed right where she was. Pulitzer had made stubbornness pay. She could too.

He relented.

'That should give you time enough to investigate Mr Zemeckis's story for the *World* and turn it into something worth reading on the 30th.'

Emily's eyes widened, but she kept her nerve.

'I'll need an advance,' she said boldly. 'I'm out of funds.'

'Our men get paid after the event, by the space they fill.'

'But I still need money to do the story,' Emily said firmly.

'Then I'll put you on our standard tryout rate– $15 a week, plus expenses. And be sure you account for everything.'

There was a very long pause indeed, as Emily weighed up what to her was a disappointing offer. But before she could protest, Pulitzer added.

'That's the deal, Miss Strauss. Mr Butes will telegraph our City Editor, Charles Hadham, to discuss your assignment. Tell him to make time to see her in the office tomorrow, Arthur.'

36

Joseph Pulitzer stood up and stretched out his hand.

'He didn't even ask to see my press clippings,' grumbled Emily as Arthur Butes showed her out. 'So what exactly do I have to do to get a permanent job with him?'

'You really want that, don't you?'

She nodded.

Butes looked at her and then at the letter from Janis Zemeckis that she still clutched tightly in her hand.

'You must find out what happened to the girl, Miss Strauss. That's the only way. *Find out what happened, get your story in by the deadline and tell it to the world!*'

DAY FOUR

Sunday October 22, 1893

6

Audit

The National Convention of any well-run organization, whatever the delegates may think, is no place for serious decision-making, because democracy and public debate have a nasty way of upstaging those who like to run the show.

The politically astute and influential members of the Audit Committee of the Old America Association were well aware of this. They generally met a few days or so ahead of the Association's two-day Convention in private chambers, so policies and elections could be neatly stitched up before it ever started.

Because the OAA's 1893 Convention was slated to be such a special one, it being that organization's twenty-fifth anniversary and also being the year of the World's Fair, it had long since been decided to hold it in Chicago's newest and finest theatre, the Auditorium on the corner of Michigan Avenue and Congress Street, on October 27th and 28th, two days before the Fair's end.

The place chosen for the all-important meeting of the Audit Committee was a prestigious one: the twelfth floor of Chicago's vast, new twenty-two-storey Masonic Temple, on State.

This year a key decision was going to be who should succeed the retiring president, Jenkin Lloyd

41

Rhys, the New York civil engineer and inspiration behind the founding of the Old America Association. But that decision was closely linked to another equally contentious one: what should the OAA's stance be on the immigration problem, as it now was perceived. The OAA, like the Audit Committee, was pretty well divided down the middle between the Rhys faction, which favored a laissez-faire approach to immigration, and the faction led by Paul Hartz, the OAA's Executive Vice-President, and his son-in-law Gunther Darke, both of whom demanded a tougher stance on immigration from Eastern Europe. Most agreed it didn't look like their day had yet come.

But as the clock chimed ten the Rhys faction discovered that it had a problem. Jenkin Lloyd Rhys had not yet arrived.

Paul Hartz put in a personal call to Rhys's hotel. He had not been seen since the night before and was not in the hotel now. Hartz therefore exercised his right and took the chair.

Alarmed by Rhys's disappearance, several senior members of the OAA saw at once that with the coming election of a new President this might well change things, weakening the position of the President's allies while strengthening that of Hartz and his anti-immigration faction. They surmised that this was an unexpected bonus Hartz could not have foreseen but one which, if he was clever, he could make use of.

A short time later, after Hartz had briskly moved the Committee through the previous meeting's Minutes and Matters Arising they moved on to finance, his own area of interest. It was all good news.

When the issue of Rhys's successor came up Hartz dealt with it smoothly but to his side's advantage.

'Had Mr Rhys been here then I am sure we could have resolved this issue. We all know who his nominee is . . .'

Hartz turned to Chester W. Allen, the OAA's long-term Honorary Secretary and Rhys's closest friend and ally, and smiled warmly. The two men loathed each other.

'. . . but I think Mr Allen would agree with me that we should now defer the matter of succession until Mr Rhys has joined the meeting . . .'

Chester Allen, a Manhattan lawyer of some eminence but also considerable dullness, was forced to agree. This was not the outcome of the meeting he would have wished for and his growing sense of unease at Rhys's absence mounted.

Where the hell was he?

Nothing more was said, but the smirks of the anti-immigration, pro-Hartz faction, who now had the upper hand, were unmistakable.

7

Zemeckis

NEW YORK Sunday October 22, 1893   12.00 PM

At noon Emily Strauss called on Mr Janis Zemeckis. She did this ahead of visiting the *World*'s offices on Park Row in Lower Manhattan in the afternoon, feeling she needed to show she had already begun work on the story.

The Zemeckis Bakery was located on the Lower East Side just off Mulberry Street. But when she got there, it was closed, the shop door locked and the business for sale.

A side door led to apartments above, while three steps down from street level there was a window which gave access and light to a basement where she guessed the baking was done.

She got some background from a tenant on the top floor. Mrs Kopecky was a Czech widow, a cigar maker from whose rooms there came a strong smell of tobacco.

Yes, she confirmed, Zemeckis owned the building but was in debt to the bank for it. His daughter was dead, or gone. Now the man himself was as good as dead too, his business for sale. But what business? *He* was the business. Good bread, healthy bread, the best she knew. But where was Janis Zemeckis now? He spent his days wandering the streets, sitting in parks, reading newspapers, filling in time, trying to forget the unforgettable.

His daughter Anna Jelena? Such a good girl. A good, strong Latvian girl who was quiet and modest, studied English properly, and could read and write so well she had got herself a job as a librarian.

Emily eventually found Janis Zemeckis outside the Aguilar Free Library on East Fifth Street. He was a pale man, hunched and shrunken rather than small, seeming unable to make up his mind how to cross the busy street as horse cars, trams, drays and carts rushed on by in either direction. She had never seen such sadness in a face, such despair. She noticed how he searched the faces of the passing crowd – still hopelessly seeking his daughter.

His eyes were shadowed, his mouth thin and each

cheek was etched with a vertical line from a lifetime of early rising and hard physical work in sunless basements.

'You wrote to Mr Joseph Pulitzer,' she began.

He looked hopeful, too hopeful.

'Mr Pulitzer thought that maybe we should tell our readers about your story . . . about how you lost Anna.'

He nodded his head and said, 'In my letter I said to him, "Mr Pulitzer, I lost my Anna but that is not why I write. I looked for her in Chicago, everywhere, and nobody wanted to know or to help. If America does not care to look after its young people what *does* it care for? My Anna, my child, was taken and nobody can tell me why. When I finally found her it was too late and she was dead. Maybe if people had been more helpful I would have found her alive. These things I said. What is your name, young lady?'

'I'm sorry. Emily Strauss.'

He reached out a hand formally and shook hers.

'Mr Janis Zemeckis,' he said unnecessarily. He looked hard at her with intelligent eyes and said, 'You are a reporter?'

'Yes.'

'Miss Strauss, it is not just young women. Men also. Children too. The city is full of predators and people disappear. Hundreds of them. Can you imagine? And no-one cares.'

He pulled a small photograph from his jacket pocket and proffered it to Emily.

It showed a girl like a hundred thousand others – dark, thick curly hair pinned up under a modest little hat; a good young figure in a pretty day dress with lace insets and wearing a distinctive crucifix – the one

45

whose discovery in the morgue had confirmed for Mr Zemeckis that his daughter was dead.

She was by no means a beauty, her face being solid and rather plain, but she had the same intelligence in her eyes as her father and something he did not have any longer, a belief in life, a joy in living. A good daughter and, had she had the chance, a good wife and mother in her own turn.

Back on Mulberry Street, the shop, as well as the bakery below, were clean, tidy, but almost bare.

'The better to sell it,' he explained.

'You don't want to make bread anymore?'

He shook his head firmly.

'An unhappy baker bakes poor bread. I came to America to forget that I had lost my wife and my son. Now America has stolen my daughter and my livelihood. Where do I go now? I don't know. I show you Anna's room . . .'

They had lived together in the apartment above the shop which was modest but comfortable.

Zemeckis needed little prompting to talk. He told her about Anna and why he had sent her to Chicago.

At one point he paused and said quietly, 'If I had known what a wicked, sinful city Chicago was – if I had seen with my own eyes those prostitutes in the streets, and the men whose eyes were so hungry for young women – I would never have sent her. Never, never, never. By the time I did it was, of course, too late . . .'

'But you had dreams for her and yourself, didn't you?'

'Yes, I had dreams before the nightmare that is now.'

He smiled and then told her of those simple hopes and dreams, and Anna's too.

'She wanted the love of a man, a good man, like all women. One to make her proud, to give her children, to look after, to share life with. She knew what her mother had been to me; she wanted the same for herself and knew it would give me happiness if she found it. But I know she would not encourage the wrong kind of man and that she would tell me or her aunt and uncle in Chicago.'

'Did she have admirers?'

'Some. I did not like them. Young, no-good men. She was too young.'

Emily smiled slightly. She had had the same conflict with her own father, but he had been less strict.

'Did she have a special beau?'

'Of course not.'

'Did she have a job to go to in Chicago?'

'I told her she had no need to work, but Anna did not want to be idle. The library here where she worked arranged a tryout for her at the Chicago Public Library. But as this was only part-time, she also took on some work in the Administration Building at the World's Fair, arranged by my sister-in-law.'

'Did she write home?'

'Yes, regularly. I show you. I show you her letters . . .'

He disappeared into another room and came back with a bundle of letters written in a neat, round, girl's hand.

'She was my *daughter*,' he cried out, 'my *life*.'

He reached into his breast pocket and produced a crucifix on a chain, it was of grey metal and quite bulky and distinctive.

'Mr Freeman returned it to me on my last visit,

once they had completed the formalities. I keep it with me now, always. I cannot forget her. She left me but she cannot leave my heart.'

By the time she left Emily felt she knew the young woman who had been Anna through and through, even though the letters seemed to contain little that was unusual and gave no indication at all of any men or women whom Anna might have known and of whom, naturally, her father would now have been suspicious.

She had got all the background she needed on Zemeckis's search – where he had been in Chicago and who he had seen or tried to see. She could not immediately think of anywhere she would have gone herself which he had not already tried. She asked if she could borrow Anna's letters to read at her leisure in case there were any clues in them they had missed. And then Janis handed her the precious photograph as well.

'Really, I can't take that, Mr Zemeckis . . .'

'It might help,' he said, closing her fingers over it with his own, 'so please, take it. Give it back when you know the truth.' It was as though in the act of giving the photograph to her he passed over to Emily the responsibility for finding out what had happened to his daughter during those lost weeks and it made it easier for himself to live with his loss.

'But do not lose these things, Miss Strauss!' he said as she said goodbye. 'They are all I have left of her . . . do not lose them!'

8

Chilled

In the pitch darkness of an isolated warehouse somewhere on Chicago's South Side, Jenkin Lloyd Rhys, president of the Old America Association, was suffering the first stages of hypothermia.

His wrists were trussed tightly behind him with twine, which was looped up around his neck and down to his ankles in such a way that when he moved his arms he began garrotting himself.

To ease the pressure he had slumped sideways to the floor, his back and hands resting against a freezing brick wall.

It was not so cold that he was likely to freeze to death, but his legs were shaking uncontrollably and his teeth chattered so much that his denture had come loose and was halfway out of his mouth.

He had no idea where he was or what had happened to him. All he remembered was leaving his hotel at around seven the evening before to take a stroll over to the Lakeshore before retiring for the night. As usual his wife had not come to Chicago with him as she did not like long rail journeys or strange hotel beds.

The weather was fine and the sidewalks crowded but somewhere on Adams, just as he came within sight of the Art Institute on the other side of Michigan Avenue a man passed him, blocked his

49

path and halted, causing Rhys to stop as well. The man was not especially tall but he was most certainly broad. He turned, apparently in apology, and the next thing Rhys knew was that his right arm was being gripped painfully tight and before he could even shout he was pushed down an alley near a saloon and . . . and that was the last he remembered.

He had woken up in the dark trussed like a goose and with no idea where he was and nothing for company but the sound of a railroad and the coming and going of locomotives and boxcars. He called out a few times but doubted if anyone could hear or would ever hear.

He lay shivering for a while before remembering that he knew enough about the cold and what it did to a man to know that he better start moving. Which was not easy with that cord round his neck.

Yet somehow or other he succeeded in turning on his front and then, getting into a kneeling position, he was able to use the wall as a prop to push himself up, hopping against it because his ankles were bound together.

All this in pitch darkness with just the sound of the trains and a chill, sweet smell in the air.

Risking losing his balance again by breaking from the support of the wall he turned finally toward the door, hoping to kick it to attract attention and to shout if he had any voice left in him at all.

'Help!'

It came out as no more than a croak.

'Help!'

He reached the door, went to kick it, but it flew suddenly open, blinding him with daylight and the brief vision of a man whose breadth filled the doorway, the same man he had met the evening before.

Jenkin Lloyd Rhys was a tough man. The son of Welsh immigrants who had come to America when he was eight, he had risen from humble beginnings in a mining community east of Pittsburgh to pre-eminence as a city engineer in New York. Like a lot of self-made men fear did not come easily to him and he knew the power of reasonable words.

He demanded to know where he was and why.

The man muttered a single word in reply, after which Rhys felt himself suddenly picked up bodily and hauled over the man's shoulder like a side of beef. For a moment he thought he was being carried back into the darkest depths of the place from which it had taken him so long to find the way out.

He tried to shout but only a frightened whisper came out of his mouth.

Then the man grunted, turned right round, and portered him out of the warehouse as if he were no more than a sack of feathers, across some rail tracks, before heaving him straight through the open doors of what he recognized at once as a refrigerated boxcar.

He carried him to the darkest end of the car past hanging sides of beef and finally heaved him upward and placed his right armpit onto the upturned spike of an empty meat hook suspended from the ceiling.

'N . . . n . . . noo . . .'

Rhys felt a pain so terrible in his shoulder that he briefly lost consciousness.

When he came round he felt two great hands grabbing at his ankles and then a brief tug down drove the hook through sinew and flesh and straight into bone and Rhys knew a pain and fear beyond anything he had ever imagined.

He blacked out again, only to be brought back to

his world of pain by the crash of the boxcar doors being slammed shut and the knowledge, as his shocked eyes stared past his suspended feet to the floor below, that the boxcar and the train of which it was part were beginning to move.

It was only then that Jenkin Lloyd Rhys, who sincerely believed he had never hurt anyone in his life, realized the full impact of the solitary word he had heard the man say to him. *Johnstown*. It was the name of a town in Pennsylvania. A name that had haunted him for the last four years.

'*Oh dear God*,' he sobbed, as he hung there in the lonely dark and the train began moving off with a creak and a groan.

9

In the Ward

CHICAGO Sunday October 22, 1893   2.07 PM

Anna Zemeckis crouched down in a state of fear on the floor of the ward on Far Side. It was a long, damp, louse-infested room inhabited by eighty women in every stage of lunacy. They terrified her.

She had just learned the hard way not to make eye contact with anyone. To do so was to invite trouble. Someone she had glanced at had hit her hard in the belly without further provocation and that had made her nauseous. It was a random act of violence of a kind she guessed would be the first of many if she did not find a way of getting out of Dunning.

Some of the inmates were strong and vicious and

lashed out if she went anywhere near; others looked weak but grew suddenly angry for no apparent reason, scratching and gouging others at random until one of the stronger ones beat them onto the floor.

Night wasn't so bad because then the women were confined to their cribs with an orderly watching over them. But in the morning they herded everybody into the day ward, which was no more than a vast wide corridor with locked doors at either end and three chairs for eighty women. The chairs were taken by women who might have been orderlies or trusties – either way Anna did not like the look of them.

When the food came the women practically fought for it and when they had a share they hunched in corners guarding it as they gobbled it down or, their first hunger satisfied, secretly eking it out, salivating, sometimes playing with it. Root vegetables became dough, the thick brown bread became mush, beans turned to paste, all of it squeezed between fingers, plastered onto mouths, spat out on the floor, trodden in and scooped up by someone else. Filthy food became an insane comfort in an insane place.

The first thing Anna learned was to look where she put her feet and when fatigue had first forced her to squat down too she chose the least filthy spot she could find. Some of the women were so demented that they did not bother to make the short journey to the water closets at one end of the ward and messed themselves where they squatted or sat.

A woman came at her suddenly, giggling. An old hag of a creature with only two teeth, her mouth opening wide into a wet gummy void when she silently laughed, which she now did. She tried to touch Anna, first her breasts and then her privates, cackling about friendship as she did so.

Anna pushed her away again and again until, when she came once too often, and Anna saw others were watching and waiting to see what she would do, an instinct to survive took over and she hit the old lady hard.

After that no-one touched Anna much or came near. She found herself crying for the terrible thing she had been forced to do.

I've got to get out, she told herself.

It didn't help that she ached through and through – outside from the blows she had received from Riley, and inside, because the swill they called food had made her sick.

Got to get out, thought Anna again, turning round with a look so determined and fierce that it was the other women who looked away from her now.

Finally she slumped back onto her haunches, glowering.

Her expression might be blank, but her mind was feverishly active. She was going to find a way out because she *had* to. There was something she had to do, outside in the real world, but . . . she frowned, clenching her fists, willing herself to recover more of her memory.

When she had first remembered her name was Anna Zemeckis during the doctor's examination of her the day before, she had felt like she had regained her soul. But the relief had been short-lived.

Since then other memories had bombarded her but they were all jumbled. All they amounted to were moments too brief and disconnected to make much sense, but which nevertheless were unpleasant and terrifying flashes of recall. The chief of these was that she was running from someone, but she did not know who. But there was something that troubled her even more: the feeling that whatever she was running from was caused by the need to protect something, but she had no idea what.

A woman came and crouched down next to her and for the first time that grim morning Anna dared to smile. It was the woman who had the crib next to hers at night and she was all right.

She's all right, Anna told herself as the woman's shoulder touched her own.

Anna closed her eyes and, feeling the touch of another human being, a tear coursed down her cheek.

She could remember she had been running, running, running before she fell into Bubbly Creek. She had seen things so shocking, so frightening, that just to have seen them was a sin for which she could never be forgiven and for which she would be better off dead. But it still didn't make any sense. There had been hogs and knives and men in white . . . butchers, killing and blood.

That's when she ran and ran, but it was hard because she was carrying something she had to protect.

'I can't remember what it was,' she whispered to the woman next to her. 'But I've got to get out of here.'

The woman stared at her and put an arm around her seeming unable to say anything, but her eyes spoke loud and clear, asking 'Why?'

A slow tear came from one of Anna's eyes.

'I've done something terrible,' she whispered.

What? her new friend seemed to say.

'I don't know,' said Anna and it was the not knowing that was her agony. *'I can't remember.'*

At that moment, there was a sudden hush right through the ward as if the women there had heard what Anna had said.

But it was something else.

Maureen Riley had walked in and she looked mean.

'Where's that Bubbly Creek bitch?' she snarled, looking up and down the ward.

10

The World

NEW YORK Sunday October 22, 1893   2.26 PM

Arriving in the foyer of the *World* offices on Park Row, Emily soon discovered that the name Charles Hadham got her straight past the uniformed concierges to the editorial offices on the eleventh floor and to the inner sanctum of the City Room.

It was a vast, cavernous place ablaze with lights even on this bright sunny Sunday, with row upon row of flat and rolltop desks crammed together in every available inch of space, most of them occupied by newsmen in rolled up shirtsleeves. And everywhere the constant din of typewriters and the click of telegraph machines. Over in the far corner near the door were a group of desks on a raised platform – the 'throne' of City Editor Charles Hadham, a big restless man who looked like he might have been more at home in a boxing ring. He sat smoking a pipe at a large untidy desk, surrounded by papers, files, two telephones, people and more people, most of them men.

Someone whispered in his ear that 'the girl reporter' was there and he looked up and waved her over.

'Haven't much time,' he said. 'JP said you'd make an appearance. Warned me in fact.'

He gave Emily a rueful grin, quickly dealt with a couple of things and then turned to her, somehow managing to make her feel she had his full attention.

She told him about the Zemeckis letter, what she had done already and what her plans were. He nodded now and then, asked a few questions and then scribbled a note and handed it to her.

'Here's an order on the cashier for your expenses. Have you booked a hotel . . . ? Mack!' he called out, turning to a man of fifty or so in shirt-sleeves. 'This lady is Miss Strauss and she's going to Chicago on a tryout for Mr Pulitzer, so you better be kind to her when she files her copy.'

Mack nodded, shook Emily's hand, but did not smile.

'God help you,' he said.

'Mack's one of our story editors and more than likely any story you file will cross his desk. He's Scottish and can only cope with very short sentences and no long words.'

Mack shrugged, looking as if he had heard it all before.

'So, *have* you a hotel? I guess you'll have a hard time finding one, the Fair being on.'

Emily nodded, eager to show she knew the ropes.

'Yes, the Annex to the Auditorium Hotel. It's near . . .'

'I know where it is. Opposite the lake on Michigan Avenue. You were lucky to find a room, but it will cost with the Fair being on.'

57

'I should say! There wasn't a room to be had in the whole of Chicago, but I know the management. I've stayed there before and did them a favor or two. When I explained the urgency, they offered me one of the maid's rooms in the attic – it was that or nothing.'

He nodded approvingly.

'Listen, Miss Strauss, don't set your hopes too high. Like as not you won't get a story. If you do, it probably won't get used. If it does you won't get a job anyway. Nobody does first time. There's a shortage of them for men round here, let alone women. As for JP . . .'

'He changes his mind about people,' said Emily matter-of-factly.

'It has been known.'

'Then I'd better do well, hadn't I, Mr Hadham?'

'I guess you better!' he replied with a smile.

People came and went, putting sheets of copy on Hadham's desk, picking up others, speaking the whole time across the conversation they were having. He nodded here and said a word there but somehow continued to engage with Emily.

'But you never know. You might find something. Might even be worth printing. If you do get something file it via Mack not me. If it's any good he'll make sure I see it. If we use it you'll get space rates. You know what that means ?'

'I get paid by the inch not the strength of the idea. Thanks. Just like the *Echo*.'

'Humph! If the idea's really good Mr Pulitzer might give you a bonus.'

'And I get a byline?'

He pursed his lips.

'Emily Strauss will do,' she said resolutely.

'Most women reporters use a pseudonym. Something

poetic or alliterative, like Lucy Locket or Bessie Bramble.'

'I like my *own* name, Mr Hadham.'

'Well maybe, just maybe – if it's *really* good and we use it you may get a byline, but no promises,' he said mock-wearily. 'Now listen. You know Chicago already so you know it's a tough city. You do *nothing* stupid. Just find out why they don't help people find their relatives; or if they *do* help people, why they're slow about it; or if they're *not* slow, why they're not faster. The Fair ends on the 30th of this month: that gives you a week by the time you get there. Our star reporter will be filing something in the *Sunday World* for the Fair's end on the 29th, but we'll still have the last day to cover on the 30th. That's your chance. But be sure to file your story by the night of the 29th. We don't *like* Chicago in this office. It stole the World's Fair from under New York's nose. Get us a good story, just to tarnish things for a bit for Chicago, get us some dirt. Just try to make sure it's half-truthful dirt and something we can use . . .'

He stopped, raised a hand and signalled someone over.

The man was in his mid-twenties, dark-haired and personable. He had a wide grin and white teeth.

'Benjamin B. Latham,' he said, shaking Emily's hand.

'Emily Strauss.'

They eyed each other and liked what they saw.

'Miss Strauss is going to Chicago for a tryout, courtesy Mr Pulitzer,' said Hadham. 'The disappearing women cover-up.'

'Didn't know there was one.'

'There's one now and Miss Strauss is going to nail it or you won't be seeing her again.'

'So maybe she'll disappear too? Sad; and possibly unpleasant,' he added coolly in a nice, clean-cut New England accent.

Emily smiled.

His grin widened.

'One of our readers lost his daughter there,' Emily explained. 'Claims there's been a lot of disappearances during the Fair and Chicago City Hall's been covering them up.'

'Course it would. Bad publicity. Doesn't want visitors to stop coming. But proving it could be difficult.'

'We'll see,' said Emily.

'And *you're* going to help her,' said Hadham to Ben Latham before turning back to Emily.

'This gentleman is an illustrator,' he explained.

'News illustrator *and* photographer,' said Ben, handing her a card.

'Yes, well . . .' said Hadham doubtfully. 'Be that as it may. I'm sending Mr Latham out to Chicago in a few days' time to cover the closing ceremony of the Fair. He can help illustrate your story too if you find something worthwhile. Meantime he can check things out for you this end if you need back up. By telegraph. Be sure to check in with him daily, Miss Strauss.'

'My pleasure,' said Ben cheerfully.

'And you can start by showing her where to get her money.'

Ben raised his eyebrows and looked impressed.

'She gets money *before* she files?'

'She does.'

Charles Hadham suddenly looked tired, or maybe he was just bored. Emily knew it was time to go. But he had some final advice. 'Don't antagonize anybody,

Miss Strauss. Stay sweet and keep them sweet. Don't go anywhere unsafe. Do *not* go risking your life trying to find out why this girl ran away or was abducted, or whatever the hell happened to her, because it will be something that's dangerous to know. We've got male reporters who do those kinds of stories. *Understand?*'

Later, having got her advance for the trip, Emily turned impulsively to Latham.

'What do I have to do to get to work for Mr Hadham in the City Room?' she asked.

'That's easy. Ignore what he said and find out what happened to the girl, why she ran away,' he said, echoing the words of Arthur Butes.

Then he got serious too.

'But if I were you I wouldn't even try. Staying alive is more important than getting a job on the *World*. Chicago's not a safe place for lone girl reporters.'

He paused and a moment's worry crossed his face.

'But whatever else you do, don't forget that deadline. *Whatever you do,* the story's stone-cold dead if you don't get it in for the October 30th edition when the Fair ends. No story from Chicago, however good, will take the gloss off the closing ceremony for the Fair once it's over and done with. So whatever you file, it better be on time. But if Hadham doesn't change his mind I'll be in Chicago with you by then so . . .'

'Whether you're there or not I'll file in time,' said Emily cutting him short.

He grinned good-naturedly once more and then impulsively stretched out his hand and shook hers.

'Welcome to the *World*,' he said.

11

Cadavers

'Dr Eels! I'm sorry . . . the women are waiting.'

'They can wait a bit longer,' Morgan Eels replied coldly without looking up from the cadaver before him. It was – or had been – a man, thin as a rail, about fifty. Its face was waxy grey and gaunt, its scalp shaved.

'How many women are left to examine now?' he asked without looking up.

'Three, sir,' said the orderly, who had just arrived.

'Who are they?' murmured Eels to Mould, his assistant, standing next to him.

'There's the Nevitt woman on whom you'll be doing a new procedure tomorrow. Then there's the Bubbly Creek woman and another, all suitable for the clinical trial this coming Friday.'

'Excellent,' said Eels as he sighed and straightened up. He arched his back into a stretch. He and Mould were both gowned up in white, from head to toe, but Eels wore nothing on his head.

Behind them, on a trolley, was another cadaver. It was female, and it too had a scalp that had been shaved, this time only partially: the top right side had been partially cut and folded back with the skull, exposing the brain, into which an instrument had been stuck, up to its thin steel handle.

The area they were working in was little more than

62

a corridor converted into a pathological laboratory. Its walls were peeling, its high ceiling cobwebbed, its single window filthy. There were two gas lights and an electric light that flickered on and off.

'I'm sorry, Dr Eels, it's Riley,' said the orderly, interrupting again. 'She doesn't like being kept waiting.'

Eels let out a grunt of exasperation and frowned.

'So I've noticed. The tail most certainly wags the dog in this establishment! *That* will have to change.'

He straightened up again.

'Inform her I shall be there to examine the patients at quarter past the hour. Have the papers ready.'

'Yes, Dr Eels.'

Eels walked round to the cadaver's head and examined its right temple.

He took up a drill.

'Hold it still,' he said.

Eels positioned his feet, and set the bit to the incision he had made earlier with a chisel, pushing firmly into the skin and on to the bone. He began to drive the bit into the skull.

Twenty-five minutes later, having removed his white robe and putting his collar and cravat back on, Morgan Eels had transformed himself from surgeon back to alienist and returned to his examination room on the floor above the laboratory.

He had three women to see and he did so briskly. Surgery, even exploratory dissection of a cadaver, always put him into a good, assertive mood and eager to get on.

The first two women were straightforward. One was an imbecile who had been at Dunning for many years and, so far as anyone knew, had no relatives or other parties interested in her well-being. Riley confirmed her identity, which both knew anyway, and Eels signed the necessary papers and prepared the record.

He thought about the second. Mary Nevitt was a younger woman of twenty, a tiresome hysteric, inclined to a whole range of nervous symptoms including crying spells, indecisiveness, suspiciousness, meticulousness of a particularly irritating sort (she was inclined in her more lucid phases to tidy up other people's clothes and shoes), negativism, obsessive talking and restlessness. He had never known a patient whose fingers twined and intertwined so much as she talked.

She would undoubtedly benefit from the procedures he proposed to carry out on her, as would society from her cure. But Mary did not want to agree to anything and was a most reluctant patient.

'I don't want you to cut my brain,' muttered Mary as Riley forced her down into the seat in front of Eels, her hands writhing more than ever.

'The only outward sign that we have operated on you will be a loss of hair because we will have to shave a small area of your scalp. But it will grow back, it really will! Now . . .'

He stood up and nodded at Riley.

Nevitt tried to speak again.

'Tomorrow, Miss Nevitt, tomorrow . . .' said Eels dismissing her. 'Mrs Riley will see you safely back to your ward.'

'*Next!*' rapped out Eels, as he sat back down in his chair.

Moments later the woman from Bubbly Creek entered the doctor's examination room, Riley's lumbering presence just behind her.

One glance told Eels the woman had deteriorated since yesterday and might well be reaching a critical point. She presented symptoms of extreme nervousness, exhaustion and obvious emotional instability.

He glanced through his previous notes on her.

Yes . . . there was something she either knew about herself and was denying or did not know but should have done. In either case intervention was called for immediately. But . . . he would deal with that matter later.

He looked at her. Instinct told Eels this woman would not be easy. She had, he guessed, the peasant intelligence that he had often found in Eastern Europeans. Being uneducated and generally lax in their habits this unfortunately expressed itself in stubbornness and an unwillingness to accept authority.

A great deal of time was being lost in Chicago, as in New York, in pandering to wantons such as these and today Dr Eels had no patience for it.

'So, tell me, do you now know your name?'

Anna hesitated, and immediately he knew she did, just as he had suspected she had the day before. It annoyed him. *He had no time for this.*

He eyed her coldly.

Since the woman had come to Dunning as a ward of Cook County Insane Court, and no relatives were known, Eels did not in fact need her full and proper name for his purposes. 'Jane Doe' would do.

Nor did he need any signature to proceed with her treatment apart from his own as medical superintendent in waiting. But . . . it rankled that she was deliberately withholding her surname when he was sure she knew it.

He relaxed, suddenly beginning to enjoy himself. He eyed the forms on his desk but did not touch them. No, he didn't need her name, but . . . it would be satisfying to see if he could trick it out of her.

65

Eels smiled: 'This need not take long. A few more questions so that these forms are complete, and then I'll explain what we are going to do.' He leaned forward reassuringly and added, 'That's all that's needed.'

'What is wrong with me, doctor?'

Anna made herself sound meek and pathetic, but her head was full of thoughts of escape.

Eels shrugged dismissively.

'It has many names but I think the one you will best understand is hysteria. It is common enough in one of your sex and age who may have suffered trauma of some kind. It is curable. And we shall start the treatment right now.'

Eels fixed his eyes hard on Anna's and said, 'I would be grateful if you could try to answer the following questions as fast as possible. There are no correct answers, rather it will help me to ascertain your level of intelligence, for that is a factor too.'

He paused.

She stared at him uneasily. She felt frail and sick. Yesterday he had seemed merely unpleasant. Now he seemed positively evil, his smile reptilian.

'First, colors. Respond as quickly as possible. Simply give the color that comes into your head.'

She nodded, puzzled.

Tree . . . ?

'Green.'

Sky . . . ?

'Blue.'

Snake . . . ?

'Black.'

Yolk . . . ?

'Yellow.'

'Excellent. Now let's try city and state names.'

New . . . ?
'York.'
New . . . ?
'Jersey.'
West . . . ?
'Virginia.'
North . . . ?
'America.'
Great . . . ?
'Britain.'
The pace was getting faster and their eyes locked onto each other, with Eels leaning forward assertively as he fired words at her. Anna was suddenly enjoying the harmless game, taking pleasure in using her mind, forgetting her dislike of him in the rush and challenge of the words.

Sweat showed on his pale yellow brow.

The sky outside changed from blue to gray and rain beat suddenly, angrily, against the windows behind him.

'Or just words that go together,' he said suddenly.
Table . . . ?
'Leg.'
Pork . . . ?
'Pie.'
'*You are?*'
'Anna.'
She gasped at the fact she had said it.

Eels relaxed and smiled again.

'Well done, Anna,' he said. 'You see there really is nothing to be afraid of!'

I must not say my surname, I must not . . .

She had the uneasy feeling that he knew something she didn't, something important.

President . . . ?

'Lincoln.'

Doctor . . . ?

'Eels.'

He smiled and she smiled too. His shining spectacles were pools of light in which she was drowning.

'Now, Anna, just repeat the number that follows the one I say. One . . .'

'Two.'

'Forty-two'.

'Forty-three.'

'One hundred.'

'. . . and one.'

'Excellent. Now let us do it for speed. Beginning simply, with numbers. One . . .'

'Two!'

'Three.'

'Four!'

'Five.'

'Six!'

He smiled and nodded approvingly, glad to see her relax. He was almost there.

'Seven.'

'Eight!'

'Nine.'

'Ten!'

'Anna!'

'Zemeckis.'

It came out before she could stop herself and she stared at him in horror.

Eels smiled with pleasure and looked smug. It was really no more than a party trick.

'I didn't mean . . .' she began, 'I didn't want . . .'

'That is perfectly normal, perfectly. I am here to help you, to find a cure. You are not well, Miss

Zemeckis, not well at all and . . .'

'I don't *feel* well, doctor. I feel sick. The food's dreadful and . . . and . . .'

His glasses shone brightly, dazzling her, and the rain on the window now shone with the sun that had come out again.

Dr Eels reached smoothly for the form he wanted her to sign. He had her now, it was just a question of timing.

'You will need to sign . . .' he began quietly.

He watched her intently, a snake watching its prey. She tensed up and immediately he went in for the kill.

'You *are* aware, are you not, that you are with child?'

Her eyes widened and her mouth dropped open.

'Pardon me?'

'You are *pregnant*, Miss Zemeckis. My examination yesterday confirmed the cause of your constant nausea. It's a common symptom.'

He was right, she had not known. Or if she had it was part of her memory loss, possibly its cause.

'I . . .'

The room whirled in Anna's head and the lights seemed to whirl as well. She began hyperventilating.

'I can help you with the baby, and with your mental distress,' said Eels, pushing the form forward to the front of his desk and reaching for a steel pen which he dipped into ink.

'You can write your signature? Yes . . . yes? Just sign, and then I will be able to help you.'

She took up the pen in a daze of shock and bewilderment.

'You . . . I . . . you can help?' she whispered.

'Of course,' he said reassuringly.

Maybe it was the thin, mean mouth; maybe the unpleasant way his spectacles caught the light.

Maybe it was animal instinct.

Anna put down the pen abruptly.

'No. I won't,' she shouted. For now she understood. It was the child in her womb that she had been trying to protect without realizing it. It was the child that had sent her running from the men that night into the blackness and oblivion of Bubbly Creek; the child that, in the end, was giving her the will to survive.

Eels visibly contained his anger.

He pulled the form back, attached it with the others on his clipboard and put it neatly to one side.

'Of course,' he breathed, his eyes cold again, 'we don't actually *need* your signature, Miss Zemeckis. But I prefer my patients to be compliant – it helps their recovery, you see. I shall recommend the treatment anyway . . .'

He turned away.

'What will you do to me?'

He stared at her.

'There will be some small discomfort but . . .'

She stared at him, still in shock but beginning to make sense at last of the physical and mental confusion she had been suffering.

I am with child and that is why I . . .

'I do not want to lose my baby,' she said simply.

'Aah . . .' he shrugged. 'But if I am to make you well again, Miss Zemeckis, then we must deal with this matter before your surgical procedure next week.'

'No! I do not want that . . .' said Anna, her voice rising as she stood up.

'There is nothing to be afraid of, Miss Zemeckis,' he said, also standing up 'I promise you, all will be well.

Riley, take Miss Zemeckis back to the ward. And be sure to take good care of her until Thursday . . .'

'I don't want you to . . .'

Riley had Anna in an iron grip.

'See she is closely watched,' snapped Eels as Anna continued to protest.

'They don't escape from *my* wards, Dr Eels,' said Riley as she manhandled Anna out of the room.

'I don't want . . .' shouted Anna, hysterical now.

'Take her away,' snarled Eels.

Later, in her crib, locked in for the night in a darkened ward, Anna lay eyes wide open, hands on her belly.

'We have to get away from here,' she said aloud. She was speaking to her unborn child and as she did so she knew that if she had to she would kill to ensure that her baby survived.

DAY FIVE

Monday October 23, 1893

12

On the Train

The following morning, Monday, October 23, Emily Strauss boarded the Exposition Express at Jersey City for the twenty-six hour journey to Chicago.

The first time she had made the journey, back in September for the *Echo*, she had been over-excited, over-dressed and had taken far too much luggage. But for a natural ability to fall asleep when she felt like it, she would have arrived totally exhausted and taken days to recover.

This time she travelled light, dressed sensibly and kept calm. After the initial excitement of departure, she settled down to go through Anna Zemeckis's somewhat girlish letters to her father, her own notes and some clippings which, as an afterthought, Ben Latham had sent to her from the *World*.

She had decided that she would initially cover the same ground as Janis Zemeckis had done, pretending, if need be, that Anna was her sister. But time being short she wanted to arrive up and running, so before she left that morning she had sent three telegraphs to contacts she had made during her previous stay.

The first and most important was to Fay Bancroft in the Woman's Building at the World's Fair whom she knew to be one of the most respected organizers

75

working under the redoubtable Mrs Potter Palmer, doyenne not only of the Fair but of Chicago society as a whole.

Fay had become a close and valued ally to Emily on her previous trip and she was the only person to whom Emily had confided that she was returning to Chicago to work on a new story for a more important paper. She did not say what the story was, but asked Fay to get her an introduction to one or two people who might have better contacts than she had been able to establish.

Fay had telegraphed straight back telling Emily to come to the Fair the day she arrived so they could talk over lunch.

The other telegraphs were sent to Mrs Markulis, Anna's aunt, and to Julia Lathrop, a contact at Hull House, the settlement house on the West Side. Emily was confident that Miss Lathrop could give her some useful leads because the ladies at that institution, who did such stalwart work among Chicago's immigrant communities, had unparalleled access to all levels of Chicagoan society. She doubted anyone at City Hall would admit publicly to any problem about women going missing – or any other problem for that matter, since they were all so busy promoting Chicago as the greatest city in America.

Mid-afternoon Emily retired to her berth for a rest and fell at once into the contented sleep of someone who has worked hard to get where they are going and deserves some rest before the real job begins.

She awoke suddenly to find the train at a standstill, a rainstorm raging outside.

'Where are we?' she asked a passing guard in the corridor outside.

'Bald Eagle Mountain, miss. Train always stops

76

here, especially when it's rough outside. Should be in Altoona by nine.'

Emily went back to her berth and glanced at her pocket watch. It was a few minutes before six and, for no reason she could think of, her mood had changed to one of deep unease.

Wind and rain suddenly lashed the carriage window so hard that for a moment she fancied it was trying to lash her too.

13

Cures and Remedies

CHICAGO Monday October 23, 1893   6.00 PM

At six that same evening, Dr Morgan Eels was pacing nervously up and down the back of the hall in which he was about to give probably the most important lecture of his medical career. It was a lecture on which not only the future funding of Dunning but also his own pioneering medical career depended. As the newly appointed Superintendent at Dunning he had been asked by OAA Vice-President, Paul Hartz, to describe to a selected audience of its members the important new research program he was about to initiate in the treatment of mental illness.

'Give 'em a show,' had been Hartz's advice. 'Say that the problem's reached dangerous proportions, offer a solution they can afford, make them understand that their help will bring honor to themselves and Chicago and trust me, Eels, they'll open their pocketbooks.'

Hartz, now in his sixties but still formidable and used to having his own way in everything, liked to be on time. He told Eels to stay at the back until he was called forward and then strode down the aisle to ready the audience.

He was a master of smooth talk and salesmanship and began his introduction right on the hour.

'Ladies and Gentlemen,' he began, 'honored guests and fellow members of the Old America Association . . . In my time, I have had the pleasure of introducing presidents and military men, archbishops and captains of industry . . . but never, not once, have I felt as excited as I do this evening as I introduce to you one of the rising young men of American medicine, Dr Morgan Eels.'

Eels stepped up to the lectern to a round of applause, and began, in a low, somber voice, like someone who has studied the world's ills and come to his conclusions only after much thought. He did not waste time getting to the point.

'America is in grave, grave danger,' he declared. 'Weakness and vice are everywhere about us, crime is outrageously rampant and the remedial measures which this noble society has devised over the years in a spirit of philanthropy, generosity of heart and democracy have proved themselves inadequate for its protection.'

He paused and then repeated, with sudden anger, '*Utterly* inadequate.'

He barked this out so vehemently that many in the audience sat up straight.

'My friends and colleagues,' he continued, stepping even further forward, 'we have allowed the idiot, the imbecile, the epileptic, the habitual drunkard, the murderer and the harlot to run riot among us. Criminals who might be deemed incorrigible by any sensible judge are set free by those of liberal inclination to commit heinous crimes again; imbeciles, who, were they denizens of the animal kingdom, would long since have been extirpated by natural selection, are allowed to be a burden on the state.'

He paused and stared, his face suffused with anger.

'A burden! To our cities and the state! To *their* own misery and at *our* great expense.'

He turned and looked behind him.

'*Curtain!*' he commanded.

At this the curtains behind Eels suddenly opened to reveal a startling scene, but one kept for the moment in semi-darkness: two slabs on which were the indistinct figures of two cadavers covered in sheets, alongside which stood a nurse in uniform; and Mr Mould, in his white gown, holding another gown and mask at the ready, obviously intended for Eels.

These living figures stood unnaturally still, as Eels had commanded them to, and were a counterpoint to the two corpses, the outlines of whose heads, shoulders, chests and lower extremities beneath their coverings were lit for now only by flickering gaslight. They were the same cadavers Eels and Mould had prepared the day before.

The audience had barely adjusted its eyes to this strange tableau before the orderly threw a switch and a bright electric light, directly over one of the cadavers, lit it up. A moment's further pause and then Mould expertly pulled away its covering.

The audience gasped.

What was revealed was the gray corpse of a man, completely naked but for some muslin placed over his genitalia and a bandage over his skull.

79

Eels went straight to the cadaver's far side and stood under the bright light where he allowed himself to be robed up ritualistically by Mould, like a medieval knight being dressed in armor by his squire before a battle.

'This evening I wish to say something about cures and remedies,' continued Eels. 'The insane fall into two categories – the chronically melancholic and what I term the psycho-schismatic, those whose mental state is so disrupted that they are unable to connect with reality.

'Alienists would have us believe that because the symptoms presented by these conditions and their variants are so different the causes are different too. So different that there is no hope of finding a single cure. It is not for me to suggest that this attitude keeps alienists in business since I myself am one!'

The audience appreciated this and laughed with him.

'But . . . I am also a trained surgeon and neurologist and it is in that capacity that I speak tonight.

'Let me explain how this may be achieved, starting with this male specimen first,' continued Eels, placing his hand on the head of the cadaver and eyeing it with what seemed contempt.

'In life this case was, regrettably, typical of many. A Bohemian, uneducated and of low intelligence, probably the product of perverted inbreeding, he arrived in this city in 1888. In a short space of time he proved himself deviant and vicious and committed various acts of robbery and violence on several upright citizens, resulting in the death of one of them.

'However, in its wisdom the Court at the Detention Hospital declared him insane and committed him to the care of this institution, where he continued to cause such difficulty that his delusional behavior, which if resisted provoked only violence, had to be controlled by physical restraint as well as opiates.

'Some among us might think it would have been best if this man had never been allowed to immigrate into this great and too-generous land by stricter laws than we presently have. For, once domiciled here, he became nothing but a danger to his fellow man and a drain on our resources.'

He paused for a moment and then added magisterially, 'In death, however, he can finally serve a useful purpose.'

With that Eels turned the cadaver's head sideways so that its half-open eyes seemed to stare at the audience.

'It has been known for several decades that there is a direct connection between the neocortex, which is that large upper and frontal part of our brain which distinguishes us from other mammals, and our behavior and emotions. Put another way, we know that changes to certain parts of the lobes of the brain affect how we think and feel and what we do . . .

'We have learned a great deal in recent years about the more detailed anatomy of the brain and in particular which parts affect which emotions and senses.'

With that, Eels undid the bandage around the cadaver's head and revealed what at first appeared to be no more than scratches on its shaven scalp and temple. Even so, the audience, already hushed, now grew deathly silent.

'Let us take a closer look . . .' began Eels, as he coolly reached toward the cadaver's temple and suddenly pulled forward an entire flap of the skin and bone to reveal a part of the gray-white brain underneath.

Someone in the audience, a lady, moaned slightly. Elsewhere a gentleman grunted. A few covered their eyes, or peeked through fingers, but most craned forward for a better look, and some at the back stood up.

'The procedures required to prepare the cranium in this way can be safely performed *in vitrio* but it requires special skill and takes time.' With a deft movement Eels now removed the entire top of the cadaver's cranium revealing much more of the brain.

'Why would we wish to gain access to a living person's brain in this way? I will tell you. Because we now have an almost overwhelming body of evidence – some accidental, some the result of deliberate investigation by myself and my colleagues in this field – that shows that quite minor physical changes in the brain can radically improve the behavior of the individual concerned.

'To put it simply, it may well be that we can quite literally cut out the problem areas and render the disturbing symptoms of insanity harmless and benign. In short, a physical cure for insanity is finally possible if only we can find out from where in this extraordinary and marvelous structure – with which as you see even the meanest and most vicious of individuals is endowed – the symptoms of insanity emanate.'

Eels eyed his audience.

'Ladies and gentlemen, there is no single word in the medical lexicon to describe this new branch of medical science. And so I have created one myself. I call it psychosurgery . . .'

The demonstration that followed was little more

than a morbid and prurient peepshow – human butchery under the guise of an educational lecture. While some ladies might have felt faint and a few gentlemen had sweated and undone their collar studs, the audience had nevertheless enjoyed the warm glow of moral superiority that came with Dr Eels's tendentious and prejudicial assessment of his subject. He pulled no punches either when he came to his second, a woman, whose head Mould now uncovered.

'This case was typical of the armies of wanton women, many no better than hysterical harlots, most of a low-grade stock, who freely roam our cities day and night spreading disease and moral corruption among our fine young men.'

He eyed the corpse, his hand resting on its lank dark hair before easing the head toward the audience.

'She was but one of the many women housed in our asylums in a state of secondary dementia who manifested various degrees of mental dissolution. From the onset of puberty her mental defect, all too common in her class, displayed itself in a chronic wantonness which meant that up to the point of her committal to this asylum she had borne no less than six children by several different men. To most of these men she gave disease, the same she passed on to her brood, several of whom are syphilitic imbeciles, who remain locked up at our expense in various institutions in the state of Illinois.

'One of her vile offspring, now eight and roaming free, is a boy of unusual animal strength, who already displays criminal tendencies. I have no doubt that he, like his siblings, will have a propensity to that excessive reproduction of the species which characterizes their kind. This case, like the first, was a recent immigrant of the type and grade that comes from certain parts of Lesser Europe. Yet . . .'

Dr Eels took one of his needles and placed its point into the woman's right nostril.

'. . . it may well be that an operation as simple as the one I am about to perform, if conducted when this woman had been a girl, would have prevented all the tragedy implicit in what I have outlined.

'If I insert the needle, so . . .'

Eels gently pushed the needle up the cadaver's nostril toward the skull and the frontal lobes of the brain. Explaining that at this point the cranium was at its thinnest he took a small steel mallet and tapped the needle into the brain.

'It is, in theory at least, simply a matter now of manipulating the insertion instrument between the lobes and the limbic mass in such a way that it severs forever the bad connections, if I may so put it, that plagued this woman's life and those with whom she came into contact.'

Eels paused to accept the audience's murmur of approval and the ripple of applause that accompanied it.

'Ladies and gentlemen, there is no doubt that poverty, disease and crime are traceable to one fundamental cause – depraved heredity. Our continued toleration of the weak and vicious in our midst will mean that such base scions of humankind not only vex their own generation but contaminate posterity through the uncontrolled proliferation of their seed until whole nations are infected.

'There is a danger – no, a strong belief based on sound demographic research – that that is what is now beginning to happen here in America.

'We should learn from nature's method for the

preservation and elevation of races, namely the selection of the fittest and the rejection of the unfit . . .'

Eels now grew deathly still. He stood as he had at the opening of his speech, his hands by his side, his feet together. But his eyes blazed behind their silver spectacles, two fierce fires burning bright.

'It is finally a matter of arithmetic. For the rejuvenation of the race we need to multiply those individuals whose dominant craving, like our own here tonight, is the altruistic sense while eliminating those whose lives are ruled by the baser selfishness. I believe we should take steps to limit the multiplication of the organically weak and the organically vicious.

'There are two approaches. The first is a program of enforced sterilization of defective men and women, procedures which are generally simple and speedy and produce beneficial side effects including a calming of the nerves and compliance with authority.

'But the surest, the simplest, the kindest and most humane means of preventing reproduction among those whom we deem unworthy of that high privilege is a gentle, painless death. This should be administered not as a punishment but as an expression of enlightened pity for the victims – too defective by nature to find happiness in life – and as a duty toward the community and our own offspring. This I believe!'

Eels fell silent and someone shouted 'Hear, hear!'

'Thank you, ladies and gentlemen, for your kind support. I am pleased to announce that later this week I shall initiate the first part of the program of investigation into surgical cures for insanity, with the help of a new group of volunteer patients, involving cerebral surgery and, in some cases, curative sterilization from which I expect speedy and excellent results!'

As Eels sat down the audience rose as one and gave him an ovation such as he had only ever dreamed of. Over the next half hour Eels and Paul Hartz between them received many verbal pledges of financial support, five significant ones coming from wealthy members of the Chicago chapter of the Old America Association.

It was, or seemed to be, an evening that opened a new chapter in the history of the Cook County Insane Asylum. Whatever Dr Eels's potential patients might suffer that night locked into their narrow cribs in freezing wards, he himself slept as comfortably as a well-fed baby.

14

Stonycreek

CAMBRIA COUNTY, PENNSYLVANIA
Monday October 23, 1893   8.11 PM

That same night, shortly after eight, a freight train pulled out of Pittsburgh and wound slowly eastward up through the steep, sheltered valleys of the Allegheny Mountains.

It had lights front and back but nothing much in the middle except for twenty-eight wagons of assorted goods and commodities bound for markets on the East Coast, including six refrigerated boxcars of dressed hogs and sides of beef. In the dark and driving rain it was hard to make much out, but the

refrigerated boxcars had *DARKE HARTZ &*
COMPANY painted in white letters on the side.

One of these meat wagons contained unexpected
human freight: one man seated on the floor; and
another hung up on a hook – Jenkin Lloyd Rhys.

The man on the floor was well wrapped up against
the chill from the air vents front and back that kept
the ice in the wagon cool. By his side was some food
– bread, ham, cheese – and a pitcher of water, not
beer.

Twenty minutes out of Pittsburgh the train ran
through the mining town of Johnstown.

The man on the floor got up and lit a lantern.
Holding on to the side of the swaying wagon with
practiced ease he moved over to have a look at Rhys,
raising his lantern so he could stare into his face.

His dry mouth hung swollen and loose now and he
stared from eyes that were nearly insane from his
hours of suffering and pain. The life of Jenkin Lloyd
Rhys, which had begun inauspiciously in a humble
cottage in the South Wales mining town of Ebbw
Vale, was coming to an unfair and terrible end, made
all the worse by him having had to dwell for the past
hours on the injustice of this terrible end to his life.

He had served his adopted country well, very well.
He had played fair by all he did business with; he had
given a helping hand to many an enterprising young
man; he had looked after his employees as he had his
own family; he was responsible for many philanthropic endeavors; he was God-fearing, a pillar of
church and community; and he was founder, leader
and president of the Old America Association, whose
worthy aims of preserving and promoting all that
was good in the way of traditional American values
surely no reasonable man or woman could condemn.

87

Suddenly a double whistle sounded.

The man put the lantern safely out of the way on the floor, pulled back the great bolts on the double door and with two great pulls opened the doors to right and left.

Wind and rain rushed in and the sides of meat swayed and pulled on their restraints. The man grabbed the shank of the hook Rhys was hanging from and with a heave got it moving one way before swinging it round on the curve at the end and back along the wagon side to the open door.

Rhys's eyes opened wider.

Often, even in the final agony, a man doesn't want to die. Extinction seems worse than any pain, even to a churchgoing man who says he believes in heaven.

Rhys's tormentor pulled out a knife and cut through the twine that had tied his hands behind his back. They swung free now but they were useless, blackened, engorged parodies of the manicured, smooth things they had been only twenty-four hours before.

Not for the first time but most definitely for the last Rhys spoke: 'Why?' he managed to say.

'Johnstown,' the man replied. It was the same answer as before.

Rhys's eyes registered protest and he even managed to mouth a few words: 'It wasn't my fault.'

The man ignored him and pulled a knife from the leather sheath on his belt. He reached forward with his massive left hand and cupped the back of Rhys's head to hold it steady against his chest.

Rhys whimpered.

Then, as the man carved four letters one after the other on his forehead, Rhys screamed. Blood blinded his eyes and dribbled down into the froth at the corner of his mouth.

His work done, the man let Rhys swing for a moment as he peered out into the dark, cocked his head to one side as if listening, waited a minute or so and then, apparently satisfied, turned back into the carriage. He put an arm and shoulder to Rhys's body and expertly hoisted him up and off the hook. Bloody drool came from Rhys's mouth; the sounds he uttered were those of an animal dying in fear and in pain.

The man carried him the short distance to the open door and held him there.

'Welcome back to Johnstown, Mr Rhys . . . and the Stonycreek River,' said the man, before heaving him out into the night. Rhys arced away into the dark, his useless hands and arms flailing helplessly at the rain as he fell into the raging waters of the river far below.

The train rolled on and not long after picked up speed for the long drop down to Altoona.

There, briefly, it made an unscheduled stop long enough to allow a man to get out of Wagon 27 and secure the doors again.

He was now carrying a small valise and wore an overcoat and curled bowler against the inclement weather. He crossed the tracks, made his way to the main part of the station and joined the few dubious characters who hang round rail depots at this time of the night.

Eight minutes later the *Exposition Express* from New York heading for Chicago hove into view, lights ablaze, like a passenger liner out on the Atlantic at night. It slowed down and a guard leaned out, looking for the man who raised a hand in acknowledgment.

The watchers were amazed to see the guard take

the man's valise and then reach down a hand to help him aboard.

'Who the hell was that?' someone said.

The others shrugged as the *Exposition Express* disappeared on into the night.

Up in the train the guard said respectfully, 'It's all ready for you, Mr Krol,' and showed him straight to the special berth reserved for directors of the railroad and their friends.

'Have a good night, sir. I'll wake you for breakfast.'

Krol nodded but did not smile.

He closed the carriage door behind him, undressed to his combinations, shook his head as if to shake off the effort of his murderous work over the past twenty-four hours and eased his huge, muscular frame onto the bunk before covering himself with a sheet and blanket.

He laid his head on the white starched linen of the pillow and closed his eyes.

Not long after that the train rattled its way across the bridge that spanned the ravine through which Stonycreek roared endlessly below, but Dodek Krol never knew that: he was enjoying a sleep so deep it might almost have been the sleep of the dead.

Nor did Emily Strauss know they had crossed Stonycreek either, though if she had she would have recognized its name at once. Not so long before it had been the scene of the worst flooding disaster in American history. The rest of America would have recognized it too. That night one more name had been added to the death toll.

But as it was, Emily Strauss, five carriages along from Dodek Krol, was as sound asleep as he was, unaware of the rain's funereal drumbeat on the roof or of the body of a good man caught in the murderous race of the rushing water of Stonycreek far below.

DAY SIX

Tuesday October 24, 1893

15

Flight

At seventeen minutes past nine the following morning Anna Zemeckis began running for her life and for that of her unborn baby, for the second time.

The first had sent her tumbling to near-death in Bubbly Creek. This time she had no idea where it would take her.

At eight-fifteen Riley had appeared, belligerent and smelling of liquor and warned several of the women to be ready to go over to Main Building to see Dr Eels at nine o'clock sharp. Anna was one of them.

She had no doubt about what they were going to try and do to her.

She grew ever more desperate to find a way out of the ward but realized there was none. The doors were watched either end by the trusties as well as the two orderlies who were already back on duty.

I am not going to let them harm my baby.

Cold anger and clearer thinking now began to replace her sense of desperation, as Anna realized that her only hope was to make her escape somewhere between the ward and Dr Eels's office. After that . . .

After that, I'll kill anybody who gets in my way.

When Riley returned Anna knew she must act compliant. So outwardly she did nothing but whimper and look scared. She wanted to lull Riley into a false sense of security, despite the fact that the vice-like grip on her arm was becoming excruciatingly painful.

They crossed the yard to Main Building and climbed the stairs to Dr Eels's surgery. A woman was already changed into her shift and was waiting. She was the second that morning.

Eels emerged, his white gown loose, looking pleased with himself. He took the gown off.

'Ah, Zemeckis! You look better today and you will be better still before long. Yes. Now, I don't suppose you have changed your mind and decided to sign the form I showed you?'

Anna looked at him, at the nervous woman next to her who was about to be 'treated', and at Riley and another orderly talking. For a moment she nearly ran then and there, but found herself saying, 'Yes, I'm ready to now, Dr Eels.'

She said this softly, head down, the very picture of compliance.

Eels beamed. He liked to win.

'Good, good!' he said, 'This needn't take long. Riley, bring her into my office.'

He opened it up, leaving the keys in the lock.

'No need to be nervous, Miss Zemeckis, the procedures are really all very straightforward.'

They passed the great camera on its brass tripod and the examination couch and went to his desk. Eels got his familiar clipboard, found Anna's form, clipped it to the top of the pile and put it in front of her.

'Please, sit down, it'll be easier . . .'

Riley got a chair and Anna sat, her heart thumping.

I can't . . . I mustn't . . . maybe it'll be all right . . .

Doubts assailed her as Eels dipped his steel pen in the ink and passed it to her.

Maybe Riley shouldn't have breathed just then and sent the stench of her vile liquor breath across Anna's face. Maybe.

Maybe it was the fact of the child inside her. Maybe.

Whatever it was, a sudden powerful rush of rage and purpose surged through Anna Zemeckis. She turned to Riley, stared at her ungiving face and instinctively thrust the nib of the pen, ink flying, straight into her right eye.

Then, as Riley screamed and brought her hands to her face Anna rose, picked up the metal clipboard and using it as a weapon whacked its edge at Eels's startled face, right into his teeth.

He grunted in pain and rage.

Anna ran out of the door, slammed it shut, turned the key in the lock and ran for her life. Behind her the muffled screams of Riley and Eels faded as she ran down the corridor, still clutching the clipboard like a weapon. She made for the stairs she saw at its far end and charged down them two steps at a time.

Nobody was about and there were no sounds yet of pursuit.

She slowed, opened the door to the yard outside, saw with relief that no-one was following and calmly went down the steps to the basement below, praying that the door would open and lead somewhere that offered other ways of escape.

Only then did she hear a distant shout and the running of feet, but it was nowhere nearby. Then an orderly's whistle, but that was a long way off too.

But Anna knew she had little time.

The basement door was unlocked and she slipped inside. She found herself looking down a dark basement corridor which seemed to run the whole length of the building. She set off down it at once, moving from door to door and thinking she could escape into a room if someone came. She went to throw away the clipboard but stopped herself. There were papers on it with her name. Besides, it had been a weapon once, and it might be again.

She ran on, passing door after door, avoiding the boxes and rubbish piled all along the corridor, crossing over intersections with other corridors off to her left.

The light at the end of the corridor grew brighter and she saw it came from another open door like the one she had first come in by.

When she reached it she nearly retched. The smell of rotting food was suddenly overwhelming.

'Garbage!' she told herself and she knew exactly where she was. She had seen piles of garbage at the end of Main Building near where the freight train delivered coal. From there they took it off to Dunning's incinerator. The door opened onto steps that led up to the trash cans and garbage put out ready for removal.

Except that some of it had slipped and slithered down the steps to the basement and, no-one having bothered to move it, it was now crawling with rats.

As she hesitated, Anna saw a silhouette at the far end of the corridor. It was large and broad and looked like one of the male attendants.

She crouched down where she was and waited until the man had gone. And then she heard it: the chuff-chuff of the freight train that serviced Dunning.

Anna cautiously climbed up the steps again and peered up into the yard. She saw the coal tips off in the distance and an incongruous line of washing nearby. The garbage lay between. Near the tip was a hut and she decided to make a run for it. When she was satisfied that no-one was in the immediate vicinity she climbed the last few steps and, still clasping the clipboard, headed for the hut only realizing a locomotive was approaching as she did so. Hoping the driver had not seen her she grabbed some garments from the washing line – a dress, a shawl, some woolen stockings – thrusting them and the clipboard with its papers into the shawl and tying the whole lot into a bundle so that it might seem she was on an errand.

Then she made a run for the hut and crept inside.

Only just in time.

The locomotive heaved to a halt, its bulk looming at the hut's little window and some shouting ensued.

'There's a woman loose,' she heard someone say. 'If you see her, grab her.'

Footsteps crunched outside the hut door and it opened. A man of thirty or so stood there staring at Anna. He was dressed like a train driver.

He put a finger to his lips. He seemed amused.

Then he said in a low voice, 'There's a hopper second from this end full of empty flour sacks and delivery crates. Get into that and avoid the other one, it's full of coal dust. No-one checks the hoppers. Climb up into it when I sound the whistle and crouch right down or they might spot you from the upper windows. Get out at the fourth stop and not before. I'll come and get you and show you where to go. We'll be gone in about five minutes and it'll take an hour or more, depending.'

She stared at him.

Her eyes were filled with gratitude and held a question: *why?*

His only answer was to shake his head and look as

if Dunning did not meet with his approval as he said with another grin, 'You're the third this month.' Then, 'Good luck, girl, you'll need it!'

In that moment of normality and human kindness clouds cleared in Anna's mind. She remembered her father, that his name was Janis and that he was a baker who lived and worked on the Lower East Side in New York where he had raised her.

The hut door closed, the driver walked away and the next five minutes were the loneliest of Anna's life.

She felt that she would never see her father or her home again. She felt utterly alone.

Then the locomotive whistle went and she remembered why she was running and what she must do. She peered out of the hut window, saw that the coast was clear and headed for the second hopper, which was open to the sky and much higher than she expected. She clambered up its rusty ladder, threw in her shawl and its contents, and then fell right in on top of a pile of empty flour sacks. Their dry sweet smell reminded her of her father once more and all that she had lost.

She followed instructions and crouched right down on the sacks. The train took off, stopped awhile for an inspection, where someone slapped the side of the wagon she was in, and then there was another shout and a whistle and the train began to move once more.

Anna stayed low, saw buildings towering above her and windows too, was rocked from one side to another as the train wound its way through the grounds of Dunning.

Then suddenly she knew it was clear of that terrible place. Maybe it was the vast blue sky she saw, maybe the tops of passing trees, maybe the prairie wind.

Whatever it was Anna Zemeckis was out of the Cook County Insane Asylum and heading back into Chicago.

'What now?' she wondered, as she made herself comfortable on the sacks.

She realized that she had absolutely no idea.

16

Everyone's Crazy

'My! Oh *my*!' cried the passengers on the *Exposition Express* as they crowded at the train windows to catch their first glimpse of Chicago after their long journey. 'Now that's a sight to see!'

In the far distance, across the waters of Lake Michigan, the air being clear from recent rain and the October sun quite strong, Chicago's mighty buildings, the highest and newest of which had been built for the Fair, rose shining, white and golden, in the sky.

'Pity the wind's in the wrong direction,' said someone knowingly. 'You'll all find out when we arrive!'

Half an hour later Emily Strauss knew what was coming when the train pulled into Dearborn Station. The noxious smell of the famous Union Stock Yard permeated everything and it had made her retch the first time she had come to the city. It was the smell of noxious black smoke from the yard's innumerable chimney stacks, of meat and offal, the fetid garbage dump and the open sewer.

But it didn't bother her now. Her story was what mattered. She was back in the fastest growing city in America, this time to write a story for the greatest newspaper in the country and nothing, absolutely nothing, was going to get in her way.

She checked for her valise and purse and then waited as the train came to a final halt.

'After you, miss!'

Someone opened the carriage door and someone else helped her out.

A porter offered to take her valise.

'I can carry this myself, thanks!' she said, 'But I have a trunk . . .'

'What a crowd!' she exclaimed, astonished as she took in the bustle of the city beyond.

'Hold on tight to your things,' warned her porter, '*very* tight!'

Only when they emerged through the depot's great red-brick entrance, blinking into the sunshine, did Emily feel able to breath again. It was already half-past eleven and she knew she had barely enough time to get her baggage to her hotel on Michigan Avenue and then take the new Elevated out of town for her luncheon appointment in Jackson Park at 12.15.

Her porter had disappeared with her trunk in search of a cab, though she had told him not to. She felt so excited to be back that, for the moment, she closed her eyes to breathe in the atmosphere of a Chicago that seemed transformed since she was last here the month before.

At that time she had left feeling a failure: rejected by her newspaper, without hope of a job, no longer convinced that she had what it took to make it in the tough, uncompromising male world of journalism.

Now everything had changed.

She had met Mr Pulitzer and talked her way into an assignment if not an actual job on the *World*. And she had a story to work on in which she believed.

'Hey! Bring my trunk back!' Emily snapped sharply as the porter reappeared having got a cab, 'I'm being met.'

The porter shrugged, rudely dumped her trunk and stretched out a hand. She gave him a couple of dimes and, muttering, he went his way.

She just had time to buy one of several of Chicago's German newspapers being hawked by newsboys when she spotted the person she was looking for, just as he saw her and hurried over.

'Miss Strauss? Miss *Emily* Strauss? For the Auditorium?'

He was seventeen or so, tough-looking, tall but still gawky. His hands and feet were large, as if his body still had to grow into them, and his gaze was quick, eager and intelligent. He wore a tight jacket with 'Auditorium Hotel' embroidered on its lapel.

'They sent me to collect you. Said if you had more'n one trunk to take a cab.'

'I've just this one,' said Emily, stuffing the newspaper into her valise.

He eyed the trunk.

'That ain't much for a lady,' he said with a grin.

He took her valise and then before she could stop him he heaved the trunk onto his shoulder as if it was no more than a bale of straw.

'Said if there was just one trunk to walk. It's quicker. You go in front, Miss Strauss, where I can keep you in sight. Don't want to lose you before we get there and you don't want to lose your things either, especially your valise. Hey, mister, leave off!'

The young man, whom Emily guessed was one of

the hotel's bellhops, stuck out his boot and stepped on the foot of a man twice his size who looked as if he was about to hustle her.

'I've got to get to Jackson Park for lunch,' said Emily anxiously over her shoulder.

'Should've said before,' shouted the young man above the din of people and traffic. 'Make a left when we get to Wabash and stop.'

The crowds were thick and came in waves, like water in a rapid. Emily battled on, until she was brought to a halt as they turned onto Wabash by a tramp as bearded as Methuselah and carrying a placard which read *EVERYONE'S CRAZY BUT ME!*

She tried to get out of his way but whichever way she stepped he mirrored her move.

'Please!' said Emily, sidestepping yet again and looking round for her escort. He was behind her in the crowd.

'I'm not crazy and I've got the papers right here to prove it, ma'am, and you better sign up to 'em or that impostor Mayor Carter Harrison and his crew in City Hall'll have every last dime you got for the tunnels they want to build right under your feet. Don't believe me?'

'I . . .'

'I got the papers to prove that too. Right here! Somewhere any rate. I . . .'

He stopped side-stepping and dug into the capacious pockets of the army greatcoat he had on and hauled out a sheaf of papers. Then more from another pocket. They had an official look about them and to her surprise Emily read the words 'City Hall' on one and 'Electoral Office' on another.

'Agree with 'im!' she heard her escort whisper in

her ear as he caught up with her, 'He ain't bad, he's Mr Crazy.'

They hurried away as quickly as they could.

'Don't worry about him, Miss Strauss, everyone knows Mr Crazy means no harm. It's just his way of keeping going. You can stop round that corner.'

She pushed her way out of the crowd to a quieter part of the sidewalk and found herself under the shining iron girders of the brand new Elevated on Wabash. She turned back as the boy barged his way through to join her. A train roared past directly overhead and its brakes began to squeal.

He nodded south down Wabash to some steps that led up to an overhead station where the train had just stopped.

'Best take the Elevated for Jackson from there. But if you come back after dark don't go getting *off* there, carry on up to the stop at Congress and Wabash and walk from there. It's longer but safer.'

He pointed the other way.

'And you'll take my baggage straight to the hotel?'

'Straight as an arrow, ma'am.'

'What's your name?'

'Johnny Leppard.'

He put the trunk on the ground, the valise on top of it, pulled himself up to his full height, which was now, she realized, a good three inches taller than herself. He reached out a hand and said, 'John H. Leppard. The H is for Hudson seeing as I was born near that great river.'

Then he added unexpectedly, 'I don't always want to work for a hotel.'

He had a dreamy look in his eyes.

'Who *do* you want to work for then?'

'Nobody. I want to own one.'

'One what?'

'A hotel, ma'am. One as big as the Auditorium. That's my aim in life. This position is just to help get me there!'

His determination and the grin that accompanied it were infectious. Emily grinned back, recognizing a kindred spirit. She could see that nothing was going to stop Johnny Leppard from reaching his goal just as nothing would stop her reaching hers. Meeting him felt like a good omen.

'I better get going,' said Emily.

'Remember, Miss, take the Elevated back to Congress if the light is even half gone by the time you leave Jackson. The streets round lower Wabash aren't for ladies after dark. They don't call it Hell's Half Acre for nothing.'

'No safer for boys either,' said Emily.

'I can look after myself!' he said with a frown, heaving the trunk back on his shoulder. 'Shall I tell 'em to expect you for dinner? Best to keep a table by. Hotel's full.'

She nodded.

'Make it for half-past seven. I reckon I'll leave the Fair by six.'

He nodded, turned, swayed under the weight of the trunk, regained his balance and was lost in the crowds on Wabash as he turned right for her hotel on Michigan.

17

Something Missing

Dr Eels's injuries were superficial. He had a cut lip and a cracked incisor.

Riley, however, was a different matter.

The human eye is more resilient than it looks, being surrounded by the sclera – the white of the eye – which is tough connective tissue designed to protect the delicate inner parts that make sight possible.

The nib of a pen can easily rupture the sclera and cause blindness or impair the vision, especially if it is loaded with ink. But to do that the point must be thrust straight into it. If it comes at an angle there's a good chance that the sclera will do its job and divert the intruding object upwards and to the rear of the eye socket where it will come into contact with the bony orbit which holds the eye.

Unpleasant, possibly dangerous, but not necessarily sight-threatening.

However, Anna Zemeckis had thrust the steel pen in hard, very hard. It had been diverted all right, sliding over the sclera, and then, because she used the heel of her hand, it hit the right orbit hard and had crunched on through into the frontal lobe of Riley's brain.

Now, over two hours later, the much-feared orderly was lying on the examination table in the doctor's surgery helpless as a child, the pen still sticking into her eye.

Eels, his lip stitched and plastered and made ugly yellow with iodine, stood on one side of the table.

Mould stood on the other, awaiting his master's verdict. It had been Mould who had attended to the doctor's superficial facial injuries and persuaded him to lie down for a while during which period Mould had got Riley onto the table. He had listened to her strange ramblings, made notes as Eels had trained him to do, and been very puzzled by what he had heard.

Finally he sedated Riley – very lightly, enough to ease the pain but not so she would lose consciousness – and had gone to get the doctor up again.

'Something's strange about her,' he said with barely concealed excitement.

'Strange?'

'See for yourself, sir,' he said.

Eels had done just that. He examined the angle of the steel pen in Riley's eye but did not touch it. He asked her a few questions and listened to the semi-incoherent answers.

It was not what she said but how she said it that excited Eels.

Her voice was soft, almost gentle.

That was something Riley's voice had *never* been.

The injury appeared to have changed her personality – for the better.

Eels studied her, and the pen, and then turned to Mould.

'Interesting,' he said, 'very.'

Mould agreed.

'She's an ugly brute,' observed Eels.

Then, raising his voice, he added, 'Aren't you, Riley?'

Riley giggled like the woman she wasn't and never had been.

'Highly interesting, I think,' said Eels. 'But more than that . . . the eye appears completely undamaged but for some peripheral bruising and, of course, the area of the orbit is sterile and therefore . . .'

'Therefore this is a far better route in than via the nostril, sir?'

'I would never have thought of it,' said Eels in a moment of wonder and rare candor. 'We access the brain by way of the orbits of the eye. Perhaps, if we angle the instrument right, we need only make one entry to cause lesions sufficient to deal with both lobes.'

They stared at the grotesque sight of Riley and the pen in her eye, both literally breathless with excitement at their momentous discovery. In the whole of America right now it was unlikely that anyone else knew better than Eels and his assistant Mould precisely what this signified.

They had found a practical method of quickly and efficiently pacifying the troublesome mental patient for good. This was the 'cure' Eels had been seeking and it promised to revolutionize the treatment of the mentally ill – worldwide.

Then, after a pause, he gave a hard, greedy look at Mould: 'Not a word of this to anyone.'

'Certainly not, doctor.'

It was not until after he had de-gowned and returned to his examination room where it had all happened that the shock finally had set in.

Eels sat at his desk and his hands began to shake.

'I'd better lie down again for a bit,' he told himself.

But he never did.

Because it was then that something suddenly came to him, something that set his heart thumping in alarm.

He got up and looked around the room.

Under the desk.

Then in the desk drawers and on the couch and under it.

Then by the camera and its tripod and then right out of the door and along the corridor outside.

Then back down to find Mould and the orderly who had come to rescue them.

'Did you see my clipboard,' he asked, with increasing urgency. 'You *must* have seen it. She had no reason to take it. Has she been found yet?'

'She will be, Dr Eels,' said the orderly, 'they always are. More than likely she'll give herself up.'

'But I need the papers on that clipboard. I *need* them. They must not fall into anyone else's hands.'

'We'll find 'em, sir,' they said.

'You'd better,' said Eels.

He began to sweat at the thought of his patron, Paul Hartz of Darke Hartz & Company, and how he would react to what had happened.

Hartz, who had been instrumental in securing Eels's appointment to Dunning, was not a man who gave people a second chance.

18

White City

Emily boarded the Elevated for the World's Fair at Wabash and Congress. En route to Jackson Park she settled back into a seat in the crowded compartment given up to her by a sharply dressed gentleman who stood and raised his spotless hat with a charming but predatory smirk.

She knew his game. Mashers like him – smart, confident, well-groomed men who knew how to charm young, inexperienced, out-of-town female visitors to the Fair – were two a dime on that route. An offer of a seat was a well-known ploy. She already knew from her previous time in Chicago, the kind of fate that awaited girls who fell into the hands of men like that and resolutely ignored him.

She got out at 40th so she could enjoy the walk to the Fair by way of the Midway Plaisance. This exciting mile-long westward extension of the Fair was a show-ground for a host of overseas and private exhibits. There were North African bazaars, Irish villages, German Bierkellers, Egyptian donkeys, a spoof volcano that erupted every hour – and just about every huckster, con artist, escapologist, trickster, quack and fraud in America worthy of the name. All of them working the Fair-going crowds for everything they could get, and charging from two dollars to go up in a balloon, to just ten cents for a trip on the sliding railway.

The fact was, as Emily had discovered during her previous visit to Chicago, the Plaisance was more fun, more entertaining and sometimes a good deal more educational than the official buildings, programs and worthy exhibits which lay beyond the Fair's formal entrance in Jackson Park. The rest of the world had worked that one out too.

But now Emily headed through the crowds determined not to be drawn into any of the dozens of attractions along the way. Even so her eyes were inevitably drawn to the most astonishing of the Midway Plaisance's spectacles – the gigantic 260-foot wheel erected halfway along it by George W. Ferris, engineer and bridge builder.

She reached the main entrance to the Fair itself a few minutes before she was due to meet Fay Bancroft and headed straight for the impressive Woman's Building. Finding a seat, Emily arranged herself as elegantly as she could, though she couldn't help noticing she was surrounded by ladies who were far more effortlessly elegant than she was.

'My dear, I've kept you waiting!' Fay Bancroft's familiar, well-modulated voice called out.

She was one of those women who, having sighted her quarry heads directly toward it with a winning smile while her eyes dart and glance about to left and right and straight over the head of the person she is about to greet, lest she miss something in the social scene around her.

They exchanged the lightest of kisses, after which Fay led Emily toward the elevator.

'We'll take luncheon in the East Indian Tea House on the third floor; the Roof Garden Café has become rather too crowded for my tastes since word got round about how competitive its prices are. It's become a victim of its own success! But the Tea House is really very civilized and the gentlemen are not allowed to spit, which is a mercy. We can talk properly there.'

The two women had not known each other long but from the first they had discovered an easy intimacy. Fay had spotted the young reporter at a tedious function in the Manufactures and Liberal Arts Hall early on in Emily's first trip to Chicago, guessed what she was and, having a penchant for nurturing rising stars, invited her to a tea party. She had been flattered when Emily had offered to write something about her role on the Educational Sub-Committee of the 117-member Board of Lady Managers of the Woman's Building, and when that piece was published in the *Echo*, had taken Emily out to lunch downtown.

Emily quickly brought Fay up to date, telling her about the stunt she had pulled to meet Mr Pulitzer.

'I am quite appalled!' exclaimed Fay with delight. 'And what was the great man like? Did you meet his sainted wife? One hears so little of her that I sometimes wish one heard something bad!'

Their food came and both were hungry, enjoying the excellent cuisine and gossiping away like old friends.

Only when their main course was done did Emily get to business. She produced the photograph of Anna Zemeckis and a copy of the letter written by Janis to Pulitzer.

'And no-one knows where she went during those five weeks?' said Fay finally and somberly.

Emily shook her head.

'I spoke to Mr Zemeckis at length. He visited Chicago three times in all and went to every police department, every hospital, every morgue, but he didn't find her. Not until it was too late, that is, and she turned up on a slab in the morgue. She was killed in a traffic accident.'

'My dear!' said Fay softly, affecting a shudder.

'The question is where was she and what was she doing between the time she disappeared from her relatives' home and when she was killed in the accident? I've heard that others have gone missing, other women, I mean. During the Fair, quite a few.'

'Have you?' said Fay cautiously, her voice dropping.

'Most are never heard of again.'

'Aren't they?' murmured Fay.

'Mr Pulitzer said that was what happened in cities and there's nothing new in it,' continued Emily. 'I heard that more have gone missing in Chicago during the Fair than might be expected.'

Fay stayed silent.

So did Emily.

'Girls like that . . .' began Fay dismissively.

'She came from a good family,' Emily interjected at once, sensing Fay's hesitation. 'Mr Zemeckis raised her right. Didn't let her out of his sight until she came to Chicago this spring.'

'Well then maybe a girl like that . . .'

'Like what, Fay? Like *me*? I'm the same, my father was no better than Mr Zemeckis. Working men trying to do right by their daughters. You can't call us all "girls like that" and sweep us under the carpet and forget about us.'

Fay reached out a hand and put it on Emily's.

'Is that why you're so interested in this girl? Something about her that could have been you?'

Emily nodded.

'And you think she was a good girl?'

'I know it,' said Emily. 'I've seen her home. I've seen her father. I've talked to her neighbors. I've read her letters. She was a girl who deserved to get the best out of life. But someone, probably a man or men, has taken that from her and now . . .'

Fay looked apologetic.

'I didn't mean to speak ill of the girl. I know your background, Emily, because you've told me. I can guess where this Anna girl came from. You know why?'

Fay leaned closer.

'Take any American woman and you know what you find not very far beneath the surface? Someone – a mother, a sister, maybe a grandparent – someone in the family who came off a boat with hardly a dime in their pocket.'

Fay squeezed her hand and smiled.

She stared into Emily's eyes and Emily stared back, suddenly amazed. Fay was talking about herself.

'But I thought your family had been here for generations . . .'

Fay put a finger to her lips.

'I *prefer* you to think that and everyone else too, so keep it to yourself. My little weakness I guess. But I want you to know that I *don't* judge a girl by the job she does because oftentimes it's the only job she can get or she can do. I judge people by what they make of their opportunities. You're right about women in Chicago and the Fair and them disappearing more than they ought. It's common knowledge. Chicago's still a frontier town for all it wants the world to think differently. It's also a dangerous place. We all know that but we don't advertise the fact. If we had we wouldn't have had the World's Fair here, and if we did now then people would stay away.'

'That doesn't help Anna Zemeckis,' said Emily.

'No it doesn't,' conceded Fay.

She sat thinking and Emily let her.

Finally Fay sighed and said, 'Emily, I'm going to try and help you find out what happened to her. Give me a day or two. I'll make some enquiries. Meanwhile . . . have you a notebook?'

Emily produced one and handed Fay a pencil.

'You'll get help from the women at Hull House. You know it?'

Emily nodded. 'Yes, I've already contacted Miss Lathrop.'

She had visited the famous Settlement House at Halsted Street on the Near West Side before, having asked for and obtained the obligatory interview with its indefatigable founder Jane Addams.

'Many girls in trouble turn to Hull House. I'm sure Julia will help you. She is a good friend of mine. She does much good among the single working girls of the West Side for whom there is so little provision and who are naturally vulnerable. I will send her a note to say you are a friend. As for these others . . .'

Fay jotted a few more names in Emily's notebook, explaining how each person might be useful.

'Now,' she said suddenly, glancing at the clock, 'There's a meeting I need to attend at 2.00 p.m. so I must go. But at four there's a reception over at the Illinois State Building which a number of the people on this list will be attending. I think you'll find it useful, so perhaps you'll be my guest for that?'

Emily agreed at once that she would be glad to.

'Till later then, my dear,' Fay said when they parted with another brief embrace.

19

To Canal Street

Anna Zemeckis stayed low in the open hopper as the train dragged out of the northwestern suburbs of Chicago toward the city center. It traveled slowly and gave her time to think.

She remembered the driver's warning to stay out of sight until the fourth stop and did not even risk so much as peeking over the wagon edge to see where she was.

Her memory was getting clearer all the time, like a puzzle whose pieces kept appearing from nowhere without warning to fill in the picture of her life. But she seemed to see it at a distance, without emotion, as if the woman in the picture was not herself.

She now knew her name, that she was with child, that she came from New York and that her father's name was Janis and that he was strict and she was scared of him. She remembered that well enough. Of one thing she was also sure: he would never accept the sin and the shame of what she had done. There was no going back.

She knew also that whatever had happened to her before she fell into Bubbly Creek was still too shocking for her to remember – or more like, to want to remember. But she knew she must try because maybe that would help her remember who the father of her child was.

The third stop brought the train into the shadow of a grain elevator and the sounds of ships on the river. She used the remaining time to tidy herself up a bit. Her dress was torn and stained from her escape. She took the one she had stolen from her bundle and, keeping low so as not to show herself over the side of the open hopper, she undressed quickly and tried it on. It was plain and a little large, but at least it was clean, as were the stockings and the shawl which she wrapped around herself.

Then she noticed the clipboard she had hit Dr Eels with. She was about to discard it, but decided to take a closer look at it for the first time.

On the top was some kind of list of names with something about 'experimental procedures' and Cook County Insane Asylum on it; underneath were several forms. All the names – twenty of them – were women's. And there, near the end, was her own – *Anna Zemeckis, age about 21* . . . She didn't stop to read any more. Rolling the list up tight together with the form with her name on it, she stuffed the papers down her bodice.

She pulled on the woolen stockings and felt less exposed after that. Her shoes were sturdy but grubby. She managed to get them clean with a piece of sacking.

That left her hair, which she guessed looked as messy as it felt, which was tangled and lank.

She tore off a part of the hem of the dress she had discarded and used it to tie back her hair.

But her hands and nails were filthy and her mouth felt rough; and still the sense of being sick was never far away.

The papers had brought her an inrush of memory of working in a library. Was it Chicago? Or New

York? Or was it both? Trouble was, the harder she tried to remember the more difficult it was.

Twenty minutes later the train finally made its fourth stop. Anna peeked over the edge of the wagon and saw the Chicago River stretching away between two high factory buildings. There was a ship, some barges and some cranes and beyond them three bridges one after the other.

Footsteps crunched along the track and she hid back down again.

'You can come down, it's safe!'

It was the driver.

She clambered back down the hopper ladder and on to the track.

'You know where you are?'

She shook her head.

'That's the North Side industrial area in that direction. You don't want to go that way. Not nice. You go *that* way.'

He pointed to a wooden fence on the far side of the tracks.

'Climb through that gap in the fence over there and you can make your way across the empty lots to Canal Street. What are you going to do?'

'I don't know. Need water first! I'm parched.'

He led her across a couple of rail tracks to a far corner of the sidings and a ramshackle hut.

He fished about under the wooden structure, found a key and opened up the padlocked door.

'Here . . .'

He gave her water and some food.

'Best bet is to get yourself beyond the reach of Cook County and across the state border into Minnesota. You can get a direct train to St Paul or Minneapolis. That'll get you out of trouble.'

'Oh, but I need to get further than that,' responded Anna. 'To Canada.' The conviction with which she said it was a surprise to her, a sudden moment of revelation. For now she remembered. 'Yes . . . my aunt, she lives there . . . on a farm, north out of Winnipeg, on Lac du Bonnet.'

'Then you'll be heading in the right direction. You can get a train straight to Winnipeg from St Paul. You got beaten up by the look of things.'

He had noted with concern her bruised face.

Then he added, 'The girls always get beaten up in the Detention Hospital; and worse. Then they get sent to Dunning.'

'My beating happened before that,' said Anna, suddenly sure it had. 'It happened before I ended up in Bubbly Creek.'

He looked sympathetic.

'Can you sew?'

'Of course.'

He nodded toward Canal Street.

'Go on past the Union Depot and down to Jackson. There's sweat work down there for anyone can use a needle and not many questions asked. But lie low. Dunning doesn't like losing patients and they'll put the police on it.'

Anna's heart missed a beat, and then some more.

'I hurt someone getting away,' she blurted out.

'Then they *will* be after you, girl. Just lie low a few days, get some money together and then get the train out to St Paul. The Fair's on and the police have their work cut out. They won't hunt you for long. Better things to do.'

He stared at her.

'Got any money?'

She shook her head and said, 'I don't want, I . . .'

He took a handful of coins from his pocket and pressed them into her hand.

'You take 'em.'

'Why are you helping me . . . ?' she stuttered.

'I was down on my luck once and someone helped me.'

He grinned suddenly.

'Why did any of us come to America if it wasn't to make things better for others as well as ourselves. Eh?'

'I'll pay you back.'

'You help someone else one day. That'll be payment enough.'

'My name's Anna,' she said impulsively.

'And mine's Tomas Steffens! Now . . . go!'

He stood there watching her, right until she had slipped through the fence and was gone.

'Good luck, Anna,' he said aloud, 'you'll need it in Chicago!'

20

The Illinois Crowd

CHICAGO Tuesday October 24, 1893   3.35 PM

The reception that Emily Strauss attended that afternoon was busy, loud and useful. Fay was as good as her word and introduced her to a cross-section of Chicagoans to most of whom Emily gave her card and received theirs in return, though she was sure with her good memory for a face and a name that she would remember most of them.

She was allowed a few brief words with the high-ups including the famous Mrs Potter Palmer the life force behind the Woman's Building, who gave her a winning smile, and Philip Armour, king of the meatpackers who smiled politely but seemed anxious to move on. Finally, feeling like one of a dozen bees around a honey pot, she shook the hand of the Mayor himself, the bearded and affable Carter Henry Harrison III. It was a chance she did not want to miss, though she would have preferred to meet him later on in her investigation.

'Good afternoon, sir. Emily Strauss of the New York *World* . . .'

One of Harrison's aides immediately closed in.

Emily ignored him. 'Any chance of a few words for the *World*?'

'Plenty,' said Harrison, 'but right now . . .'

He was smiling as he moved away.

'. . . about women visitors disappearing during the Fair.'

The moment she said it Emily knew it was too much, too soon. Harrison showed no alarm or irritation but his aide swiftly stepped in.

'Another time, Miss . . . ?'

'Strauss.'

'Another time, lady.'

But Harrison turned back.

His smile was genuine. He had not been elected Mayor five times for nothing.

'Sure there's been women going missing, Miss Strauss, and men too. But Chicago's got no monopoly on disappearances. In fact, it's about the one thing we *don't* have a monopoly on!'

There was general laughter and it was good natured.

'People go missing all over. Even in New York, as your boss Mr Pulitzer knows. As for Chicago, we do what we can for those that go missing in our jurisdiction, and with a fair amount of success. But . . .'

Someone tugged Harrison's sleeve. Emily had had her two minutes' worth.

'Maybe I can call on you at City Hall, Mr Mayor?'

'You do that. My office and my home are always open to genuine inquirers. You won't find me hard to find. But right now . . .'

He shrugged mock-helplessly, reached out a hand and shook hers again.

'Gotta go.'

He went, his entourage with him, and Emily was left feeling he was a good man who had given her more time than most.

'Did he really mean that?' she said to someone standing next to her. '. . . about his door always being open?'

'That's *exactly* what he meant. Everybody knows where the Mayor lives on South Ashland Avenue. I reckon it's the secret of his success; he makes people feel he's accessible.'

Emily watched after him. 'I just might take Mr Harrison up on his offer . . .' she said to herself.

Meanwhile the Illinois crowd swelled about her and she continued on her round of shaking the hands of the great and good of Chicago. These were mainly businessmen, their enterprises ranging from real estate and finance to steel, groceries and pharmaceuticals. There were women too: some no more than pretty things on their husbands' arms, others more formidable, like Hannah Horner, the German-born widow of Henry Horner, the grocery magnate of South Water Street. In no time at all Emily had out of her the story of how on Henry's premature death in the late seventies Mrs Horner took over the business and grew it yet more.

'That's enough about me!' declared Mrs Horner adding 'Time for you to meet the Illinois Crowd!' as she introduced Emily to a group of women whose hands she shook and names noted: Harriet Isham, Kate Field, Mrs Frederic Eames, Mrs Christiane Darke, Mrs John Jacob Glessner and several others, any one of whom might be useful in the days to come.

A while later Fay reappeared.

'That photograph of your girl,' she said, 'there's a place you might usefully display it and I have obtained permission for you to do so . . .'

Emily followed her to a notice board at one end of the Great Hall in which the reception was being held. It was filled with advertisements of various kinds and in one section titled 'Looking for . . .!' there were dozens of cards, slips of paper with names written on them and a few images in the form of *cartes de visite* of visitors to the Fair, all for people who were looking to contact each other.

Emily pinned up the spare copy of the photograph of Anna Zemeckis she had had made before leaving New York and scribbled her name as well as her own and her contact details, asking for any information anyone might have about her and the weeks when she went missing.

Eventually, as the numbers in the hall suddenly fell away and she saw the sun was dropping low on the horizon outside, Emily realized she had stayed later than she intended. Chicago was not a good place for a single woman to be out after nightfall. She decided to head off back downtown for her hotel supper and an early night.

*

Meanwhile, elsewhere in the hall of the Illinois State Building a middle-aged, mustachioed man, his face tough and resolute, his eyes intelligent and questing, his form muscular, his jacket of thick tweed, his boots a little scuffed and grubby, had been watching the crowd carefully.

Now it was thinning he finally he emerged into the light still contriving to seem more a shadow than a real man.

He spent his days watching people, and noting what he saw and sometimes what he didn't and was in the Illinois State Building of the White City at a reception to which he hadn't been invited.

But then no-one noticed, so it didn't matter.

He went to the notice board and examined it quickly and systematically. Then seeing the picture of Anna Zemeckis and Emily's note, he quickly and calmly removed them both and placed them carefully in an inside pocket.

Nobody objected. He did not look the kind of man one should challenge.

Then he turned away and vanished into the gathering gloom outside.

As for Emily, her hopes for an early return downtown were dashed. The end-of-day queues at the terminus for the Elevated seemed a mile long and the trains were running slow.

21

Sweatshops

Anna Zemeckis did what Tomas Steffens the engine driver advised and set off at once to find a sewing job in a sweatshop. It wasn't easy.

She started on Canal Street which ran north–south on the west side of the Chicago River and Chicago's downtown area. It was a street of busy intersections with trains crossing over at either end and the Union Depot right in the middle.

Anna hurried southward through its clamor of wagons and carts, busy warehousemen and shouting porters, keeping her eyes to the sidewalk and her shawl tightly wrapped round her.

She felt safe in the anonymity of its crowds but these petered out after she had passed the depot and continued on toward Van Buren Street and the garment quarter. She knew she needed to find employment if she was to pay for the board and lodging she must find.

She stopped and huddled in a doorway to count the money Tomas Steffens had pressed into her hand: a dollar and fifteen cents. It was more than generous and her gratitude was equaled by her determination that she would somehow find a way of paying it back.

She hurried on.

At Jackson she saw a man coming over the bridge

carrying a bundle of half-sewn black cloaks on his shoulder tied together with twine and impulsively turned in the direction from which he had come.

It took her straight on to South Market Street and in whichever direction she looked she saw evidence of the garment trade – tailoring establishments, a cravat factory, wagons with bales of cloth and some men outside a doorway with rails of dresses and some boxes of newly made men's pants.

She was just debating whether or not to approach them for a job when she saw a notice in a window on the far side of street. The establishment was called Taylor Kirk and Co., and the notice read *HANDS WANTED FOR FINE HATS*.

When she got closer she saw that someone had added the word *Experienced* at the top and *Use the Back* at the end.

Plain sewing she was sure she could do, but 'Fine Hats' she was less sure of. She passed on by in the hope that if one place wanted hands another surely would.

She was not wrong. A block further on she saw a huge hoarding on top of a seven-floor factory which read *INTERNATIONAL TAILORING COMPANY*.

The door at the side of the premises also advertised for hands, this time for 'finishers'. Anna went on in.

The dingy interior still hummed and vibrated with the sound of machinery, the working day in this part of Chicago not ending till seven. There was no light but what came through the door.

A boy stood by a lift which was open and piled high with garments.

'You gotta use the stairs,' he said.

'Who do I ask for?'

'Depends.'

'For work.'

'Just ask,' he said. 'Third floor.'

He spat tobacco juice on the floor at her feet.

The wooden stairs were steep and uneven and the noise got worse with each one until, arriving at the third floor, Anna could no longer hear the sound of her own breathing.

Her interview lasted seconds.

'You experienced?'

'Not very but I can learn.'

'There's no-one to learn you. Show me your hands.'

Anna held them out, conscious of her stubby, dirty nails.

'Yer'll not last long here. Too soft. Try two blocks on. There's always smaller firms wanting.'

Again and again it was the same story until one of the girls she met said, 'If you can hand sew Brennan's is worth a try. Always looking for hand finishers. Pays well if you can get in. It's on Clark Street. Can't miss it – Brennan's Tailoring Emporium.'

Anna set off once more.

Brennan's had a shop at the front and a workplace at the back and their products were plain to see as Anna made her way through the gloomy stock rooms: ladies' cloaks, men's jackets and pants, and Brennan's specialty – cravats, slip-ties, dude ties, flat scarves, four-in-hands and bow-knots in colorful profusion.

The forewoman, Mrs Donal, was a formidable Irish lady. She said at once she was reluctant to take Anna on, explaining that pressure of work was so great that there was no time to learn green hands.

'But I'm dextrous and trained,' said Anna, responding to a grin and a wink from one of the girls nearby. 'I'm experienced with cloaks and coats.'

'Then why not get work in one of those trades? They pay better than us.'

'You could try me for a week,' said Anna.

'Try you for a year and you'll not learn it if you don't know it already.'

Anna sat there hopefully.

'I'll let you have a cravat and see what you can do,' said Mrs Donal. 'What's your name?'

Anna froze momentarily, remembering she must not betray her true identity, 'It's Jelena . . . Jelena Markulis.' Her mother's name had been the only one to come to her in that desperate moment.

It was a beginning and Anna set to, secretly watching another woman working on a scarf to see what she did.

The workshop was breezy and roomy and the hands had chairs and were allowed to talk: men one end, women the other. Mrs Donal ambled over an hour later and looked over Anna's work.

'Passable, I suppose.'

'What will I get paid?'

Mrs Donal snorted and walked off.

'That's a sample,' explained one of the other women. 'Don't pay you for samples. That's her privilege. She'd have told you to leave if she didn't like it. Finish it and ask for some more . . .'

Mrs Donal accepted the sample and gave Anna more cravats to do.

'Forty-five cents a dozen,' she said, 'and it's eight o'clock sharp in the morning or you're fined.'

Anna accepted the terms, grateful for what she had got.

'You German then?' said one of the girls. 'We're mainly Irish here.'

Anna shook her head.

Another asked, 'Where are you staying then?'

Anna explained that she had yet to find accommodation.

The woman nodded, having guessed Anna's situation right.

'Try the Mission of Hope,' she said. 'You Catholic?'

Anna shook her head, 'No, Lutheran.' But something made her reach instinctively for her neck.

She remembered she had had a crucifix once. Her mother's crucifix, the one she never took off.

She felt a pang of loss and sadness.

'I had a crucifix,' she said suddenly. 'But it's gone . . . and I can't remember where I lost it.'

'They'll give you one free at the Mission,' said her new friend without enthusiasm. 'It's on Monroe and South Jefferson. Mrs Donal'll give you a letter. They only take girls in employment so you'll be all right.'

22

Dead Man's Alley

CHICAGO Tuesday October 24, 1893   7.10 PM

The going-home queues for the Elevated at Jackson Park were so long that it was gone seven in the evening before Emily finally found a seat and was on her way back downtown.

No sooner had she done so than she fell asleep.

Others did the same. A day at the World's Fair brought on tiredness quicker than any sleeping draught.

The trouble was that when she woke, which she did with a start, the carriage was emptying of its last passengers and a guard was prodding her.

'Train stops here. Got to get off.'

'Where are we? I need to get to Congress.'

'So do other folk. You'll have to walk like them.'

'Where are we?'

'Twelfth. Stay on Wabash and you'll be all right. It ain't that far. Now . . .'

The guard helped her off.

Maybe Emily was still half asleep, maybe she was just confused, or maybe Chicago, having given her a warm welcome and an easy afternoon, wanted to remind her of its darker side.

Within half a block she knew she was lost, the steps down from the Elevated confusing her into thinking she was going north, which she needed to do for a couple of blocks to find her hotel, when in fact she had turned west . . . or maybe . . . or possibly . . .

She couldn't make sense of where she was at all except the more she looked around the more she did not like what she saw.

The better-dressed ladies she was used to seeing downtown had all disappeared, and had been replaced by looser-looking women with garish dresses with bodices set too low and hems set too high. They stood in groups, staring at passing men.

The men were worse still: some well-dressed but furtive, others looked like young clerks out for an evening's fun. Others hung back in the shadows, bowlers at an angle over their eyes, keeping a predatory eye on the passers by.

Emily dug into her purse for the Rand McNally map of the city she had brought with her, but knew it was a mistake the moment she unfolded it and held it under the nearest light, which came from a saloon window.

Men already lurking on the sidewalk took the map as an excuse to stop.

'Can I help you, ma'am . . . ?'

'No,' said Emily firmly, hurriedly putting the map away and walking on.

She stopped by a stall that sold newspapers, or so it seemed, to give herself time to think.

'They come by the half dozen, ma'am,' grinned the stall-holder.

She looked more closely. The 'papers' were a cover for something else: postcards with pictures of women in every stage of undress.

A big, rough-looking man with a curly bowler loomed over her, his smile as reassuring as a streetcar with a wheel missing.

'No, I . . .' she hurried on, realizing it was best to keep moving. She had to find a more private place to study her map.

If she could only find the Elevated again she could orientate herself. If only she could see a street name . . .

'Hello, miss!"

She crossed the road, hoping she was heading north, knowing the hotel could not be more than a block or two away. On the sidewalk on the far side she spotted another road which she only realized was a filthy dark alley when she had turned right into it.

She saw its name too late: Dead Man's Alley.

Turning back immediately she found herself face

to face with three or four men grinning unpleasantly at her.

'Lookin' fer someone, lady?' growled one of them.

Emily was terrified.

'Or somethin'?'

Her heartbeat was thunder in her chest.

'*Leave her be!*'

Another man, bigger than the rest, and better dressed, loomed out of the dark and faced the men down. He carried a cane which he only had to raise slightly before they retreated back into the seething crowd.

'Thank you, sir. I was trying to get to the Auditorium Annex.'

He smiled but she couldn't see more than his teeth in the dark.

'That's not far. Come from the Fair? The Elevated stop short?'

'Yes,' she said, glad he understood. 'At 12th. I just want to get to my hotel.'

'It's just a block from here, ma'am,' he said, taking his hat off and offering an arm.

'Which way?' she said nervously.

'I'll show you. Down here's the quickest. Be there in less than three minutes. I'll show you.'

His voice was the purr of a big tom cat.

'Where?' said Emily faintly as he led her back into the alley, the way she had not wanted to go. 'I don't think . . .' Ten paces on he took her hand off his arm and held it in his hand, his grip like steel.

'Let me go,' she said.

'Don't think so, lady,' he said, forcing her forward almost off her feet.

Again she tried to scream, but failed. She looked desperately back toward the light of the street and saw the figures of men watching.

Emily Strauss, cub reporter, who thought that at twenty-two she knew the ways of the world, had fallen for the oldest trick in the book. Accepting help from a welcome stranger because a group of men are threatening, not realizing he's the one in charge.

She tried to call for help.

His hand tightened on her arm still more and her cry turned into one of pain as the shadows closed in around her.

23
Mission of Hope

CHICAGO Tuesday October 24, 1893   7.45 PM

Over on the Near West Side, two hundred yards down Jefferson at the corner of Monroe, stood the dour-looking Catholic Mission that was about to become Anna Zemeckis's unlikely new home.

It was built of yellow brick in a dreary, straitlaced way with a formidable, solid oak door in heavy gothic style, its hinges massive, its lock huge and with a mean metal grille, blanked off with a wooden slat which could only be slid open from the inside.

There was a range of plain rectangular windows covered in black metal bars facing the street – to stop intruders presumably, but Anna wondered irreverently if it was also to stop the holy sisters getting out and having a good time downtown.

The place did not exactly inspire feelings of warmth and none at all of hope, even though a side

134

extension to the building had *MISSION OF HOPE* painted on it in big black letters.

Anna approached the door and, before deciding whether to raise the knocker or pull the metal bell-pull, read the two notices displayed.

Charity handouts only on Saturdays 5.00-7.00 p.m. read one of them, *Working girls only need apply* read another.

Anna rang the bell, which clanged loudly.

Almost at once the wooden slat slammed open and two cold gray eyes stared at her from behind a metal grille.

'You should use the door-knocker after seven-thirty,' the owner of the eyes said in a thin, harsh voice.

The slat slammed shut again but after a moment bolts were drawn and the door was opened. Anna found herself staring down at a diminutive, rotund nun with gray eyes and a thin, wet mouth.

'Follow me.'

Anna was tired and just wanted to sleep. She signed some forms; she met three sisters, including the one who opened the door, who was Sister Agnes. The others were the superior, Sister Ursula, old, crabbed and stooped; and Sister Dolores, younger, bad-tempered looking and bossy.

Who did what Anna had no idea. She knew only that Sister Agnes ran through the Rules with a capital R, the breaking of any one of which meant immediate expulsion from the Mission and the forfeit of all monies received and Sister Dolores demanded fifty cents from her 'against breakages' and opened a cash box that was overflowing with money.

'Must you have the fifty cents now?' Anna managed to say.

'Yes,' said Sister Ursula, reaching out for it.

Anna's pitiful supply of money from Tomas Steffens suddenly halved.

Sister Agnes took her to a dormitory and showed her the cot that was to be hers. There were no other women in there at all, presumably because they were all having supper. Anna could smell the sickly aroma of overcooked vegetables and overstewed meat. It made her stomach turn.

Finally, left alone, she lay down on the cot and closed her eyes.

'Boots *off!*' a voice shouted in her ear.

It was Sister Dolores, the younger one, appearing out of nowhere.

'The Rules are *very* clear on *that* point,' she said.

Anna took them off and lay down again.

She closed her eyes and drifted into worried half-sleep, images of the long day dancing before her, the noise of the crowds on Canal Street now soft, now loud, and then blending in with the clatter of the machinery at Brennan's, before that too melded into something else: the arrival of women in the dormitory, their boots resounding on the wooden floor, their voices subdued.

For the first time during that long and terrible day, Anna Zemeckis allowed herself to shed a single tear for the crucifix she suddenly missed so much. The one a long, long time ago her father had given her when her mother died, which was the first thing she could remember; and she experienced again the grief she had first felt at the loss of her mother and how her long journey to America with her father had begun.

Janis Zemeckis.

He was always so strict. He would never forgive her now. *Never.*

Before sleep overtook her, she lay for a few minutes contemplating the religious images hung in frames along the walls of her dormitory. There was the Virgin Mary and Mary Magdalene and in a far corner a picture of Jesus at a door holding a lantern, representing the Light of the World.

But strangely, in the gathering gloom, out of all these images, it was Jesus' crown of thorns that showed up best.

24

Run!

CHICAGO Tuesday October 24, 1893   8.08 PM

Dead Man's Alley was dark, dank and stank of water-closets and filth, of cheroots and beer. And there were noises too: fits of raucous laughter, of rowdy men carousing in nearby saloons and, somewhere, closer, a drunken woman's voice warbling Mr Harris's 'After the Ball is Over' to an out-of-tune piano.

The grip on Emily's arm was powerful and her helplessness was made worse by the fact that the man had hooked his left arm around her shoulder, pulling her tightly into his side.

'You try screaming again, lady, and I'll stick you,' he said savagely.

Her left leg collided with a trash can which went flying.

Even if she had tried, which she didn't, Emily could not have screamed. Her mouth was dry, her throat knotted up with fear.

She tried to turn away and saw, in a half-open door, a man standing against a woman. His pants were half off, her hand was at his privates, his hand was up her skirt and her thighs above her stockings all bare.

The prostitute stared at Emily indifferently and went about her business.

From the direction in which she had come, she could hear the normal sounds of people in the street and the clip-clop of hacks passing by.

'Where are you taking me?'

The man hit her on the side of her head and it hurt.

Ahead she saw an open door against the side of which a girl wearing next to nothing was leaning, drunkenly mouthing the words of the song Emily had just heard to the sound of a piano from within.

She knew as certain as night followed day that if he got her in there she wouldn't be coming out again.

'*Hey! Mister!*' someone shouted.

Emily's abductor stopped in his tracks and looked back the way they had come.

A lump of sawn wood came out of the darkness at him. It smashed straight into his groin. The man screamed in pain and let go of Emily. A hand reached out to support her. It was Johnny Leppard, the young bellhop from her hotel, and he looked like a demon out of hell.

'Run!' he shouted, '*Run!*'.

Ten minutes later, they finally slowed.

Johnny took her arm gently and helped Emily on.

'Come on, miss, it ain't far now.'

'How did you know where to find me?' said Emily.

'Heard the Elevated was stopped at 12th and went down to meet you. Other guests have had trouble when that happens so I thought . . .'

Emily felt tears coming.

'It's all right, miss,' said Johnny, his hand comfortingly firm on her arm, 'you're safe now.'

'I'll get some supper sent up,' said Johnny ten minutes later when they reached the Auditorium hotel. 'Don't expect you'll want to come to the public restaurant now.'

'No,' she said, then, 'It's Johnny Leppard, isn't it?'

'You got a good memory, miss.'

She stared at him. He looked so young but he looked tougher than any man she knew.

He grinned again.

'I never forget a name and a face,' she said, 'and I'll never forget yours. Thank you.'

'We can't go losing our guests, Miss Strauss, or we'd have no trade. Your supper's on the way!'

Then he was gone with a grin and an engaging swagger.

Emily breathed deeply, cursing herself for being such a fool. She would not make the same mistake again.

Her home city of Pittsburgh had been rough and tough. New York was worse. But Chicago? It was something else.

She picked up the paper she had bought that morning at the depot, the *Chicagoer Arbeiter-Zeitung*, and skimmed through it, hoping to find something pleasant to lighten her mood, but it was full of obituaries, accidents, lost children and a new story about the body of a man found dumped on 15th and Halsted. The horror lay in the fact that he had been eviscerated and none of his internal organs were to be found.

Someone in the Harrison Street Police Station had

told the reporter that, 'It wasn't the first of this kind. It looks like the Meisters. They do it to their own, as a punishment, and to intimidate others.'

She put the paper down.

She frowned, gritted her teeth and looked at her hands.

They were steadier now.

She breathed some more.

Finally she said out loud, as though the whole city were listening: 'You know what? Chicago's not going to beat Emily Strauss.'

DAY SEVEN

Wednesday October 25, 1893

25

Deadhouse

At eight the next morning Emily took a streetcar from Harrison and Wabash for Cook County Hospital. It was a twenty-five-minute trip over the river to the West Side, against the run of traffic for that time of day.

The tall, red-brick buildings of the hospital with their colonnades, mansard roofs and lofty central tower were less than twenty years old. But it seemed to Emily that their ornate gothic style, pale sandstone facings and oppressive ornament already looked out of date in a city that was advancing so rapidly toward the twentieth century.

The morgue, or deadhouse as Chicagoans called it, was a different matter. It lay through the main building on the east side of the huge site in an extension hurriedly added to accommodate a need that reflected the city's exponential growth.

The deadhouse had a solid oak door and a hall that smelt fresh, looked clean and at that time of morning was still nearly empty. There was a reception desk with a male attendant but he was busy talking.

It gave Emily the opportunity to look around. Along the entire wall of an adjacent corridor, she saw a series of notice-boards that carried dozens of images of the faces of the dead, some head-on, some in profile, some in both. Most were head shots but a few were full body, minimally covered.

A number were quite disturbing, the features distorted in death or maybe by the manner of death.

'Some of them don't look too good, do they?'

Emily turned to find herself facing a man fifty or so. His beard was trim, his eyes bright and humorous, his clothes good quality.

'I've seen worse,' she said.

She had already worked out that she was going to get nowhere in the deadhouse if she played the weak woman.

She explained she was from the New York *World* and a few minutes later found herself in the presence of Alan Freeman, the hospital's senior mortician.

Freeman seemed genial and was willing enough to help, if he could. He listening quietly as Emily told him what she knew about Anna Zemeckis's disappearance and her father's attempts to find out what had happened to her.

'He said he came here . . . to identify her body,' she said. Light dawned on Freeman's face.

'A little Latvian man from New York.'

'That's the one,' said Emily.

Freeman jumped up, disappeared for a couple of minutes and came back with a file and sat down again.

'It's a terrible thing, Miss Strauss, to happen to a young girl like that. I have a daughter myself and can't begin to imagine how he feels. This city's a hard place.'

He opened the file and glanced through the autopsy report on the girl's body.

Outside in the corridor a bell rang. Then again.

'Day's beginning,' said Freeman matter-of-factly.

Another man in a white coat appeared.

'See to it, Eugene, would you,' said Freeman, 'I'm busy.'

He led Emily to an office off the main autopsy room. Its walls were lined with shelves holding large, thick ledgers. He pulled one down.

'Cases like hers where cause of death is known and properly witnessed only need a brief autopsy report. She died as a result of cranial and chest trauma sustained under the wheels of a streetcar.'

'May I see the report?'

Freeman passed it to Emily. The report was no more than a hastily written page recording answers to standard questions on the body of the deceased. It confirmed all Freeman had said, but, nevertheless, Emily read it through twice.

'What does "Other indications irrelevant" mean?' she asked, pointing to a final line before the report was signed off.

Freeman hesitated. He took back the ledger, read the line again and looked at her.

'You're a journalist, not a relative?'

'That's right.'

'You must not publish what I am about to say. Some things are very hurtful to the next of kin. We find things out which it is better they do not know.'

'Like?' said Emily.

'This Zemeckis girl. She wasn't a virgin. But this has no relevance to the cause of death, so we make no special deal of it. Mr Zemeckis did not need to know this unless it was relevant or he had asked specifically.'

Emily was frowning. There was absolutely nothing in Anna's history that remotely suggested this. Everything she had heard suggested the opposite – that Anna was a good and virtuous Lutheran girl.

'So what happened to Anna's body?'

'She was buried in the potter's field out west of the city. It's the usual procedure. After the father came and confirmed it was his daughter, he claimed the effects and put in an application to have the body exhumed so she can be taken back to New York for burial. But that won't be for a couple more weeks.'

'Mr Freeman, there are photographs of dead people on the wall out there.'

Freeman nodded.

'You take photographs of all the deceased?'

'Most, but not all. We can't store the unidentified bodies for more than a few days, especially in the summer months, so we need to keep a record in case relatives turn up later.'

'Did you take any photographs of Anna Zemeckis before she was buried?'

Freeman nodded. 'I guess so.'

He looked at the file.

'A couple,' he said.

'Did Mr Zemeckis see them?'

'Sure he looked, but he found it traumatic. Hers was not a pretty death. The streetcar had mangled her body terribly. But his relative came too and confirmed the identification . . .'

'Mrs Markulis?'

'Yes. They went on the crucifix and the dress she was wearing.'

'May I see the photographs?'

'I guess so. But . . .'

'It's all right, Mr Freeman. I know what to expect.'

She didn't. And it was a shock.

The two photographs Freeman produced from a file and laid on the table in front of her were grotesque. One was of the face, split virtually in two, the flesh peeled back, only one eye visible. The mouth gaped open and ugly. The black hair was matted with blood. It looked like no man's daughter. It was monstrous.

The other was of the upper torso. The right breast and rib cage were horribly crushed. The shoulder looked as if it had been nearly wrenched from the body. The crucifix, which Emily recognized at once, lay just above the left breast and with the chain intact. It looked incongruous on such a mangled corpse. No doubt such a photograph would have been enough to rock any man's faith, let alone that of the God-fearing Janis Zemeckis.

Emily didn't need to look for long at the images. She could see why they would have disturbed Mr Zemeckis but . . .

But . . .

Freeman took them back.

But . . .

'What is it, Miss Strauss?'

'Can I take a second look at the one of the head?'

She did so, this time more dispassionately. In among the horror of distortion and disfigurement something very ordinary indeed had caught her eye and it was untouched by the accident.

'Did you make a note of all discriminating marks and scars on the body?'

'Yes, we always do.'

'Do you have a magnifying glass?'

'Yes, but . . .' Freeman protested as he rummaged in a drawer and handed her one.

'Why, have you noticed something?' he continued.

'Yes . . .' whispered Emily, as she hunched intently over the photograph.

'. . . she has pierced ears.'

Freeman looked at his report and said, 'Correct. She did have. Most women do these days.'

'That's right, *most* do, but *not* Anna Zemeckis,' Emily said.

'Pardon me?'

She studied the photograph again. Finally she looked up and said, with absolute conviction, 'I don't think this is Anna Zemeckis. Her father told me quite clearly that he refused to allow her to wear any jewelry apart from the crucifix, and that only because it had belonged to her dead mother. So unless she's had her ears pierced since she came to Chicago, this isn't her.'

Freeman picked up the picture of the dead girl and examined it himself.

'We have to be sure these marks on the ears did not occur as a result of the accident. Is there any way you can check out what you've just said?'

'Sure,' Emily replied. 'Her aunt, Mrs Markulis, who came here to identify the body. I'll ask her. But, having met the father I'm telling you now there's no way this girl would have gone against his wishes.'

Alan Freeman thought for a moment, and then said softly, 'If this is not Miss Zemeckis, then who is it?'

'. . . and why was she wearing Anna Zemeckis's crucifix and dress?' said Emily.

They sat in silence without any answers.

'I'll have to give it some thought, Miss Strauss. If I come up with anything more I'll let you know. Now . . .'

He got up to show her out.

On the way, through another open door, Emily spied a man in uniform standing by a table on which lay an uncovered corpse. It was gray-colored, the body of a man. Fortunately the head was turned away. But the body cavity was open, and, even to Emily's inexpert eye it looked empty of organs. Another man, short and gray-haired, was sketching it. A third, the pathologist probably, was at a sink washing his hands.

Emily suppressed a lurch of nausea, then remembered the newspaper story she had glanced at the night before.

'Sir, may I ask you, is that the man found yesterday on Halsted Street?'

'The Meister killing. Yes, they do it to scare people.'

'Who are they?'

'Butchers,' he said shortly.

She was unsure if he was being pejorative or was simply describing their line of work.

'They're a gang,' he added, 'who work out of the Union Stock Yard.'

As they parted he said, 'You know there's really not a lot of difference between our two professions – mortician and journalist – in the way we have to find answers to difficult questions. Is there?'

'I suppose not,' conceded Emily.

But she was thankful, as she walked out on to the street, that her own questions generally related to the living and not to the dead.

26

Brennan's

Anna Zemeckis made sure she was on time for her first full day's work at Brennan's Tailoring Emporium. But the moment she sat down at her worktable in the second-floor back room she sensed a change in atmosphere. The women, who had been talkative before, now worked in silence, heads down.

Anna soon discovered why.

It seemed that she had been lucky to come looking for a job on a Tuesday because that was the one day of the week when Mr Brennan Jr, who was in charge of the Clark Street outlet, attended to matters in his father's more classy store over on State.

Now he was back, he seemed to have something to prove and Anna could see why everybody was subdued. He was tall, thin, with a long neck and prominent Adam's apple above his tight, white collar. He seemed incapable of saying anything pleasant to anybody and reduced a woman twice his age to tears just after Anna's arrival because she was two minutes late. She hadn't been able to cross the bridge at Van Buren, it being raised for the passage of a ship.

'Should've thought of that and come the other way round! Fined half a day!'

'But . . .'

'You answering back? *Eh?!*'

He stood over her, his pale brown eyes furious, his mouth tight with anger.

'You carry on and it'll be money at day end, if there's any due. Eh?'

'Money at day end', Anna guessed, meant being fired.

Anna settled down to her work hoping Mr Brennan would take no notice of her.

And nor did he, until nearly twelve.

Then, 'Who's this, eh? *Eh!?*'

Anna looked up to find him towering over her.

'Mrs Donal said . . .'

'I know what she said, girl. Don't need to be told that. Where are you from?'

Anna hesitated, knowing it mattered. This was an Irish place and she guessed others weren't as welcome.

'Europe,' she said non-commitally but very quietly. Louder and it would have been seen as insolent.

She judged him right. The answer was passed over as he impatiently grabbed the item she was working on to examine it. He grabbed so hard and fast that the needle went straight into her finger and some stitches ripped as he pulled the garment, and the needle, free.

Her eyes watered with pain but she said nothing.

He peered at Anna's work.

'It'll do,' he conceded, 'but I keep a close watch on girls I don't hire myself and don't you forget it. And don't stare. Get on with the work. I *said* get on!'

Anna got on.

Only when Brennan got diverted with queries from the shop, or with the models who came up to his office to try on cloaks and other things, did the women dare talk. Then only in furtive whispers.

151

'We get thirty minutes break at half past twelve,' she was told. 'There's water to drink but you need a cup of your own. You can share mine. You eat in there if you've got anything *to* eat. Only place to get clear of him.'

Anna had nothing but a slice of bread she had secreted that morning at the Mission of Hope. Not that she wasn't hungry, she was. But she preferred to save something for lunchtime.

She still felt sick but that didn't matter so much now; her mind had moved on to other things.

Sitting at her bench sewing she started to remember a lot more, making sense of the jumble of other images and memories she had of her life before Dunning.

Images of her father kept recurring and they weren't all bad. There had been happy times: him holding her close on a great big ship; him standing one morning in his bakery, laughing, his face covered with flour; his hand in hers when she went to school.

No, it wasn't all bad. But it was the memory of her mother that upset her because she knew she needed her and she wasn't there and never would be. And she couldn't ever go back to her father and tell him. He would not forgive her.

Thinking of her mother, Anna's head drooped low over her sewing as she struggled not to cry.

A hand touched her arm. It was the woman who had lost half a day's money. She gave her a smile and a look that said, 'I wish I could help . . .' It was a mother's look, her head a little to one side.

'I'm Jelena,' whispered Anna.

'I'm Eileen, I . . . ssh! He's coming this way. He's in a specially bad mood today.'

'Why?'

'City Hall inspector. There's one coming this afternoon.'

'Is that bad?'

'Ought to be but they never do anything. And it's good for us.'

'Why?'

'Brennan'll pick on some of the girls to take a "break" for a couple of hours, to make the place look less overcrowded. He gives us a dime for the privilege.'

'Why?'

'Keep our mouths shut.'

'Ten cents!' said Anna. It seemed a fortune. If she could have done her sewing with her fingers crossed that she might be chosen she would have done so.

27

Riley's Men

CHICAGO Wednesday October 25, 1893   12.11 PM

Dr Morgan Eels had had a bad night and a worse morning. All he really wanted to do was keep on monitoring Riley's progress so he could work out exactly what had happened to her. A steel pen thrust accidentally into the eye of a hospital attendant in his own surgery might look like criminal negligence to most people but to Dr Eels it seemed nothing less than a passport to a glittering future international career. He wanted to seize the moment.

Instead, he had the more immediately pressing problem of Anna Zemeckis to deal with. No trace of her had been found, nor of the important papers she had taken inadvertently. Eels had come to the conclusion that she had escaped the grounds and therefore constituted a real threat to his future. He made an appointment to see his mentor Mr Paul Hartz at his office downtown.

Meanwhile Donko O'Banion, driver of the Dunning paddy wagon, showed up. He had come to inquire about his sister, Maureen Riley.

The notion of Riley having a brother at all took Eels by surprise, she seemed such a monstrous one-off. But on looking closer at the huge frame of Donko and his piggy eyes, he could indeed see a physical similarity between the two.

'Well then . . .' he began.

'And her husband wants to see her too . . .'

'She's *married*?' gasped Eels. That seemed impossible. Everything seemed to be getting worse.

Riley's husband was waiting outside. He turned out to be a uniformed officer from the Harrison Street Police Station. He too was large and lumbering.

'James Flaherty Riley,' he announced. 'Where's my wife? I want to see her.'

'You must be careful not to disturb her,' said Eels hollowly as he escorted the two men to Far Side.

The problem was not so much 'disturbing' Riley as the fact that nothing *could* disturb her. When they arrived at Far Side they found Riley sat up in a chair, glassy-eyed and immobile.

'Apart from the bruising around her eye she's physically well . . . there's nothing actually wrong with her, but . . .'

Donko waved a fat hand in front of Riley's eyes. She did not respond. She remained slumped in the

chair, her legs stretched out before her, her huge arms
hanging down to the floor, her hands limp, her
mouth half open.

But she did seem aware there was someone there.
For a moment there was the glimmer of a childish
grin when she saw the two men. Then she lost interest
and looked away to the middle distance.

'She ain't Riley no more,' pronounced James Riley
without emotion.

'Who did this to her?' asked Donko.

Eels saw an opportunity. He told them what had
happened, reminding Donko that it was he who had
taken Anna Zemeckis to the Detention Hospital and,
after she had been processed and committed,
conveyed her on to Dunning.

Donko squinted and then frowned which was his
way of remembering things.

Light dawned.

'The ugly bitch out of the Creek? The one I picked
up on Benson Street who smelled like shit. That one?'

Eels conceded that it probably was. He was now
quick to mobilize their help on his behalf, and
through them, that of the police.

'I have a photograph of her,' he said helpfully, 'as
I have of all new patients. Perhaps . . . ?'

He showed them.

Officer Riley smiled grimly.

'You give me enough of these and there won't be a
patrolman downtown who isn't looking for this girl.'

'Nor anyone in our whole community,' added
Donko.

By 'community' Donko meant the Irish and that
was a very considerable number of Chicagoans
indeed, incorporating as it did most of the Near West
Side and a good few suburbs beyond.

155

'She won't last twenty-four hours without being caught,' said Donko.

'And she won't *want* to last twenty-four hours beyond that!" said Riley unpleasantly. 'Not alive at any rate.'

'She'll wish she was back in Dunning,' growled Donko.

'Which is precisely where I want her,' said Eels smoothly, pleased with the way things had gone. Mr Hartz *would* be pleased.

28

Home Sweet Home

CHICAGO Wednesday October 25, 1893   1.30 PM

The Markulis hardware store was a slow, two-streetcar journey from Cook County Hospital up to the North Side. Tired of sitting, Emily got off early and walked the last three blocks, glad to catch a glimpse of the clear sky above Lake Michigan at the far eastern end of North Street.

Anna's uncle and aunt lived above their store on the corner of North and Larabee Street and, at first sight, it looked an impressive establishment. Taking full advantage of its corner location the building had an octagonal turret set off by wings on both sides. But close up Emily could see that its once-bright fabric was grimy from the soot and smoke that wafted across from factories on the south side of North Street. The front windows, which had not been cleaned in a while, were cluttered with goods.

There was an air of carelessness about everything, as if the store had seen better days.

The half-moon step up into the store was also dirty with dust and litter. The interior of the shop was as dingy as its windows and the male assistant who greeted her was not exactly solicitous. Mr Markulis 'never being here at this hour', Mrs Markulis was fetched from upstairs. She greeted Emily somberly, in acknowledgment of the unfortunate circumstances of her visit.

'Please, Miss Strauss,' she said rather formally, 'come upstairs to the parlor and we can talk.'

She was a pale, wispy woman in a tight-corseted, rather old-fashioned black silk dress. She wore a simple silver brooch at her throat and a thin gold wedding ring.

Her manner seemed rather strained; her eyes were more hunted than warm, and her handshake too quick, as if she did not like physical contact.

'Please,' she said again, indicating some stairs behind the counter.

Mrs Markulis relaxed a little after she served coffee as Emily began to get her talking about Anna's family history.

She had heard something of it already from Janis Zemeckis and knew that his wife's brother Hendriks who had been a book-keeper for a timber firm in Riga, had emigrated to America in 1870 to help run his firm's office on the Chicago River. Hit by the panic of 1873 he had moved into hardware and in no time met and married Liesel Hoffmeyer, the only child of a successful German hardware merchant on the North Side. The substantial premises owned by the Hoffmeyers had been erected in the late seventies by Mrs Markulis's father who had astutely acquired the lot after the Great Fire of 1871. When Mr Hoffmeyer died unexpectedly in 1878 Hendriks Markulis had been left in effective control of a thriving business.

But his and Liesel's two children had both died at birth, after which Hendriks had tried to persuade his sister and her husband, Janis Zemeckis, along with their daughter, to leave Riga and join them in Chicago, even offering to cover the costs of travel. He was homesick and wanted some more Latvians nearby. He said there were plenty of opportunities for bakers in Chicago.

But Janis Zemeckis was cautious and finally only made the journey to the New World after his wife died in 1882, refusing his brother-in-law's offer of financial help. He had also decided against the option that Anna would have preferred, of moving to the Canadian state of Manitoba to be near his wife's sister, Anna's Aunt Inga.

After considering his options carefully, Zemeckis decided New York's Lower East Side, with its strong Lutheran community, offered better opportunities than a remote farm in Canada or the additional strain of traveling out to the Midwest. Now, comparing Zemeckis's well-ordered bakery in New York and this untidy run-down establishment in Chicago, Emily guessed that, so far as the Markulises were concerned, there had been a temperamental difference between the two men as well as a religious one.

Emily knew that, though Janis was an advocate of temperance, it was not something he especially advertised in his Lower East Side home.

But in the Markulis household it was different. It was difficult to avoid the fact that Mrs Markulis was an active member of the Woman's Christian

Temperance Union, starting with the little white ribbon she wore above her thin bosom as a sign she had taken the pledge.

Hanging on the wall, not far from the picture of the late Mr Hoffmeyer, was a framed sampler in the shape of a cross. The frame itself was painted in shiny and forbidding black shellac and the beautifully cross-stitched words read: 'For God and Home and Native Land' in English, but rendered in high German gothic-style script.

'I made it myself,' said Mrs Markulis, adding with a touch of self-satisfaction, 'and the frame too.'

'Really!' exclaimed Emily, aware that some appreciative surprise was needed.

Finally Emily steered her toward what she really wanted to hear about.

'I guess Mr Zemeckis was rather strict in general?' she suggested.

'He is a good man, God-fearing. I know that.'

'But strict?' murmured Emily, following her instinct, for she felt that in some way this had been an issue – for Anna and maybe for Mrs Markulis too.

'Too strict, I think. Most certainly liquor was to be discouraged at all costs. But a social life . . . a growing girl needs that. How else is she to meet the right young man?'

Emily paused; she had at last, unwittingly, been given an opening to the one thing she most needed to find out about.

'Tell me, Mrs Markulis, . . . did Anna have a beau?'

The response was unequivocal. 'She had no male friends in particular that I knew of. Any friendships she had with young men were of the harmless kind, like her colleague John at the library.'

'Oh yes, the library. Mr Zemeckis mentioned it,' replied Emily, 'You arranged that for her, did you not?

'Yes, through my good friend Mrs Jane McIlvanie who is wife of the Deputy Librarian of the Chicago Public Library and a colleague of mine at WCTU.'

'So . . . how close was Anna to this John?' Emily probed further. 'What did you know about him?'

Liesel Markulis seemed more than happy to fill Emily in about John Olsen English, about whom Anna had, apparently, talked often and openly. He was one of the more senior librarians but their work brought them only into passing contact. They were opposites. She was gregarious and relaxed; he solitary and almost terminally shy. But despite the differences they had struck up a firm friendship.

Anna had soon learned John's unhappy history from her workmates and from Mrs Markulis, for it was common knowledge in WCTU that John lived with and looked after his invalid, widowed mother on the Near North Side who made his life utter misery. His father had been killed fighting for the Unionists at Chattanooga in 1863 when John was two years old. He had left Mrs English well enough provided for, and from that day on, she had lived a life of modest and self-centered indulgence with a succession of maids, a son to do as he was told and long-suffering friends from the congregation of the nearby St Patrick's Roman Catholic Church on West Adams Street to listen to her endless complaints.

After John had left college, his mother had found him a librarian's job in Chicago to ensure that he remained at her constant beck and call. His occasional attempts to break free were ridiculed and promptly suppressed by his domineering mother.

It was something about which Mrs Markulis and Mrs McIlvanie frequently gossiped, for the latter's husband had found Mrs English's tentacles reached as far as the library itself, in the never-ending demands she made on her son.

'So . . .' ventured Emily finally, 'even if Anna and John had had romantic inclinations, Mrs English would have put a stop to it.'

'Undoubtedly. Besides, Anna's a Lutheran, and he's a Catholic'

'Tell me, Mrs Markulis. Did Anna really *want* to come to Chicago? Or did she do so because her father wanted it?'

'Anna was happy to come here under our care but she was always honest enough to say that her real dream was to live with her Aunt Inga, that's my husband's sister, in Canada. I think perhaps . . .'

'Yes, Mrs Markulis?''

'Perhaps Anna and John might have been very well suited. For he too had dreamed of being a farmer, like the Olsens, his forbears on his mother's Swedish side of the family. I think Anna agreed to come to Chicago in the hope that it would be a first step to earning her father's permission to go north to Canada. But she would never have gone without his approval.'

'Is there any chance she would have gone there without his permission? I'm thinking . . .'

'I know what you're thinking, Miss Strauss. Frankly, when she first disappeared the same thought occurred to me: that she had run away to her Aunt Inga, perhaps because she was unhappy here.'

'*Was* she unhappy?'

Mrs Markulis hesitated, then said, 'I don't think so.'

Emily did not for one moment believe her. Anna

had been unhappy, the question was why.

Mrs Markulis continued quickly, 'Regrettably none of that matters now. When I saw . . . when . . .'

Emotion overtook her.

Emily poured her a coffee.

'On that dreadful day when I saw Anna in the morgue . . .'

'You're sure, are you? Sure it was her?'

'Of course I'm sure. The dress, she made it herself, here in Chicago. I helped her. And she was still wearing the crucifix her mother had given her. Yes, I'm afraid there's no doubt it was Anna, no doubt at all.'

29

Portraits

CHICAGO Wednesday October 25, 1893   1.55 PM

At five to two precisely Dr Morgan Eels was already sitting waiting in the main foyer of Stock House, the administrative building of Darke Hartz & Company in downtown Chicago. New, opulent and glossy, it rose up on the north side of Washington between La Salle and Fifth, opposite the site of the half-completed Chicago Stock Exchange: a testament to the extraordinary success of the company over the last twenty years.

Eels was feeling nervous. Like a lot of physicians who spend too long in the reassuring confines of the charitable public institutions they run, he was uneasy in the world of big business and especially with men like Paul Hartz, whose offices were designed to impress and sometimes to intimidate.

A neatly arranged set of newspapers, journals and commodity reports – local, national and international – lay on the table near where Eels was told to wait, but he looked at none of them.

He was thinking about what he was going to say to Paul Hartz, whose gilt-framed portrait in oils stared down at him from the right-hand side of the main staircase to the offices above. He wore a dark suit and cravat and looked as fine a man of business as ever was. Hartz was now more than sixty, but the artist had presented him as still young enough to be eternally on his way to the top.

He made a pleasant contrast to his partner Hans Darke whose portrait hung nearby. Darke had started life as a butcher with a single horse and cart in Richmond, Virginia. He had built up his business from there, diversifying into cattle breeding and setting up a stud in the Midwest, where he made his name as a breeder who knew his product second to none and his markets too. Moving to Chicago, he had added meatpacking to his growing operation, following Philip Armour's lead in the efficient slaughter and dressing of cattle and hogs and Gustavus Swift's in the use of refrigerated boxcars.

Darke was notoriously taciturn and curmudgeonly and the portrait showed it: his dour, thickset face and stocky form did more than hint at Teutonic origins. So ingrained was the German ethic for hard work in Hans Darke that it was said he drove his people like an army at war on limited rations, and his two sons, Gunther and Wolfgang, hardest of all. In recent years, Wolfgang had taken increasing charge of the

Darke Hartz killing floors in the Stock Yard, and all other matters to do with butchery, while the older and more urbane Gunther had moved onto the distribution side of the meat-packing operation.

The fact was – and it was well known throughout the industry – that Darke and Hartz loathed each other. They rarely communicated with each other or spent more than five minutes in the same room except at essential board meetings and the annual stockholders' convention.

But despite all that, they ran one of the most successful businesses in Chicago.

Eels looked back across the stairwell to the more appealing picture of the urbane Paul Hartz. No sons there, just the daughter – Christiane – Gunther's wife. Paul Hartz was a firm believer in keeping money and business in the family, and even though there was as yet no heir on his side, the fact that Gunther was his son-in-law now and disliked his father and brother so much gave Paul the balance of power.

The clock chimed the quarter hour and a clerk appeared.

'Dr Eels? Mr Hartz will see you now.'

Paul Hartz was in an expansive mood and greeted Eels warmly, though he didn't get up.

He sat in a large, open-plan office with two clerks at stand-up desks at the far end and an oval conference table in the middle at which a group of men sat talking informally.

There was a bottle and some glasses on the table and the air was heavy with the aroma of expensive cigars. It looked as though a meeting of some kind had just broken up.

Hartz, it appeared, was the one who had a liking

for portraiture, for he had no less than three Presidents of the United States, in oils, looming on the brocaded walls behind him: James A. Garfield, Chester A. Arthur and the recent former president, Benjamin Harrison – all staunch Republicans like Hartz himself.

As Eels advanced across this imposing chamber, the men already gathered there nodded friendly greetings in his direction, waiting for Hartz to make the introductions, which he did not do at once. Instead he signalled Eels over to his desk and invited him to take a chair adjacent to his own so that the two men could talk confidentially.

This invitation into the inner circle of Darke Hartz & Company bolstered Morgan Eels's confidence. He abandoned his carefully rehearsed words and decided to come straight out with it. He told him of Anna Zemeckis's escape and the lost documents, putting himself at Hartz's mercy without attempting to attribute blame.

Hartz listened without expression.

When Eels had finished he said, 'I was already aware of all this. If you had said differently you would have been on the train back East, Eels. But . . . we all make mistakes and I respect a man who freely admits his.'

Hartz's eyes grew hard.

'But you're only allowed one mistake Eels. No more. Eh? I shall order my own people to deal with it. But if they do not find the girl and take her back to Dunning in the next forty-eight hours then your job is on the line. Understand?'

Eels nodded. He felt both gratitude and fear.

'Yes, Mr Hartz,' he said. 'I hesitate to say this but in my own self defense . . . when I formally assume my full responsibilities at the Insane Asylum at the end of the month, there will be certain reforms of my predecessor's regime that will be necessary. Security will become paramount, to protect the public from any dangerous patients who might get loose.'

Hartz nodded his head absently.

'Meanwhile, I have seen to it that the police have initiated a search for the girl,' said Eels.

He smiled ingratiatingly, feeling that these few words had shifted the blame for the escape to the inefficient regime of his predecessor, Dr Brown, while establishing that he, by contrast, was a man of action.

Eels was so pleased with himself that he failed to read the sudden shadowing in Hartz's eyes.

'The *police?*' repeated Hartz with chilly emphasis.

One or two of the other men in the room began paying attention.

Eels explained about Riley's brother and police officer husband and how he had given them copies of the photograph he had taken of Anna on her admission to Dunning. He said nothing about steel pens in eyes or scientific breakthroughs but already he was talking too much, giving Hartz too much detail. Dr Eels had not yet learned that it is best to let a man like Paul Hartz dictate the pace.

'A photograph?' said Hartz.

Eels produced the image he had taken of Anna Zemeckis.

Hartz barely glanced at it. He liked girls but the ones he liked had class. Then he looked again, reminded of something he had long since lost touch with. Despite the bruising round her eyes the girl had an endearing look of innocence combined with pluck.

'How the hell did you lose a girl like that?' he said, seeming finally to make light of it all. But he didn't wait for Eels's reply, turning instead to the room at large. 'However, I was forgetting, you gentlemen haven't all met Dr Eels, have you? Those of you not able to attend his lecture at Dunning two nights ago missed a treat.'

Eels relaxed.

He was asked a few questions about his research work at Dunning and responded with what came close to a lecture.

'Interesting,' said one of the younger men seated at the table.

He was tall, broad shouldered, beautifully dressed and every inch the coming man. He stood up, smiling coolly, the one person in the room who, so it seemed, was not overawed by Paul Hartz.

Approaching Hartz's desk, he reached out a hand and offered it to Eels.

'Gunther Darke,' he said. 'I guess Mr Hartz agrees with you on almost everything?'

'I . . . well . . . I would certainly like to think he does.'

'It's more than I do.'

'Oh,' said Eels, deflated.

'You shouldn't mind him,' said Hartz coldly. 'My son-in-law likes to play the role of devil's advocate.'

'The logical conclusion you appear to be suggesting, Dr Eels,' continued Gunther Darke, unperturbed, 'would seem to be the clinical elimination of the insane.'

'I think there is a strong case for that in certain circumstances,' said Eels.

'Such as?'

'Where an inmate of my establishment, after due process through the Insane Court, is adjudged to be not only insane but beyond cure.'

'Then what?'

'Then if the nuisance they cause society and the cost of their maintenance is such as to be prohibitive I think elimination is a reasonable and justifiable course.'

To Eels's relief, from the looks on their faces, the rest of Hartz's colleagues seemed to agree with him.

'And by what method would you eliminate these costly incurables?' asked Gunther Darke.

'It wouldn't be my decision, Mr Darke, but the Court's,' said Eels. 'But I think most physicians who have studied the subject would agree that, given the large numbers likely to be involved in such a cull of the socially worthless, then in carbonic acid gas we have an agent which would efficiently and humanely do the job.'

Paul Hartz stood up.

'There speaks the true man of science, gentlemen! Truthful and objective but politically impractical – for now. Those who agree with me on this issue, as on the general need to protect native Americans from the incursions of the lower class of immigrant, will need to fight a strong and persuasive battle.

'I regret – because he is and was my friend – that the founder of the OAA, Jenkin Lloyd Rhys, did not have the stomach for that fight. Now that he is not with us – and we hope he is physically well even if, as I suspect, he has suffered some kind of mental breakdown – we will have to put forward our own candidate against the one he nominated.'

'You should stand yourself, sir!' someone cried enthusiastically.

Hartz raised a hand modestly and then, to Eels's horror, laid it to rest on his shoulder, causing consternation among several of those present.

Hartz laughed.

'Don't worry, gentlemen; it is not my intention to nominate Dr Eels for the position of President of the OAA! We need him for more important work!'

Eels gulped and looked pale, which made everyone laugh even more.

'I shall name my man in good time,' said Hartz smoothly.

The informal gathering broke up and Eels, confident that he had handled a difficult situation well, and somewhat puffed up with the sense that he was making a mark among men who mattered, took advantage of the dry weather and an off-lake breeze that had cleared the cavernous city streets of smoke and smog and sauntered down to the Adams Street Bridge and over to the Union Depot for his train back to Dunning.

It was only when the journey was almost over that he remembered that he had left the photograph of Anna Zemeckis on Paul Hartz's desk.

30

Secrets

CHICAGO Wednesday October 25, 1893   2.23 PM

'I really don't think there is any more I can tell you about Anna,' said Liesel Markulis, as Emily continued to ply her with questions.

It was, self-evidently, the kind of probing she had dreaded. The shock of Anna's disappearance and death was written all over her face. That and for some reason a sense of shame, as though it had been in some way her fault.

This woman, Emily realized without the need to say more, had been given the sacred charge of looking after someone else's child and it had all gone terribly wrong.

'This is so difficult,' Liesel began. 'Since . . . since then . . . I have talked to no-one except Janis when he was here but he . . . he said little because he was so upset, you know . . . and my husband, he says nothing and I . . .'

'But what was Anna really *like?*' asked Emily, hoping to divert Liesel Markulis from a torrent of words that looked as if they were heading for tears again.

It worked.

She pulled herself together, sat up straight and looked Emily in the eye. 'She was a good girl, a happy young woman, so excited to be here in Chicago at the time of the World's Fair. She was clever and adaptable and she enjoyed working in the library. Her part-time job there had left her with enough free time to see the Fair. And then there was my work with the Woman's Christian Temperance Union . . . she took a great interest in that too.'

'She was already a member?'

'No, I persuaded her to join. She came to the meetings quite regularly. She met other women there and also through her work at the Administration Building on the South Side where she later started doing volunteer work one day a week.'

'Anyone in particular? Did she have any special friends?'

Liesel Markulis's face darkened.

'She was rather close about such things. We had

words about it. I explained that, for her own safety, we needed to know who her friends were.'

Emily smiled and asked, 'Did you ever meet any of these friends?'

'Eventually. At the Administration Building Anna worked under the supervision of a woman called Marion Stoiber, who, we were wrongly informed, was married. She was not. I cannot say I liked her. Rather vulgar, rather too knowing. Anna fell under her spell. They used to meet for lunch occasionally on a Saturday, at Mrs Clark's Lunch Room on Wabash.'

'Marion Stoiber,' repeated Emily. 'Sounds Polish.'

Mrs Markulis nodded.

'As a matter of fact, despite my initial misgivings about her, since Anna's disappearance Marion Stoiber has been most kind and supportive and she even comes to WCTU meetings. There's hope for everybody, I think.'

'And she admitted she wasn't married, but separated?'

'Eventually, yes. She said it was unfortunate. Her husband had been incapable of holding down a job, got into debt and had deserted her. She preferred to say no more than that. I felt sorry for her, Miss Strauss. But as for Mr Markulis . . . well, he said she was a fraud.'

'I'd very much like to meet her,' said Emily.

'She will, I hope, be at our annual WCTU convention tomorrow. Would you like to come? I'll introduce you.'

Emily agreed she would attend.

'Mrs Markulis,' continued Emily after a pause, 'do you think perhaps Anna hid things from you, that she had secrets she did not want you to know about?'

Mrs Markulis's eyes widened in horror at the suggestion. She shook her head.

'No. I think no. Her father was so strict and we were under very clear instructions about where Anna could go and what she could do and who she could meet. We even had to persuade him to allow her to join the Turnverein.'

'Gymnastics?'

Emily was surprised. Turnverein clubs were usually the domain of boys and men.

Liesel Markulis smiled.

'As I explained to Anna's father, the Nord Chicago Turnverein is progressive and prides itself on promoting healthy living for all, boys and girls, men and women and we at WCTU support it in doing that.'

'But I thought most of the Turnvereins were little more than German drinking clubs. They are in Pittsburgh. My father was a member of one!'

'Most are, I believe. But the NCT is a temperance club and its members consume no liquor. Maybe that's why they have produced the most successful team in Illinois.'

'And Anna was a member?'

'Yes. She enjoyed the activities very much and the social contact, I think.'

Janis Zemeckis had mentioned none of this. Maybe Anna and Mrs Markulis had thought it best not to tell him.

'May I see Anna's room?' asked Emily.

There was nothing much to see and nothing personal left in it, or so it seemed. There was a homely German picture on the wall of the kind Emily knew well and a souvenir calendar from the Fair, adorned by a picture of the Woman's Building, the same building Emily had been in the day before.

'What happened to Anna's things?'

'Zemeckis asked me to pack them, which I did. But I found nothing that would give any clue as to why she disappeared.'

They stood in the room staring at nothing in particular.

It was as if Anna had never been there.

But then Emily noticed something. 'Look,' she said, moving to the opposite wall, 'she's circled some of the dates on the calendar.'

'Yes, I made some engagements for her,' responded Mrs Markulis. 'I circled them to remind her. And she marked others herself.'

'Seems to be Wednesdays and Thursdays . . .' said Emily.

'Yes, the Turnverein every Wednesday evening and WCTU meetings on Thursdays.'

'. . . and a few others too.' Emily looked more closely, '. . . on Saturdays, mainly.'

'Yes, those were her lunches with Miss Stoiber. In fact, she had lunch with her the day she disappeared. See, here, September 7th.' Mrs Markulis pointed to the calendar.

'And there's another one here, a Friday in June and it has something written by it . . . "lecture" . . . A lecture about what?'

'What date did you say?' asked Mrs Markulis, suddenly looking flustered.

'June 16th. Can you remember exactly what she did that day?'

Mrs Markulis hesitated. 'June . . . yes . . . I think that is the day she attended a lecture on the Chicago meat trade and did the tour of the Union Stock Yard.'

'Did she tell you about it afterwards?'

'I can't remember her saying very much. But I think

she did not like it . . . the killing floors, I mean . . . the blood. She seemed upset when she got back. But . . . tomorrow . . . you must come along to the WCTU Convention.'

Mrs Markulis took an invitation from the mantelpiece. 'Please! Take it, I can arrange another seat for myself.'

Emily knew she was being steered away from the subject and that she would not get any further with Mrs Markulis today.

'It's being held in the Woman's Temple on the corner of La Salle and Monroe Streets starting at eleven, in the Willard Hall. It should be most enjoyable. Members of the Turnverein will be giving a demonstration. Everybody will be there.'

'I'm not a member.'

'Then you'll have an opportunity to join! But meanwhile . . .'

Liesel Markulis retreated back into herself as memories of Anna returned.

'. . . are you seeing any other people today apart from myself?'

'I am,' said Emily, 'in two hours or so. I'm going to see if the good ladies of Hull House can shed any light on the disappearance of girls like Anna in Chicago.'

'You will find them most welcoming and, I am sure, helpful. Until tomorrow then . . .'

They shook hands rather formally but Emily, seeing how forlorn Mrs Markulis looked, gave her an impulsive hug.

'Until tomorrow!'

31

Friends and Acquaintances

Late that same afternoon, Anna Zemeckis found
herself enjoying a welcome respite from her work in
the unlikely setting of the rubbish-strewn embankment of the Chicago River with her new friend
Eileen. Mr Brennan had, as expected, given them a
break for an hour, along with seventeen other girls,
while the City Hall factory inspector paid his
regular visit.

Jackson Street Bridge was a cacophony of people
and wagons high above their heads as they sat
enjoying the last of the sunshine.

'It's quieter down here,' explained Eileen. 'We can
chat.'

They had bought an apple strudel to share. As they
ate it Eileen was trying to exchange the kind of
confidences that Anna steadfastly wished to avoid.

Steamers were unloading their cargoes. Launches
plied their trade between barges, and everywhere
there was the drift of smoke.

'You're in some kind of trouble, aren't you,
Jelena?' Eileen's probing continued.

Anna nodded.

'Why don't you tell me about it?'

'It doesn't look very safe round here,' said Anna
nervously.

Further along two bums sat by a smoldering fire.

They looked up in the women's direction but minded their own business.

Buildings towered up about them. Across the river the Armour grain elevators were modern cathedrals against the skyline; and further along, the Kirk Soap Factory belched out its foul-smelling fumes.

'It's okay at this time of the day,' said Eileen. 'But in summer it stinks to high heaven down here. Now, you were saying . . .'

Providence smiled once more on Anna Zemeckis in the form of a tall male figure with a booming voice.

'Ladies! Good day and good riddance I say to all but good folk such as ourselves who are honest and stick to our principles. May I join you?'

Anna got up from the little seat they had found and was ready to flee when Eileen, with a groan but grinning all the same, took hold of her arm.

'It's alright,' she said. 'It's Mr Crazy. He don't hurt a fly.'

Anna looked at him and at once relaxed. He exuded bonhomie and an easy confidence with himself and the world around him.

He took a seat a yard or two away from them and produced some waxed paper and proceeded to untie the string that bound it. Once open, he laid the parcel daintily on his knees as though the paper were the best linen napkin. Anna saw that it contained some dark rye bread, sliced sausage and a couple of pickles.

'Want some?' he asked.

'No, thank you,' said Anna.

'Who is he?' she whispered to Eileen. While the big man tucked in, Eileen explained.

Mr Crazy, it emerged, was not exactly a hobo, nor exactly a street vendor. And despite his strange appearance he was far from being one of Chicago's low-lifes.

He was, in fact, one of the city's best-known, benign eccentrics. Nobody had been able to discover his real name, and those who had known it had long since died or moved on. So he was generally known as 'Mr Crazy'. He was a man of very strong, outspoken opinions, informing all who cared to listen that the folk in City Hall, and in particular, Mayor Carter Henry Harrison, were cheating the citizens they were meant to represent in all sorts of ways.

He was not quite the city's mascot – he was too proud, too intelligent for that; and far too strange and quirky. But he was most certainly one of its treasures. Tall, bronzed, with a long white beard and always dressed in a greatcoat that went down to his boots (some said he looked like an old Civil War general), he was always, despite his threadbare clothes, extremely clean. He had the great booming voice of an orator, and would constantly reiterate, to those who would listen, his familiar, much-repeated mantra: 'I have the papers to prove it!' His claims seemed preposterous and were never-ending.

For the past few months his latest assertion had been that the City Fathers of Chicago intended to tunnel under the city, which would make the great new skyscrapers fall down. The year previously it had been that the World's Fair would end in disaster – which very obviously it had not. For the year following he was predicting revolution in Illinois state.

Meanwhile . . . nobody much minded or cared, but they liked to see Mr Crazy about and would often give him the price of a meal. They also bought the pipes he carved down at his Lakeshore den from driftwood that he foraged for among the acres of garbage that had accumulated in that noisome no-man's-land.

If there was one extraordinary thing about Mr Crazy, it was this: he might live in a ramshackle hovel, but he always kept himself immaculately clean. And if there was one eccentricity for which he was a legend in Chicago, it was his early morning ablutions in the Lake, which he did in the nude, all the year round, informing anyone who challenged him that his beard was the only covering he needed.

The Lakeshore was Mr Crazy's domain, and from its garbage-strewn wastes he emerged daily in all weathers to do his rounds. When the City Fathers were in session he sat in the Public Gallery, as was his right, and listened in, sometimes challenging the proceedings. Harmless though he seemed, Mr Crazy was not someone to cross in matters of Liberty, Justice and the Law. His knowledge of civil issues in Chicago was encyclopedic and he was right. He knew the law books back to front and upside down. So much so that as the years had gone by he had earned the unique privilege, encouraged by the more open-minded of local Democratic politicians, of actually being listened to on points of order and procedure.

But he was never ever a nuisance. He never drank. He was never rude to anyone, and if he came across someone in trouble he would take them to the Harrison Street Police Station or the Pacific Garden Mission or the Cook County Hospital.

It was rumored he was rich, which surely was not the case, because he always gave away what he had, including the pipes he supposedly made to sell. Probably no-one in all Chicago except the man he had designated his arch-enemy – Mayor Carter

Henry Harrison himself – could have relied on more people's support than Mr Crazy, had he ever asked for it. Which naturally he never did.

Right now Mr Crazy was having his afternoon tea.

Anna noticed that he carried a placard he had obviously made himself. The lettering was beautifully rendered. It read, *SAY NO TO MAYOR HARRISON; SAY NO TO THE TUNNELS.*

Then in smaller letters it said *Apply here for the proof.*

'See, he's crazy,' whispered Eileen. 'Whoever would go tunnelling under the city? The buildings would fall down.'

'She's right, madam,' said Mr Crazy, moving back into earshot again. 'And you'd do well to remember that, though I'm old, my hearing's as good as the next woman's. The tunnels will make everything fall down and then I'd be a poor man.'

'Thought you were already, Mr Crazy,' Eileen riposted.

'Poverty is relative, young lady.'

'So why do you live on the Lakeshore!'

'Because my cabin is the finest residence in all Chicago, but meanwhile . . .'

He approached Anna, and, before she could say no he put a neatly made sandwich of rye bread and salami on her lap along with a gherkin.

'You look hungry to me. Eat.'

'Thank you, sir,' she said.

She dared to look up and found him beaming down at her, looking just like Saint Nicholas – the Santa Claus of the old Latvian storybooks she'd loved as a child. He certainly had the red cheeks and twinkly eyes, just no sack of presents.

Then he moved off to join the other two men further along the embankment.

'You can't eat it,' said Eileen.

'Oh yes I can,' said Anna firmly.

She was thinking not just of herself but of the child she was carrying as well. She was thinking too that what Mr Crazy had shown was something no-one else had shown her in a long while: kindness and courtesy.

So eat it she did.

32

Child

CHICAGO Wednesday October 25, 1893   4.15 PM

Emily approached the once-elegant, but now dowdy two-storey mansion that was the main building of the Hull House Settlement with a sense of excitement. There was always something going on at Hull House – a social event in progress, a new philanthropic venture being discussed or some educational lecture about to begin.

Hull House was a welcoming haven and had been since Jane Addams and Ellen Gates Starr had established it four years previously. Its team of earnest and often privileged middle-class supporters provided welfare, education, childcare for working mothers, counselling and hot dinners for the poor – mainly Italian, Jewish and Greek – of the Near West Side community that surrounded it.

It changed peoples' lives in unexpected ways, but

Emily was not prepared for just how suddenly and dramatically that could happen.

On arriving she had asked if she could see Julia Lathrop.

'I'm very sorry, I'm afraid she's not here. She's out of Chicago and . . .'

'Sheets! Are there any *sheets!*?'

The young assistant who had been talking to Emily froze.

'Well *someone* must know where they are!'

The speaker was small, dark and wiry, like a bull-terrier in skirts.

Her eyes settled on Emily.

'Do *you* know?'

'Just arrived,' said Emily, 'but I guess sheets are normally upstairs and not down.'

Since no-one else made a move, Emily went upstairs herself, poked her head into a couple of rooms, searched along the corridor and found a linen cupboard. It was full of sheets.

She grabbed three and came back down.

The woman who had asked for them was outside on the verandah overlooking Halsted Street talking to a slip of a girl dressed in barely more than rags. She looked dirty, destitute and desperate.

'Good,' said the woman, grabbing the sheets.

She looked appraisingly at Emily and said, 'You'd better come with me since I'll need some help. Follow the girl!'

They hurried after the little thing, soon turning off Halsted into a side street and off that into another. The atmosphere soon became foul.

'What's your name?' asked Emily, raising her skirts and side-stepping the mire.

'Katharine Hubbard, Julia Lathrop's new assistant. And yours?'

'Emily Strauss, New York *World*. Where are we going?'

'To deliver a baby.'

'But I . . .'

'There's no but about it, Miss Strauss, we'll have to go and help her ourselves because no-one else will. The girl tells me a friend of hers in the tenement house she lives in is having a baby all by herself.'

'Yes, miss,' interrupted the girl 'and she's hollering something fierce: my mother says it's disgracing the whole house, she is!'

'And the sheets, Miss Hubbard . . . ?' queried Emily as she rushed to keep pace with her.

'You don't imagine there'll be anything clean or hygienic where the poor creature lives, do you?'

'Er, no,' said Emily.

The maze of alleys they had entered smelled of a thousands things, all of them as rotten and bad as the waste, human and animal, that lay in festering puddles along their length. Emily rapidly lost all sense of direction.

The muddy ground underfoot had never been paved, though it might have once been boarded. For the most part it was not even recognizable as mud, but rather a foul viscous muck across which it was only possible to pass, thanks to the judicious placing of a boulder, or broken barrel-side or a few crushed tins.

The tenements on either side were no better than shanties, built so badly, so meanly, that most leaned one way or another. All were dilapidated almost beyond repair, and several had literally collapsed where they stood.

Suddenly the alleys opened out into a kind of square in the middle of which two men, with bowlers and waistcoats over their dirty white shirts, were harnessing two horses by a heap of manure. Nearby a huge bonfire smoldered, giving off the foul stench of scorched carpet and gutta-percha. Beyond was a brick-built tenement, five storeys high. In they went, clambering up several flights of stairs until they arrived at last at a one-room apartment no more than eight feet square with the smallest of small windows set high in one wall.

Although they could hear her screams, it was hard at first for them to make out where the mother-to-be lay, because she had slipped between the wall and her greasy mattress in the final stages of her labor. She now lay there in the filthiest of shifts which had ridden up to her breasts as, legs open and baby's head showing, she screamed out the final moments of her lonely labor.

But what shocked Emily perhaps more than anything else was that when her eyes finally adjusted to the murk the woman giving birth seemed herself no more than a child.

Of the next quarter of an hour, Emily afterward remembered every single detail – of the lice-infested bed, now stained with all the waters and blood of childbirth, of the girl's touching gratitude that she was finally alone no more, of the way Katharine Hubbard galvanized all around her to do what was necessary to see America's newest citizen safely into the world. But at the time it was just a haze.

Emily did what she could, marveling at her companion's composure and compassion and her seeming indifference to the all-pervading squalor.

The clean sheets they had brought were laid on the decrepit bed, the girl was eased onto them and boiling water and a towel were summoned up from somewhere. Eventually, one of the curious women out on the landing by the stairs was sufficiently encouraged by the appearance of the 'Hull House women' to step forward and offer her services as makeshift midwife, for she had delivered her sister's baby back in Ireland. Once her hands were washed by Katharine she eased the baby out when it seemed to get stuck at the last moment and delivered it safely on to the sheet. A moment or two later, using a pair of sewing scissors, the cord was cut.

'There's more,' said the woman to Katharine softly, and for a horrified moment Emily thought she meant more babies . . . But it was the placenta she was referring to.

As Emily, her help no longer needed, stood back, she was moved by the way the young girl reached out instinctively to hold her baby. It was something as ancient as time – the mystical bond between mother and newborn.

In that eternal moment Emily Strauss knew something else, or thought she did.

It came at her so powerfully she actually gasped.

It was about Anna Zemeckis and what it was that might have made her leave the safety of her uncle's house and go into hiding. She was going to having a baby. *That's* what it was. Somehow, no doubt through a combination of ignorance and innocence, she had got herself with child. That's why she had disappeared. She wasn't dead, she was in hiding somewhere.

Emily's heart began thumping as she looked around this dreadful place. This, or something like it, would be the inevitable outcome for Anna.

Or, worse still, an abortion in a back street somewhere thereabouts.

She's alive . . . and I've got to find her . . . Emily told herself, *I must find her now.*

The belated arrival of a doctor jolted Emily out of her thoughts. Mother and baby had no need for him by then. But he still demanded his fee and it was Katharine Hubbard who paid it.

'What will happen to them?' asked Emily, as they made their way back through the maze of alleys to Hull House.

Katharine Hubbard shrugged.

'We'll keep on eye on them. But . . . you've seen for yourself. The tide of poverty and suffering comes in and goes out and it is something not even a thousand Jane Addams and their Hull Houses can do much about.

'But . . . if we refused to respond to a poor girl in the throes of childbirth,' Katharine continued, 'it would be a disgrace to us for evermore! If Hull House does not have its roots in human kindness, it is no good at all.'

It was only when they were back on the front steps of Hull House that Katharine turned to Emily and said, 'Now, what is it that we can do for you?'

Emily told her about Anna Zemeckis, how her father had misidentified her body in the City Morgue, how she was convinced she was still alive, and in serious trouble, possibly pregnant.

'It's only a guess, but after what I've just witnessed . . .'

Katharine Hubbard nodded.

'Fits the facts,' she said somberly. 'I'll see what more I can do to help and be in touch if I hear anything.'

33
Turnverein

The imposing, red-brick headquarters of the Nord Chicago Turnverein, Chicago's largest and most successful gymnastics club, were situated on the North Side, off Goethe Street.

The club's extraordinary success in competition was legendary and down to one simple thing: the quality of its leadership. From its founding in 1863 by the late Johan Sackler, who had organized it with Prussian efficiency, the club had realized the importance of gaining support from local businesses and this tradition had prevailed. Sackler himself had been in the grain business but he had passed the baton to a meatpacker, Mr Richard Whetton, a passionate advocate of the Turner movement.

On his death Whetton's company was bought out by Darke Hartz & Company and these new owners had donated the Whetton japanning factory on the North Side to the Turnverein, on whose lot the new building had been erected in 1889. All the club then needed was a new director.

It settled on one of the finest gymnasts and strongmen in the state of Illinois, a man as popular as he was feared. He demanded a high salary and got it. He also demanded total discipline from club members, and got that too. And he demanded loyalty, which he got in spades.

The only trouble was that in two day's time he was leaving the club, and no-one knew it. Because he had a second career, a secret, more lucrative and fulfilling one. And he had decided the time had come to pursue it full-time in a city bigger than Chicago.

The club's director was Mr Dodek Krol and his second career was as a hired killer. He was the man who had murdered Jenkin Lloyd Rhys less than forty-eight hours previously; and for the last few minutes he had been in a very bad mood indeed.

He had been given a commission of the kind he disliked, but which he could not easily refuse. He had been asked to kill a girl. To make matters worse, it seemed that the initial task of finding her had been put into the hands of the police and a few thugs in Chicago's Ward No. 1.

A note had been delivered from one of his clients at the Old America Association, a very fruitful source of business. Rhys had been on his client's list. He was not the kind of man to say no to.

The letter came with a photograph of a girl called Anna Zemeckis who was on the run from Dunning. Krol had no interest in young girls, especially mad or bad ones. He had no interest in why she was being sought. He had better things to do.

He made the requested telephone call.

'I have your message but I really . . .'

'We need her disposed of.'

The man he was speaking to ran one of Chicago's newest and most rapidly growing businesses: the trade in pornographic images.

It was not a trade Dodek Krol liked or respected.

He had never had an interest in such images and he did not like the men who made them, forcing girls to do things they should not do; paying men to be photographed doing things they should not do either.

So now he listened in silence and the more he heard the more his instincts were against it. And Krol trusted his instincts. Chasing after such a girl in Chicago was neither easy nor profitable.

'The only practical way is to put the Meisters on it . . .' he said.

'Exactly. They will listen to you, Krol.'

'As they will to you. But . . . why not simply let her go?'

'I have my reasons for wanting her found and . . .'

Krol listened again but heard nothing persuasive.

'But there are so many girls like this one, a never-ending supply. They arrive here in America from Europe daily, in their hundreds and thousands. They surely cannot hurt you. It will be cheaper to let her go.'

His client swore.

'Put the best Meisters on it, Krol. And when you've found her, let me know. If you won't take it further than that . . .'

'I won't kill her myself if that's what you mean.'

'. . . then *I* shall have to see it's done. Just find the bitch.'

There was a pause. The only sound to be heard was the tap-tap-tapping of Indian clubs from the gymnasium below.

'What the hell's that?' his client asked.

'A rehearsal, for a display at the WCTU conference tomorrow. Will *you* be there?'

'Not if I can help it.'

The telephone clicked, leaving Krol scowling.

He put his hand under the edge of his oak desk, and with one great explosive wrench, sent it spinning across the room. It crashed into the wall and fell to the floor, one leg breaking off.

Down below in the gymnasium of the Turnverein, fifty people stopped what they were doing and looked up at the ceiling.

They had heard thunder in the heavens. Their god was angry.

DAY EIGHT

Thursday October 26, 1893

34

Suspicion

The following morning, over on Clark Street, Anna Zemeckis just made it to her worktable at Brennan's with a minute to spare. Mr Brennan was none too pleased. He was a stickler for punctuality and a minute early felt like half an hour late to him. He had even been known to fine girls half a day's wages for arriving at the last moment, on the dubious grounds that it caused others anxiety, meaning himself.

'We start at eight prompt,' he told Anna, 'and that means you need preparation time before that. I'm warning you right now, girl – next time you'll be fined.'

Anna knew enough not to argue.

'Sorry Mr Brennan, sir,' she said meekly.

She stole a glance at Eileen, who winked. They'd get a chance to talk later.

Anna was late because she had woken up feeling sick and had decided to take a streetcar. Not knowing the stops, she had missed the right one and had had to run back along Jackson Boulevard to Clark Street to get to work.

Rushing had made her feel even worse and she was now pale and sweating, her hair half undone. But despite this bad start to the day she felt more secure than she had for days.

Dunning seemed far behind her now and if only she could stick with the work for a little longer, she would have enough money to pay the train fare to St Paul in Minnesota, away from the jurisdiction of Illinois and the Cook County Hospital. From there, Tomas Steffens the train driver had told her she could get a train to Winnipeg and travel on to her aunt's farm by Lac du Bonnet.

'Jelena? Jelena! We're stopping for five minutes to oil the machines.'

Momentarily, Anna failed to recognize her unfamiliar name when Mrs Donal the supervisor roused her from her reverie. Around them the sounds of the machines had suddenly died into silence and the roar and rattle of Clark Street intruded once more.

'You've worked well this morning, Jelena. This is not half bad.'

This was praise indeed coming from Mrs Donal. But what followed was unnerving and sounded more like a question – of the kind Anna had been dreading.

'You seem unwell.'

So far Anna had confided her condition to no-one but she was beginning to find it a strain.

'I *have* been unwell, Mrs Donal. I had a cold that went straight to my stomach. '

'Hmm. Take the air in the street for a few minutes, but be back on time. Mr Brennan likes to keep everyone on their toes.'

'Thank you, Mrs Donal.'

Anna slipped off downstairs, Eileen with her. They sat against a wall by the back entrance, enjoying the sun.

'Did you really have a cold?'

'Yes,' said Anna firmly. 'They always go to my stomach and make me feel sick.'

'Hmm,' said Eileen, just as Mrs Donal had done.

'Eileen . . .' began Anna. She wanted to confide in her, to tell her about her pregnancy, 'I . . .'

But something stopped her.

'Mmm?'

'I think we better go back in.'

'It's not such a bad place,' Anna told herself as she puffed her way back upstairs to the machine room, 'if only I can stay here undisturbed for a couple more weeks.'

But that was unlikely.

For at that moment, a few blocks away at the intersection with Lake, four men stood conferring with a fifth. They had grim, unforgiving faces and wore curled bowler hats and had the kind of aggressive attitude that told passers-by that they were not the kind of men to mess with.

Any Chicagoan with eyes in his head would have known them to be members of the gang that did the dirty work for the bosses of Ward No. 1, or a favor, when needed, for corrupt policemen such as James Riley. And today Riley was calling in a favor. He needed their help in finding the girl who had done bad things to his wife Maureen up at Dunning.

The men asked a question or two of the fifth man, Maureen Riley's brother, Donko O'Banion, committing to memory the face on a photograph he held, before breaking up to systematically work their way down the establishments on either side of the street.

It was going to be a long and tedious task but sooner or later they would get to Brennan's.

35

RHYS

The body of Jenkin Lloyd Rhys had fetched up in a
tangle of barbed wire and timber sometime during the
previous night beneath the railway viaduct just south
of Johnstown, Pennsylvania. Two days had passed
since Dodek Krol had pitched Rhys out of a
refrigerated Darke Hartz boxcar a few miles upstream.

When it was finally spotted at 9.46 that morning
the sheriff was called.

Rivers like the Stonycreek and the Little
Conemaugh, which together form the Conemaugh
River along whose banks Johnstown is built, deal
with bodies harshly when they are running high with
October rain.

Rhys's head was stove in, an ear was nearly torn
off, the torso and legs were swollen and the flesh all
blanched. All the body had left in the way of covering
was one woolen stocking, a pair of drawers and an
expensive shirt whose pearl buttons had mostly
popped free.

Yet for all that, Johnstown's sheriff had no trouble
identifying the corpse. That was because four letters
were carved nice and neat in its forehead and the
name they spelled was RHYS. Clearly the killer had
wanted his victim to be identified and in Johnstown
the name Rhys was very well known indeed.

Four and a half years previously Johnstown had been the scene of America's worst natural disaster. A heavy storm traveling east from the states of Kansas and Nebraska had hit the Allegheny Mountains on May 30th, 1889, bringing with it a torrential downpour on a scale never before seen, and this in an area already notorious for heavy rainfall. In the following twenty-four hours, ten inches of rain had fallen. The little creeks in the mountains above the town had gone into spate and began ripping up trees and rocks. By the 31st the Conemaugh River was bursting its banks and beginning to flood the town, which was hemmed in on either side by its deep valley site.

Meanwhile, fourteen miles upstream the Conemaugh Lake, held back by a cheaply built seventy-two-foot-high dam, had filled to capacity. Nobody worried too much, least of all the moneyed members of the elite South Fork Fishing and Hunting Club who owned the lake and had responsibility for maintaining the dam. Many of them lived in their big, safe houses fifty-five miles away in Pittsburgh overseeing their steel, coal and railway enterprises. The members included some of America's wealthiest: Andrew Carnegie, Philander Knox and Henry Clay Frick.

. . . And Jenkin Lloyd Rhys too, who, unluckily for him, had been elected three months earlier to run the Club's sub-committee responsible for site maintenance and was maneuvred into the no-win task of managing a belated program of dam strengthening.

But the storm beat them to it. The dam burst on the afternoon of May 31st, propelling the lake's contents downstream in a terrifying, death-dealing wall of water which, hemmed in by the narrow valley, rose to sixty feet high.

Over two thousand people in Johnstown, including nearly four hundred children, were taken by surprise. They didn't stand a chance: if they weren't drowned they were crushed and horribly injured. If they escaped something worse awaited them. They were carried downstream to the Stone Bridge, and hurled against over thirty acres of debris that had piled up in only a few hours.

The living soon became the living dead because caught up among the debris were miles and miles of barbed wire, washed down from the yard of a wire factory upriver, along with great logs of timber and thick black oil.

Rescuers watched helplessly as the injured survivors, caught up in the wire and covered in oil, were consumed by fire when the waters receded. Their agonizing screams for help were heard throughout the night and into the dawn.

Inevitably the disaster needed scapegoats: the South Fork Fishing and Hunting Club and the members of its committee. None more so than Jenkin Lloyd Rhys who in vain protested his innocence – the problem had been building up for years and he had been on the Club's committee only a short while.

For a time it seemed that Rhys would lose everything and would even be removed from his presidency of the Old America Association. But until Dodek Krol caught up with him friends in high places had made sure he survived.

When, that morning, word spread through the town that the body fished out of the water was that of Jenkin Lloyd Rhys, there was widespread satisfaction. The town's law officers were not going to trouble themselves unduly about how or why he had ended up dead at Johnstown. There was a certain poetic justice in the fact that the river that had killed so many had finally claimed him too.

The death was quickly and conveniently marked down as 'accidental', which seemed a tall order, given the letters carved in his forehead. But maybe that was post-mortem, someone suggested helpfully.

Given the state of the corpse, an early burial was called for, the exact time depending on the response from the next of kin, Rhys's wife, who was immediately contacted in New York.

'Get him out of here as fast as you can,' said the mayor nervously.

'Can't do anything till we get a response from the family,' said the coroner.

'Then we'll have to put a guard on him. We don't want trouble.'

'It's kind of hard to lynch a dead man.'

36

WCTU Ladies

CHICAGO Thursday October 26, 1893   10.30 AM

Emily Strauss arrived for the Woman's Christian Temperance Union meeting at half-past ten to find a crowd of drunks and ne'er-do-wells from Chicago's many saloons and bars heckling delegates as they arrived.

Their jibes at those entering the Woman's Temple – a 'temple' to women not to God – were of the jokey kind. 'Keep yer spirits up!' one of them shouted at a well-upholstered, prosperous matron, pulling out a bottle of malt and waving it in her face. 'Cos I'm sure as hell looking after mine.'

All Emily attracted were a few appreciative whistles which she affected to ignore.

The crowd was already spilling off the sidewalk, determined to make things awkward for the delegates as they passed under the great banner displayed over the front entrance, which read:

WOMAN'S CHRISTIAN TEMPERANCE
UNION
CHICAGO BRANCH
ANNUAL CONVENTION
'For God and Home and Native Land'

Just as Emily herself reached the entrance the mood changed for the better. The Mayor arrived, mounted on a white horse, looking both resplendent and jovial. He had timed his regular ride round the city to perfection. Emily had heard that Carter Henry Harrison was a master at managing the electors: it seemed he knew a thing or two about managing mobs as well.

Once inside, she found the great lobby buzzing with women. The ticket that Liesel Markulis had given Emily gave her a seat in the main Lecture Hall in which the event was to start at eleven.

The chatter of the throng was loud in that high, excited way that attaches itself to crowds of sociable women intent on changing the world. Emily also noticed that there was a fair scattering of men. Many looked like ministers of religion, lawyers and members of the teaching profession, judging from their sober demeanor and clothes.

'Miss Strauss!?'

It was Liesel Markulis.

'Goodness! I thought I'd never reach you through this crush! What a wonderful turnout!'

She pointed out where Emily's seat was and explained that she herself would be sitting near the front with her local board members.

'I have arranged for Miss Stoiber to come and sit next to you. Remember I mentioned her. She'll tell you what she remembers about Anna. I think you'll find that she has a sensible head on her shoulders and if anyone can make sense of what has happened she can. But, excuse me, I must go . . . !'

'Mrs Markulis?'

Emily's suddenly serious tone stopped Liesel Markulis in her tracks.

'Did you notice anything different in Anna's behavior in July?'

Emily thought she detected a glimmer of guilt in Mrs Markulis's eyes.

'I really don't know. Maybe she was homesick now and then, for her father, but no . . . nothing in particular. Except she couldn't bear the heat.'

Emily nodded.

'Did Anna have her ears pierced when she came to Chicago?' she asked.

'Why no.' Mrs Markulis looked genuinely puzzled. 'Why do you ask?'

'Another time,' Emily said, 'the meeting's about to begin . . .'

As Mrs Markulis moved off, an usher tugged at Emily's sleeve and she took her seat. The woman next to her introduced herself as Marion Stoiber. She was in her early thirties and her handshake, like her expression, was cautious, and without warmth.

'We'll talk about Anna in the break for luncheon,' she said. Emily opened her mouth to respond but

Marion frowned, put a finger to her lips and nodded toward the stage. Moments later a tall, elegant woman on the platform rose up, looked around like a college headmistress intent on bringing order to unruly students, took up a gavel and firmly beat it thrice on the table, bringing the good ladies of WCTU to order.

37

Mr Toulson

CHICAGO Thursday October 26, 1893   11.03 AM

At about the same time that the good ladies of WCTU began settling down to the serious business of the day, a telephone rang in an obscure, out-of-the-way downtown office.

It had been established only a few months before by William Pinkerton, son of the founder of the Pinkerton Detective Agency, as a base for certain specialized covert operations, about which his regular staff needed to know nothing.

Strictly speaking the office was not part of Pinkerton's at all; the only people who knew of its existence and used it were ex-Pinkerton men of the very highest caliber, discreetly returning from 'retirement' to undertake assignments of a very particular and dangerous kind that required their expertise.

The phone rang again.

A tough-looking thickset individual picked up the receiver. He had taken off his jacket and sat with rolled up sleeves and wide suspenders at a pigeonhole desk, a waste basket to one side and a shiny brass spittoon to the other.

'Yes?'

'You have a call from New York. A Mrs Rhys.'

The man sighed.

'Okay, put her on.'

There was a brief pause, a few hollow clicks, and then the distant sound of a woman, breathing heavily, the voice tremulous. 'Mr Toulson?'

'Yes.'

'He's been found . . . as you warned he might be. He . . .'

Jenkin Lloyd Rhys's wife, Ellen, began to weep.

For a tough-looking man who had seen and occasionally had to do some horrible things in his nearly fifty years of life, Toulson had remarkably gentle eyes.

'I'm so sorry, Mrs Rhys.'

She wept some more.

'I'm sorry,' she said eventually, 'I . . .'

'Take your time.'

The sobbing at the end of the line continued and then, eventually, Ellen Rhys said, 'He was found in Johnstown, Pennsylvania. They say it's accidental death. He was in the river, it . . .'

'Just try to give me the facts, Mrs Rhys . . . as best you can.'

Ellen Rhys repeated what the sheriff in Johnstown had told her over the telephone. She was not to know that his version had not included everything.

'Who identified him?'

'The sheriff himself. They all know Jenkin in Johnstown . . .'

Her voice faded.

'*Accidental death?* Who's fooling who?' Toulson was incredulous.

'That's what the sheriff told me.'

'And what do you think?'

'I don't believe a word of it. JLR knew that everyone in Johnstown hated him.'

She broke down again.

Toulson consulted a tome on his desk and looked up a name.

'What else did Sheriff Bastable say?'

'He strongly advised me that in the interest of public safety my husband should be interred as soon as possible. As a precautionary measure . . .'

'You mean they fear reprisals?'

'Yes. News of the discovery of his body is all over town. In view of the situation, he wants me to telegraph permission for Jenkin to be interred in secret, given his unpopularity in Johnstown. Then, at a later date, they'll bring him back home to New York for a proper burial. But I don't know . . . What do *you* think?'

Toulson was silent at the end of the phone.

'Sheriff Bastable wanted me to call back very soon . . .'

'I'm sure he did,' said Toulson heavily.

He thought a moment more.

'Mrs Rhys, this is a very serious matter. I am most grateful for your cooperation and your courage. In time I think it may come to matter a great deal. Let me look into the situation and get back to you.'

After repeating his condolences, Toulson hung up, only to pick up the telephone again immediately. He gave an instruction that very few people in America, bar the president, could ever give.

'Get me Mr William Pinkerton on the line.'

The phone rang a few minutes later.

'Fifteen seventy-one?' Having set up this additional, secure office in Chicago, William Pinkerton abided strictly by its rules, addressing Toulson by number only.

'It is,' said Toulson. 'Sir, I have an urgent question. Who do we have in Pittsburgh? Needs to be someone very good.'

'They're all good.'

'I mean able to deal with troublesome sheriffs.'

'Where?'

Toulson hesitated.

'It doesn't matter, I don't need to know,' said Pinkerton, 'just give me a moment.'

There was the rustling of paper before Pinkerton came back on the line.

'I have someone. He's very good.'

'Name?'

'Van Hale.'

Toulson's eyes lightened.

'I thought he was in San Francisco.'

'He moved. He's in Pittsburgh clearing up the mess left after the Homestead strike.'

Toulson said nothing. There was nothing to say about that ignominious debacle which had left the reputation of Pinkerton seriously damaged. Toulson and Van Hale had both warned against that operation and now they were among the few senior men who had survived the shakedown that followed.

'He's perfect. Can he do it personally?'

'I'll see that he does. I'll talk to him right away.'

Toulson put the telephone down and reached for a box file. It was number ten of nineteen. They stretched right across one wall of his office. He opened it and prized free a folder, which he took out and put on his desk.

He opened the folder and pulled out some photographs, eying them with extreme distaste.

The he reached for another box file and another folder. It also contained photographs – of women and men – just ordinary pictures that could be of any passer-by in the street. Only these were of the missing, the dead and the murdered.

Impatient that he would have to wait for some time for the operator to set up his call to Pennsylvania, Toulson turned on his desk lamp, positioned it closely over the photographs and with a magnifying glass began making comparisons between these and the other photographs.

Twenty minutes later the phone rang again.

'Fifteen seventy . . .

'For Chrissake, Gerry,' interrupted the voice at the other end. 'Is that you?'

Toulson grinned and laughed.

'Hello Van,' he said. 'You busy?'

'Don't have to be.'

'How soon can you get over to Johnstown?'

'Within an hour.'

'Heard of Sheriff Bastable?'

'Jesus,' said Van Hale.

After briefing Van Hale on the situation in Johnstown and what he wanted him to do there, Toulson was about to end the call but changed his mind.

'Van, there's something else . . . You know anything about the illegal trade in pornography?'

'Not something I've investigated personally, Gerry, but it's a growing problem. We all know that.'

'Yes, and I have reason to believe there are links to Chicago . . . and possibly the Old America Association too. I need you to check a few things out for me. Here's what I want you to do . . .'

When the call was over Toulson returned to the photographs on his desk.

Moments later, he let out a long, slow sigh of satisfaction.

Leaning back in his chair, he pulled two photographs clear of the pile.

One was as lewd as photographs of its kind ever got.

The other was of Anna Zemeckis.

It was the one he had removed from the board in the Illinois State Building. Attached to it were the contact details of someone Toulson had never heard of: Emily Strauss.

38

Starr Turn

Emily Strauss soon discovered that, as far as annual conventions were concerned, the WCTU ladies liked to run a tight ship, with a well-oiled procedure, punctuated with Christian songs and prayers led by a succession of obliging and acquiescent ministers of religion. Emily had been raised to be distrustful of dogma and officialdom, and was too restless for organized volunteer work. To her mind the vigorous ladies running the show made the gentlemen present seem rather weak, as if their manliness took a poor second place to their Godliness.

The program had begun with some formal

speech-making, involving self-congratulation and anti-saloon rhetoric, followed by the pleasant diversion of the Turnverein spectacle.

Marion Stoiber unstiffened a little as the intervals between speeches and activities came and went, during which, Emily noted, everybody else chattered away like shoppers along State Street on a Saturday.

'Of course, our President, Frances Willard, is not able to be here today . . .' explained Miss Stoiber with a pursing of the lips and a note of disapproval.

'Why not?'

'She's in England convalescing. She was taken ill after her mother's death last year. She has sent someone to address us on her behalf instead.'

The program indicated that Miss Willard's representative was one Amelia M. Starr.

'She's an English cousin of Ellen Starr who helped Jane Addams found Hull House over on the West Side, so I suppose that's in her favor. I believe she's just come over from England to help at Hull House for a while, bringing with her Miss Willard's latest message to the membership.'

'Which one is she on the platform?' asked Emily.

'Well, I've not seen her before but I know all the others up there by sight, so she must be the one over on the right . . . in fact she looks quite like Miss Willard herself!'

The woman she pointed out was not much to look at: of medium height with a plain, pinched face adorned by steel spectacles and with hair somewhat haphazardly pulled back into a bun. She seemed like a bookish type, pale and rather lost among all the other committee ladies in big hats, who looked so much more colorful, better dressed and altogether more formidable than her.

Or at least most of them did.

There was a second row of ladies on the platform, behind the more important officials and main speakers, and among them Emily spotted two or three of the women she had met at the World's Fair. One in particular interested her because she looked as awkward and as nervous now as she had before in the Illinois State Building, which was unusual in one of Chicago's social leaders.

'That's Christiane Darke, isn't it? Do you know her?' she asked Marion Stoiber.

'Not personally, she's one of our wealthier ladies, I believe, both by inheritance and marriage. She's the daughter of Paul Hartz, one of our leading industrialists, of whom I daresay you've heard.'

Emily nodded.

'So she married into the Darke side of the business?'

'She married Gunther, one of Hans Darke's two sons. He's over there.'

Marion Stoiber pointed to a row of seats on the right positioned sideways on to the hall. In fact Emily spotted her friend Fay Bancroft before she saw Gunther Darke and smiled inwardly, unsurprised that Fay had obtained one of the best seats in the hall or that she was exchanging a few words with one of the best-looking men in it.

Gunther Darke was in his early thirties, olive-skinned and clean-shaven but for a fine black moustache. He wore his expensive suit with easy grace and when he sat up straight after leaning forward to speak to Fay, Emily could see he was well made and noticeably taller than those around him.

Emily brought the conversation back to Anna. 'You worked together at the World's Fair, I believe?'

'Yes, in the Administration Building. Many of the part-time staff, like Anna, were volunteers.'

'But you were paid?'

Marion nodded.

'I'm a trained stenographer and clerical assistant. I jumped at the chance of a job at the Fair. It was a once-in-a-lifetime opportunity. Anna joined us in mid-May, a couple of weeks after she got to Chicago. You know, she came here from New York?'

Emily nodded. 'I went to see her father. He wrote to the New York *World*.'

She explained the assignment that had brought her to Chicago but Marion seemed unmoved.

'I doubt that I can be of much help.' Her tone was decidedly unencouraging. 'But in any case . . . not now, the speakers are about to continue.'

Emily turned back to look at the stage. The first of the three keynote speakers was approaching the lectern. But Emily's eyes were drawn to the right, toward Gunther Darke. He was talking with Fay and smiling broadly as he did so.

'He's a fine-looking man, don't you think?' whispered Emily, noticing Marion's interest.

'I suppose so,' responded Marion, her gaze wandering again, brusquely adding, 'If you take an interest in other women's business.

Feeling admonished, Emily glanced at Christiane Darke up on the stage. She looked stony-faced and rather desolate.

'You wouldn't think, would you, that her husband is one of the stars of the World's Fair!' said Marion suddenly.

Did Emily detect something odd about the way Marion Stoiber said this? She thought she did.

'Why so?'

'Once a week he leads the Master Butchers of Darke Hartz in a demonstration of the art of dressing hogs and steer at the Agricultural Hall.'

Whatever Emily had expected, it was not that.

'But you won't get a ticket to see it, Miss Strauss. It's a sellout!'

'What, men cutting up meat!?'

'You should see it and you'd know why.'

'You have, I presume?'

Marion Stoiber nodded.

'I got a ticket because of my work for the Fair.'

But Emily didn't have time to get Marion Stoiber to elaborate. The gavel banged on the table upfront once more and the audience fell silent as the keynote speaker took the stage.

After a brief and none-too warm introduction by the lady chairman, who made a rather pointed reference to Miss Willard's absence, her stand-in, Miss Amelia Starr, took the lectern. She was not physically impressive but her voice had that rare quality in a speaker, especially a female one. It commanded instant and absolute attention.

Her accent betrayed her English roots but it had none of that pretentious arrogance that East Coast ladies, conscious of their English antecedents, feel it necessary to assume. It was soft, yet carried clearly right to the back of the hall and she wasted no time on idle introductions, false modesty or extravagant praise.

She paused for a moment, looked right round the hall and then gave a self-deprecating smile.

'I stand here today only because Frances Willard herself cannot be here. But it matters not who I am or what I may be. I am simply that thing which is at once sadly weak and fiercely strong; that thing that must run with the waves yet be a rock to the tide; that thing despite its many despairs that must forever cling on to the single faith that all in the end will be good and true.

'In other words I am what most of you are: a woman. Before that I am what all of us are – you good men included – I am a human being. And that is all you need to know about me . . .'

From that moment Miss Starr had the audience in her grip. Of the speech that followed Emily ever after remembered the spirit rather than the content, which was angry yet humane, modest yet rousing, thoughtful yet provoking in its assertion of woman's valuable contribution to human society and in the continuing campaign for prohibition.

Holding up her hand to the audience, Amelia Starr drew to her conclusion.

'The coming change in which our movement is a great and glorious part, and in which we women play an essential role, has until recent years been like this open hand: a weak thing without purpose. Now, bit by bit, starting I believe with the discoveries we made about our own abilities in the magnificent work we did to mitigate the horrors of our Civil War, we have come together as fingers that form a fist; and that fist, – which is ourselves so long as we combine with clear goals and shared faith – must be directed with ever greater purpose and power.

'That is our task now and in the years ahead. It is a great task and one which requires that anger of which I speak to remain strong, just as our faith in our purpose and our God stays strong. We must remain united in preserving our humanity in the face of that great social evil that threatens us all – alcohol, a scourge which undermines the very heart and soul of the family.'

The audience clapped and cheered. Some of the delegates, including even some men, rose to their feet.

But the speaker raised her hand, stilling the audience one last time.

'The road to prohibition, to female suffrage, to liberation and proper equality, will be a very hard and a very long one. It will be, I fear, many years before we women take our proper place at the helm of state . . .

'Ladies and gentlemen, on Frances Willard's behalf, I thank you for all you have done in the past year, all you are doing and all you will surely do in the days and weeks, months and years to come, for that fragile, sometimes lost, but always most wonderful thing – humanity. And as you do so, never forget that one great, guiding principle: that everything we do is for God, and Home, and Native Land!'

As the audience rose to give Miss Starr a standing ovation, Emily Strauss, who was not much given to prayers, found herself uttering two silent appeals to whatever God was looking down on the proceedings that day.

One was for Janis Zemeckis, that his daughter would be returned to him. The other was that Anna remain safe until she could rescue her from whatever trouble and danger she was in.

39

Escape

As the long morning's work drew to a close at Brennan's Tailoring Emporium Anna Zemeckis grew more and more tired.

A sudden and unseasonable rise in humidity had meant she had spent the morning battling against waves of nausea. Her sense of anxiety at being noticed was made worse by the fact that something in Eileen's manner toward her had changed.

They were late breaking for lunch that morning because the shop had sent in an urgent order and they had had to complete it. By the time it was done the machines were overheating and had to be stopped for a while. So Mrs Donal let the women go and take their break in the cooler air of the yard for twenty minutes. Mr Brennan, seeing the exhausted women slumped against the yard wall, chose to be soft for once as he came on by.

He glanced at his silver pocket watch.

'Twenty minutes more!' he said. Which gave them an additional ten minutes. Nobody complained.

He loosened his cravat and on the way up in the freight elevator took off his jacket. He was in a good mood.

'Get it done, Mrs Donal?'

She nodded toward two piles of garments neatly tied up with twine.

Silence and no complaint was the nearest her boss ever got to praise.

Then, 'Anything doing, Mrs Donal?'

'I got a cake, sir. In your office.'

He nodded complacently.

'You saw I let the girls go outside for some air.'

'I did.'

He came closer, a glitter to his eye.

'Come here,' he said.

She went up to him.

He wasted no time putting a hand on her breast. Then a hand on her thigh as he felt for her stocking top through her skirt. He took one of her hands and pulled it to his stomach and pushed it down a shade.

She let her hand go further down until it found his member and held it through his pants the way he liked.

'Nice, Mrs Donal?'

'Yes, sir.'

She played with him until he got hard. Then he slid his hand up her skirts to her bare thigh. Then more.

'Nice?' he said.

'Yes,' she sighed.

Behind them the freight elevator whirred into life.

Brennan grunted but it wasn't with irritation.

'Where's that cake?' he asked, pulling away.

He wasn't quite smiling; he never went that far. But his eyes had a look of satisfaction in them and his mouth hung loose.

'On your desk.'

He cupped her breasts a final time and then disappeared inside his office.

Moments later a man appeared on the stairs.

'You in charge?' he asked Mrs Donal.

'Mr Brennan is. He's in there.'

'Short of staff or somethin'?' the man said, looking round the empty sewing tables and idle machines.

It was meant to be a joke and Mrs Donal, recognizing the kind of man he was, half smiled.

'They're in the yard taking a break. It's the humidity.'

The man had a dark suit, a tilted bowler and scuffed thick boots. Mrs Donal noticed his sizeable hands.

He looked like one of the Ward No. 1 boys. So she didn't argue when he barged into Brennan's office.

Shopkeepers along Market Street never said no to this gang of thugs when they turned up on their doorstep. There wasn't much happened along those streets without everyone knowing about it. And when they were after someone it was no use trying to hide.

As one of the gang stood talking to Brennan, the girls were crossing the yard and coming back up the stairs, an exhausted Anna trailing behind them.

Eileen tried to hurry her. 'Hurry up, Jelena or you'll be late and they'll fine you . . . Oh, do come on . . . *Whatever* is wrong with you?'

'You go on ahead,' Anna said wearily. 'I'll be up in a minute.'

There was a closet in the yard; she felt sick and needed to use it.

Two minutes later as she started mounting the stairs, she sensed that something wasn't right.

Minutes before, the girls had been talking and laughing; then there had been a moment's eerie silence that she couldn't explain before the machines kicked in again.

She knew nothing of the Ward No. 1 gang but something – her animal instinct as a woman carrying a child perhaps – made her sensitive to bad smells in the air. And these men smelled very bad indeed.

So she slowed as she reached the last steps up to the sewing floor and peeked through the banisters to see what was going on.

She saw Brennan.

She saw Mrs Donal.

She saw the back of Eileen's head hunched over her machine.

She saw a man with a bowler and a thick cane in his hand.

They were waiting for someone.

Then she heard footsteps from below.

'Hey! Corm! *Corm!*'

It was another of the gang calling out to Cormack Hanlon, the man in the bowler, and he was coming up the stairs behind her.

Mrs Donal, more used than any of the others to distinguishing one sound from another above the clatter of the machines, glanced toward the door to the stairs and saw Anna's frightened eyes peeking through the banisters.

Very, very slightly she shook her head.

'*Corm!*'

Anna shrank back against the wall, went up the last few steps and then carried straight on up toward the storage floor above.

'Where's the girl?' she heard Brennan say.

'She's on her way up,' said Mrs Donal.

Anna froze just out of sight.

The man reached the top of the stairs, saw his friend, and joined him on the sewing floor.

As he turned his back Anna slipped down the stairs behind him, heart thumping, skirt raised to stop her tripping.

'So where is she?' she heard one of the men say.

Anna was off down the stairs in seconds, but even so it was too late. Maybe they saw her shadow at the door; maybe one of the girls gave the game away. More like they heard the sound of her feet running down the wooden staircase below.

She heard a shout as she ran straight past the boy at the door.

'Where you goin'?' he shouted.

As Anna made a right out of the building and then another right up Clark Street, she heard the men run out of Brennan's behind her, shouting and giving chase.

This was enough to attract the attention of the three other gang members working their way down the premises on the other side of the street. One of them spotted Anna, shouted out and went to cross the road in pursuit of her. But the traffic was slowed almost to a stop and his passage was impeded by a streetcar.

Ahead, as she ran toward Monroe and made a left to the safety of Market Street, Anna saw a jumble of horses and overturned vehicles surrounded by a noisy crowd. It was the fracas the officers at the Woman's Temple had been sent off earlier to sort out.

Seeing several police officers at the scene, she slowed immediately, lowered her skirt, pushed her way through the throng and moments later turned east with the crowds on to Monroe.

When the Ward No. 1 men reached the intersection moments later she was nowhere to be seen.

40

Guessing Game

It was only when the morning session at the WCTU congress broke up that Marion Stoiber and Emily found the opportunity and a quiet corner to talk in.

'So, what do you want to know exactly?' asked Stoiber.

'In her letters to her father Anna mentioned a friend – a man – she met at the Library. Did you know him?'

Emily already knew the answer to that question because Mrs Markulis had told her about John but she wanted to see Marion's response.

It was unequivocal.

'His name was John Olsen English. I met him only once, on a Fourth of July picnic outing that the library arranged to the Lakeshore. Anna invited me along. His mother's the notorious Mrs Hester O. English.'

'Notorious?'

'She's well known on the Near West Side as a self-centered dragon who likes to give just enough money to St Patrick's Catholic Church to have the good Fathers and the congregation dancing attendance on her. John was the same; always did his mother's bidding. I told Anna not to waste her time with him, he would never make a good match. But . . . she didn't want to listen!'

'What kind of beau did you think Anna needed?'

'A man, not a boy,' said Marion knowingly.

'And you found her one?'

Emily slipped the question in quickly and quietly to see what would happen.

Marion was quick to respond, 'I did . . .', only then to try and cover her tracks . . . 'I mean to say, I did think she needed a wider circle of male acquaintances . . .'

'Of the kind you had?'

'That's a rather forward question, isn't it?'

'I'm a forward kind of person,' said Emily with an engagingly frank smile, 'and I'm just trying to do my job and find out what life in Chicago was like for a girl like Anna Zemeckis.'

'Well it's a city that offers more than Mr John English, that's for sure.'

'You mean things are different here for girls?'

Marion hesitated.

'Well, I could mean that, yes. I suppose I could. I have a much wider circle of friends than my mother ever had.'

'You mean men friends?'

'I mean friends.'

The conversation seemed to have reached an impasse and as Marion was looking restless Emily decided to change tactics.

'I guess you and Anna did things together?'

'Sometimes. On Saturdays. We used to meet for lunch at a place on Wabash.

'Mrs Clark's Lunch Room?'

'You're well-informed.'

'Mrs Markulis told me. She also said you did some exciting things together.'

In fact she had not said that, but Emily reckoned it

was worth a try. Marion wasn't saying much and she could let her wonder what Mrs Markulis *had* said.

'I guess we did. The Fair, for one thing; that was endlessly fascinating to Anna. And a couple of theater shows, but we had to have an escort for those. Mrs Markulis insisted.

'There must have been other things.'

Marion stared at her and Emily stared back. It was a game of poker, a game of bluff, a guessing game. Marion was wondering what she knew; and Emily knew she didn't yet know enough. She just needed a chink of light to work her way to a clearer picture.

Suddenly it came.

'I think what she was most excited about – and it took some arranging because tickets were hard to come by even back then in the early days of the Fair – was a special tour of the Union Stock Yard.'

'I thought you just applied at the Main Gate off 47th on Exchange Avenue,' said Emily. 'That's what I did when I came to Chicago for the Pittsburgh *Echo*. Cost me twenty-five cents.'

'Sure, you can do that,' said Marion, 'but if you want to see the real thing close up you need a special ticket.'

'The real thing?'

Marion Stoiber hesitated and an almost lascivious expression passed across her face.

'The hog wheel,' she said, 'sticking the hogs.'

Her eyes gleamed.

Was it the blood, the death, or something more?

'And you thought innocent little Anna Zemeckis would enjoy that, did you?'

'She . . .'

Stoiber wasn't telling the whole story but Emily sensed in her hesitation that perhaps she wanted to.

'Everybody enjoyed the tour, women especially,' said Marion, 'and Anna was no exception. Didn't you enjoy it, or didn't you get that far?'

The tables were turned, because on her own tour Emily had had only had a cursory look at the killing floor. So if Anna had found it so fascinating, why had she never mentioned it to her father in her letters?

'Look, I've got to go,' said Stoiber, 'but . . . I haven't minded talking to you . . .'

'There's more, isn't there? You know more.'

Marion suddenly looked sad and rather lonely – and maybe guilty . . .

She nodded mutely.

'We could meet for lunch tomorrow,' said Emily. 'You could tell me more.'

'We could . . .'

'You're working at the Fair, aren't you? The steps of the Woman's Building at 12.30?'

'My break is from one.'

'One it is then,' said Emily.

'Yes,' said Marion uncertainly and then, more brightly, 'Yes.'

By the time she had finished her conversation with Marion Stoiber Emily found that all places for luncheon in the restaurant at the WCTU Temple were taken, so she decided to make her way back to her hotel for refreshment there.

But as she left the building Emily found herself face-to-face with a wall of sound and seething humanity. The crowd outside, good humored when she had entered two and a half hours previously, had turned as ugly as she had feared it might. It was drunk, it was disorderly, and it meant trouble.

Worse, the police seemed to have it barely under

control so that people leaving for the luncheon break had once more to run the same gauntlet of unpleasant shouts and jibes.

The crowd swayed back and forth, the police swore and used their nightsticks, people pushed past Emily in their haste to grab one of the queuing cabs, or simply to get across Monroe and out of harm's way.

Since that seemed the best option it was what Emily tried to do too. But the crowd of people at the Woman's Temple thickened, the mob pressed closer, and before she knew it someone had tripped and tumbled in front of her and straight into the mob itself.

Emily went at once to see if she could help the woman, whose hat had gone flying and whose purse was already in the grasping hands of one of the rabble, while another seemed bent on kicking her.

'Leave her alone!' shouted Emily at once, wading straight in. But her voice was as nothing against the mob's baying shouts.

Then she felt a hand on her arm and a voice saying, 'Leave this to me.'

It was then that she realized that the woman on the ground was Christiane Darke and the man who had come to her rescue was her husband, Gunther.

He looked anything but charming now.

His face was suffused with anger and his tall frame, which brushed against Emily as he pushed by, was taut with fury.

He reached out a hand and lifted the man kicking at his wife off his feet and threw him back into the crowd. He lashed out powerfully with his left arm and then with his right. Men and women shouted in pain and fell back.

Then he bent down and picked up his wife as if she was a child.

'That woman's taken her purse,' cried Emily, pointing.

Gunther Darke looked at her. To her amazement he smiled calmly while the entire world around was in chaos.

'Look after her for a moment, ma'am! Take her back inside!' he said, and thrust Christiane into Emily's arms.

She hurried Christiane, who felt as thin as a rail, back to the entrance itself. Other hands took her from Emily's safe grasp and she had time to look back at Gunther Darke. He had a tight grasp on the woman who had tried to steal his wife's purse while the mob fell back still further.

With horror Emily noticed the man who had tried to kick Christiane Darke. He was slumped in a shadowy recess by the side of the steps into the Temple. Another man, taller even than Darke, in a long black frock coat and bowler was now kneeling over him, his fist raised. The man on the ground looked terrified. The fist drove into his nose and mouth. The man lay still.

There was blood dripping from his assailant's fist as he stood up and walked off calmly into the crowd.

Ten minutes later, a shaken Christiane Darke was insisting that Emily stay with her. Her husband agreed, having shepherded the women toward another, quieter side exit from the building. A tall man – Emily thought it was the one she had seen earlier hitting the man outside – appeared and spoke quietly to Gunther.

'There's a cab out back,' he said to Christiane. 'I'm sending you home in it.'

He turned to Emily.

'You won't mind accompanying my wife, to see she's safe?'

'Of course not!'

As they turned to leave Emily heard footsteps in the corridor behind them. It was Fay Bancroft.

'Wait, I'm coming with you, Christiane . . . Ah, I see you've met Emily Strauss.'

41

Charity

CHICAGO Thursday October 26, 1893   1.35 PM

The moment she left Brennan's Anna realized that if she was going to retrieve her paltry possessions from the Mission then she had to do it right away. Sooner or later the men who were after her would get there too, because one of the girls at Brennan's would blab.

Spotting a carrier on Market Street whose wagon was piled high with furniture, she impulsively stepped out into the street and flagged it down.

'Sir! Please. I'm with child and feeling bad. I need . . .'

'Where you headin'?'

'Jefferson, over the river.'

'It's on my way. Come on, young lady . . . easy . . .'

He leaned down and gave her a hand, heaving her up into the wagon behind him.

'You find a place down there . . .'

She huddled against a wicker chair and some brooms.

'When's it due?' he called down to her.

The truth was Anna had no clear idea.

'February.'

He said no more and the wagon heaved and creaked its slow way westward across Jackson Street Bridge and, for the time being, away from danger.

Anna's mind was racing. The little world she had struggled so hard to create for herself had collapsed in moments and now she must start all over again. But she had to go back to the Mission first – to retrieve the fifty cents the sisters had demanded she hand over against breakages. She needed that money to get out of Chicago. She had no other possessions bar a cheap nightgown and change of stockings she had bought in the market, and – if she could call it that – the two documents she had taken from Dr Eels's clipboard. Instinct had made her keep them though she still had no idea of their significance. The previous night she had covertly rolled them up tight and stitched them inside her bodice with a needle and thread stolen from Brennan's.

The wagon lurched, the brooms rattled beside her and the wheels clattered over the cobbles. Anna felt more and more sick and then, thankfully, the driver gave a command and a yank on the reins and the horses pulled over and stopped.

'Jefferson, miss. At your service! Here, I'll give you a hand.'

He held Anna steady as she stood up and clambered down the awkward steps on to the sidewalk.

'Thank you . . .' she began.

But the man grinned and waved and was gone.

A short while later she was outside the Mission of Hope, its exterior as unwelcoming now as it was the first time she had seen it.

She knocked at the door, then pulled a bell cord which produced a distant ring.

The wooden slat snapped open and two cold gray eyes stared at her. It was Sister Agnes. Not good. Sister Agnes was as chilling in her character as in her demeanor, but at least the door opened at once.

'Yes? Anna Zemeckis, isn't it?'

Anna started at hearing her own name spoken out loud. It wasn't the one she used at Brennan's where they all knew her as Jelena. How could she have been so foolish that night she arrived after escaping from Dunning? She should never have used her real name.

'I know I shouldn't be here now but . . .'

She stuttered out her excuses, playing the role of abject stupid girl as best she could. She made up a story about a relative having moved to Chicago and offering her accommodation. The sister said nothing.

'So, I've come to collect my fifty cents . . .'

'Sister Ursula is on duty today. She's in the office. Go and see her when you've got your things.'

She bolted the door behind them.

Anna groaned. Sister Ursula was no pushover. She was old and crabbed and followed the rules. Anna guessed it would be hard prying fifty cents out of her. She had heard other girls say as much.

But at least she had got in without challenge and so, breathing a sigh of relief, Anna hurried to her dormitory and grabbed the nightdress and spare stockings she had left hanging on her peg. She took a quick look round what had briefly been a home of sorts to her and said a quick goodbye. Then she was off down the long corridor to the Mission's office.

When she arrived, Sisters Agnes and Ursula stepped to one side, conferring together in a low whisper. In the background, in a smaller room, she was surprised and worried to see a third Sister replacing the handset of the Mission's telephone. One of the girls had told her they had invested in this modern device because at hostels like these the Sisters sometimes had the need to summon police help with troublesome girls.

Anna began to realize something was wrong. They had let her in too easily. Far too easily. Sister Agnes had been quick to lock the door behind them and had not accompanied her to the dormitory. She had left her alone so she would have time to consult with the others. The telephone call . . .

Politely and contritely Anna explained there was a change for the better in her circumstances. She thanked the Sisters for their kindness, and asked for her fifty cents.

'I would be grateful if you could hurry. I have to meet someone,' said Anna finally.

'And I would be grateful if you would mind your manners, young woman,' said Sister Ursula without looking up. 'There is a procedure to be gone through. Sister Dolores, fetch the box.'

The younger sister retreated into the other room and came back with a metal cash box. She opened it. It seemed to Anna to be overflowing with coins and bills.

The clock ticked louder still.

'Sister Agnes, please go to the dormitory and see that all is well. See that Anna has unmade her bed and deposited her bed linen in the laundry.'

Anna knew she had not, she had not been asked to. Her heart thumped. She had to do something but had no idea what. Maybe she should just cut and run. Now . . .

Ominously, the phone rang again.

'Sister Ursula,' said Anna, her mind suddenly clear, 'if you do not give me my fifty cents now and let me go I shall hit you. I shall hit you hard.'

Sister Ursula's face faded from yellow to white.

'I *shall*!' said Anna, stretching out her hand. 'Give me my money!'

Sister Ursula looked terrified.

'Give it me *now*!' Anna screamed.

Her hands shaking, Sister Ursula fumbled at the cash box. It was the final straw. Anna grabbed at the box. She got her money and charged out, slamming the door behind her so hard that a plaster image of Mary Mother of God that hung above the door to Sister Ursula's office crashed into pieces on the floor behind her.

Anna raced down the corridor. Sister Agnes, approaching from the other end, could do little but let out a squeal and raise her hands helplessly as she was forced aside.

Anna headed straight to the front door, pulled open the bolts and was about to rush through when a thought occurred to her. Seeing the large key on a metal ring which always hung by the door, she grabbed it, slammed the door behind her and locked it before throwing the key across the street.

She looked first one way and then the other. Lower down the street a black covered wagon was coming up Jefferson from Jackson and it was traveling fast. It struck terror in Anna's heart.

She had seen the man driving it before, and the wagon too. It was the paddy wagon from Dunning, the one with Cook County Insane Asylum painted on its side.

She crossed over to the shadowy side of the street

and headed north. As she did so, she looked back once more. Sure enough, the wagon had pulled up at the Mission and Donko O'Banion and his assistant were rattling at its door.

She walked on, head down, and did not look back.

42

Post-mortem

Rorton Van Hale had once been one of the Pinkerton National Detective Agency's top men. In the normal course of things, had Allan Pinkerton not had two exceptionally able sons to take over the business, he might have ended up running it himself.

As it was, he was now one of that rare group of former agents, who although no longer on the official books of the Agency, served as covert operatives on a variety of special assignments. Gerald Toulson was another, and the two knew each other well and trusted each other absolutely.

Neither had been tainted by the appalling mishandling of the Homestead Riots of June and July 1892, which had all but destroyed Pinkerton's reputation and brought labor relations in the iron and steel industry of Pennsylvania to an all-time low.

Now, fifteen months later, Van Hale was in Pittsburgh quietly picking up the pieces for Pinkerton. The trip out to Johnstown for a less sensitive assignment had come as welcome relief.

'Almost like old times, Gerry,' said Van Hale when he called Toulson back around half past two that day. 'Got here just in time to stop the local coroner labeling it officially as "accidental". The body's been buried in secret, temporarily. They'll get it out to New York when the dust has settled.'

'You're sure it's Rhys?'

'Absolutely. For one thing, the Sheriff, Mayor and half the townsfolk had crowded into the morgue to gloat. They all recognized him.'

'Second, his name had been carved on his forehead, just so there was no doubting precisely who he was. Never heard of that kind of thing happening accidentally, have you?'

Toulson agreed he had not.

'So?'

'So I took one of the Agency's tame pathologists along from Pittsburgh, like you said. Rhys drowned after a fall from a height, probably onto rocks.'

'You mean he was thrown into Stonycreek?'

'Probably from a train. A rather special train.'

'Go on.'

Van Hale was on a roll.

'He had a wound in his right armpit. He had been hung up on a meat hook.'

He paused before adding, 'Remember the Gubner killings in Philadelphia?'

Toulson's eyebrows raised. Nobody involved was ever likely to forget them.

After a clash between rival firms in Cincinnati for control of the meat trade there, the five-man board and one of the main suppliers of Gubner Meat Trading Company had been found in an obscure icehouse by a railway siding east of the city. One was still alive, just, and that was old man Gubner himself, one of the best-known meat men in the Midwest. The older generation were a tough breed.

What was noteworthy about the murders was that all six men had been hung on meathooks and left to a long, lingering death, watching the ice around them slowly melt.

The leading suspect in the case was one Dodek Krol, an employee of Darke Hartz of Chicago.

'How do you know for sure Rhys was dropped from a train?'

'You try dropping a body into the Stonycreek River any other way. It's just not possible. Which means . . .'

'Which means,' said Toulson, 'that I'll check out train movements this end. How long was he in the water? Let me guess: three days?'

'Spot on.'

43

Hull House

CHICAGO Thursday October 26, 1893   3.01 PM

Anna Zemeckis decided her best refuge after fleeing the Mission of Hope was the Hull House Settlement she had heard so much about. But she approached it warily, unsure what to expect. She had never been there but she knew it was a place where ladies, some from the richer and better parts of Chicago, helped those of the city's most underprivileged. Nervous of using the grand-looking front entrance, she edged round the side like a nervous cat until she came upon a wide-open door that led to a kitchen.

There were a few chairs, a table or two and a woman, one of the Hull House volunteers, making coffee at a range and who immediately offered her some coffee and a cookie.

The woman did not question Anna but left her alone to drink her coffee, no doubt aware from experience that a caller such as Anna, so obviously nervous and under stress, was easily frightened away if approached too directly and too soon. But it was not hard to guess what her trouble might be. For Anna did not realize that in the last day or two her baby had shifted in her womb and her rounded belly had become noticeable.

'Why don't you sit here and I'll find someone to come and have a chat with you?' Another coffee was poured for her and another cookie was tempting indeed.

. . . And there she might have stayed had Anna not heard a voice call out from the hallway, 'Hello! Is anyone there?'

Someone had come in by the front door and, finding no-one around, had walked through toward the back. The woman went to answer her and Anna got up at once, fear in her eyes.

'Is Miss Lathrop anywhere to be found?'

Oh yes, Anna recognized the voice immediately.

She followed the other woman to the door she had just gone through to see for herself, peeking round it carefully.

It was Sister Dolores from the Mission.

The volunteer offered her a coffee.

'No time for that,' interrupted Sister Dolores imperiously. 'We've lost a girl . . .'

Anna Zemeckis did not stay to hear more, but turned tail and ran back out across the courtyard and onto Halsted as she wondered what options she now had left.

'The Union Depot,' she told herself.

A rail depot was a good place to lose oneself in a crowd and if she could get there without being spotted, she could stop for a few hours, perhaps until dark, and consider what to do. She dodged between the traffic on Halsted, crossed to the other side and headed north once more.

44
Darke Party

CHICAGO Thursday October 26, 1893   3.15 PM

Once Emily and Fay had got Christiane Darke away from the Woman's Temple to the safety of Fay Bancroft's grand house on Park Street overlooking Lake Michigan, she relaxed.

A change of dress was found for her and a light luncheon served for them all. Then, as a mark of gratitude to Emily for what she had done, Christiane invited her to an At Home that her father-in-law Hans Darke was holding that same afternoon.

'But . . . I believe you don't get on particularly well with your father-in-law?' suggested Emily, 'Or indeed that he is the partying kind!'.

'Both things are true,' Christiane replied frankly. 'I've known Hans all my life and he's a hard man to like. It doesn't help that he favors his younger son Wolfgang and that I am married to Gunther, his older son.'

234

Emily said nothing, for there was the hint of something she could not quite put a finger on.

'Of course, I mean I must . . . I must stand by my husband.'

Again a pause, again Emily and Fay stayed silent.

'Mustn't I? Yes . . . Yes . . .'

Emily felt she had never seen a woman at the edge of such pain. It was surely obvious that she stood by Gunther only out of duty not love. But that was a common enough dilemma.

'Well it should be a most interesting occasion!' Emily murmured. 'I'd heard that despite the firm's success the two partners of Darke Hartz barely talk to each other?'

'My father's tried many, many times. But a few minutes in Hans Darke's company and you'll see the problem. He's not interested in small talk. And since his wife died five years ago, well . . . he's retreated into himself.'

'What does your father think?'

Christiane shrugged.

'My father doesn't think about it anymore. I guess all he cares about are that his holdings in the company are the same as Hans Darke's – thirty-five percent each. Gunther, Wolfgang and I share the rest . . .'

Christiane smiled and, as she paused, Emily did some quick calculations.

'It's all right, all Chicago knows about the split,' continued Christiane. 'I'm not revealing any great secrets. Anyway, as you've probably worked out, whichever one of the partners gets the support of two out of the three of us children gets to control the company. Hans Darke always assumed that meant he was in control because he thought his two sons would support him. Well, not any more. Gunther's on my father's side and of course I am too – well he's my father, isn't he!'

She gave a brittle little laugh.

Even when making light of things, Christiane came across as an unhappy woman.

'Maybe it's better not to mix families and business,' said Emily, deciding it was better to change the subject. 'What is the reason for the At Home?'

'It's to give people the first opportunity of seeing Hans's newly built house,' explained Christiane. 'He has a thing about the rising school of young Chicago architects, you know, and commissioned it specially.'

'Will I have heard of the architects?'

'Of Louis Sullivan possibly. His partnership built the Auditorium of which your hotel is the Annex. So you'll know the kind of decoration?'

Emily nodded. Rich, intricate, organic. She liked the style.

'This time Sullivan has worked with someone called Frank Lloyd Wright. Gunther says he's a nasty, arrogant little man so I can't wait to meet him!'

Christiane laughed mischievously and even managed to look light-hearted for a moment. Fay offered them more tea.

The house was on Astor Street, north of the Chicago River. As Fay's carriage drew up outside, Emily could see that it was all clean lines and plain windows.

'Gunther thinks it's just terrible,' said Christiane as they got out of the carriage. 'All that money, and his father, true to form as he sees it, has put up something perverse. But I don't think it's so bad, is it! It's certainly a lot less claustrophobic than my father's great pile on Prairie Avenue.'

'Hartz Castle, they call it,' said Fay.

236

It was evidently a shared joke and they laughed gaily.

Inside, the décor was plain and the furnishings were nearly nonexistent compared to most of the over-ornate houses of the rich she had been in before. Such color and variety as there was came from Louis Sullivan's intricate pastel decorations and arts and crafts metalwork.

Everything was oak and light and polished reflections. Hans Darke might be an ogre, but his cave was a palace of understated beauty and modest charm.

'Welcome, Christiane!'

It was Hans's niece, Elfrieda, his hostess for the occasion.

She was short, dumpy, warm and informal. She gave Christiane a kiss on her cheek and did the same to Fay.

'Good to see you again!'

Then turning to Emily she said, 'And this is your friend from the New York *Times*?'

'The *World*,' said Emily.

'It makes no difference, I read both and my uncle reads neither.'

'What does your cousin Wolfgang read?' asked Emily playfully.

'Wolfgang?! *The Drover's Journal*, the *Grain News* and the stock market reports. He's as bad as his father!'

'Now listen,' said Elfrieda. 'You can roam anywhere on the first and second floors since for the time being Hans is still not living properly in the house. Hans himself is probably hiding away up there right now practicing the speech he feels he must make later. That will be at around 4.00 p.m.'

The doorbell rang.

'Wolfgang's prowling about the place somewhere,' said Elfrieda, '. . . that must be the first arrivals . . .'

Christiane and Fay, having other things to talk about, left Emily to explore the house by herself. Taken by the sight of the balcony on her arrival, she mounted the stairs and went out on to it.

Later, retreating back into the room, she bumped straight into somebody.

It was a man and he looked displeased.

'I'm Emily Strauss,' she said brightly, offering her hand.

He was in his late twenties, broad, stocky, with a shock of black hair. He looked more like a tradesman than the kind of society gentlemen Christiane and Fay had led her to believe would be attending the party. His face was without expression.

'Well then,' he said grudgingly, 'I suppose I am to say you're welcome? You are, of course. Sorry, I am not so good at this kind of thing, but I have been told to play host.'

Light dawned.

'You must be Wolfgang Darke!' said Emily.

'I am,' he said, brows beetling. 'I don't recall us meeting before?'

'We haven't. I arrived with your sister-in-law Christiane and Fay Bancroft.'

'Yes,' he said again, unhelpfully.

'My father's going to say a few words,' Wolfgang managed to blurt out. 'I came to get everybody. It's to be downstairs. Now.'

The hall was already full of people and more were crowding at the doors of the two rooms at either end of it, and in the panelled alcoves by the front door.

An older man, so like Wolfgang that she had no doubt he was Hans Darke, stood in the hall to her left holding a folded piece of paper with some scribbled notes on it. Emily was grateful she had the good fortune of a prime position from which to observe that rare sight – the Darke-Hartz dynasties gathered together.

But not a single member of the family was standing next to another. Christiane was with Fay at the far end of the lobby. Wolfgang had passed by Emily and stood now to her left, some way from his father.

Emily spotted Gunther to her right by the door into the nearer of the two living rooms. The only person she was unsure of was Paul Hartz, whom she had never seen before. Then she spotted someone who looked like an East Coast gentleman sitting in one of the alcoves, almost out of sight. On closer inspection she saw how like Christiane he was; and then she realized too she had seen his image recently, in an illustration in one of New York's Republican newspapers, alongside President Benjamin Harrison, one of whose supporters she knew Hartz to be. He certainly was every inch the power broker: urbane, patrician, confident.

Hans Darke, and his speech, were the opposite, but at least it was short. Emily was intrigued by the contrast between the man and the house he had commissioned from two such young and modern architects.

'Who is that gentleman your father is talking to?' she asked Gunther Darke, who was suddenly at her side. She was glad to finally have the chance to talk with him.

'Louis Sullivan. Bit too colorful for me, I'm afraid.'

'The man or his interior design?'

'Both, as a matter of fact. Champagne?'

Gunther's eye twinkled as he reached for two glasses on a tray offered by a maid.

Emily meanwhile could not take her eyes off Hans Darke. There was something strangely and unexpectedly touching about him. Here, in the midst of the idle chatter and everyday pleasantries of Chicago's social elite, she observed how he reached a hand to take Sullivan's arm and turn his attention to the dado along the wall behind them.

Darke's butcher's hands, large and clumsy as they had seemed when he was speaking so self-consciously, were now gentle. The two men bent down and Darke ran a solitary finger over the intricate form of the pattern Sullivan had designed, as he traced one of the dado's sinewy elements, smiling with pleasure as he did so.

Behind them, looking on, and then turning abruptly away, was a thin young man, quite short, rather stiff.

'Frank Lloyd Wright,' murmured Gunther Darke in Emily's ear, 'not a happy man, I think.'

'Why not?' said Emily.

'Sullivan's just fired him for poaching his clients.'

'Mr Darke . . .' began Emily, deciding to grab the moment and ask him for a ticket to his forthcoming demonstration at the Agricultural Hall.

'Gunther, please,' he said, coming flirtatiously closer. Emily could see why Christiane might feel jealous; she could also see why other women found him attractive – she did herself, very. It was rare she found herself with a man as agreeably tall and broad, rarer still a man with such humorous eyes and a beguiling charm.

'Er . . . Mr Darke, I wanted to ask you a favor . . .'

He smiled broadly and nodded his head.

'You want a ticket to my final demonstration at the World's Fair, don't you?'

'I do,' said Emily frankly.

'I'll get one sent over to your hotel, which is the Auditorium Annex, I believe?'

She looked surprised.

'However did you know that?'

He continued to smile but his eyes hardened.

'I like to keep myself informed about journalists who come to events I am involved with. As far as the ticket goes, consider it done.'

'Thank you!'

'I trust you won't faint at the sight of freshly slaughtered animals?

'I don't think so.'

His eyes hardened and his mouth tightened again. He looked suddenly quite fierce.

'It has been known for ladies to faint during my lecture,' he said.

Two hours later, after circulating among the gathered guests and exchanging a few dull pleasantries with Mayor Carter Harrison, whom she had already briefly met at the Illinois Building, Emily decided that the Hartz At Home, though interesting, was not yielding what she had hoped. All she had got was a lot of bland comments about how Chicago was really not as dangerous a city as people said. The reports about rising crime and people going missing were exaggerated.

'. . . by papers such as your own, Miss Strauss,' said one male guest belligerently.

She began to think it was time to leave.

Emily tried to turn away but the man grasped her arm.

241

'It's meddlesome journalists like you who are trying to take the gloss off the greatest event in American history and this city . . .'

Emily was alarmed, but before the man could open his mouth and berate her further, another man appeared and he was sent on his way.

'So, Miss Strauss, what are you doing in Chicago?'

Emily had never seen the gentleman before but it seemed only polite to answer his question.

'I'm trying to find out what happened to a girl from New York who disappeared here, Mr . . . ?'

'And you think a house in Astor Street is the place to start?'

'I haven't just started, and my presence here is far from accidental.'

'Really?'

'I'm sorry,' said Emily, 'but . . . ?'

The man produced a card and gave it to her.

It read, 'Gerald M. Toulson, Director, Letwin & Company, Engineering Consultants.'

'Thank you for rescuing me from . . .'

'Nobody,' said Toulson.

Fay Bancroft appeared as he was about to say something else.

'My dear . . . oh, excuse me, sir. I was wondering if my friend would like a ride back downtown.'

Already bored and realizing she had nothing useful to gain by staying, Emily accepted the offer but refused to allow Fay to take her right back to her hotel.

'Wabash will be fine. Drop me there. I can walk where I'm going.'

'Where exactly *are* you going? You reporters lead such secretive lives.'

'I need to check out a couple of things,' said Emily without elaborating further.

'It seems to me,' said Fay, tired after the exertion of being bright and sociable for several hours, 'that you do far too much walking.'

'Ah, but you see so much more from the sidewalk than from a carriage,' said Emily as they arrived on Wabash.

'Call on me for tea tomorrow afternoon,' said Fay, 'I've something to tell you!'

'Tell me now!'

'Tomorrow!'

Emily made a wry face, called out her thanks again and set off down Wabash.

Half a block away, a man paid off his cab and stepped down on to the sidewalk, but hung back in the gathering shadows until he was satisfied that Fay's carriage was well out of sight.

Only then, as the street lights lit up the main boulevard and sunset fell over the city, did he set off in pursuit of Emily Strauss.

45
Union Depot

CHICAGO Thursday October 26, 1893   7.51 PM

It was a near impossibility for a woman loitering by herself with no obvious intention of either catching a train or leaving the concourse to go unnoticed for very long at Chicago's Union Depot on Canal Street. There were too many watchful eyes seeking out the weak and the vulnerable.

No wonder: dozens of rail tracks converged at the Union Depot, which got its name from being built to unite the termini of five different railroads at one central point in downtown Chicago. Three hundred and fifteen trains came and went daily, transporting over sixty-five thousand people.

That meant a constant flow of potential victims for the predators who lurked there.

But as it happened, the management of the Union Depot was legendary among rail men right across America, for its efficiency, its firmness, and the benign way in which it took care of its customers, so long as they were within the Depot's jurisdiction.

The Depot was lucky. It's well-known and much-loved Depot Master, Mr John Crapsy, had trained his assistants, gatemen, ticket agents, ushers and special policemen to keep a watchful eye out at all times so that the Depot's reputation as a crime-free zone was maintained, even during the maelstrom that was the World's Fair.

On the evening of October 26th, even though Mr Crapsy himself was on leave through overwork until November 1st, the system was running like clockwork under the able leadership of Assistant Depot Master Bob Storey.

So it was that at five-thirty that afternoon he had been alerted by one of the ushers to the presence of a woman on the east side of the concourse who seemed in some distress but was causing no problems. That was normal. Probably someone had failed to meet her and she was just anxious. But she lingered on.

At ten minutes past seven Bob Storey sent one of the matrons in charge of the women's waiting rooms over to talk to her.

'Won't you tell me your name?'

'Jelena, but I'm not in trouble.'

'Well, my dear, so long as you are here you are safe, but after eight you may not stay unless you have a ticket to travel on one of the later trains. If it is accommodation you need then we can help. These days we can contact most of the reputable hostels by telephone to find out if they have a vacant room.'

'Thank you, I'm all right.'

She gave her a list of hostels and refuges and then let her be.

Anna Zemeckis glanced at the list and frowned. It included the Mission of Hope.

At around a quarter to eight each evening, it was Bob Storey's habit to do his own round of the Depot with a particular eye on any people who might need help but who, regretfully, might have to be shown off the premises into the darkness of Canal Street outside. It was often at this point that young women, reluctant until then to accept help, yielded to encouragement and advice and took it.

It was a strange fact about the Union Depot that, though its watchful attendants had strict orders to keep tramps, mashers, loose women, hotel touts, salesmen and street vendors – male and female – and much of the rest of Chicago low-life off the con- course, there was one particular person – and one only – who had been given free passage to come and go at will.

. . . And that was Mr Crazy.

Mr Crazy was well known to Bob Storey and even better known to John Crapsy, who had given strict instructions that no member of his staff was to meddle with him or try to eject him from the Depot, so long as he was causing no obstruction and doing nobody any harm.

There was a good, perhaps an extraordinary, reason for this. Mr Crazy was one of those rare individuals who was not only harmless but had the knack of spreading goodwill and good cheer wherever he went. He was also, as both Crapsy and Storey knew, an intelligent and articulate man who had a gift for making others feel at their ease. No-one in Chicago bore him ill will, and no-one ever harmed him, however dangerous the places he wandered in and out of.

In the Fall Mr Crazy often chose to end his day in town, before heading home to the Lakeshore, with a mug of well-stewed coffee with Mr Crapsy. But today it was Bob Storey's pleasant duty to provide the big man with a coffee, after which Mr Crazy tagged along, as he often did, when Storey did his last round of the Depot. It was during such rounds that Storey had discovered Mr Crazy's facility for persuading difficult customers to do what they should when all else had failed.

That particular evening Storey pointed out the young woman sitting on the concourse and said, 'She's been there a couple of hours or more now. What do you make of her? We think she may be in trouble of some kind but, when Mrs Morgan spoke to her, she denied it. But it's nearly eight now and she's still here . . .'

Mr Crazy studied the woman.

Eventually he said, 'I've seen that one before, a day or two back. Can't remember where now, I see a lot of people. She's barely more'n a girl. She ain't in trouble, she's in doubt.'

'What about?'

'Search me. I'll go and ask her.'

'Wish you would. But go easy on her, I doubt if she wants to hear about your legal claims.'

'Not claims, rights. I've got the papers to prove it.'

'See if you can get her to go to the Diocese Home if she's nowhere else to go.'

Mr Crazy nodded; then, in his roundabout way, like a knight moving purposefully but indirectly across a chessboard, he finally worked it so that he was sitting next to the young woman.

'They tell me,' he said slowly, 'that your name's Jelena.'

Anna stared at him and then relaxed.

'Mr Crazy.'

'And I notice . . . Shall I tell you what I notice, Jelena?'

'If you must,' said Anna with a gulp.

She looked at the man more closely and felt reassured. 'I notice you keep looking at the Western Union. It closes shortly, so if you want to send a telegraph you better get on with it.'

'How did you guess?' said Anna. That was exactly what she had been trying to summon up the courage to do for hours. The truth was she had hoped time would run out and the decision would be made for her.

'Years of practice reading the signs. You wouldn't be the first not to know what to say. Who's it to?'

'My father.'

'Run away from home, have you? What do you want to say?'

'Don't know. And anyway . . .'

Mr Crazy dug into his coat pocket and pulled out a dollar in change.

'There you are, now you've no reason not to send it.'

He reached over and put the money in her hands.

'Don't need that much.'

'I don't need any of it,' Mr Crazy said.

Impulsively, Anna got up and went across the concourse to the Western Union.

Mr Crazy watched after her.

Behind him, the 8.10 from Milwaukee pulled in a quarter of an hour early. A whole crowd of travelers got off and poured out on to the concourse, obscuring his view of the office.

When things had cleared ten minutes later the Western Union office had closed for the night and the girl called Jelena was nowhere to be seen.

46

On Wabash

CHICAGO Thursday October 26, 1893   8.15 PM

After leaving Fay, Emily walked down Wabash in search of a rather particular photographic studio.

It wasn't easy. Wabash was the most subterranean of all downtown Chicago's streets. The tall buildings either side were one reason, the new Elevated Railway that ran almost its entire length was the other.

Together these shut out the stars in the night sky above and created shadows and blind spots between its steel girders below. The noise the trains made didn't help a girl think either.

Emily had been up since six that morning but she wanted to find the photographic studio of Henry Robinson, *'Photographer to Society, studios in Chicago (Wabash Avenue), New York (Sixth*

248

Avenue), London (Strand), Paris and Berlin. Most commissions undertaken. Prices reasonable.'

That's what it said in gold lettering on the back of the *carte de visite* that Anna had sent her father from Chicago and which Emily now held in her hand. She hoped Mr Robinson might still be in his studio and that he or one of his assistants might remember Anna's visit in the summer.

The studio turned out to be a modest affair: a solitary window display showing the standard kind of portraits and list of prices, and next to it a narrow green door. The words PHOTOGRAPHIC STUDIO were painted on a panel that stretched across the top of both the door and window. Below was the simple inscription *Henry Robinson FRSP (London) Proprietor*.

The studio was part of a low four-storey building of no merit, one of the older buildings erected shortly after the 1871 fire, of the kind that Chicago's real-estate men were now busy knocking down to make way for much taller, grander structures. It seemed likely that this building would not last much longer: there was a builder's handcart propped up against the wall of the adjacent alley, and in a second-floor window, just legible, a 'To Rent' sign that had slipped sideways as if in acceptance that these were not premises in which anyone saw any future.

Emily pulled the photograph of Anna Zemeckis from her purse and checked the details on the back against the shop-front before her. She had the right place.

She moved nearer to the window and looked at the display. She peered closer, beyond the display. Inside, she could just make out a small counter. The wall behind was of frosted glass, beyond which she could see movement.

In the window itself were two notices. The first read, 'No *unaccompanied women. Parent or designated chaperone preferred.*' That seemed perfectly reasonable and proper. But as for the second: '*Wide variety of stock photographs. Sight on application,*' Emily was not at all clear what that meant.

Just as she was about to ring the bell and open the door, an arm reached out at her from the passing crowd and grabbed hold of her waist. Before she could resist, the palm of a hand had gone over her mouth and she was hustled with considerable force straight past a couple of newsboys, their mouths agape in horror, and pushed into the shadows of the nearby alley, stumbling over the handcart as she went.

A voice at her right ear said, 'Miss Strauss, I would be grateful if you did not struggle, scream or in any way draw attention to yourself. You will come to no harm.'

That was all very well, but for Emily Strauss this had been a long day and it was the second time in forty-eight hours someone had dragged her down an alley.

She let her knees buckle, crooked her elbow and brought it violently back straight into the man's abdomen.

He recoiled in pain but did not let go. In fact, his grip tightened and he lifted her up so her feet could get no purchase on the ground. She tried to bite his fingers where they clenched over her mouth but he only clamped them harder.

'Miss Strauss,' he repeated, breathing a shade more heavily, 'if you go into that studio and start asking questions, which I believe is what you were about to do, not only will you cause a great deal of trouble but your life will be in danger. Now, we wouldn't want that, would we?'

Emily tried to speak but could not.

'Would we?' The hand clamped across her mouth so hard that she felt she was beginning to suffocate.

She managed to shake her head.

'Promise?'

Emily nodded.

Very slowly the man took his hand away.

'You won't try anything again?'

'No,' she said, glowering in the dark.

She recognized his voice but could not place it.

The man's grip loosened from behind but she still could not see his face.

'I believe that the studio is being watched. I don't wish to alert the person watching that you or I are interested in the place, or they will be down here and after both of us.'

'How do you know?'

'No explanations. Not right now. Just do precisely as I say and follow me, because we're not going out the way we came in.'

'Why should I trust you?'

'Because you want to live.'

With that the man marched off ahead of her down the dark alley, with Emily blundering after him.

A few minutes later, after a tortuous journey down alleys between buildings, among ashcans and piles of garbage, Emily emerged on to State Street and the evening crowds. Only then did the man finally turn round.

She knew him at once.

'It's Mr Toulson, of Letwin & Company, is it not? Somewhat different circumstances than our previous meeting this afternoon, don't you think? . . . So this is your night job, is it?'

Toulson smiled grimly. 'Your elbow packs a punch.'

'Give me a bit more practice and it will pack a better one.'

'We need to talk, but not right now. You're staying at the Auditorium Annex, top floor, maid's room?'

'How do you know that?'

Toulson shrugged.

'I'll contact you in the morning. I'll come to the hotel. Don't do anything stupid between now and then.'

'Meaning?'

'Meaning don't go knocking on doors which open onto worlds you know nothing about.'

'You know about Anna Zemeckis, don't you?'

'Maybe.'

'You going my way?' asked Emily as she hailed a passing cab.

He shook his head, helped her in and shut the door behind her.'Got a job to do,' he said

'Consultation?'

'You could call it that,' he said, turning back into the gloom of the alley they had just come down. Then he was lost to view before Emily could ask anything more.

47

Sanctuary

Half a mile away Anna Zemeckis finally found a refuge for the night. She had made her way back to Tomas Steffens's shack by the rail track where she had last seen him.

Remembering where she had seen him hide the key under the wooden front step, she retrieved it, opened the door and went in. There wasn't much she could make out in the dark. Not much at all, but it suddenly felt like home to her.

She found some remnants of food on a table – stale bread, some sausage wrapped in paper – and a pail of water and helped herself, apologizing to Tomas as she did so.

One day I'll pay you back, she whispered.

She ate and drank and she even dared open the little window and stare out onto the backyard of a city that was not her own but which, in its own strange, frightening way, felt like it was trying to protect her.

She thought of the telegraph she had finally found the courage to send her father and repeated its final words: *Forgive me, Anna.*

Then she lay on the floor and wrapped her shawl tightly around her. She felt around in the dark for the old copies of the Chicago *Tribune* that she noticed Tomas kept in a pile and then lay herself down on the rag rug in the middle of the floor. With difficulty, for they kept sliding off, she spread the sheets of news-paper over herself.

She lay for a moment and listened to the world, remembering she had left the window open only when she was settled. But she left it as it was. She was afraid of nothing anymore.

Then, putting one arm under her head as a pillow and the other round her middle for comfort, she began to drift into sleep.

Which was when, for the first time, she felt her child move. No more than a flutter, a tiny touch of almost nothing at all. Except that it was everything.

'We're going to live,' she whispered, '*live* . . . Even if no-one in the whole world cares.'

48

Bad Night

CHICAGO Thursday October 26, 1893   9.30 PM

But there was someone who did care, and his name was Gerald Toulson.

Having returned to the photographer's studio on Wabash after seeing Emily safely on her way, he had a brief and forceful 'consultation' with Henry Robinson. That was now over, and he was making his way back to his room at the Grand Pacific Hotel with a package in his hand.

It contained images of several girls, among them Anna Zemeckis. Unpleasant pornographic images which, he reckoned, the girls had been coerced into posing for.

Yes, Toulson most certainly did care about the girl called Anna Zemeckis. If he could find her alive she might well prove to be the crucial witness he was looking for.

Provided he could keep her alive for long enough.

In Chicago that was never easy, as Mr Henry Robinson was in the process of finding out.

Not long after Robinson's unpleasant visit from Toulson a figure with a large bag over his shoulder appeared in an unlit doorway right across from the premises on Wabash. Obscured by the nearby uprights of one of the Elevated's supporting steel piers, the man had watched as Henry Robinson, his day's work finally done, turned off the studio lights and came out of the door.

As he did so, the man eased himself from his hideaway, crossed under the Elevated and reached him as he turned to lock the door.

'For heaven's sake, you're too late' said Robinson. 'We're closing. You'll have to come back tomorrow . . .'

His eyes widened in fear when he saw who it was.

The man was tall, dressed in a black frock coat over a white shirt with a black cravat.

'Lukas . . .' Robinson stuttered.

The Meister grasped Robinson by the scruff of the neck, opened the door and pushed him back inside. Robinson half turned, protesting, but he was unceremoniously pushed on past the counter and into the back studio.

Lukas did a lot of dirty jobs. This was one of them. He dropped the bag he was carrying by the door.

'Turn on the light,' he ordered.

Robinson did as he was told.

Lukas put a photograph on a table.

'Her name's Zemeckis,' he said. 'I want to see you destroy all the plates you have of her, every one. Now.'

'But . . . why's everyone so interested in this girl. She's not . . .'

'*Now* . . .'

One by one, using a hammer he normally used for framing pictures, Robinson did as he was asked. There was no point in mentioning the recent visit from Toulson. He knew when he had finished he was going to die and nothing would save him.

'Faster,' said Lukas, taking off his coat and laying it well clear of where they stood. Then he rolled up his sleeves.

'But Lukas, how long have we known each other?'

'Too long. Finished?'

'Y . . . yes.'

Robinson turned and stared at the butcher's knife and the rolled up sleeves.

'Please no,' he said. 'Not me.'

Lukas lunged at him, sticking him straight in the throat like a hog. He held him at a distance so his clothes were not stained by blood, though his right arm was. He bent him struggling and gurgling over the broken plates and let the blood pour on to them.

Then he turned Robinson round, saw he was still alive, and stuck him again in the neck.

As Robinson's body fell limply against him, Lukas lowered him to the ground.

He put the knife to one side and ripped Robinson's shirt wide open to the undervest. He undid the pants and pulled them down.

Slitting the undergarment straight down with his knife, Lukas revealed his victim's bare chest, a pale, pigeon thing. With a skilled twist of the wrist he slit open his abdomen and heaved the body over so that the guts spilled on the floor.

Lukas cleaned his knife carefully on a towel after running water over it at the studio sink. He washed his hands and checked himself in the mirror.

Going over to the bag he had left by the door he took out a fresh shirt but did not put it on immediately. Instead he took out a can of kerosene.

He walked to the basement below and worked his way up by way of the studio, and the front, taking the trail of kerosene all the way up to the shop door.

He washed his hands again and finally put on his clean shirt.

Then he struck a lucifer and set the fire in motion. He was calmly walking away when he remembered something.

Going back into the burning studio, Lukas retrieved the photograph of Anna Zemeckis and put it in his bag.

Then he walked off calmly into the Chicago night.

DAY NINE

Friday October 27, 1893

49

Goose Island

The next morning, Anna was woken by a bright shaft of sunlight shining straight in her eyes through the tiny window at the back of Tomas Steffens's hut. Screwing them up, she shivered and turned the other way. She was stiff and cold but otherwise she felt refreshed. She had woken twice in the night from nothing in particular except worry and had lain listening to the distant sound of rolling stock and the soft hoot of shipping on the nearby North Fork of the Chicago River.

Somewhere a church clock struck. It was seven and time for her to go.

Anna's plan was still to get to Canada as quickly as she could. The money Tomas Steffens had given her had helped buy food for her first couple of days and pay the fifty-cent deposit she had recovered from the Mission. Aside from that, all she had were a few cents short of a dollar left over from the loose change given her by Mr Crazy at the Union Depot.

She reckoned she needed just one more dollar to get out of Chicago to the safety of St Paul and she knew where she had to go to get it. The girls at the Mission had said that if there was one place in Chicago where you could guarantee a job that paid cash at the end of the day, no questions asked, it was Goose Island. Not a nice place, nor a safe one, but it was either that or the streets for a girl with nowhere else to go.

She tidied her hair in a scrap of mirror on the wall but did not see what she had become: gray-faced, gaunt, hair greasy, eyes like those of a hunted animal. If she had, she might have given up there and then.

As it was, all she could think of was getting to St Paul. After that she'd have to think again.

She left a note of apology and thanks for Tomas Steffens, carefully shut the hut door and headed back across the tracks to the gap in the fence, as she had done three days before. But this time she headed toward the North Side.

Goose Island was less than half a mile north of where Anna emerged on to Canal Street. It had become an island when the Illinois & Michigan Canal was built in the 1850s to the east of the winding North Fork of the Chicago River between North and Chicago Avenues. This had left a piece of land cut off by the canal on one side and the river on the other, which Chicago's entrepreneurs realized offered useful waterfront sites to industries needing a ready supply of water. These were mainly smelly, polluting ones like tanneries, paint works, breweries, stinking gas works and soap factories. Desperate for the employment offered, impoverished immigrants, mainly Irish and later Bohemian, moved in, finding what space for living they could among the factories. The geese these residents kept gave Goose Island its name.

By the 1890s, the Irish had moved out and the less particular, or more desperate, Poles had moved in, building yet more shacks and hovels amongst the factories and more regular houses – more slums within slums.

By that October morning when Anna Zemeckis walked up Canal Street to Goose Island, it was a dark and dingy industrial maze in which little thought was given to the facilities needed by the humans, whether residents or workers, who inhabited it. There was no main drain, so the streets and alleys stank of human waste. There was no enforcement of the ordinances concerning the proper construction of dwellings, most of which were no more than tumbledown hovels, nor had there been for many years. The wooden sidewalks were dangerously rotten, more than one toddler and not a few drunks had drowned in the mud when the sidewalk gave way. Goose Island was a place where people, ground down by their environment, were never naturally friendly to each other and even less so to strangers.

Yet at the start of each day a tide of poor, desperate, half-starving men, women and children made the trek from west and south, up Halsted and Canal and across to Goose Island, in hopes of finding employment – even if just for the day.

The streets they found themselves in were largely unpoliced, the factories unregulated, the atmosphere so thick with smoke and the stench of chemicals and waste that newcomers often turned back, their hands to their mouths and nostrils; while those familiar with the place bent forward as if into a noisome wind, eyes on the ground, hands close to their bodies, women and men alike, pulling up their skirts and pants respectively to keep them clear of filth, watching each step they took for fear of stepping in the mire; cautious of each wagon that passed, for fear of being deluged with mud and excrement.

It wasn't hard to find work there, provided you weren't choosy. Permanent signs could be seen outside the sorry, sagging buildings that passed for factories with advertisements by employers seeking labor: *Work available: Generous Payment on Results. Inquire within.* Others had beaten Anna to it at the first three places she inquired. The fourth got a result.

Maybe the company had had a meaningful name at one time but now it had reduced itself to initials only: E.K.M. & Co.

It was five rickety storeys high and boasted a freight elevator.

'Top floor, lady,' said a man loading boxes on a wagon. 'Ask for Groats.'

He nodded toward the elevator.

'Use it if you want,' he said. 'Keep yer hands and feet and head inside, otherwise you'll lose 'em.'

The elevator had no doors. It swung a bit but did not move. Anna saw a lever and pulled it. The elevator dropped an inch or two.

'Other way. Slow at the top.'

Regretting she had climbed aboard this contraption, Anna juddered her way to the top, the open floors sliding past inches from her nose, briefly revealing scenes of increasing activity, noise and mayhem.

The place was a garment factory specializing in cloaks, by the look of things, so she was confident she would get work if any was available. It was several times the size of Brennan's and en route to the top floor she saw all sorts in storage and being made: jackets, sacques, circulars, dolmans and plain cloaks.

She stepped into the murky, dismal fug of the top floor none too soon because the elevator, having a life of its own, started moving back down before she was quite out of it, causing Anna to fall out onto the wooden floor.

Close up, she saw it was covered with lint, cut threads and fleas – lots of them. She got up fast.

The sewing room made Brennan's look like the foyer of a smart new hotel on Michigan. It was crowded to bursting point with tables, clacking sewing machines and something like one hundred and fifty girls, mostly younger than herself, some no more than children.

The smell from the recently dyed cloaks – mainly brown, blue and black – was foul; but that emanating from a nearby pile of English plaid made her want to retch.

The pressing table stood in the center of the room with gas stoves on which the irons were heated for girls to take them off and sponge and press the garments, each operation accompanied by steam carrying the acrid smell of scorched cloth.

It is true there were fans, but these merely blew the moist, hot air about, adding to it lint and occasional strands of cotton which made some of the girls cough.

'Groats' turned out to be a man who had the thin, yellowed creased skin and sunken cheeks of a smoker. The whites of his eyes were yellow too and rheumy. He wore slippers and a filthy shirt hanging out over his pants, the suspenders pulled down over his hips. The only sign of his authority was the slouch hat on his head which, amazingly, looked brand new.

Anna told him what she wanted and what she could do.

But his first question was not about work.

'Where you from?'

'South Halsted.'

'Original like?'

'Romania,' she lied.

He looked at her in silence for a moment. It was impossible to tell if he believed her or not.

'Can you work a machine?'

She shook her head.

'You can sew?'

She nodded.

'Good or bad? Don't lie. I'll know soon enough.'

'Good.'

He nodded with satisfaction and offered her twenty-five cents for every dozen cloaks she made. A quick glance at a pile of these told her that standards at E.K.M. & Co. were not high.

She took the job and moments later found herself sitting between two young girls.

'We're to work short threads,' said one of them warningly, without looking up. Anna knew that meant slower work. Short threads were for when conditions we so crowded that longer threads in a needle threatened the eyes of girls sitting to your right and left.

Anna settled to the work but after thirty minutes felt uncomfortable.

'Are there water closets up here?' she asked her silent neighbor.

'Behind. Can't yer smell 'em?'

Anna got up, unsure if she would be reprimanded, but she was not. Anyway, Groats was nowhere to be seen.

There were six closets, all unutterably filthy and used by men and women alike, it seemed. There was water and carbolic soap and one towel, wringing wet. No-one was in the murky place and even had they been they could not have seen much. Anna took the opportunity of washing herself as best she could without removing her dress and shook her hands dry.

Then, feeling better, and pleased that the speed at which she worked was faster than the girls around her, returned to her place.

'Where yer from?' asked one of the girls.

'Romania,' lied Anna again.

'They're looking for a girl from Latvia.'

Anna's heart thumped but she said nothing.

'Where's Latvia?' said another of the girls.

'A long way from Romania,' said Anna, too quickly.

It was not the right thing to say. Too smart. Too quick. Too noticeable.

Without saying anything more, she bent her head to her sewing and let her mind wander to thoughts of her final escape from the hell of Chicago, and a new life in Canada.

50

Messages

CHICAGO Friday October 27, 1893   8.22 AM

It was nearly half-past eight and Emily was sitting in the dining room of the Auditorium Annex with a view of Lake Park and the water beyond, contemplating several messages brought to her table from the front desk by Johnny Leppard, who lingered for a few moments and then went off humming cheerfully.

She watched him, a half smile on her face, not quite sure if he was a boy or a man and deciding that maybe she warmed to him because he seemed an example of that special kind of male who was always going to be a bit of both.

'Johnny!'

He turned back, a question in his eyes. For a moment they stared at each other in silence, Emily not sure why she called out to him so impulsively.

Then: 'I just wanted to say thank you for what you did the other night.'

'Said it already, Miss Strauss. Didn't need to then, don't need to now. You need something, you just let me know.'

This time his face didn't hold a boy's grin but a man's smile. It was the smile of a young man who was going places.

Emily wished she had a clear goal like Johnny, who wanted to run his own hotel by the time he was thirty.

Me? she wondered. *Travel and see the world writing great stories as I go.*

She turned to her messages.

The first was from Gerald Toulson, telling her to expect him at ten.

The second was from Ben Latham, confirming his arrival at the hotel at about the same time. That might be no bad thing, thought Emily.

Ben also reminded her that he needed a room because if she had not found him one it was going to be a park bench.

The third message was another from Mr Toulson saying something had come up and he might be a little late. He would get a message to her if he was further delayed.

'Humph!' Emily said to herself. She was not at all sure about that particular gentleman or whether his story about the photographer's studio being watched and a dangerous place had been a deliberate ploy to interfere with her investigation. But at least his coming later would give her time to brief Ben.

A fourth message was from Gunther Darke in the form of an expensive-looking envelope with Darke Hartz & Company, Chicago, embossed in glossy black print in its top right hand corner and bearing the hand-written instructions *For Miss Emily Strauss of the New York World, By Special Invitation, Gunther Darke* across the front. It contained an impressive printed card: the promised invitation for Darke's lecture and demonstration at noon that day in the Annex of the Agricultural Hall.

Emily glanced at the dining room clock and saw she still had a good hour before Ben was due to arrive.

She left the dining room and went in search of the ever resourceful Johnny. She found her young friend soft-soaping a guest about to leave and receiving his reward in the form of a substantial tip. Emily waited until he had completed his business and called him over.

He had discreetly pocketed the money before he reached her.

'If I ask reception for a room for a friend,' she said, 'what are they going to say?'

'No.'

'Supposing I offer them money?'

'It would need to be an awful lot. It's the end of the Fair. Every hotel, every room, every park bench in Chicago's taken.'

'You're saying it's impossible?'

'I never say that word, Miss Strauss. Never will till the day I die. The day Saint Peter sends for me is the day I'll say impossible. Too much living to do, too many mountains to climb with great views.'

'You're a bit of a philosopher, aren't you? Listen, I've got a colleague from the *World* arriving in about an hour. I've got to find him a place to sleep.'

'Colleague or close friend?' Johnny eyed her frankly.

Emily flushed.

'Colleague. He certainly can't share my room. I've got to find him somewhere.'

'He can have my bed, going rates,' said Johnny promptly.

'And where will you sleep?'

Johnny stared a bit more and Emily flushed again. Then he laughed and so did she.

'I'll find somewhere, don't worry,' he said archly. 'Tell him to see Mr . . .'

He nodded toward the concierge.

'That's the man he pays.'

'Not you?'

'Don't work that way, Miss. It's the concierge that runs this hotel. Best-paid man in the establishment. He gets a cut of everything, including my room if I let it out.'

'Who's floor will you sleep on?'

Emily was curious. She was thinking that maybe there was a story in the way hotels were run.

Johnny stared at her again, then he grinned.

'A close friend,' he said.

To her astonishment Emily felt a small pang of jealousy. About Johnny Leppard?

She needed some fresh air and decided on a quick walk along Michigan Avenue. But once outside and finding herself waiting for the traffic to clear enough for her to get across, she turned west. She was curious to see what Henry Robinson's studio looked like in daylight, and she decided it would be interesting to put Toulson's warning to the test.

As Emily turned into Wabash, a uniformed boy from the Western Union almost bumped into her.

Moments later, as she was swallowed by the crowds on Wabash, he entered the Auditorium Annex and went up to the clerk at the front desk.

'Telegraph for Miss Strauss,' he said, pulling a buff envelope from the leather pouch on his belt, 'and it's urgent.'

51

The Color of Blood

CHICAGO Friday October 27, 1893   9.02 AM

Ever since Anna Zemeckis had inadvertently revealed to Dr Morgan Eels what seemed the perfect cure for certain types of insanity, he had been living in a heady world of dreams of international glory and a consequent state of dangerous self-denial.

This explained his inability to face the fact that his recent interview with Paul Hartz had carried a nearly palpable threat that if the missing girl, Zemeckis, and the documents she had stolen were not found then he, Eels, would be in serious trouble.

But the doctor was now only three days away from his official ratification as the new Medical Superintendent of Cook County Insane Asylum, and since the missing documents had not turned up, his earlier worry transmuted itself into certainty that they were

271

now destroyed or lost and would not come back to haunt him.

Meanwhile, Dr Benjamin Brown, his predecessor, had obliged Eels by vacating his splendid offices early, wisely making himself scarce before his successor attached too much blame for another patient's escape to himself. There had been a brief farewell party full of eulogies for the affable and ineffectual Dr Brown, a private word between the two men and a handing over of keys. Then Brown was gone as if he had never been.

Eels now had more important matters to attend to than Zemeckis, namely the series of what he hoped would be ground-breaking surgical procedures on a succession of twenty or so patients.

He started early that morning. But just after nine, when he had successfully completed the procedure on the second patient and was taking a break in his examination room, an orderly arrived in a fluster. Dr Eels was wanted urgently. A gentleman had arrived demanding to see him.

The calling card that the orderly handed to Eels read *Mr Dodek Krol, Physical Culture Director, Nord Chicago Turnverein* followed by an address.

Eels was incandescent. 'A gymnast! Demanding to see *me*, here and now! Didn't you tell him I'm in the middle of some important operations and cannot be interrupted.'

'I did, sir, but he was very insistent. Said it was imperative he spoke to you.'

'Tell him to come back tomorrow.'

'Sir, the gentleman . . .' the orderly hesitated, unsure what to say. '. . . the fact is, sir, the gentleman is not the kind one can easily say no to without very good reason . . . he seems well, quite . . . er . . .'

Eels's pale face suffused with sudden rage.

'Tell this . . . *gymnast* . . . that the Medical Superintendent of Cook County Insane Asylum is busy right now and that he should have made an appointment.'

The orderly retreated, but a few moments later he returned.

'Mr Krol says he does not like to wait.'

'Then he doesn't have to! He can damn well go back to Chicago and make a proper appointment if he pleases,' said Eels.

At which point the door to Dr Eels's surgery swung slowly open. The orderly took one look and fled.

Dodek Krol stood calmly in the doorway eyeing Eels, who rose from his chair, anger turning swiftly to alarm.

Krol's shoulders were nearly as wide as the doorway. His curled bowler was set neatly at his side in one of his huge hands. His overcoat was undone, but being well cut and of the finest cloth, it hung loosely but elegantly. His boots of the thick-soled, well-made European kind, were clean but not over-polished.

He projected confidence, success, certainty of purpose and menace

'Sit,' Krol said in a low voice.

Eels did as he was told, his heart thumping painfully.

He saw that Krol carried a stick in his left hand. It was a thick malacca cane of the kind sporting gentlemen carry for their own defense. It looked to Eels very like a sword cane.

'What do you want?' he croaked, trying to recover his composure. 'This is . . . I am . . . this is a hospital, sir, and I am its director.'

'I have come to talk to you.'

Eels's throat tightened and dried.

'W . . . what about?'

Eels could not stop his voice shaking.

'Missing papers.'

'I told Mr Hartz . . . I sent the police . . .'

Then for a wild, heady moment Eels thought he had misread the situation entirely.

'Is it possible,' he gasped, 'that you have them, Mr . . . er Mr Krol?

Krol's mouth hardened, his eyes crinkled slightly into a dismissive smile.

'I haven't. But we need them.'

'What for, sir?' said Eels, recovering himself a little.

Krol sighed the sigh of a man used to seeing men disintegrate before him.

'You sent Mr Donko O'Banion in search of the girl?'

'I . . . he . . . well, I didn't exactly send him. He works with the police. His brother-in-law . . . I thought . . .'

'That was deeply stupid. O'Banion's one of a gang who work Ward No. 1. They're all stupid. That makes you stupid too.'

Eels spluttered wordlessly like a turkey cock.

'Mr Paul Hartz gave you forty-eight hours, I believe. Your time has run out.'

Eels's heart nearly stopped in his chest.

'I shall have to find the girl myself,' said Krol, 'which I do not like. We will have her within twenty-four hours. You better hope she has this document. Now, Dr Eels . . .'

Krol looked around for somewhere to put his hat. He found a chair and pulled it to the side of Eels's desk. The chair looked as if it might disintegrate under his weight.

'. . . I want you to show me exactly what this document looks like. I need to know what we are looking for.'

'It isn't much,' bleated Eels, 'it's just, it's . . .'

'Show me,' said Krol.

Eels showed him.

'How many names will be on it?'

'Twenty.'

'And the papers are pale yellow?'

Eels nodded. A thought made its way into his beleaguered brain.

'You do not propose to dispose of the girl?'

Dodek Krol said nothing. About such things he never said anything.

'It is better that she is brought back here,' said Eels. She is one of these twenty. She will need to be properly accounted for, otherwise she will be perceived by my fellow scientists as a mortality. That will not be good. It is a matter of statistics. I need her back here.'

'My client will decide what to do with the girl, not you.'

'You mean Mr Hartz.'

Dodek decided he did not like Dr Eels.

'I mean my client,' he said. He paused and then added, 'If we do not find the document, Dr Eels, then it will be necessary to visit you again.'

Eels's eyes widened as Krol loomed over him, massive and bestial.

'Sir,' he croaked again, 'what shall I say to Mr O'Banion? He is coming here this morning for further instructions.'

'He already came,' said Krol, 'and you can say what you wish.'

He folded the yellow sheet of paper and put it in his inside pocket. Then took up his hat and his cane and turned toward the door in silence.

Eels stared after him.

It was only then that Eels noticed that Mr Krol had a stain on the bottom of the left leg of his pants. Eels's eyes widened as the door swung shut.

He sat for a while in his chair, shaken and fearful in the knowledge that his world, so nearly won, might easily collapse about him.

When he felt stronger he got up, went to the window and looked down at the graveled expanse which faced the main entrance to the Insane Asylum.

No-one was about, not even Donko O'Banion, whose paddy wagon was standing on the drive, its horse untethered.

Eels looked more closely.

The horse stood idly, tail switching at flies.

The wagon's door was ajar and from it something dripped onto the gravel below. It was the color of blood.

52

Negatives

When Emily reached Henry Robinson's photographic studio she found a crowd of onlookers just dispersing, and a policeman checking the ropes that cordoned off the front of the studio.

A fire had gutted the bottom floor of the flimsy

building, blackened the outside of the three floors above and had almost spread to the small pharmacy next door.

Toulson had been right to warn her off the place.

'What did I miss?' she asked a gawking delivery boy.

'Someone set fire to the place. And killed the proprietor.'

'They took his body away in the night,' added a middle-aged man.

'Policeman said his throat was cut,' added his wife. Her eyes were excited, her face flushed.

'Ear to ear,' added a newsboy matter-of-factly. 'By the time the Fire Department got here he was all burned too.'

Emily wished that the remaining officer on duty would move away, which, to her surprise, he suddenly did. A wagon that had passed her moments before, mounting the sidewalk as it tried to turn sharply into Adams, had shed its load onto the street. The officer went to sort out the mess, so she crossed Wabash, slipped under the ropes and in through the blackened door.

The floor was a mess of burnt papers and glass over which, lifting her skirt, Emily stepped gingerly. There was a window on one side which afforded some light but the place was murky from soot still hanging in the air.

As her eyes adjusted to the gloom, she was startled by a sudden sound further into the ruined building. A timber settling perhaps, a draught of air through a shattered window?

Emily crept forward and tried to ease open the studio door. But it swung wide open beyond her grasp, the hinges having been distorted by the fire. It hit the wall behind, bringing a shelf crashing to the floor.

Through the murk Emily spied a hunched and hooded figure with strange legs standing at the far end of the studio and silhouetted by a red glow.

She was about to retreat fast when a bright explosive flash stopped her short. It was followed by the sudden acrid smell of burning.

Staggering back, temporarily blinded, she heard the figure crunch across the floor toward her. For the third time in as many days it looked like someone was going to grab her. She lashed out blindly but it made no difference; a hand loomed out of the darkness and grasped her arm.

'What the hell . . . ?' a half-familiar voice began.

Emily's sight came back in strange starry strands until finally she saw the face of the man in front of her.

It was Ben Latham.

He was holding her upright with one hand and rubbing his cheek with the other.

'Where did you learn to hit like a man?' he said.

'What are you doing *here*, Ben . . . ?' was her reply.

'Train arrived early. Thought I'd take a look at the studio where the photograph of our girl was taken. Found the place cordoned off. Said I was an official illustrator and they let me in. Horrible.'

'That flash . . . ?'

'Fire didn't get to the camera. It had a plate inside. Just testing it out but overdid the magnesium powder a bit. Nice camera but out of date. I was trying to take a photograph of the wreckage but you got in the way. Here, let's shed some light on the situation.'

Ben crunched his way back across the studio and picked up the source of the red light, a lantern.

'These places always have 'em. For developing . . . red light doesn't spoil the images and it's just about possible to see what you're doing by it.'

He turned up the lamp.

'Someone killed the proprietor, Robinson, the man who took Anna Zemeckis's photograph,' said Emily. 'Can't you make that thing cast a more normal light?'

Ben removed a curved piece of red glass and cursed as it burnt his fingers. But the whole room brightened at once.

The studio was large and rectangular, everything in it filthy with soot and dust. There was a couch and some other props, a backdrop of painted trees with a lake on a roller, some chairs and the huge portrait camera on a tripod. The roof had large slanting glass windows to allow in the maximum light.

The floor was covered in blackened glass.

'Photographic plates,' said Ben. 'Whoever was here was either looking for something or destroying something, possibly both.'

'Like what?'

'I can guess, but it's something a nice girl like you wouldn't want to know about.'

Emily frowned.

'Like *what?*' she repeated, with menace.

Ben grinned.

'See the notice in the front window, what's left of it?'

Emily had but couldn't remember what it said.

'It's an invitation to customers who want to see "stock images". That's code for dirty pictures. Pornography. This place sold it, so . . .'

They were interrupted by a shout. It was the officer returning.

'Buy me some time,' said Ben. 'I want to look

around a bit more. I'm pretty sure I know what they were looking for.'

Emily went to the front of the shop, pulling the studio door shut behind her.

The officer seemed surprised to see a woman.

She introduced herself – taking her time about it. She showed her reporter's pass. She told him she was only doing her job. She just kept on talking and talking as loud and long as she could.

Finally, when the officer could get a word in edgeways he said, 'Ma'am, you shouldn't be here.'

It was a pity that, in the brief moment of silence that followed, Ben stepped on some glass in the studio.

'One of your friends?' growled the officer, reaching for his nightstick.

As Ben appeared, Emily said, 'But officer, we're . . .'

Just then, a second man arrived on the scene, ducking under the ropes.

'It's all right, she's known to me.'

'If you say so, Mr Toulson,' muttered the one holding Emily by the arm.

Hitching his bag over his shoulder, Ben said, 'I'm real hungry. Any chance of some breakfast?'

'So, you're an officer of the law, Mr Toulson?' said Emily as they left the blackened building.

'Am I?' said Toulson.

'Is he?' Emily asked the officer, ignoring Toulson.

'If you say so, ma'am,' he replied unhelpfully. 'Now, get the hell out of here, *all* of you.'

'The restaurant at Marshall Field's does a good breakfast,' said Toulson coolly as the three headed out onto Wabash, 'and a lady will help us look respectable.'

'I'll do my best,' said Emily.

53

Snitchers

The girls at E.K.M. & Co. did not take to Anna Zemeckis: she was older and smarter as well as being quicker and better at the sewing.

These girls were young, half-starved, ill-dressed, ignorant of life, and had suspicion written on their faces as well as the weary resignation of the eternally exploited.

Anna realized she had arrived nearly at the bottom of the bottom of the pile and knew if she did not get out fast, and that meant hours not days, she too would begin to slide down into the wretched place they were already in.

Just before ten, Mr Groats patrolled the sewing tables checking the girls' work. He grabbed the work of the girl next to Anna and ripped it apart.

'Not good enough,' he said. 'Improve or leave. I can give your space to a new girl anytime.'

When he reached Anna he examined her work and then declared, 'Too fine! Custom work! Don't need to be so good on such cloaks. You stay and I'll move you to better work when there's a gap.'

As he moved on, the other girls looked at Anna resentfully.

'Where'd you say you came from?' said the one who had already asked that question.

'Romania,' repeated Anna.

281

'Never heard of it,' she replied, glancing at the other girls and smirking.

Anna decided the best thing to do was ignore them.

She was surprised when a few minutes later, needing to press her work out to carry the stitching on neatly, another girl whom she had not seen before stopped and asked her where she was from.

She repeated her lie and the girl seemed satisfied.

But, a short time later, a third asked the same question. It was time to ask why.

'Been told to,' the girl said. 'There's a dollar in it.'

'A whole dollar?'

The girl nodded and said, 'They're watching out for someone.'

'Who?'

The girl shrugged.

''Bout your age. From Latvia.'

'Where's that?' said Anna.

'In Russia, I think.'

'Latvia,' repeated Anna softly. The very word made her want to weep.

She returned to her worktable knowing she had to get out of Chicago fast. She had been lucky twice. A third time . . .

She made the decision to leave when she had earned another fifty cents and with any luck, if Groats accepted her work, that would be by the end of the day. Meanwhile she had to try to lay suspicion to rest.

She sewed harder and faster still, listening to the girls around her, waiting for an opportunity.

It seemed that one of the reasons the girls resented her was that they had liked the girl whose place she had taken. She had fainted a couple of times and the other girls had kept it from Groats. The third time he was standing right next to her and she was out the door at once.

'Was it hunger?' asked Anna quietly, the first time she had talked in a while.

No-one replied but she guessed they wanted to. Maybe they weren't so bad after all, just young and simple and already half-beaten up by overwork and under-nourishment.

She waited a bit, then said, 'I'm going to have a baby.'

There was a combined gasp of curiosity, sympathy and relief from the group nearby.

'When?'

'February.'

'Are you . . . ?'

'I'm not married.'

For a moment she forgot why she had said it, basking in the fickle way in which the girls' attitude to her had suddenly shifted from rejection to empathy.

'I had to move from my last job because of it.' Then, as offhand as she could, 'There was a Latvian girl there . . .'

The interest level rose palpably.

'Anyway,' asked Anna nonchalantly, 'why are you so interested in a Latvian girl?'

'She's wanted.'

'Yes, but why . . .'

'There's a dollar in it for the girl who let's them know.'

'Maybe *I* should . . . Who do I tell? Mr Groats?'

'If you tell him, it'll do no good. He's not a snitcher. You tell Agda Akesson.'

Someone pointed at a woman on the far side of the room, older than the others and Anna too. She was dark for a Scandinavian, sour faced and very pale. Her hair was pulled back tight and her mouth looked permanently turned down.

'Doesn't look very nice,' observed Anna.

'A dollar's a dollar.'

'I liked the Latvian girl, she gave me some cake. Don't see why . . .'

'If they found out you knew and didn't say . . .'

'Who'd tell her?'

The girls fell silent and looked at each other shiftily.

Anna decided if anyone was going to snitch round here it would be her. She'd elaborate on her story about meeting a Latvian girl where she worked before.

She glanced again at Agda Akesson.

'I'll tell her the moment I get a chance,' she said.

54
No Deal

'So,' said Emily, taking the initiative when they reached the restaurant, 'you're with the police, Mr Toulson?'

He looked grave and moved his head in what might have been a nod or possibly a shake.

'You haven't introduced me to your friend.'

Emily did so.

'So . . . ?' tried Emily, a second time.

'I *was* with the police,' said Toulson finally. 'So

284

naturally I *know* the police. But I am not with them now. That's not important, though. What *is* important is that your inquiry into this dead girl is becoming a nuisance because it's interfering with something much bigger.'

'Which is?' said Emily.

He ignored her question.

'How many girls have you interviewed since you've been in Chicago?'

'A good few,' said Emily cagily.

Not nearly enough, she was thinking.

'What do you know about the Comstock Act?'

'Of 1873?'

He nodded.

'It was to stop the dissemination of pornographic literature about birth control and sex education, wasn't it?'

Toulson nodded, 'Dissemination of immoral literature in paper form – books, magazines, pictures, drawings, that sort of thing.'

'What's all this to do with Anna Zemeckis?' asked Emily. 'Or Mr Robinson for that matter?'

'I think Mr Latham can make a fair guess.'

'He was probably taking pornographic photographs on the quiet,' said Ben, 'which means he was selling them to select customers from his own premises or distributing them in some other way. Quite a few photographers have been caught doing that, usually because their bribes to the police have not been enough. That's my guess, and maybe that has something to do with why he was killed.'

'But is there really much money in such a filthy trade?' said Emily, genuinely surprised.

'Far more than you'd think,' said Toulson.

'Are you seriously telling me that Anna Zemeckis

was in some way involved with this kind of thing?' said Emily. 'She came from a good family. I've met her father.'

'Don't care if her father was Mr Comstock himself,' said Toulson, 'I *know* she was involved.'

'Even if that were true,' continued Emily, 'which I don't believe, you're not going to get me to abandon my investigation just because it might take me into dangerous territory.'

'There's no "might" about it, Miss Strauss. Pornography of the type I'm investigating is a filthy, nasty, dangerous business, closely linked to white-slave trafficking, in which young girls get abused, raped and murdered. Which is what probably happened to Miss Zemeckis.'

'Let's get this straight,' said Emily. 'You want me to help you investigate something you haven't yet convinced me is actually going on?'

'That's just about it,' said Toulson.

'Then I need something in return if I'm going to cooperate.'

'Like what?'

'Evidence. Right now. You *got* any?'

'You don't give up, do you, Miss Strauss?'

'No,' she said, 'I don't. It's my profession. It's what Mr Pulitzer hired me to do.'

Ben looked uncomfortable, Toulson dubious.

A penny suddenly dropped and it made a loud clang in Emily's head.

'So what *exactly* do these pictures show?' she asked.

'They show,' said Toulson heavily, 'what goes on behind closed doors between consenting adults.'

'Sexual intercourse?' said Emily.

''Fraid so,' said Toulson.

'You're telling me that so-called red-blooded men not only like pictures like this but haunt the alleys and side streets of the Levee buying and selling them?'

'I'm afraid so. You'd be naïve to think they don't.'

'I'm no more naïve than most of my readers but I'm learning fast. You're saying Anna Zemeckis was in some way involved in this?'

Toulson nodded.

'A nice, decently brought-up Latvian girl from a good home in New York, willingly allowed herself to be photographed having sexual intercourse?'

Toulson shook his head.

'Not quite, because I doubt what she did was done willingly. She was probably one of the reluctant ones, taken against her will and dosed with chloral. That's why she's probably dead.'

'What exactly do you want me to do?'

'I need help identifying some of these girls. Maybe you've come across some of them in your investigation. What would it take to get you to look through a file and tell me if you can put a name to any of the girls whose photographs are in it?'

'Prove Anna's involved and tell me who you're working for.'

'It's a deal,' said Toulson.

'Here and now,' said Emily. 'I've got a luncheon appointment at Jackson Park to get to, so I don't have long. Let's start with this so-called proof.'

'That's easy enough,' said Toulson, pulling a file from his briefcase, 'but I'm warning you, you might be shocked by what you're about to see.'

'I don't shock easily,' said Emily.

He produced a folder and took out a head and shoulders shot of a girl and placed it on the table in front of Emily. She looked at it long and hard.

'That's Anna Zemeckis all right,' she said eventually, 'but this image by itself proves nothing. Why she's wearing a feather on her head I can't imagine. Was she in a theatrical performance of some kind?'

Toulson laughed cynically.

Ben examined it.

'It looks like it's been cropped,' he said, 'Where's the whole photograph?'

They looked at Toulson.

'Miss Strauss . . .' he said uncertainly.

'Show me,' said Emily grimly.

He handed her a picture. It showed two women and a man. The man and one of the women were naked. He was on top of the woman, his whole body shown from behind.

She lay beneath him, her face toward the camera.

They were having sexual intercourse and she did not look unhappy. But that woman was not Anna.

The other woman, dressed in a tightly laced pink corset and black silk stockings and, somewhat incongruously, wearing a hat with a large ostrich feather in it, appeared to be acting as their handmaiden. She held a great fan above them made of the same feathers.

She too looked at the camera. But her face was solemn and unsmiling.

It was Anna Zemeckis. The head and shoulders shot of Anna that Toulson had first shown Emily was taken from the same image.

'Yes,' she confirmed, 'that's Anna.'

She handed back the folder.

'Now, Mr Toulson, you want me to look at some other photographs and help you identify those involved? First, you were going to tell me who you're working for. I know it's not the engineering company printed on your card; and you've said it's not the police.'

'I guess you could say I'm a Pinkerton man,' said Toulson. He reached out a hand. 'Let's agree to work together on this.'

But Emily did not take it.

Instead she got up from her chair.

'We're going, Ben,' she said.

Ben looked astonished, but got up.

Toulson look flabbergasted.

'Let's not shake on it, Mr Toulson,' she said coldly.

'Can I ask why . . . ?' He had rarely had an interview go as wrong as this so fast.

Emily stared at him without expression.

'Ever heard of the Homestead Strike?' she said. 'Pittsburgh is where I'm from. People from those parts don't like Pinkerton men. Especially me. My father died of wounds received at the hands of a Pinkerton. *That's* why.'

Toulson did not flinch.

'We all have a job to do, Miss Strauss. Sometimes we have to do things we don't approve of. We make mistakes, like the Pinkertons did at Homestead. But sometimes too we do things that prove more dangerous than we realize. Trust me, if you get in too deep in this investigation, you and Mr Latham will find yourselves with nowhere to go. The men who run this business are vicious and very dangerous. They're disciplined and well led. You should go nowhere near them or anyone involved with them. You . . .'

Emily did not let him finish. 'Goodbye, Mr Toulson,' she said briskly and turned and left. Ben followed with an apologetic shrug.

Back on Michigan and nearing the Auditorium

Annex Emily was still walking so fast and furious that Ben almost had to run to keep up with her.

'What the hell was all that about?' he said.

Emily stopped short in the street.

'Pinkerton men are the opposition,' she said angrily, 'and I like to steal a march on the opposition.'

'And what's *that* supposed to mean?' said Ben, exasperated.

'He never asked me about the other woman in the photograph with Anna.'

'The woman who was . . .'

'Yes, the one who was having sexual intercourse.'

'What about her?'

'I'm having lunch with her today,' said Emily.

55

Alive

CHICAGO Friday October 27, 1893   10.58 AM

'When Emily and Ben returned to the Auditorium Annex after their encounter with Toulson there was a message waiting for Emily to call Donald Stadler, Night Editor of the New York *World* at once.

By the time she got through, Stadler had gone so it was the assistant to City Editor Charles Hadham who gave them the news.

Janis Zemeckis had received a telegraph from Anna the previous evening. She was alive but gave no details of her whereabouts. Western Union indicated that the telegraph had been sent from Chicago's Union Depot, but that was all they knew.

The telegraph simply read, '*Am safe and well. Please do not worry. Forgive me, Anna.*'

'We've got to find her,' said Emily as she put down the receiver.

She and Ben had barely begun to consider their options before the clerk from the front desk came up waving an envelope. It was a handwritten note from Katharine Hubbard of Hull House.

Dear Miss Strauss,

You asked me to let you know if I could find out anything more about your missing girl, Anna Zemeckis. Yesterday, someone matching her description showed up at Hull House – or at least, we think it was her, from all you told me and the distressed state she clearly was in. Most unfortunately, I was not here and this information has only just been passed on to me. I understand she was asked if she needed help but declined and then slipped away leaving no other details. She seemed exhausted and unwell – and was visibly pregnant. But at least she is alive. I have instituted a search for her through the network of refuges and mission houses which we know cater for women in such distressed circumstances. She will certainly need help sooner rather than later. Do please get in touch – I shall be here today and tomorrow morning.

Sincerely yours, Katharine Hubbard.

'Well, I was right,' said Emily and let out a long sigh. 'We need to move fast and check out who might have seen her at the Union Depot yesterday evening. And I must go and talk to Mrs Markulis again. I'm sure she knows more than she's been saying . . . Only there's this too.'

She pulled out Gunther Darke's invitation to his lecture.

'What about your lunch at the Fair?' reminded Ben.

Emily thought for a moment, working out how best to use her time, fighting against the impulse to rush off to the Union Depot just because that was where Anna had been only a few hours previously. She would be long gone by now.

'Stoiber's important, I'm sure of it. She's the only one who might know the truth about Anna, and where she's likely to be,' said Emily. 'So I have to meet her. Gunther Darke's lecture I could do without but . . . well, we know Anna went to the same event and she did the Stock Yard Tour too, because it was marked on her calendar. But I don't have time to go to the Stock Yard then to the Union Depot and then to the North Side to see Mrs Markulis, and then go back to Fay Bancroft's.'

'Tell you what,' interrupted Ben. 'You take in the lecture at the Agricultural Hall and meet me at the Electricity Building before you have your lunch with Our Lady of the Night, and we can compare notes. I can go to the Stock Yard this afternoon and look around while you follow up on other things. Meanwhile . . .'

Ben put the battered briefcase he had been hugging on to the table. He looked pleased with himself.

'What's in it?' demanded Emily.

He opened the briefcase and produced some bulky packages wrapped in newspaper.

'While you were keeping that officer at bay in Robinson's place I grabbed as many of the broken plates that looked interesting as I could. I know someone at the Electricity Building who will help me develop them,'

Emily got up.

'I need to see them, but let's do that later. I have to get to Jackson Park.'

56

Inner Caucus

Dodek Krol took one of the three service elevators at the rear of the Masonic Temple to reach the small private room on the twelfth floor for his eleven o'clock meeting with Paul Hartz.

The meeting was the culmination of the previous seven months' work. But there was something else, something unexpected, and it was troubling him. Krol needed to raise the matter directly with Mr Hartz.

Their first subject was the matter of Jenkin Lloyd Rhys and that did not take long, just a matter of loose ends.

'There will be no connection made with the OAA, I can assure you,' said Krol.

'Good.'

'Before we go any further, Mr Hartz, there is something I must tell you,' said Krol.

Hartz looked faintly surprised. Krol was never a man to volunteer confidences.

'No-one else knows this,' continued Krol. 'I am leaving Chicago on Friday. For good. I shall work out of New York from now on. Independently of the Meisters. They have become . . . corrupt.'

Once again Hartz's face registered surprise.

'I thought you were a Chicagoan through and through now. How many decades is it?'

'Two.'

'Makes you a native of this city.'

Krol smiled slightly. But he was not in the mood to discuss things further. There was something that irked him.

'There is another matter, Mr Hartz. I do not like chasing after young women. I mean the Zemeckis girl.'

Hartz sighed. 'It is a mess. Dr Eels made a serious error.'

'It is not he who has instructed me.'

The two men stared at each other, an unspoken name hanging between them.

'Why not leave the young lady in peace?' said Krol. 'Escaping from Dunning is an act of sanity.'

Hartz shrugged and looked weary.

'I suspect there are things about Zemeckis we neither of us need to know. But whatever else, those documents can harm us.'

'I will find her but not harm her, that is what I have said. But . . .'

'Mr Krol?'

'You asked me once to consider another commission. I refused. But now . . . now I might reconsider.'

'The circumstances have changed,' responded Hartz tartly. 'He is on my side now.'

Krol shrugged.

'If matters change again . . .' he said softly.

'You would do it?'

'I would, Mr Hartz, if the commission came from you personally.'

Hartz nodded without expression.

Murder was always an option but it could be a blunt instrument. He changed the subject.

'Why New York?'

'I like the anonymity a big city gives.'

'Chicago is big, Mr Krol.'

Dodek shifted his massive frame in his chair.

'Not big enough,' he said.

The meeting was over. Both men had much to do.

Krol stood up and reached out a hand to shake Hartz's as he too rose from his chair.

'It was a pleasure meeting you, a pleasure doing business with you,' said Krol, keeping hold of Hartz's hand. 'Thank you.'

Such a moment of uncharacteristic social grace from the big man puzzled Hartz.

'Goodbye, Mr Hartz,' said Krol with some regret, for he was an intelligent man and in Hartz he recognized someone, in essence, very like himself.

'Goodbye, Mr Krol,' murmured Hartz aloud after the Pole had closed the door and his footsteps receded down the corridor. He pondered the handshake and the nature of the goodbye but finally shook his head, his puzzlement seeming misplaced. The man was a Pole. They did things differently, didn't they?

But not always. They too, it seemed, could change their minds.

Back on the street, Krol's cab was waiting for him, with two Meisters standing alongside it.

Krol, who did not like sidewalk conferences, climbed into the carriage and leaned forward as the two men came to the window to confer with him.

'You have found her?' he asked in a low voice.

'She was hired this morning.'

'Where?'

'Garment factory called E.K.M. Halsted and Cornell.'

'Don't know it.'

His men screwed up their noses. 'Goose Island,' one of them said.

'Who's the informant?'

'Reliable.'

Krol thought a moment more.

'We need her alive.'

'Alive and kicking,' said one of the men, with a grim smile.

'You both go. When you have her . . .'

'We know what to do.'

They looked at their pocket watches and agreed on a time.

'Good.'

Krol dismissed them with a nod. As his carriage set off south he kept his head down, eyeing the street on either side. He saw no-one and noticed nothing unusual, just plenty that was familiar, not least the familiar sight of Sol Bann's saloon, an institution in this part of Chicago. Krol eyed the faces in its windows without much interest, the usual riff-raff, he guessed, none looking his way. His cab passed on by. Sol Bann's place had no further interest for him: he was not a drinking man.

A few seconds later Gerald Toulson emerged from Sol Bann's onto State. He looked north after Krol's two men and south after Krol himself, then hailed a cab and instructed it to follow Krol's.

'Where we goin', sir?'

'No idea,' growled Toulson.

57

Beast of the Field

Emily arrived at the Agricultural Building of the World's Fair just in time to examine the audience before the lights went down.

There seemed to be a preponderance of women, many of them quite young and certainly unmarried, most of whom sat in the front rows. They were well dressed for the occasion, some coquettishly so. Fay Bancroft had said that was normally the way when Gunther Darke gave his demonstrations.

As the lights dimmed to darkness, the chatter of the young women at the front gave the occasion a sense of barely restrained excitement.

Emily's seat was a good one, a little to one side of center but no more than fifteen or twenty yards from the stage itself, the layout of which was extremely unusual, though she had had only the briefest glimpse of it before the curtains were drawn shut, leaving only a raised dais with lectern to the right-hand side, not unlike the pulpit from which a sermon is delivered in a church.

What she had seen before the curtain closed was a stage set low with rows of tables on it which reminded her of images she had seen of the medical school theaters where anatomical dissections took place.

Suddenly, a spotlight illuminated not just the lectern but the left-hand side of the stage where the Master of Ceremonies appeared.

'Ladies and Gentlemen, in this, his final appearance, giving what has proved to be one of the most popular talks in the extensive program of educational lectures at the World's Columbian Exposition, please welcome a director of Darke Hartz & Company, Present Convener of the Guild of Master Butchers of America and a recent past World Champion Master Butcher – Mr Gunther S. Darke!'

The clapping began at once and the spotlight moved from the MC, who retreated off stage, to the lectern to the right. At first, the only thing that could be seen of Gunther Darke himself was his hands, which grasped the oak sides of the lectern on which his notes lay. Somewhere above, out of the direct glare of the spotlight and therefore only dimly visible, loomed the powerful head and shoulders of the man himself.

He raised his hands momentarily to indicate to the audience that he intended to begin and it fell silent at once. As he did so Emily saw, with an unexpected thrill, that the tops of two fingers of Gunther's left hand were missing.

Butchery, it seemed, was a dangerous trade.

As Gunther leaned forward to glance at his notes Emily had a glimpse of a strong nose and chin. Then he pulled back into the darkness once more and began to speak.

'America is a great, pure country in which the beasts of the field . . .'

His voice was more deep and gravelly than she remembered, like a rough wind in the dead of night. The auditorium was filled with sudden, nearly dazzling light, as a shutter was opened in the lantern projector behind the audience and the first slide was projected onto the screen. It was a magnificent view of the wide open prairie, its grass limitless, the sky above vast and great herds of cattle stretching as far as the eye could see.

The slide had been hand-colored, and superbly so.

Indeed, the image was so arresting, so inspiring, that as Gunther Darke continued there was sporadic clapping and someone shouted, 'God Bless America!'

'. . . in which the beasts of the field, I say, and the hard work of America's finest men in taming them and bringing them to market have, in a short space of time, created the greatest meatpacking industry in the world. Men like Mr Joseph McCoy who founded the city of Abilene in Kansas as one of the first great American cow towns, a railroad shipping depot for longhorns from Texas to our stock yards. Men such as he have been inspirational in our work here in the Midwest. In this great city. In Chicago!'

His voice became more than arresting, it became masterful. The audience, and Emily too, seemed to want to shrink back from its challenging strength and potency while at the same time surge forward and submit to its allure.

Emily sat breathless and mesmerized. Never in her life had she seen or heard anything like it. She had come as a journalist but she leaned forward now and listened as just another member of the audience – and as a woman.

'But greatness is not achieved without difficulty, without trial, without discipline,' continued Gunther Darke, more quietly, '. . . and most certainly not without great cost.'

A new slide appeared, then another and another, each telling a story of hardship and sacrifice across the frontier, of settlers harvesting their crops on hard-won land, of cattle dying and of men dying too, in their efforts to keep their livestock healthy and productive . . .

Throughout this dramatic tale of American hard work and enterprise, Gunther's voice rose and fell, grew sometimes harsh, sometimes soft, as he took his audience on a journey through history and across America that culminated finally in Chicago itself, rising out of the ashes of the Great Fire of 1871 to supplant Cincinnati as the Porkopolis of a newer, bolder and more modern America – and of the world. Only rarely did any feature of Gunther Darke's face become visible, and then only briefly: a flick of his dark hair, a chin, a nose, a cheek, and just once or twice a shadowed, staring eye. But always, no matter how fleeting, there was a sense of strength of body and mind reflected in his silhouette and the power of his words.

The slide show turned finally to the work of Darke Hartz & Company itself in the present day, and its efficient slaughtering and meat production process, from the killing of the hogs at the great hog wheel on the Darke Hartz killing floor right through to the dressing of their carcasses for market.

Throughout this section Gunther Darke stood impassive and unsmiling, better lit now, his black, glittering eyes transfixing his audience, his hand with its missing fingertips, steady as a rock.

'Butchery,' he concluded, 'is one of Man the Carnivore's oldest skills because it has grown out of his most basic instinct: survival. We kill to eat; we eat to live; we live to kill once more . . .'

As Emily stared at Gunther Darke and his eyes and full mouth, the sensuous form of his body, the overwhelming strength of his gaze, the power even of his silence, she tried but could not stop herself remembering the images Toulson had shown her earlier that morning.

Somewhere among the female audience in the seats in front of her a girl sighed despite herself and a woman gasped aloud, carried forward by the same impulsive emotions as Emily's. She was brought back to reality and a sudden stark and terrible realization. She now knew for certain what it was that Anna Zemeckis, so young and inexperienced, had felt when she had sat in this same auditorium and seen this same presentation. She had been confronted by the raw life and energy and the masterful brutality that was Gunther Darke and the bloody industry of which he was both a disciple and Lord.

The curtain opened, lit by a new spotlight, and there, just beyond the tables, hung the newly slaughtered, skinned carcasses of a steer and a hog.

They swung very slightly, the throats of both cut and gaping, as the audience, men included, gasped. The last drops of their lifeblood dripped lightly onto the sawdust below.

As the audience took in this extraordinary sight there emerged from the darkness of the back of the stage, like a small disciplined army, ten men, carrying between them a selection of knives, choppers, saws and billhooks.

Gunther Darke introduced them as Darke Hartz's leading master butchers who would give a demonstration of the art and science of dressing meat. In other words, they would demonstrate the rapid and efficient reduction of the carcasses of a steer and a hog into cuts and joints ready for the market and the consumer.

The men were dressed in sleeveless undershirts which exposed their muscular shoulders, arms and hands; dark pants and heavy boots – 'studded, you will observe, to stop them slipping on the blood,' explained Gunther Darke; and long, so far, spotless aprons.

They stood like soldiers with weapons at the ready awaiting the order from their commanding officer to go into battle.

'Normally,' said Gunther, 'it would take longer to dress a steer than a hog but, at the men's specific request, I have assigned the fastest and most experienced butchers to the steer and those with less experience to the hog to see if the former can still keep pace with the latter. Chicago has been built on healthy competition, which roots out the weak and allows the fittest to survive. We of the meatpacking industry, especially at Darke Hartz & Company, pride ourselves on our winning streak, don't we men?'

The butchers uttered a strange guttural collective grunt, their boots grinding on the boards of the stage, their knives and choppers glinting.

'So . . . let us see which team wins! And ladies and gentlemen, don't blink or you'll miss the action.'

The two teams of men immediately went to work on the carcasses in the way that predators hunting in packs might descend on a solitary prey.

In moments, as it seemed to Emily, the carcasses were opened up, eviscerated, split down the spines, with short and long sweeps of the knives, with rapid application of the saws. With strokes of chopper and billhook, and quick thrusts and cuts of the knife, as the men moved rhythmically, in synchronization, at their specialist tasks, the sides of meat were rapidly and effortlessly dressed and laid out, as if for market, on the table nearest to the audience.

Throughout the demonstration Darke maintained

his commentary, explaining a cut here, a process there and making the general point, in the case of the hog especially, that his company found an economic use for every part of the animal except for the squeal.

So far as the team race was concerned – Emily suspected a fix – they finished together and to tumultuous applause.

Gunther Darke now drew his lecture to a close:

'Ladies and Gentlemen, in state after state, right across our great land, Americans have worked to produce bloodlines of cattle and hogs that are perfect and pure. How have we done it? By rooting out all that is weak and deficient, by preventing the corruption and disease that can so rapidly destroy livestock just as it can destroy people. This is an achievement of which Americans should be rightly proud – and which it is surely every American's right to protect!'

The obvious analogy between stockbreeding and unbridled immigration and the need for stringent controls were all too plain – and appreciated by many in the audience.

They clapped and cheered, as Gunther Darke, like a conductor at the end of the performance of a symphony, raised his hands and said, 'Ladies and Gentlemen, I give you the art and the science of the most modern industry in the world's most modern city in the greatest country in the world. God Bless America!'

The audience erupted into clapping, stamping and cheering, which continued for quite some time; but Emily was not one of them. As the crowds began to disperse, a good many of the eager and impressionable young ladies in the audience had begun congregating at the front, reaching up to Gunther

Darke and the other butchers on stage and asking for their autographs on their programs and, in return being given what looked like cards or passes for some other event.

'What were those cards?' Emily asked of a fellow member of the audience, a man.

'Passes, nearly impossible to get hold of otherwise.'

'Passes for what?'

'A special visit to the premises of Darke Hartz & Company in the Stock Yard. Best advertising trick pulled by anyone at the World's Fair. Make something seem desirable, make it seem scarce and then make it available, but only to a chosen few. But that's Chicago, boostering all the way!'

'And those girls,' said Emily, who was quite sure that Anna had once been one of them 'they're allowed to go alone?'

'Lambs to the slaughter, Madam,' came the cynical reply, 'but then . . . this is Chicago!'

58
Out of Time

CHICAGO Friday, October 27, 1893   11.45 AM

Anna always knew the clock was ticking against her but when she saw Agda Akesson whispering in Mr Groats's ear and looking in her direction and then him nodding she guessed her time had run out.

Something or someone had given her away.

Maybe they could see she was with child.

Maybe it was just that she looked scared.

But the moment the snitcher Akesson quietly headed in the direction of the freight elevator Anna felt a jolt of alarm and her stomach started churning. She waited a minute or two, hoping she had gone somewhere else on the floor or was in the water closet. When she did not return to her place Anna began to feel sick with apprehension.

She knew that if she had been snitched on she had little time. These were not the kind of girls to let her leave the building easily if there was a price on her head. If she could have waited until the lunch break it would have been easier, but she had no time for that. The best thing was to do it so fast and so quietly that no-one guessed she was leaving until after she was out of the door. After that she would just run.

She got up muttering something meaningless to indicate irritation that she had to get up at all, walked in the opposite direction away from Groats, then, head up, as though she were going to consult someone across the room about her work, she walked calmly to the door and the stairwell.

She heard someone say, 'Where's she . . . ?'

Then a mild shout after her, 'Hey, you . . . !'

Then she was running down the stairs two at a time. Halfway down she saw Agda Akesson coming back up in the elevator shaft.

'You . . .' she heard her call out.

But Anna was already a floor below, and after that she was right outside on the street.

She hurried to Halsted, taking a couple of turns north and then west to put them off the scent.

But it didn't work. When she looked back again a tall man dressed in black was hurrying after her. She turned and started running once more, her mind racing and desperate.

Where was there left to go? Who to turn to?

John Olsen English, her former friend at the Public Library, was the last man in the world she would have wished to go to for help, the *very* last. But she had no more options. For the sake of the child she carried she would swallow her remaining pride and go and ask him to loan her some money. She was out of time and had nowhere else to turn.

She slipped round another corner and headed back downtown.

59

Miracle

CHICAGO Friday October 27, 1893   12.35 PM

Just after midday on Friday, October 27, Anna reached the one remaining place in Chicago where she thought she might find help.

The Chicago Public Library, currently housed in a temporary building on Haddock and Fifth, was not far from the South Water Street fruit and vegetable market, which meant that her grubby dress and lank, untidy hair, screwed up into a sorry-looking knot, went unnoticed. There were many other bedraggled people loitering about the street, along with a multitude of street urchins, all rooting for the free pickings of bruised and damaged fruit between the stalls, around the boxes of produce and among the piles of garbage that littered every corner.

Indeed, Anna herself had earlier spotted a half-eaten apple, scooped it off the sidewalk before a couple of squabbling boys got there first and gobbled it down as she continued walking.

When she reached the entrance she made her way to the main inquiries desk, her head down and pulling her shawl up over it hoping she would not be recognized in the place she had worked until so recently. She need not have worried. She looked like a hundred thousand other girls off the street.

'Yes, miss?'

She said she needed to see Mr English.

'It's personal; a matter of great importance.'

The clerk exchanged a brief glance with one of his female colleagues.

Then he said, as Anna knew he would, 'Mr English, like the other librarians, does not receive personal callers during library hours.'

'Although it *is* a personal matter, I am not a personal caller. His mother has been taken ill.'

There was a very slight titter between the two women behind the desk. The male clerk frowned at them and turned back to Anna.

'I'm afraid the Deputy Librarian, Mr McIlvanie, has given strict instructions. You see . . . Mr English's mother has, well . . .' he was searching for a polite way of saying that the demands of the hypochondriac Mrs English were a nuisance the library had long since learned to deal with.

Anna knew that too.

'She's dying,' blurted out Anna.

'She's done that before too,' the librarian said discreetly, drawing Anna to one side as two people approached the desk with books. 'I'm sorry, but Mr McIlvanie's instructions are very clear about Mr English's mother.'

'I . . . *please* . . .,' she said suddenly, 'I do need to see him most urgently.'

Perhaps her doubt and uncertainty showed on her face; certainly her abject misery did. The librarian was taken aback by such a direct appeal. This young woman was clearly not a troublemaker even though her appearance was decidedly bedraggled. But, there was something about her that he distantly recognized.

'Why?' he said suddenly and impulsively, 'What are you to him?'

'Nothing,' said Anna, 'I am nothing . . . nothing at all.'

She felt weak and hopeless and in despair. Her strength had all run out. She turned away, trying to steady her growing dizziness from fatigue and hunger, knowing that once she went back through the door to the world outside she had no-one left to turn to.

'I am nothing,' she said again softly, no longer able to find the words to explain herself, and began walking toward the door.

She had barely gone more than a step or two before the desk clerk took pity on her.

'Miss . . . *Miss* . . .'

She turned back.

'Miss, I think, knowing Mr English as I do, he would be upset for you to be turned away. I really do. You had better sit out there in the hallway, in case you are seen. I will get Mr English myself. Can I give him a name?'

'Jelena,' whispered Anna.

'And a surname?'

'. . . Jansons' she said, frantically hoping John Olsen English would remember how often she had talked of going to Canada to live on her aunt Inga Janson's farm. 'Please, I do not want to cause him trouble. I better go . . .'

'Sit over there,' said the clerk firmly, but kindly. 'I will give him your name and let him decide. It is the best I can do. Meanwhile, if a tall gentleman with a beard and white hair should come stalking about then you're to say you're on your way out and were simply taking a rest. Yes?'

Anna nodded.

She didn't need the clerk to tell her who this was. Everyone knew Mr McIlvanie.

Meanwhile, in his upstairs office, John Olsen English sat lonely and still grieving. He looked terrible. His face was gray, his eyes dark and blank, his posture listless. He wore a black armband and moved at his tasks slowly, a man in a nightmare of confusion and loss.

The disappearance of his would-be sweetheart was one thing; her death another. If only he had known why any of it had happened he might have been able to come to terms with his troubled relationship with Anna. Her sudden death had given him the opportunity to do neither.

Until very recently, that is.

Light, terrible and cruel, had begun to dawn and it had happened as a result of one of Mrs McIlvanie's typically brisk, no-nonsense observations. Could Miss Zemeckis, she ventured to her husband at home one evening, could she just possibly have been 'in some kind of . . . trouble'? Woman's trouble, that is. And of the worst kind?

It was a version of this remark, turned into a question, and overladen with a certain diplomatic ambiguity on the part of Mr McIlvanie, that had alerted John English to a grotesque possibility.

The implication, when it finally got through to him, not only shocked him, it galvanized him into doing what he did best: think hard and seek order out of chaos.

He went back over his many conversations with Anna and remembered something he had paid no heed to at the time: a much vaunted visit she had made in mid-June to the Union Stock Yard, to the killing floor of one of the big meatpackers.

What was puzzling was that afterwards the normally talkative Anna had said nothing about the visit, and had got quite angry when he had innocently asked about it. From then on her inexplicable moods and the alienation between them had accelerated.

John English considered the problem as objectively as he could and came to the conclusion that something had happened during that visit, something terrible, and that as a direct result Anna was in serious trouble.

He also tortured himself with the thought that he had not been good friend enough or wise enough to know how to get her to talk in time to save her from whatever had afterward led to her death.

He was cataloging some books when his colleague from the inquiries desk knocked at his door.

'Mr English, a word in private, please,' the new man whispered discreetly, hovering at the door.

'P . . . pardon me?' said John, looking up from his work.

'I did not wish to draw your colleagues' attention to the fact, but . . . there is a young woman to see you. In the lobby.'

'I believe that M . . . Mr McIlvanie has made it q . . . q . . . quite plain that I am n . . . n . . . not to see anyone bringing messages from my m . . . m . . . m . . . mother.'

'I believe the young lady is here on her own account.'

'I do n . . . not know any young ladies.'

'She says her name is Jelena . . . Jelena Jansons.'

John Olsen English's eyes widened and he stopped what he was doing.

'P . . . pardon me?' he said again. His mind raced and grappled with that name. He recognized it at once, the surname that is. But the given name, Jelena, why that was . . . The clerk said again, 'Miss Jelena Jansons.'

'I . . . d . . . do not understand.'

'She is sitting in the front hall, hopefully out of sight of Mr McIlvanie . . .'

'I b . . . b . . . better come.'

'Yes,' said the librarian.

'I'd b . . . better c . . . come right *now*,' John said again, more calmly now because he realized that this must be one of Anna's Canadian relatives. Perhaps Anna had mentioned his name to her Aunt Inga in one of her letters. She had often read him her aunt's letters, full as they were with descriptions of farming life in Manitoba of the kind after which they both hankered.

John Olsen English entered the hallway and saw the bedraggled woman sitting on the bench, her head down, as though she were looking at something on the floor.

'M . . . M . . . Mrs Jelena . . . Jansons? I'm sorry, perhaps it's M . . . M . . . Miss?'

Anna turned her face to him: 'It's Anna, it's me, *Anna*.'

John stared at her open-mouthed, his already pale face growing paler still.

He could hardly breathe.

It was not her form he recognized, for that was utterly changed and shockingly so, it was her voice and her eyes.

'John,' she said, 'I need your help.'

If she had ever doubted what kind of man John Olsen English was, the expressions that passed now so rapidly across his face: of surprise, recognition, shock, relief – indescribable relief – left Anna in no doubt at all. It was as though, without question, he instinctively knew and understood everything.

Which was indeed true. For he gazed at her with such compassion and surely saw at once the nature of the 'trouble' she was in.

His face showed no anger toward her at all, but alarm and a sudden, overwhelming protectiveness.

Then, for the first time, Anna saw a look on his face that she had never seen before: a look of utter rage on her behalf and of near-murderous intent.

'Anna,' he said, his voice as terrible as sharpened steel, 'who has done this to you?' Suddenly, miraculously, the stutter had gone, as it always did when he was in her company.

He sat down, took her in his arms and held her tight and cared not at all if anyone saw or what anyone might think. She was alive and safe and here now with him.

'Tell me . . . please tell me, who has done this to you?'

'We can't stay here,' was her only reply as she broke free of him, 'We mustn't stay. I might be found.'

'Anna . . .'

'Please. I don't want to cause you any problems. I just need some help, a loan of a dollar or so, and then I'll never trouble you again. But we mustn't stay here.'

'Never trouble me again!' He laughed almost manically.

'*Never trouble me again!*'

'Please . . .' she said, pulling at his arm.

He saw then that she was utterly terrified.

'We shall find somewhere safe nearby and I will explain . . .'

Whatever library rules John broke he didn't care at all. He got up and followed Anna and the next time the clerk who had first summoned him looked their way he saw no-one at all: just a swinging door to the outside world.

60

Positives

CHICAGO Friday October 27, 1893   12.45 PM

Emily caught up with Ben Latham in the Electricity Building shortly after Gunther Darke's lecture ended. It was quarter to one and she had fifteen minutes before she was due to meet Marion Stoiber on the far side of Jackson Park.

They met by the General Electric Company's distinctive Tower of Light, the roof-high display made up of thousands of miniature lamps which produced a startling kaleidoscope effect that stopped the hundreds of visitors, Emily included, in their tracks.

313

Ben held up a sheaf of images on photographic paper.

'Here,' he said, taking her arm, 'come over behind the Earthquake Laboratory, it's the only quiet spot in the building! But prepare to be shocked.'

He glanced around, made sure no-one was looking and handed her the photographs one by one.

'There's eight here,' he said, 'and more on the way. Not easy getting them done, given the nature of their content. Did these myself and a friend of mine working at the Eastman Kodak exhibit, which has a darkroom facility – he's reliable, won't tell a soul – is doing the rest right now while everyone else is at lunch. But these tell us enough to be going on with.'

Emily looked at them. Most were cropped at odd angles where the glass plate had been broken. One or two were nearly whole. They showed naked girls in lewd poses, men with the girls in lewder poses still and . . .

Emily did a double take.

'A hog wheel?' she said.

'Yes,' said Ben.

'But . . .'

'It's a slaughterhouse,' said Ben as evenly as he could.

'As a location for pornographic pictures? That's bizarre,' she said again faintly.

'I guess some men like that kind of thing.'

A new and even more horrible thought came to Emily as she remembered the scenes of barely contained excitement – sexual excitement she suspected – among the young women at the butchery demonstration she had just come from.

'Death, sex, blood. I guess some women find that exciting,' she heard herself say.

Ben's eyes widened. It was his turn to be shocked.

They turned back to the image in question.

It showed a group of three men, all only partially clothed, their members erect as they stood in an obviously staged way as if about to penetrate a woman on a butcher's table. She was lying across it in a corset and striped stockings, displaying herself obscenely, as if inviting the men to ravage her. From the knives the men carried, and the white undershirts and pants half-off, she could see they were, or were pretending to be, butchers of the kind she had been watching less than an hour before.

'So far as I can make out,' said Ben, 'and I'm not an expert on such things, this is one of a sequence. I've two more fragments, both yet to be developed. The men are cutting the girl's under garments off with their knives as if they were gutting her. If it weren't so ridiculous it might be frightening.'

'It *is* ridiculous,' said Emily.

The photographs were high quality and well lit, even if the subject matter was disgusting, and yet . . .

Emily could not help letting her gaze drift back to the men's privates. She had never seen such an image in her life before, let alone the real thing and was unsure what to say next.

'Take a close look at the background,' said Ben, sensing Emily's embarrassment, 'and at that window especially. These pictures are well made – they use artificial *and* natural light and the depth of focus is good too. What do you see through the window?'

'Um . . .'

She hesitated to look again. But it was unmistakable. In the window frame, rising up into the sky outside, was something as close to a representation of a phallus as there ever could be.

'What is it?' asked Emily faintly.

'Good question,' said Ben cheerfully, unaware of the highly confused drift of Emily's thoughts, 'and one I asked my friend not fifteen minutes ago. It's the water tower of the Union Stock Yard. Nothing else in Chicago like it apparently, except for the tower that is part of the Water Works on North Michigan.'

'How do you know it's not that one?'

'It's bigger,' said Ben matter-of-factly. 'Much bigger.'

'Really?' said Emily, trying to keep her eyes from wandering over the picture again.

'And these other photographs, they show the tower too. Can't think why the photographer wanted to get it in so much, though I suppose it gives depth. But it also gives the game away. I'll take my camera and my sketch book and go and look round the Stock Yard while you have your lunch with Stoiber and I'll see what I can find out.'

'Right,' said Emily, 'I'll see you back at the hotel at six.'

61

Opening

CHICAGO Friday October 27, 1893   1.10 PM

Marion Stoiber arrived for her lunch with Emily ten minutes late, looking anxious and abstracted.

She insisted they find a restaurant outside Jackson Park on the Midway Plaisance. It was so busy with the last days of the Fair that they ended up at an open-air Chinese restaurant.

When Emily had met her the day previously at the WCTU meeting, Marion Stoiber had been dressed smartly, but soberly. By the light of day and in the open air she seemed rather less smart: the garish colors of her day dress clashed somewhat and there was, Emily thought, a rather brassy edge to her whole appearance. She looked older, strained even, her face betraying dark circles of tiredness under the eyes and a pinched, pale expression which even the rather indiscreet use of a powder puff and lip rouge could not disguise.

She looked like a woman who had seen too much of the dark side of life and it was now finally catching up with her.

'Well then,' said Marion finally and a little aggressively, having started to pick at a bowl of noodles, 'what more was it you wished to talk to me about?'

'Your friend, Anna, as I explained to you,' said Emily easily, 'and maybe anything else you'd like to tell me about how single women cope with living in a big city such as Chicago. You know . . . the difficulties they face with men.'

'Ha!' expostulated Marion with unmistakable bitterness. 'The only thing you need say on that subject is that women must give and men will take.'

'You have a low opinion of men?' Emily ventured quietly.

'Not all men,' said Marion defiantly. 'Some men. A few, yes. Yes, I have.'

Emily sipped her tea and said nothing while Marion poked a few more noodles around her bowl, glowering – and brooding, it seemed, on the topic at hand.

'I don't want to talk about *that*,' she said eventually.

Emily nodded empathically.

'Anna found it hard to get out and meet young men, I believe. Her father . . . ?'

'Did she . . . ?' Marion didn't say more. She picked at her food, eyes not engaging with Emily's. She frowned, she pursed her lips, she sat back trying to relax. She glanced around at the people either side and then behind her.

But there was nothing there, just the great arc of the Ferris wheel, almost a silhouette against the brightness of the sky, turning slowly, endlessly, going nowhere.

'You must miss her as a friend,' said Emily, struggling to get the conversation moving.

'Must I?'

Emily saw the smallest shadow of hurt. There was heart in this woman somewhere yet. And there was regret and sadness too.

'Yes, I think you must.'

'She was a good, kind girl,' began Marion, 'she . . .' Her eyes filled with tears and they were genuine

She doesn't know Anna's alive, Emily told herself.

'It shouldn't have happened to her. For some women it wouldn't have mattered, but for a girl like Anna . . .'

What shouldn't have happened? And which women . . . ?

Emily guessed she didn't mean Anna shouldn't have died, it was about something that had happened before that false news came out. As for *which* women, Marion Stoiber surely meant women like herself, loose women, wanton women, willing women: not women like Anna.

From behind Marion came the sound of laughter and screaming, distant and from on high. It was three girls on the Ferris wheel enjoying the feeling of danger that was part of the thrill.

'I never did get to ride it,' said Emily.

'Neither did I . . . Look, there's really nothing I can add to what I said before. This lunch was a mistake. I can't tell you anything.'

Emily decided to go for the jugular.

'You know Anna's not dead, don't you?'

Marion simply didn't take it in, not at once. Only slowly did what Emily had just said register with her and when it did her expression was one of utter disbelief.

'I don't think I heard you right.'

Emily repeated it, her voice hardening, 'I said you know Anna's not dead.'

'Of course she's dead, don't be silly. She was identified. She . . .'

'That wasn't Anna.'

'It must have been, they said . . .'

'Did Anna ever wear earrings? Did she have pierced ears?'

'No, she wouldn't.' Marion instinctively reached up and felt the gaudy earring in her own right ear. 'I tried to get her to have them pierced but she refused. Her father . . .'

'The woman in the morgue they thought was Anna had pierced ears.'

'She couldn't have.'

'She did. What happened to Anna, Marion, you have to tell me.'

'I don't know . . . She can't be alive, I don't know what happened . . .'

'*What happened?*' Emily continued to press her.

'I don't know, I wasn't there.'

Marion Stoiber's voice was turning into a wail.

'Where, Marion? Where did it happen?'

'I don't know. I . . . I . . . '

Emily watched as Marion visibly regained her composure. She wanted to talk but she was too terrified to do so. That was the truth. That was it.

'Is she really still alive?' asked Marion very quietly.

'She was yesterday, at eight in the evening, because that's when she sent a telegram to her father from the Union Depot. Whether or not she is now I don't know. But she's in danger, isn't she?'

'Yes,' said Marion.

'Very great danger?'

'They will kill her if they can, or silence her.'

'Who will?'

'I can't tell you that, they . . . they . . . '

The terror had returned and Stoiber looked right and left again while the Ferris loomed above her, turning and turning and making the whole world seem as if it was on the move and the wheel was the only solid thing around.

'*Who?*'

Marion was silent.'

'What did you let happen to Anna?'

'It wasn't me, I wasn't there. It wasn't my fault. I thought, I only . . .'

Emily knew she was losing her again and that Stoiber was about to get up and go, to flee from her and from the truth and from the demons of guilt inside herself. She remembered the picture of Marion lying beneath a man. She remembered Ben saying a short while before that it was taken at a slaughter-house in the Stock Yards.

She remembered the one thing Anna had never told her father, of all the many things she wrote about in her long and rather dull letters home, had been her special visit to the Union Stock Yard. It was the one thing she had never mentioned.

'It happened at the Union Stock Yard, didn't it?'

Stoiber stared at Emily, terrified.

'You encouraged her to go there deliberately, knowing something would happen, didn't you?'

Marion shook her head desperately.

'No, no, if I'd known, if I'd even thought, but he promised, he promised . . .'

'Who promised?'

'I can't, I can't . . . they will kill me, like . . .'

'Like what, Marion? You owe it to Anna to tell me. Maybe we can still save her life. Who?'

Marion shook her head.

'Then just tell me what happened. You don't have to name names.'

'I . . .'

Emily reached a hand across the table to Marion's.

'Tell me,' she said gently, 'You must. Because it happened to you too, didn't it?

And Marion Stoiber, head down, nodded.

'Yes,' she whispered.

And she began to talk.

62

Measure of the Man

CHICAGO Friday October 27, 1893   1.40 PM

Once Anna Zemeckis and John English were clear of the Chicago Public Library, Anna muttered wildly that she was being watched — and hurried off down

Haddock Street, like a madwoman it seemed, forcing John to run after her.

'We mustn't stop' she said, 'we mustn't be seen.'

'But Anna . . . *Anna* . . .'

She didn't listen, but headed up into the safety of the crowds of the produce markets along South Water Street and refused to say another word. That John was with her, she was relieved and overjoyed; that he might come to harm as a result only compounded her terror. No wonder Anna almost ran, bumping into people as she went, even causing some to swear and shout after her.

She crossed through the market stalls, dodged a cart or two, then a huge wagon pulled by two great horses and came to an alley at the end of which rose the masts and rigging of a freight schooner.

'Down here,' she said, hurrying ahead once more.

'*Anna* . . .'

It was not the kind of area John English made a habit of visiting, not that it was especially dangerous or criminal on the surface, but in Chicago one could not be too careful. Fortunately, there were folk enough about dressed as poorly as Anna for her not to be noticeable, and men engaged in the maritime and produce trades well dressed enough for John not to look out of place.

'Here,' Anna had said finally, finding a quiet spot where they could sit on two upended barrels in sight of the shipping moored along the banks of the dark and ever-dirty river. The atmosphere was thick with smoke and a strange and not entirely unpleasant mixture of coal, timber and engine oil. But there was also a more welcoming smell – of cooking – for on a nearby brazier a woman was brewing coffee for the workers along the embankment and next to her a street vendor was selling hot Italian sausages.

'I'll take four,' said John English.

Then, thrusting them all at Anna, he said, 'Eat first . . . *then* talk.'

Anna hungrily consumed the four sausages as she tried to tell him the thing she most dreaded.

'John, I'm in trouble, big trouble. I'm . . .

'I know, Anna, I know what's wrong . . . I guessed as much,' he interrupted, 'and I can see. There was no other logical explanation. But you're alive . . . just tell me what happened. *Tell* me.'

If Anna could have done so she would have told him, but she could not remember, not even who the father was; not even how and when it had happened . . .

So she talked about the moment when she and John had first met and how she had felt the same attraction he had until the terrible course of events began that had led to . . . to *this*.

'I can't remember,' she sobbed, 'I . . .'

'There's no need to speak of that now. We must go to the police and . . .'

'No. No. Not the police. You don't understand, John. They don't let anyone stand in their way, they . . .'

' "They", "they",' repeated John impatiently, 'you keep saying that but you won't tell me who "*they*" are.'

'I don't know! One of the girls at Brennan's talked about the Meisters. I think maybe it's them . . . but why? Why me?'

'I know exactly *who* they are,' said John, 'I've read in the *Tribune* about their murderous attacks on people. I know how they terrorize and intimidate with their knives . . .'

'It's all right,' Anna said, cutting him short. 'It's

over and done. Now I must think of my child. I cannot go to my father, you know that. I cannot stay a moment longer in Chicago because they are looking for me. My only hope is to get a train north to St Paul and find some kind of job there until I can save enough money to get to my aunt in Manitoba. All I ask is that you let me have the money to get me out of Illinois . . . I'll pay you back . . .'

But she stopped, eyes widening as something moving along the wharf behind John attracted her attention.

John English, misunderstanding her look, moved closer and began, 'Anna, you have no need to repay me for doing what any friend would, I . . . *what is it?*'

He turned and saw what she saw.

Two men, tall, spare, well built, cleanly and soberly dressed in the kind of long black frock coats and polished boots usually worn for church on Sunday, had just emerged on the wharf from the direction of South Water Street.

Except it wasn't Sunday and there was no church in sight and the mean, purposeful look on their faces had nothing of godliness about it. They were standing talking on the wharf and indifferent to the stares their formidable presence attracted until, careless of those nearby, one of them slowly drew a knife.

It was thin bladed and so well-honed to perfect sharpness that the blade was worn fine and concave.

And now they had seen Anna and John and began walking toward them. People nearby, sensing the men's air of menace, retreated into the shadows and round the nearest corners.

Anna's stomach knotted into a hard ball of fear.

John English's likewise.

The Meisters. They both knew it instinctively.

He pulled her up from the barrel and, if the measure of a man is to think clearly and act coolly when every instinct is to run, then the mother's boy from the Near West Side now, at last, proved himself a man.

He looked to either side of the approaching men and saw there was no possibility of escape back in the direction of South Water Street. Behind him, he had already observed, the wharves widened out to stacks of empty boxes, barrels, capstans and the metal girder bases of derricks, as well as all the other paraphernalia of the river freight trade. The only way to safety lay out there, along the wharf.

'Anna,' he said quietly, not taking his eyes off the men as they came nearer, 'stand up, turn around and run, down the wharf. Just *run*.

'But . . . you . . . ?'

'I'll follow.'

The men were no more than fifty yards off. Before Anna could protest further, John turned and pushed her hard in the small of her back.

'Run and don't look back. I'll be right behind. Now!'

He pushed and she started running, as though the devil himself was in pursuit of her.

Then John turned and blocked the path of the Meisters now running toward him. It was then that he discovered that something odd and unexpected happens in a man's mind when he finds himself facing extreme peril: the world slows down and the most trivial-seeming thoughts and feelings intrude.

Because, as a knife was held against his gut John English remembered that he had failed to do the one thing he should have done – give Anna the money she needed to get safely out of Chicago and on her way to a new life with her aunt in Manitoba.

I should have done that, he told himself as the second man closed in.

63

Ferris

Marion Stoiber's story of what happened to Anna Zemeckis, and her own part in it, began with an account of her early life in Chicago before she met up with Anna in May. It combined self-pity with self-justification in equal measure but Emily listened politely with occasional nods and murmurs of sympathy.

Marion's family background had been unhappy and she had made some wrong choices, including marrying young to escape a dictatorial father. Her husband had turned out to be a wastrel incapable of holding down a job and eventually had deserted her, leaving her with a pile of debts.

But she had managed to start again by training as a stenographer and working in one of the downtown banks. Discovering she had a flair for administrative work, she had gained a good position with the organizers of the Fair when it was still in its planning stages.

'But to pay off the debts my husband had left me with I had to take extra work . . .'

'What kind of work?'

'Artistic,' said Marion with deliberate ambiguity.

'You mean . . . ?

'I do not mean what you think I mean. I worked as an artist's model. The practicing members at the Art Institute were always looking for models and they paid well, particularly if you were prepared to pose undraped. I've never been ashamed of my body and having been married, I . . . well, I was not as embarrassed as a younger, unmarried girl might have been. Anyway, it paid well and did not interfere with my other work as I could do it in the evenings and on weekends. It gave me my freedom and enabled me eventually to find a little apartment of my own.'

'Naturally, some of the artists were more friendly – over-friendly, if you like – than others; and equally naturally some of us models found a little flirtation appealing.'

'You didn't mind the work?'

'I enjoyed it,' said Marion frankly. 'After a bad marriage it was flattering that people should want to draw and paint me. Anyway, I needed the money.'

'Then, about a year ago, one of the artists asked if I might be interested in some photographic work, at an even better rate of pay, for a photographer he knew in the city center who was looking for high class models. I went to see him. He was older, more sophisticated. He flattered me and said that very few models were suitable. The work was easy and well paid. At first I posed draped; later not.'

Marion looked at Emily with the same bold frankness as before.

'I do not mind admitting that I enjoyed that too. Of course, I had no husband, nor any beau, so I was free to do what I liked. I found it rather exciting to be soberly dressed in the staid world of business during the day and transform myself into something more alluring by night.'

'Did you not ask what the photographs were for?'

'I knew exactly what they were *for*, Miss Strauss. They were *poses plastiques* – for men, men with money.'

'But what I did *not* know was that some of the men who made a habit of collecting these kinds of photographs also made a habit of collecting, if they could, the models who posed for them.'

'Collecting?'

'Meeting.'

'*Meeting?*'

Marion stayed silent but so did Emily.

Finally Marion said, 'Well . . . having relations with them.'

'And men wanted to meet *you?*'

'Yes. It seemed they found me very . . . provocative. I began to find it exciting. I bought the most alluring under garments to pose in – oyster silk satin chemises and drawers, fine silk stockings from Paris. The men reportedly liked the photographs and several of them asked to be introduced to me.'

'And you met them, these . . . clients?'

'A few of them.'

'Did they make . . . advances . . . to you?'

'I think you know the answer to that question.'

'And you found that upsetting?'

Marion Stoiber smiled and leaned forward.

'Forgive me, Emily – may I call you Emily? – but only someone who does not know men and who is a little naïve would ask if it was "upsetting". Sexual relations do not have to be unpleasant, you know.'

Emily flushed.

The interview was getting closer to home than she

wished. Ever since Gerald Toulson had shown her the file of erotic images and then Ben had developed those from the Robinson studio, she had been unable to get them out of her mind.

Marion was right: Emily knew little about men and had not had relations with one beyond the normal flirtations and occasional kisses of her teenage years. Her mother's generation had liked to pretend that female sexuality did not exist and that if it did and bordered on the pleasurable, then it was a matter for disgust and shame.

As it was, she must now contend with these new and turbulent feelings and if she did feel a touch of guilt it was because, if she were honest with herself, she wanted Marion Stoiber to tell her more, much more. And if she, the normally cool and clear-headed Emily Strauss, found herself wanting to know more, then what kind of effect had this older, sexually knowing woman had on the younger and impressionable Anna Zemeckis?

It had become increasingly apparent to Emily over the last few days that Chicago was full of predators ready to exploit the innocence of the many hundreds of single young women like Anna who had found themselves in the city during this extraordinary year of 1893. But not all these predators, it seemed, were men.

Though whether Mr Pulitzer and his editors will allow me to say as much in my story, when I write it, I somehow doubt! Emily told herself ruefully.

'Oh dear,' said Marion rather shamelessly, 'have I embarrassed you?'

'No, no,' said Emily hastily, feeling not unlike a maiden aunt. 'I prefer you to be frank . . . What I wanted to ask was whether perhaps you regretted that these activities took you in directions you did not wish to go?'

Marion Stoiber thought for a moment and then finally said, 'All right, that's true. I regret it now. But at the time it was like indulging greedily in a large bowl of ice cream; each mouthful is really good, but finally you end up feeling sick.'

'But you needed the money?'

'I did. Have you any idea how *much* men pay for pictures of women in provocative poses, Emily, and how *many* men do so?'

'It is illegal, is it not?' added Emily, now more serious.

'It *is* illegal to disseminate such material through the US Postal System. Mr Comstock saw to that with his law of 1873 but laws never stopped men making money, especially when the profits were so good. What I didn't know was that the images of me proved so popular that they were disseminated all over the United States and, I believe, Europe as well. Had I been a piece of real estate I would have been worth a fortune!'

She said this with a degree of bitterness.

'I was not compensated for anything like my true worth. But I did meet one, special man who gave me something I do not regret having experienced.'

Her expressive face changed again to a curious mix of longing, of loss, of sadness and, Emily was certain, of love as well.

'Sexual relations with the right man are not sinful, you know; or anything to be ashamed of. What I did not know or even imagine until I met this man was that relations with the right one can bring a woman total ecstasy . . .'

'But you won't tell me his name?'

Marion shook her head.

'He meant a lot to you, didn't he?'

'Yes. But he destroyed my life. Though I cannot say that I regret meeting him. For a few brief weeks, when I was his and I thought he was mine I knew a happiness and fulfillment like no other . . .'

Once more Marion was transformed before Emily's eyes, as her face softened and she smiled.

'What was so special about him . . . ?'

'You really want to know?'

Emily could see that, with a perverse kind of pleasure, Marion really wanted to tell her.

'Yes,' breathed Emily, her heart beating faster despite her desire to remain objective.

'It wasn't to do with any special quality, like goodness or kindness or good looks even; it was a presence, a power, something utterly overwhelming. I was persuaded to meet him in a private suite at the Chicago Athletic Club, which made it all the more exciting because women are not allowed there. But . . . men like him have power and wealth of the kind that women like us can only dream of.'

'Were you nervous?'

'Yes, but he put me at my ease. His first words to me were, "So, you're the famous Evangeline."

'"Pardon me?" I replied, having no idea what he was talking about.'

'"That's the name the photographer has given you for the purposes of his excellent work," he explained. "Now, Miss Stoiber, for that's your real name, isn't it? I am going to show you what I like in a woman."

'His voice was strong and purposeful and his presence from the first I can only describe as masterful, in ways that women find both alarming but also hard to resist. He made no secret, either by look or word, of his desire for me and to be honest I could see it despite the fact that he was, at that point, fully clothed.'

She smiled and it was her turn to flush. 'But as for the rest, Miss Strauss . . . well, that you will discover for yourself – sooner or later – so long as you find the right man.'

There was no doubting the provocatively teasing tone of Marion Stoiber's voice and the glitter of sexual knowingness in her eyes.

Emily found herself in a state of utter confusion: part repelled by Marion's unrepentant sexuality but also, as a sexually uninitiated woman herself, wide-eyed and curious. She shifted in her seat, picked up her pen and reminded herself that she was a reporter and she had a job to do.

'Then if you really won't tell me his name, Marion, will you at least tell me the name of the photographer?'

Marion paused a moment and then said very bleakly, 'It doesn't matter now. He's dead. His name was Henry Robinson. I heard this morning that they have killed him, as they will surely kill me and anybody else they think is a danger to their valuable trade. That is why they will want to find Anna.'

'Who's "they" Marion?'

'You must have heard of the Meisters? They're an elite guild of master butchers who operate from out of the Stock Yards. They're not all bad. But there's an inner core of hard men among the Meisters who now control the pornography trade here in Chicago.'

Emily was shocked at hearing Robinson's name again so soon and thought of the gruesome scene at the shop on Wabash. It was all beginning to add up. Robinson had introduced Marion Stoiber to the sexual *demi-monde*, innocuous enough at first for a sexually experienced woman such as her, but it had set her on the slippery slope to something far darker and more sinister. She, in turn, had exposed Anna Zemeckis to it.

'And this is the world you introduced Anna to?'

Marion's eyes grew serious and she shook her head.

'If it had been just that, then no harm would have come to her, or me for that matter. To start off with Henry took her photograph for a *carte de visite* to send home to her father. It was all very innocent. It was only later that she, like me, was lured into something quite different. Then she was blackmailed . . . like I was.'

'And who blackmailed her, Marion? Who lured her? Was it him . . .? Was it your "special" client?'

Marion's answer was tight-lipped and unequivocal: 'You would do well not to inquire.' She paused, then added rather vaguely, 'Anyway, he's gone away. He, he . . .'

'He's left Chicago?'

'Yes. He's gone away. To Kansas. He has business concerns there . . . in Abilene' she said.

Emily could tell that Marion was improvising as she went along.

'And he's not coming back?'

Marion deflected the question.

'He became more demanding. He suggested I might have more pictures taken – with other men, never with him, of course – or I would never see him again. I agreed. "Just poses," he said. "They will be worth a lot of money and no-one in Chicago will ever see them."'

Emily thought of the sexually explicit photograph of Marion she had seen that morning.

333

'Well, "just poses" meant more, much more, but by then I would do anything and the liquor and drugs they plied me with made me do more still. Until, worst of all, I was persuaded to procure other women for his pleasure and theirs.'

'Was Anna one of these?'

Marion nodded.

'I did not think he would take a fancy to her as he had to me. However, there was something about her virginal simplicity that attracted him and a certain spirit he wanted to master. There was one particular occasion . . . at the Union Stock Yard.'

'The private tour?'

'Yes. Anna thought she was simply going to see the hog wheel and the killing floor, as so many before. He was there and she caught his eye and he took her off by herself and I guess . . . well . . . excited, flattered, plied with liquor and chloral, which make a girl compliant to almost anything, he took her. I do not think rape is too strong a word.

'Afterward,' added Marion, 'she was blackmailed into going back there again and forced to pose for some pornographic photographs taken by Robinson. They even made her pose in some of the photographs they took of me. But it was all very much against her will, whereas I, well . . .'

'She told you what had happened?'

'Only briefly at the time. She was much distressed and when she discovered she was with child I felt jealous but I also knew the danger she was in, for it could be no other child but his she was carrying. That was not good at all. I advised her not to tell him but, very foolishly, she did. He summoned me and insisted I had the matter seen to by a woman known to be good and safe at such things. She has rooms up near the Levee where there is a considerable call on her services.'

'So Anna had an abortion?'

'No, she did not. We visited the woman, but Anna was terrified and left. She couldn't go through with it and I agreed with her, I who had so wanted to have a child of my own. It is a terrible thing for a woman to have to do.'

'But it is also a terrible thing to have a child out of wedlock conceived in that way, especially for a girl like Anna raised by a father like Janis Zemeckis,' observed Emily.

'It is. But she was determined. A mother's instinct. His reaction was different, as you would expect. The abortionist told him what had happened and Anna had to go into hiding or he would have dragged her back there. She ran away from the Markulises and came and hid in my apartment. Our plan was to get her out of Chicago . . . She has an aunt, Inga . . .'

Emily nodded.

'Yes, in Manitoba.'

'But then she had this mad idea that she might be able to persuade him to support her somewhere away from Chicago until she had the child. I told her not to go near him, but nine days ago, on October 18, I came back from work and she was gone. I never saw her again and then, I saw the notice in the *Tribune* that she had died in a traffic accident. I had no reason to think she could still be alive. I assumed that she had been running, probably running from someone sent after her by him.

'But the body, Marion . . . it *wasn't* Anna.'

'But her father identified her, did he not?

'Yes, both he and Mrs Markulis identified her as

Anna,' said Emily, 'but only, I suppose, because the woman, who was horribly disfigured in the accident, was wearing Anna's dress and crucifix and had dark hair like her.'

Marion's eyes widened and she put a hand to her mouth in astonishment, a sudden revelation coming to her.

'She what . . . but . . . I know who that was!'

'Who, Marion, who? You must tell me.'

'Anna and I used to go to the public bathhouse on Dearborn, always at night so as not to be seen. A week or so before she disappeared Anna left her things in the changing cubicle as usual one evening. The crucifix was in her pocket. While she was in the bath someone stole her dress – it was a good one, she'd made it herself. I had to leave her there shivering and run back for one of mine.'

'Well, whoever stole it got run down by a streetcar,' said Emily matter-of-factly. 'And by then the crucifix was round *her* neck.' . . .

Suddenly Marion tensed. 'Oh my goodness, it's after two, I have to go . . . I'm late, very late . . . Though, I suppose it doesn't really matter. When I saw the report this morning about Henry's murder and the fire, I decided the time had come for me to get out of town.'

She got up. 'I'm going West, this evening, to San Francisco and I'm not coming back.'

She reached out a hand to shake Emily's.

'So this is goodbye. It was good talking to you, Emily. I feel better for it.'

'And you still won't tell me who he is . . . ?'

'No. But if Anna survives, and you get to her in time, I'm sure she will. It's as much her right to talk as it is mine to stay silent.

'I might find out another way.'

'Then if you do and you meet him again perhaps you'll understand. But be warned . . .'

Marion Stoiber glanced right and left and then all around as if expecting to see her executioner right there in the midst of the throng of people on the Midway Plaisance. And then she hurried off into the crowds and was gone.

Moments later, Emily saw that, in her rush to leave, Marion had left her purse behind on the table. She grabbed it, stood up and called out after her. It was too late.

She took out more than enough bills from her own purse to pay the check, placed them on the table and ran off in the direction Marion had gone, east down the Midway toward the Ferris Wheel.

She thought she caught sight of her gray hat and called out, but the crowds were so thick and the noise of them and the attractions nearby drowned out her call.

She pushed on through, trying to keep Marion in her sights, until, quite suddenly, the hat was gone.

Emily climbed onto the steps of a nearby attraction to get a better view.

She saw what she thought must be Marion's back – certainly the hat was the same – moving into the shadow of the Ferris wheel. A man, a good deal taller, seemed to be close at her side.

Emily went cold.

'Marion . . . !' she shouted out, in alarm this time.

As she battled her way through the crowds on the Midway Emily heard a sudden scream. She thought it was the groups of girls up on the Ferris wheel, as before. She stopped and looked up.

As she did so the wheel ground to a sudden, jolting

halt. There were more screams and the whole crowd slowed and massed in confusion.

Emily pushed her way through them toward the massive base of the Ferris wheel.

A man in uniform who looked like one of the operating engineers stood looking ashen and helpless by the door leading into the area that housed the winding gear of the wheel.

She pushed past him, ducking her head and found herself surrounded by cogs and chains and pistons. The world outside faded away as her eyes adjusted to the dark.

Then she saw her. Marion Stoiber was deathly still in that hot and airless enclosed space and seemed to be embracing the very cogs of the machinery.

Which is exactly what she was doing.

For someone had pushed her straight toward them as they turned. She had thrust her arms out to try to stop her fall but they and her clothes had become entangled in the cogs, which, continuing to turn, had dragged her half into the machine itself, her head pressed at an unnatural angle against a metal beam. The short, unhappy life of Marion Stoiber had been crushed out of her by the eighth wonder of the modern age and her broken body had stopped it turning.

64

Factory

The Union Stock Yard consisted of six hundred acres of livestock pens, market buildings, railway lines, livestock causeways, killing floors and the canning houses of every major meatpacker in the world.

The place vibrated with activity beneath a sky darkened by a constant pall of smoke occasionally made lurid by open flames from the many boiler houses on the site. Ben Latham's only clues for the location where the photographs were taken were the images he had developed from the broken plates gathered up from Robinson's studio floor.

He approached the Union Stock Yard cautiously. It was well gated and a visitor pass was needed to go inside. He was lucky and found a talkative, relaxed guard.

When asked what his business was, he used a dodge that had worked before, showing his reporter's badge and pointing to the leather case of his Kodak Daylight Camera, an item so modern that it impressed all who saw it, especially men, and said he had come to take photographs for the New York *World*.

'Help yourself,' he was told, 'but there won't be many folk around in an hour or two anyway, seein' what day it is.'

'Why, what day *is* it?'

'The Friday before the Fair ends. Tomorrow's American Cities Day and the closing ceremony's on Monday and most of Chicago and half the world besides will be there to see the fireworks and celebrations. There's a lot less livestock coming through the yard for the next three days.

Ben headed west down Exchange Avenue, the Armour building to his left and Nelson Morris to his right. No-one paid him any attention, not even when he paused to take a photograph of the scene.

Closer up he caught sight of the processing plants of the other two major meatpackers, Gustavus Swift and the relative upstart that was Darke Hartz & Company, which was now one of the most successful in the world because of the aggressive way it had developed its distribution system by rail and sea.

He passed on down between the Swift and Darke Hartz factories and found himself among a maze of buildings, rising up to a gray sky of drifting smoke.

Down in these industrial depths his city clothes and even more, his camera, caught the attention of the busy men who hurried back and forth, many in white cotton coats covered in red-brown bloodstains. But no-one stopped him.

He reached another opening and was able now to look back at the water tower he had found in the images recovered from Robinson's studio and deduce that the building he sought was somewhere off to his left, on the northwest side of the yard.

It took him a while but eventually he found the building he believed he was looking for. It looked derelict and had the name of the company that once occupied it: A. F. Whetton & Co., Meatpackers.

He found a broken window into the basement.

The place smelled different from outside and he

thought he knew why. The site backed right on to the banks of the Chicago River. He could not see it, but the dead, damp smell of sluggish polluted water hung in the air.

The moment he found steps up out of the basement to the first floor Ben saw he was in a long-disused slaughter house. But the meat-dressing tables were still there, with dusty ropes and pulleys for heaving sides of meat hanging from the beams overhead. There was even a neat row of black gutta-percha aprons hanging on hooks, now eerily elongated by a combination of the damp air and their own weight and increasing rottenness. They looked like the aprons of giants.

Then Ben remembered he had seen such aprons before and, searching among his images, he found one which showed a half-clad girl standing against a row of them. But this wasn't the right killing floor.

He carried on along the corridor until finally he found a viewpoint similar to the ones in the images. After careful examination he concluded that he was a little to the right of where he needed to be, retraced his steps and found a walkway through to the next building.

He opened the first door he came to and was greeted by a curious sight. A room that had once been some kind of office was now derelict but for a chaise longue, some upholstered chairs, a potted plant or two and a few faded velvet drapes at the window. This was clearly the improvised location for some of the less salacious photographs he had developed from the Robinson plates. Pulling out his pad he made a few quick sketches before moving on, the light inside being insufficient for a photograph. When he entered the next door along, he found himself entering another killing floor. It was very clean, even if the beams above were as dusty and cobwebbed as those in the previous rooms. As for the meat-dressing tables, they were all covered in dust too, but for a couple near the hog wheel.

This towered above Ben but he was more interested in the heavy chains that hung from the wheel and which he knew were for the purpose of attaching the hind leg of the hogs as it turned, so hoisting them off the ground, the more easily for their throats to be cut. He stopped again and did another quick drawing.

Then, just as Ben moved from the wheel toward the windows to check out the view, something moving against the thick, wooden wheel caught his eye.

He took a closer look.

It was a single pink feather, caught among one of the chains and fluttering in the almost nonexistent breeze. It was the kind that vaudeville girls used in their stage acts; or that whores in bordellos on the Levee fanned themselves with on hot, sultry evenings. He reached up for the feather and sniffed it. Cheap perfume.

He impulsively took hold of one of the chains and looked more closely at the metal cuff and smelled that too.

Very cheap perfume.

Confident now that he had the right location, he took out the best of the photographs and paced back and forth until he had the exact same view of the table in relation to the chimneys through the window way across the Stock Yard.

This was the very table, he guessed, on which sexual intercourse between Marion Stoiber and an unknown man had taken place.

Opening up his Kodak, and hoping there was sufficient light, Ben took some photographs replicating the views, the hog wheel and the dressing tables. He wondered how any men could be aroused by sexual images of women put on display in such a disgusting environment. But there were clearly big bucks in the trade in photographing them and he wanted to find out more.

He climbed now to the upper floor, where he found some evidence, from the blurred patterns of dusty footprints on floor and stairs, of recent use. And then he noticed a new and different smell. No, it wasn't the dank smell of the river, it was something much more acerbic. Sulfur.

As he turned a corner into a darker corridor, the odor hit him harder and he knew it at once: sodium thiosulfate, better known as hypo, the fixing agent used in developing photographs. He pushed open a door and the smell was overwhelming, but the room was pitch black.

He felt around for a source of light but found none, which did not surprise him. But he knew there must be a window somewhere, probably with special blackout shutters and blinds. He propped the door open with his bag to get some light and felt his way gingerly across the room in what he hoped was the direction of the window. But as he did so, the door being too heavy for the bag, swung shut, putting him in pitch darkness.

'Damn!' he said aloud.

He felt his way ahead, his hands touching what he knew to be developing tanks, taps, and even, at eye level, a light chain with clips on it of the kind used to hold photographic prints while they dried.

Then he stilled, his heart beginning to thump. He had smelled something new: the not unpleasant aroma of fresh tobacco. He felt along the nearest bench for something that he might use to defend himself and found a pair of scissors.

His eyes strained round at the darkness. Somewhere from across the room feet shifted slightly on the floor.

Then he saw the sudden red glow in the dark of a small cigar.

There was a slight, polite cough and then a voice. 'Mr Latham, I guess?'

The voice was deep, assured and sounded slightly amused. Ben thought he knew it. But his natural desire to retake the initiative asserted itself.

'Who are you, sir?' he cried out as boldly as he could, his heart in his mouth.

The shutter of a lantern was suddenly opened and a shaft of yellow light illuminated the face of the other man in the room.

'Gerald Toulson, and I should be very glad to know how you worked out exactly where to come.'

Ben stood stunned.

'Let's shed some light on the scene,' said Toulson, opening one window shutter after another and throwing up the blinds until the place was filled with light.

'I'd also like to know,' continued Toulson, 'exactly what a professional photographer such as yourself makes of all this – and incidentally there's no need to hold those scissors quite so aggressively. I have no intention of shooting you. I need you as an expert witness.'

Ben put down the scissors and surveyed the room, which was even larger than he had thought. There was tank after tank for the developing and fixing of photographs, a store of bottles containing chemicals, mainly white pyrogallol powder, some of which had spilled out from an overturned bottle onto the work surface and the floor. There were also dozens of drying chains and racks and all the paraphernalia of a darkroom, but on a huge scale.

'Good God,' said Ben, 'this isn't a dark room, it's a factory for producing photographic images.'

'For the growing market in pornography,' said Toulson heavily.

Ben crossed over the room to where Toulson stood.

'You gave me one hell of a shock.'

Toulson smiled apologetically.

'In my line of work it's better to be safe than sorry. I don't make a habit of announcing myself when I'm trespassing. Anyway, you had me standing up here in the dark for a very long time after I first saw you approach the building. What were you doing?'

Ben showed him the images from the Robinson studio and explained how he had found the location.

'Impressive,' said Toulson.

'So how did you find the place?'

'We persuaded someone to give us the information. We got in round the back.'

'We?'

'My colleague and I,' said Toulson, glancing toward a still-shadowed part of the room.

Ben looked and once more his heart missed several beats. A man just as solid and tough-looking as Toulson was standing there.

'Rorton Van Hale, Pinkerton National Detective Agency,' he said by way of introduction, 'but be kind enough not to inform Miss Strauss of that or even of my existence. She doesn't trust Pinkertons, I gather.'

'What are you doing here?' asked Ben, still feeling shaken.

Toulson gave the answer.

'Mr Van Hale is here by way of reinforcement as I wrap up my investigation. A lot of nasty things could happen in the next twenty-four hours and I have a feeling both myself and Miss Strauss, though she doesn't know it yet, will need some backup.'

Ben looked out of the window at the rail tracks below and could see a locomotive and a string of refrigerated boxcars lined up, each with the words *DARKE HARTZ & COMPANY* painted in large white letters.

He stared at the fetid stream beyond and along its course to the South Fork of the Chicago River, screwing up his face in disgust.

'It looks as filthy as it smells,' he said.

It was sluggish, filled with garbage and a thick, foamy chemical effluent, which seemed to make it churn as it moved.

'You know what folk back of the yards call it?'

Ben shook his head.

'Bubbly Creek,' said Toulson.

65

Ashes

CHICAGO Friday October 27, 1893   2.50 PM

Anna's flight from the Meisters had been an instinctive act of survival. Having seen the men coming and the knife one of them was wielding, she had frozen in a state of such fear that it had needed John English to give her an almighty push and order her to run. But she didn't know where to. All she knew was that it had to be some place – *anyplace* – where they were not.

The wharves were not an easy place to run in a straight line, being stacked with goods and boxes, piles of lumber, coils of rope and ships' mooring lines, which meant she continually had to jump and dodge and occasionally duck, none of which was easy and comfortable for a woman in her condition.

She rapidly grew tired and was tempted to try to find a way back up to South Water Street, but John had told her not to go back that way.

So she blundered on, turning round only once. She saw that John had fallen and was lying on the ground and that the men were now running her way. Her blind fear returned; there was no way she could go back and help John now.

Then she came to a point where the wharf sloped suddenly at a dry dock where a ship was being over-hauled. It led inland with a twenty-foot drop onto mud. Anna ran round its edge, grateful that there was nobody much around. Beyond, the wharf turned to the right following a bend in the river and took Anna, as she quickly realized, out of sight of the men. Then she saw an alley to her right leading straight up on to South Water Street but turned instead toward two barges moored alongside the wharf and covered with tarpaulins.

The first stank of rotten vegetables so she went to the second. It didn't smell, so she slipped under its tarpaulin and dropped down inside, thinking it would be a matter of a few feet. It was more like nine or ten before she hit the bottom with a soft but abrasive bump and found herself in a pile of still-warm ash as clouds of dust arose around her.

The men, when they came a few minutes later, sounded bored and irritated. She heard one agree to check the market while the other came toward the barges.

'Jeez!' she heard him say, as he lifted the tarpaulin off the first one, 'what a stink.' Nevertheless, she could tell from his occasional cussing and his footsteps that he was giving the barge a thorough going-over.

Anna stayed right where she was. She tried to quietly scatter more ash over herself, but that only set some sliding down from a pile behind her. She held her breath in terror as the man's footsteps approached on the boardwalk above her.

Then, unexpectedly, his pace quickened along the wharf but he went straight past, and shouted at someone he had seen on the next craft along, a schooner.

'Say, seen a girl running on the wharf? 'Bout twenty. Black hair?'

Someone on the schooner shouted back that, no, he hadn't. Just as he did so a tug chugged past on the river and its wash hit Anna's barge, rocking it and sending ash and spent coke sliding in little avalanches all around her. She took advantage of the boat's movement to roll as far away through the ash and out of sight as she could on the other side of the barge.

The man now started systematically raising the tarpaulins above her one by one and searching the barge, starting at one end and working his way to the other. Despite the fact that Anna lay only partially covered by ash and clinker, he didn't spot her. It was deep and gloomy and dusty down there and her dress, fortunately, was dark gray.

Silence followed for a while, until the two men met up again, right on the wharf above Anna. They argued about whether to continue their search or not. They checked the barges again, half-heartedly, and once again they missed her. Then they headed back to Market Street.

Anna stayed right where she was. Even though the Meisters were gone, someone else was now moving about on the barge, whistling and doing something with ropes.

Only much later did she dare peek out from under the tarpaulin to see if the coast was clear so she could get back on dry land.

Except, to her horror, she saw there was nowhere to go. Quietly, without Anna noticing, the two barges had been roped up, one behind the other, and had now floated out some fifteen feet from the wharf edge, attached, she saw, to a tug in front.

An engine started and slowly, the barge, with Anna Zemeckis trapped inside, started moving off downriver, toward Lake Michigan.

What had happened to John? She hoped the Meisters had not harmed him and that he was all right but she was now far too exhausted to feel anything. Her eyes remained blank, without expression. Not a single tear made a channel through the ash that covered her cheeks. Her hair and hands and clothes were thick with ash too, but it didn't matter any more. Anna Zemeckis collapsed back down onto a pile of ash and clinker. It seemed that no matter what she did she caused nothing but trouble to those who tried to help her.

The tug pulling her barge hooted but she did not bother to drag herself up to the side to see why. She did not care what happened to her or her child anymore. She was tired, so tired of running.

She sank back into the warm ash and slept.

66

In Pursuit

It took Emily over an hour to make her statement to the Columbian Guard, who handled security matters at the Fair, and get back downtown following Marion Stoiber's murder.

There were two more visits she needed to make before returning to the hotel and her meeting with Ben. So she sent a note warning him she might be delayed.

The first visit was to the Chicago Public Library to interview John Olsen English. She arrived to find him in Mr McIlvanie's office, bewildered but calm after his experiences on the wharf that afternoon.

Anxious to do anything that might help find Anna, he agreed to take Emily to the place by the Chicago River where he had been attacked and Anna had disappeared.

Now they were standing on the wharf next to the same barrels where he and Anna had been sitting when the Meisters had spotted them.

Emily took in the scene. 'Show me the direction you saw Anna run in.'

They walked along the wharf until they reached the dry dock.

'She had a head start so I guess she would have got this far and round the corner of the dock before they did,' said John.

350

Emily moved on ahead, mulling things over out loud.

'So . . . where the dock curves to the right, the men would have lost sight of her . . .'

She walked faster and suddenly began running, John struggling to keep up.

'She would have . . . gone right . . . round . . . here . . . and guessing she had a few seconds' grace before they had her in view again . . .'

Emily stopped abruptly to think, John nearly bumping into her.

'But they were fit men and she's pregnant and exhausted. They would have been gaining on her fast. She would either have had to turn up an alley away from the wharf toward Water Street . . .'

John looked and agreed.

'Or what . . . ? She certainly could not have carried on along the wharf. There's much less cover that way and they would have quickly caught up with her.'

John agreed with that too.

'So, she must have found somewhere to hide . . .'

They both looked around. There were two schooners docked on the wharf but otherwise the mooring was empty.

'Doesn't look the same,' said John. 'Hardly surprising, I'd just been knocked out. But when I came round I did manage to walk down this far to see if there was any sign of Anna or the Meisters.'

'What's different about it? Please try to remember,' said Emily. 'Might be important.'

'I don't think there were two schooners there. Something smaller, lower . . .'

'I guess river craft come and go all the time here,' said Emily.

It was plain they could get no further.

'Listen, John, I'm running out of time,' said Emily, 'I have a meeting back at the hotel at six and other things to do before that. I'll be in touch as soon as I can.'

As they emerged onto South Water Street she hailed a cab and climbed in.

'By the way,' said Emily, 'Marion Stoiber told me you had a stutter. What happened to it?'

'I've been wondering that myself, Miss Strauss. In fact, I've been wondering about a lot of things of late.'

'Don't tell me,' said Emily, 'tell Anna when we find her.'

'*Will* we find her?'

'Yes,' said Emily firmly, 'because I need her for my story. So I reckon we're going to have to, aren't we?'

67

The Eels Procedure

CHICAGO Friday October 27, 1893   5.00 PM

Dr Morgan Eels was a happy man. His eyes were bright and his normally pallid skin had a certain color to it.

He had just completed the same surgical procedure on ten patients in as many hours with the gratifying result that nine had been entirely successful – so far as one could tell in such a short space of time – and only one had presented a slight hitch.

This 'slight hitch' was that a male patient had died on the operating table from, Eels suspected, a simple malfunction of the heart. He had left Mould to ascertain the cause of death for purposes of the official record.

The other patients, already largely recovered, manifested the same benign behavior as Riley had after the accidental stabbing she had received at the hands of Anna Zemeckis. They were quiescent, not complaining, and were able to answer simple questions. They had become, in short, manageable.

Yes, he told himself as he completed his rounds and stood surveying today's ten patients in their comfortable beds and then contemplating the empty ward next to it where another ten beds would, after completion of next Friday's procedures also be occupied.

Or more accurately, he was confident that nine of the remaining patients on his original list would be lying there. As for the last one, Anna Zemeckis, he had earlier that afternoon received a message from Mr Dodek Krol that she had been spotted downtown and he expected hourly that she would be apprehended.

Eels suddenly felt weary. He went and sat on one of the beds in the empty ward considering his necessary attendance, as a stalwart member, of the OAA convention the following day in order to witness the election of its new president. He had been greatly honoured by being asked, in a short note from Mr Paul Hartz, if he would be so kind as to be proposer of one of the new vice-presidents, namely Mr Gunther Darke, Hartz's son-in-law.

A good night's sleep was essential and he would turn in early.

Mould appeared.

'Talk to me as I walk,' said Eels. 'I have one last thing to attend to. I need to check on Mrs Riley's progress on Far Side.'

As they crossed the courtyard Mould confirmed that his initial conclusion was that the patient who had died earlier that day during the operation had died of heart failure.

'Could we have predicted this?' wondered Eels aloud with a moment's uncharacteristic concern.

Mould thought not.

'Very well. See that the family is informed. If there is one.'

'You must be tired after your exertions, Dr Eels,' said Mould. 'But may I say that I consider it an honour to have been witness today to the birth of a new medical procedure.'

Eels gave him a wan smile but said nothing. His mind was now on other things, as the two men entered the ward on Far Side where Riley was kept with Mary Nevitt and the two other women.

'Nurse Lutyens tells me you are gaining weight,' said Eels to the silent Riley, whose rictus grin was belied by the now permanent look of fear in her eyes.

Riley said nothing.

She sat in a large chair, facing Mary Nevitt across the ward, staring at her hands, and her long sharp fingernails which once more had begun chattering like crickets in her lap.

'I understand, Miss Nevitt,' said Eels benignly, crossing the ward to her, 'that you are much better now? And that you help with Riley?'

'Yes,' said Mary, 'I feed her.'

'Good,' said Eels.

Riley made a choking sound behind them and moved her fat, hairy legs beneath her shift.

'Well then,' said Eels, 'we'll need your help this weekend, Mary, seeing as the Fair's coming to an end and we're short-staffed.'

Mary Nevitt eyed Riley with unfeigned pleasure. Her nails now danced and chattered even more in her lap.

'Yes, Dr Eels, sir,' she said.

Neither Eels nor Mould noticed the terror in Riley's eyes as they left; or recognised her gurgles as screams.

They could not even guess at the nature of the hell on earth Riley had inflicted on the likes of Mary Nevitt over the years that was now being inflicted on her, and might be for years to come.

Dr Eels and his assistant headed cheerfully back to Main Building.

'I was thinking, Mr Mould,' said Eels, motioning him to sit down in his office, 'that though we succeeded in dealing swiftly with ten patients today, if one computes that rate against the total number of the mentally disturbed in this country in need of similar surgery, the task would be impossible for one man to achieve.

'I will need to cut down the operation time and find ways to disseminate my procedure. Next Friday we have nine patients – or ten if all goes well regarding our missing one – and my intention is to achieve an even better time than the thirty-eight minutes per patient we achieved today.'

Mould smiled.

'By the way, sir,' he inquired unctuously, 'have you decided on a name for your procedure?'

Eels sighed with feigned weariness.

'I have made a few notes but have not yet come to any decision. Perhaps you would care to see them?'

He pushed a piece of paper in Mould's direction

containing a list of words and phrases, some crossed out, others changed.

'It's scientific tradition of course to used a Greek or Latin derivation if at all possible, and certainly several come to mind to describe the procedure. It is, after all, simple enough . . . all we are doing is making specific lesions in the frontal lobes in such a way as to permanently reduce the patient's level of emotional disturbance and cognitive distress. So we might use the Greek equivalents of words like 'cut' or 'cutting', 'white' – the color of the brain tissue – and of course 'lobe', 'frontal' and the like . . . the permutations are many. I have my favorites which I have circled . . .'

Mould eyed the list of words, none of which had any resonance at all for him.

'They seem strange, sir.'

'That is because they are unfamiliar. However, there is no doubt that the one we chose will go down in medical history. But which one?'

Mould eyed the two words Eels had circled.

'Leucotomy? Very odd.'

'But the kind of thing my predecessors would have chosen. It's taken from "leuco" meaning white in the Greek and "tomy" . . .'

'. . . meaning cut or cutting,' added Mould.

'How do you like it?'

'I don't, sir. Not quite grand enough.'

'And the other?'

'Lobotomy.'

Mould dared to laugh.

'Well I'm sorry, sir, I know what your intention is, but I really think that such an absurd-sounding term as that can never catch on!'

'I agree, Mould!' said Eels, breaking into laughter too.

There was a knock on the door. It was Nurse Lutyens.

She eyed the two laughing men disapprovingly.

'A joke?' she said.

Eels explained that it was not, but that perhaps Nurse Lutyens would care to venture her own opinion.

'Leucotomy? Lobotomy?' she repeated doubtfully, 'Both sound quite wrong. In any case, sir, I would have thought the name must be already settled.'

'Really?' said Eels.

'I think it should be called the "Eels' Procedure". It should be named after the man who invented it.'

Dr Eels stood up, walked to the window and pondered a moment.

Then he turned back to his two loyal acolytes, the greedy light of ambition shining in his eyes. He now took on the manner of a man rising to speak as guest of honor at a gathering of the world's top medical men. 'Very well,' he said magnanimously, ' "The Eels' Procedure" it shall be!'

68

Women of the World

CHICAGO Friday October 27, 1893   5.03 PM

In Fay Bancroft's drawing room at Park Street, Emily Strauss was still trying to come to terms with the violent death of Marion Stoiber. She did not find her surroundings conducive to relaxation. The house was decorated in the kind of fussy, eclectic style that independent society ladies with time on their hands and plenty of money like; neo-classical French with a touch of the *fin-de-siècle* – lots of silks and tapestries and furniture with irritating curly arms and legs and imposing ornate vases of a too-delicate kind that worry big people when they come into a room.

'It really is beautiful,' said Emily without much conviction.

Fay laughed at her insincerity.

'You really don't have to try to like it, my dear, or please me in matters of taste . . . Now, come on, have another brandy and try to relax.'

'But there's one thing about Marion Stoiber that I just can't puzzle out,' said Emily. 'She was absolutely determined not to reveal the identity of her well-to-do lover. It seemed to me a misplaced kind of loyalty, for I doubt, even had he known, he would have cared one little bit.'

'And you have no idea who he might be?'

Emily did not, though for a moment she almost let slip the most important thing she'd found out about this man – that according to Marion he was behind the lucrative pornography trade operating out of Chicago. But in light of what had happened to Marion, and because of what Toulson had said about how dangerous such men were, she decided it was fairest to Fay if she kept that part of the story to herself.

Emily did not like to be underhanded but she needed to see if Fay could help her work out the man's name.

'She gave two clues I cannot make sense of,' continued Emily.

Fay edged closer.

'The first was that she suggested I had met the man before. But though I've racked my brains I cannot work out . . .'

'And the other clue?'

'Marion said the culprit did not live in Chicago now, not very convincingly, I thought. I'm sure she was trying to put me off the scent, but people don't pluck names out of thin air. She said he'd gone to Abilene, Kansas. Now, why would she say that?'

Fay's eyes widened and she put down her drink.

'What is it?'

'It's nothing,' she said, but it was an obvious lie.

Emily stared at her, puzzled, but then something quite different came into her mind. Something so shocking in its way that it was her turn to put down her glass.

'What?' it was Fay's turn to ask.

'I've just remembered something.'

'*What?*'

'Marion Stoiber forgot her purse. She left it on the table. I picked it up and ran after her, but of course . . . I never gave it back. I suppose I should have given it to the police.'

'Where is it now?' asked Fay.

'Here,' said Emily, opening her valise, pulling out a notebook and pencil and then a small beaded drawstring bag.'

'Well, *open* it,' said Fay.

One by one, Emily put its few contents on the table.

A handkerchief, neatly folded.

A small gilt mirror.

A handful of dimes and quarters.

Two keys on a ring.

'And . . . ?' said Fay, craning forward to see the last

359

thing Emily had found. It was a silver locket without a chain in the form of a little book.

She opened it.

'*Well?*' said Fay.

Emily looked at the two images inside, which faced each other. They had been cut to fit from larger photographs.

One was of Marion, smiling.

The other Emily simply stared at without a word until she whispered, '*Of course.*'

Fay took the locket from her hands.

'Gunther Darke,' she said.

Emily stared at her astonished and not quite understanding.

Fay's reaction was entirely different.

She started laughing. Then she got up with mock resignation, went to a cabinet, opened a small mahogany box and took from it an unframed photograph. She handed it to Emily.

'What's this?'

'It's me. But the question you should ask is where was it taken and by whom?'

Emily looked at the picture. It was Fay, in a riding habit, looking younger and holding a horse. She was standing by a pen full of steers.

'Where is it?'

'Abilene,' said Fay. 'Darke Hartz has a cattle stud out there.'

'Who took it?

'Gunther Darke,' said Fay, smiling.

Then, quite shamelessly, she added, 'It's where he likes to take his older, classier ladies.'

Words failed Emily completely as a frisson of cold horror came over her. The only consolation was that

Fay obviously knew nothing about Gunther Darke's involvement in pornography.

Fay sat down again, oblivious to what she was thinking.

'You see, I am not without my charms,' she said lightly. 'Another brandy? I think you're going to need one by the time I tell you what I intended when we first arranged this little tea.'

'I think I need another brandy right now,' said Emily.

69

Lakeshore

CHICAGO Friday October 27, 1893   5.10 PM

Anna Zemeckis had no idea where barges filled with ash and garbage offloaded their cargo so she sat on top of the pile of ash in trepidation. Maybe it was in the middle of Lake Michigan, in which case she would either drown or be apprehended.

So when the tug made a sharp right before heading toward the horizon and pulled alongside a wooden jetty on the far side of the rail tracks from Michigan Avenue she was mightily relieved. She had arrived at the city's largest landfill site, a moonscape of accumulated garbage consisting of ash, rotting vegetables, household waste and a huge quantity of scrap paper which fluttered about on top of the garbage and drifted off onto the water, swirling around in the air with the ducking and diving of the gulls.

She slipped out from under the tarpaulin and dropped down into the shallows and waded ashore before the tugman, and others operating cranes, could see her.

But any hopes she had of quickly getting back to the Lakeshore proper were almost immediately dashed. The area was extensive and ran southward parallel with the great expanse of rail tracks that ran along the edge of Lake Park.

She could see the tops of the mansions and public buildings that fronted Michigan Avenue and, in the fading light, make out the tallest silhouettes of them all, the tower of the Auditorium Theater and Hotel, neither of which she had ever visited.

Beyond the sea wall that bordered the rail tracks and on into Lake Park she could see the lamplighter was already out turning on the gas lamps.

Anna felt a rising sense of panic. In an hour it would be dark and she had absolutely no idea of where to go or what to do.

Out here, away from the freshly dumped, still stinking garbage, there was no smell, except of the fresh water of the lake. The scrubby vegetation that grew on the dry and desiccated soil whispered in the light evening breeze.

Although from a distance the ground seemed flat, when Anna started making her way across it she found it full of dips and hollows that were virtually impassable in places and so deep that the horizon kept disappearing and she continually had to reorientate herself.

Worse still, the land was riddled with water courses of various kinds, some fetid and foul, others surprisingly fresh, but slippery and boggy and not easy to cross.

She soon got tired and finally sat down, resigned to the fact she was about to spend a night out in the open. But as she felt herself drifting off into exhausted sleep a shadow fell across her face and a voice boomed at her, 'Is it friend or is it foe? Answer is, I don't know!'

Anna opened her eyes in fright and found herself staring into the warm, weather-beaten face of Mr Crazy, in the same long coat Eileen had told her he always wore, and the same boots and the same black hat.

'I am impressed,' said Mr Crazy, taking a comfortable position on the pile of congealed rubbish next to her, 'because I reckon that for most folk this place is harder to get to than the moon.'

'I came by barge.'

'By invitation or by accident?'

'Accident.'

'Ah! I am not so impressed. But then . . . that means Fate herself has brought you here and I guess that's impressive in another way.'

'I'm rather thirsty,' said Anna.

'Then follow me.'

'Mr Crazy, am I safe out here?'

'From prying eyes? Yes. Though folks in some of the mansions have telescopes, I do believe. They watch me at dawn and much good may it do them.'

'Why?'

'That's when I conduct my daily ablutions in one of the biggest and best baths in America.'

'What about the winter?'

Mr Crazy laughed.

'I make a hole in the ice like an Eskimo.'

'You could freeze to death.'

'I do not think so. They don't, I don't. I thought you were thirsty.'

'I am.'

'Then follow me.'

They walked for ten minutes or so to what Anna realized was an older part of the tip, the vegetation being thick and more established.

There, in the midst of it all, they arrived at the strangest house Anna had ever seen. It was located in a hollow not far from the Lakeshore itself, the water lapping no more than twenty yards off. It had an old metal pipe for a chimney, a couple of haphazard-looking windows and a door. The windows were set in walls built higgledy-piggledy from the staves of old barrels and the roof was a piece of salvaged tarpaulin of the kind she had been under on the barge, black with tar. It was attached like a tent to the sides of the makeshift hut by thick ropes stretched out in all directions and pegged down by stones. A variety of items hung from these ropes – washing, some pots and pans, a dead rabbit, wires and fishing lines, a net with a long handle. Beyond stood a rickety jetty, constructed from assorted flotsam and jetsam clearly salvaged by Mr Crazy from the Lakeshore.

'Watch you don't trip,' he said, as he wound his way between the stones and ropes, ducking down as he brought Anna finally to the front door. On either side, like the front porch of any respectable home, stood two comfortable chairs.

'Sit,' said Mr Crazy.

Anna did so gratefully.

He disappeared inside and reappeared a short while later carrying a tray with some unexpectedly refined-looking cut-glass tumblers and an earthenware pitcher of water. There was also a hunk of fresh bread.

He poured her some and handed her the glass. Then he had a glass himself, smacking his lips with evident glee.

'The finest wine in the world,' said Mr Crazy, 'and it's free. Eat this. I'll cook something soon. You better tell me what brought you from the Union Depot where we met yesterday evening all the way here, Miss Jelena.'

'You recognize me?'

'I most certainly do. I have a good memory for almost everything, unfortunately. But first you better clean yourself up.'

In no time at all he had shown her where to wash herself and given her a scarlet one-piece gentleman's undergarment to wear, the legs of which sagged down over her ankles. She put one of his shirts over it for modesty.

No gentleman from the finest family in Chicago could have done it all with such tact, thought and proper concern for her as a woman.

'Warm enough?' inquired Mr Crazy.

'Yes. Very. Thank you . . . That's the cleverest bathroom I've ever seen. Do I look ridiculous?'

'You look . . . like a Christmas decoration. As for the 'bathroom', I thank you for the compliment. Water's the first thing you have to think about when you build a place to live. I found a little run of water from a broken water pipe in Lake Park.'

'Mr Crazy . . . I've got to wash my dress and stockings so they dry by morning . . .'

'Wash tub's over there near the fire. I always keep a kettle or two boiling,' he said, pointing to another part of the site. 'The mangle's on the right.'

'You've got everything.'

Mr Crazy smiled rather wanly.

'Everything but my wife and child,' he said. 'Lost them in '71.'

She stared at him.

'In the Great Fire?'

'Yes, and my home too. But I never wanted to rebuild it, never wanted to live there again. So . . .'

'Where did you go?'

'Here, or rather over there . . .'

He pointed toward Lake Park.

'They filled it in, so Mr Crazy moves his home because he likes the water. Best view in Chicago. Best bit of real estate too. Best site in my portfolio, if I choose to call it mine, which I don't.'

Anna took her dress over to the rusty old wash tub and started pouring water on it from the kettle.

'Oh my goodness!' she called out suddenly. 'I forgot, I nearly soaked it through. Have you some scissors Mr Crazy?'

A pair were produced and Anna carefully unpicked the lining of her bodice where she had sewn in the papers she had stolen from Dunning.

Mr Crazy watched her with growing interest.

'That looks like paper.'

'It is.'

'Has it got words on it?'

She nodded.

'So it's a document?'

'Yes.'

He looked excited.

'So you've the paper to prove it?'

'Prove what?'

'How do I know? Show me the document and I will tell you what it proves.'

'It's got my name on it. I took it from Dunning, I . . .'

He raised a hand.

'Wash that dress while I get some food and coffee. Then you can tell me what you have to and I will tell you what your document proves. Was it made in Chicago?'

'Dunning. Cook County Hospital. It's from there.'

'That's good, very good. I'm good on New York, excellent on Cincinnati, but Chicago, why there's not many documents you can't show me for which I don't have something that went before.'

'I don't understand.'

'You don't have to. That's the bit you leave to me.'

He disappeared inside his house, humming.

Then she heard him say, 'A document from Dunning! Well! That's almost a first.'

Anna meanwhile washed her dress as best she could but it was heavy and unwieldy. She felt strangely content until, quite unexpectedly, her old fear came back.

'Mr Crazy?'

'Yes?'

He popped his head out of the door.

'I just wanted to be sure you're still there.'

He tugged his beard and tapped his head.

'Seems so.'

'I . . . I meant . . . it's getting dark. Where can I . . . ?'

'Here,' he said, 'you can sleep here. It's clean as a whistle and warm as toast.'

'But where will you sleep?'

'In my winter residence.'

'Where's that?'

'Fifty yards back. The water rises and a cold wind blows in from the lake in winter. And then it freezes. So I do the sensible thing and move out of the way.'

'I . . . '

'It's all right, Anna Zemeckis. Unless Fate decrees otherwise you'll come to no harm here.'

70

Taking Counsel

CHICAGO Friday October 27, 1893   6.12 PM

Emily Strauss arrived back at the Auditorium Annex to be greeted by Johnny Leppard dressed in a rather more important-looking uniform than when she had seen him last. She was in a state of growing shock as she realized the implications of what she had learned about Gunther Darke and the situation Anna was in.

But, as usual, Johnny Leppard was irrepressible and the fact was she needed some light relief.

He leapt forward from the Concierge's desk the moment he saw her, 'Your guests have arrived. They are waiting with Mr Latham in one of the small conference rooms.

'Guests, Johnny?' interrupted Emily.

'A Mr Toulson and a Mr Van Hale. I took the liberty of showing them all in there.

'Ah, rather more than I expected.'

'Light refreshments are on the way. If you need anything more, Miss Strauss, you only have to ask.'

'You look very grand today, Mr Leppard!'

He grinned his usual boy-man grin.

'I'm on a tryout as a temporary Assistant Concierge, till the Fair's end. They're so short-staffed that I offered my services in this new capacity and they accepted them.'

'More money?

'Not yet, miss.'

'You're a very upward sort of person, aren't you?'

'Like you, I think, Miss Strauss.'

She smiled.

'I suppose you have your eye on the Concierge's position – next month maybe?'

'I'll show you to the conference room, madam,' he said with mock formality, answering her question the moment they were out of earshot of the Concierge.

'Dead man's shoes as far as that position's concerned,' he said in a low voice. 'Time to move on. I have my eye on something else altogether.'

'Care to share those ambitions with me?'

'Ambitions don't put dollars in your pocket, only grasping at opportunities when you see them.'

'And one's come along?'

Johnny nodded.

'London, miss. That's why I'm learning French.'

'They speak English in London, Johnny.'

'Maybe they do, but in the hotel trade the coming language is French. The Manager of the Savoy Hotel, London, is one of our guests for the closing ceremonies for the Fair. I suggested to him that he would be missing an opportunity if he did not offer me a job.'

'And did he?'

'He's thinking about it, but he will.'

'And he's French?'

'French-speaking.'

'What's his name?'

'Mr César Ritz.'

'Never heard of him.'

'You will, Miss Strauss.'

'Or maybe he'll hear of me?'

'Nothing would surprise me about anything.'

'Nothing would surprise me about *you*, Johnny Leppard.'

He opened the door and then, as though he were an MC at some civic gathering:

'Gentlemen, Miss Emily Strauss, correspondent of the New York *World*. Refreshments will be served shortly.'

He closed the door behind her.

'*Thanks, Johnny*,' she said under her breath. '*One day soon you'll be doing that for real.*'

Emily cut straight to the chase.

'I think perhaps I was over hasty in my unwillingness to cooperate before, Mr Toulson. I have come into some information which suggests that Anna Zemeckis is in as much danger as you suggested, maybe more. And also . . .'

She paused and looked inquiringly at Rorton Van Hale.

Introductions were made.

'You were saying?'

'Let's deal with Marion Stoiber first. She was the other woman in the picture you showed us.'

'Ah . . .' said Toulson with satisfaction. 'You recognize her. Would you happen to know where I can find her?'

Emily looked surprised. She had somehow thought he would have already heard about Marion's death.

'You'll find her, by now, in the deadhouse, I should think.'

The three men looked astonished.

'I had lunch with her today,' said Emily rather

blankly, 'and immediately afterward . . . I mean moments after she left me . . . I mean . . . she . . . she . . .'

Emily did not want to weep but she did so, openly and for a short time uncontrollably. She had wanted to stay strong, unmoved, unaffected. Surely this was just a story, a job, but . . . *but* . . .

It was Gerald Toulson who got up and put his arms around her and Rorton Van Hale who got fresh coffee and Ben who, listening to the story that tumbled out of her and especially the revelation that Anna was pregnant by Darke, was the one who best summed up the man they were up against.

'He's a monster.'

Emily quickly recovered but in those few moments a bond had been forged between the four of them.

This wasn't a story, it was real life; it wasn't a job any more. It was a matter of trying to save someone's life, and maybe the lives of many others too.

'The time has come,' said Emily finally, 'for us to share what knowledge we have and to pool our resources.'

'I agree,' responded Toulson. 'My investigation is drawing to a close and you and Ben have uncovered important evidence.'

'Something's going to happen in the next twenty-four hours,' Toulson continued, 'and it won't be pretty and it won't be good. Unfortunately, there's no point calling in the Chicago Police Department because they're overstretched enough and have been for months. In any case, there's hardly a man among them downtown to be trusted, eh Van Hale?'

Rorton Van Hale nodded.

'City Hall's not going to be much use either for the next few days, from Mayor Carter Harrison down,

371

because they're all polishing their boots and dusting off their hats for the big closing ceremonies for the Fair. The worst of it from my point of view is that I was never hired to investigate anything more than the possibility of one man's involvement in an illegal trade.'

Toulson drew his chair closer to the conference table.

'We better tell you what we discovered at the Stock Yard . . . along with Mr Latham here.'

Ben produced a sketchbook from his pocket and the folder of pornographic photographs he had shown Emily earlier, developed from the broken plates salvaged from the Robinson studio. Toulson and Van Hale examined them and nodded.

'Yes, it's more of the same I showed you this morning,' said Toulson as he examined a box of cigars that Johnny had thoughtfully procured for the meeting, selected one, and lit it, eyes narrowing.

'It's part of a huge network in which Anna Zemeckis was one innocent pawn.'

'And Marion Stoiber too,' interjected Emily.

'The trouble from our point of view,' said Toulson, 'is that your girl, Anna Zemeckis, is right in the middle of this mess and I don't doubt that what happened to Stoiber will happen to her if we don't get to her first. But that also gets in the way of my investigation.'

Emily was forced to agree.

'It would help if you told us a bit more about what Marion Stoiber said to you . . .'

Emily did so.

'We don't know if the Meisters have got to her yet,' she continued, 'but as a woman I somehow think not. That girl's a survivor. I think she's still alive and between us all we have to figure out where. As for Anna's involvement in the pornography trade, she must have been lured to the building you men found. It must have been from there that she went missing. John English said she didn't remember anything much about the last day or so before she arrived at Dunning. But whoever's after Anna now it sounds like Darke is calling the shots.'

'Maybe Hartz too,' said Toulson. 'He's Darke's father-in-law, remember, and both men are members of the Old America Association. And I suspect one or both were involved in the death of Jenkin Lloyd Rhys.'

'Rhys?' repeated Emily.

Van Hale filled in that part of the story.

'Seems Rhys's death was mighty convenient timing for Hartz, given that if Rhys had still been in office it's likely his man and not Hartz's would have taken over the presidency.'

'And now?' asked Ben.

'It looks like Rhys's candidate's for the taking – he's a big wheel on the New York Mercantile Exchange. But since Rhys was got out of the way Hartz is in with a chance to place his own man. The Convention is on today and tomorrow, in the one place in town big enough to hold the OAA membership – the Auditorium Theater right next door. Both sides have summoned every member they can track down to attend tomorrow's election. God knows who'll come out of the woodwork. Whoever gets the presidency will wield a lot of power through the membership across the United States and Hartz knows that better than anybody. If Gunther Darke takes control of the OAA, even if indirectly through Hartz, then it will be very hard to stop the trade growing.'

'So what's the connection between the OAA and pornography?' said Emily.

Toulson glanced at Rorton Van Hale and said nothing.

'I thought we were pooling our resources,' said Emily. 'Don't forget, if I find Anna Zemeckis she may be your only material witness to all of this.'

'Yes, she may well be,' said Toulson, retreating a little. 'Look, I didn't undertake my investigation and you didn't get into yours to pit our wits against one of America's most powerful organizations. I'm doing a job for a private client and his name doesn't need to come into this at all . . .'

'A man you haven't named!' cut in Emily.

'But you're on special assignment for Mr Pulitzer and if this gets into the public domain they'll come after you, Miss Strauss."

'But Mr Pulitzer's kind of a useful person to have on our side, wouldn't you say?'

'He would be,' conceded Toulson.

'Then give me a break ahead of everyone else on this story and I'll deliver a damn good one that might just help your investigation now and maybe later too. Don't and I'll still deliver my story, but it won't be one that'll do you or your anonymous client any favors.'

'You talk tough, Miss Strauss.'

'I'm learning to. Now . . . if I'm to get to the root of what's been happening to Anna Zemeckis and why everybody seems to want her out of the way I need to understand the precise link between the OAA and pornography. I thought it was a nationwide organization of the middle-class, respectable and God-fearing, who wouldn't know the difference between a *pose plastique* and a postcard.'

Toulson sighed.

'Very well, but you don't use what I'm going to tell you without my say-so. And you mention it to no-one. These men do not play games. So you can put that notebook away. You commit all I say from now on to memory.'

Emily nodded.

'The real power in the OAA is held by the so-called Audit Committee. Before Rhys's death, he chaired it and he controlled it. Now Hartz is in temporary control until Rhys's successor is appointed tomorrow. But the balance of its members is clearly shifting Hartz's way. What the Audit Committee decides to do the OAA follows.

'What I didn't know until I began looking at Gunther Darke's involvement with pornography was that the OAA conducts certain what you might call covert activities. Originally under Rhys, for all his bonhomie, the main purpose of these activities was to do whatever it took to get the OAA's way over a range of political and commercial issues across a range of states.

'Since Hartz has been on the Committee – that's four years now – those activities have taken a different turn. It began with harmless bolstering of lobby positions in Washington over anti-immigration policies. In the last two years, however, it's got a lot more sinister. The intimidation of those who support immigration has been sanctioned by the Audit Committee. Now, with Rhys's disappearance, the Committee's muscle has been turned against the OAA's own people – the ones that are, or would have been his supporters.'

'But what has this to do with these obscene photographs?' said Emily.

'Simple,' said Toulson. 'Any idea how big this business really is?'

Emily and Ben shook their heads.

'In America, over a million dollars annually and rising very fast; worldwide, and that's mainly Europe, you can treble that figure. They're much more sophisticated about that kind of thing on the other side of the Atlantic, particularly in London, Paris and Berlin. I know for a fact that Robinson had links with a flourishing trade in pornographic literature and photographs conducted in London . . .

'Of course,' interrupted Emily, 'it said on the back of Anna's *carte de visite* that he had studios in other cities.'

'Yes, in London, just off the Strand.' continued Toulson 'The back streets round there have been the center of the English pornography trade for decades. But don't worry, Miss Strauss, America's catching up fast and, thanks to Gunther Darke, Chicago has been spearheading this lucrative new market.'

'We're pretty certain that some of the OAA's more unpleasant activities are funded by the pornography trade, but of course the membership at large has no idea and would be horrified. There's a hard core of barefaced profiteers who run it, headed by Mr Gunther Darke, Paul Hartz's son-in-law.'

'. . . and that's always been convenient for another reason,' said Emily.

'Which is?' murmured Van Hale.

'Who ultimately controls Darke Hartz. I believe things will change soon in that respect.'

'You seem to have discovered a lot of things in a short time, Miss Strauss,' said Toulson.

'It's pretty much common knowledge why Darke and Hartz don't talk to each other and that Hartz will make a bid for control of the company when Mr Darke retires at the end of the year. But in any event, he himself unwittingly set the whole thing in motion several years ago when his daughter married Gunther Darke.'

'Well, I have my own version of those events, Miss Strauss. So I'd quite like to hear yours,' said Toulson.

'The Darke and Hartz Families go back to when Hans Darke's father had a business on the East Coast and banked with Hartz of Boston and New York. Hans opened their meatpacking business in Chicago in 1865 when the Union Stock Yard opened and he thrived. But he couldn't compete with the big boys, Armour and Swift, and after 1878 he needed capital if he was going to survive.

'That's when Paul Hartz bought into the company, wanting a fifty–fifty split. Hans resisted and they ended up with a thirty-five percent stockholding each, with Hans's two sons, Wolfgang and Gunther, having ten percent each and Paul's daughter Christiane having the remaining ten percent, making a fifty-five to forty-five split between the families.

'Hans was a brilliant stock breeder and master butcher, but its Paul's financial know-how that enabled them to survive against the bigger meat-packers and final emerge as one of the big four in 1890.

'So far, so good. Then Christiane, whom everybody thought had a soft spot for Wolfgang Darke – one of the most uncharismatic men I've ever met incidentally, but what do I know? – went and fell for the charms of the older brother Gunther. Naturally Paul encouraged the match because by then Gunther had fallen out with Hans and seemed to favor working with Paul. His support would give Paul the majority interest.

'That's about it, except that last year Hans, who'd been ill with heart trouble, announced he wanted to retire and give his holding entirely to Wolfgang. This caused growing dissent in the Darke–Hartz enterprise, added to the fact that from the first the marriage of Christiane to Gunther had been a disaster.'

'When is Hans due to retire?'

'End of the year. Since Gunther doesn't get on with his brother either it looks likes Wolfgang – who's a chip off the old block, a master butcher but not a money man – will be out in the cold. Unless, of course, Gunther divorces the woman he appears not to love and Christiane marries the man everyone thinks she should have married.'

'You mean poor old Wolfgang?' said Ben, looking bemused.

'I do. But it won't happen. Gunther will never set Christiane free. And they will never have a normal marriage either. Christiane found out very quickly about Gunther's promiscuity and his womanizing. She was fearful of contracting an infection from him. They haven't had sexual relations for years. Which is why there is no heir to the Hartz half of the Darke Hartz empire.'

'You seem very well informed on all their family secrets,' said Van Hale. 'What's your source?'

'One of Gunther Darke's former lovers. But let's get down to the fundamental issue, Mr Toulson. Let me ask you, for a second time, who's your client?'

'I'm afraid that is one thing I am not at liberty to reveal. It breaks my code of conduct.'

'You guys have a code?'

Toulson flushed.

'As a matter of fact we have, Miss Strauss and it's a hell of a lot more meaningful than any you newspaper people might have, if you've got one at all.'

'I apologize, Mr Toulson.'

'Accepted – and as a matter of fact so do I.'

They grinned at each other.

'Does my view of Darke Hartz square with yours, Mr Toulson?'

'Yes, it does.'

'A former lover's not a bad source,' said Emily, trying not to look smug. 'Though of course she knows nothing of Gunther's involvement in pornography. If she did, she would be horrified.'

Toulson grinned.

'So, Mr Toulson. You know my source. Care to reveal yours?'

'Sure. Mr Hans Darke.'

It was Emily's turn to grin.

'Now that's really very interesting, Mr Toulson. He wouldn't happen to be your client too, by any chance?'

'You're too clever for your own good but I'm beginning to understand why Mr Pulitzer employed you.'

Johnny Leppard knocked and entered.

'Message for Miss Strauss. The gentleman who delivered it is waiting for your reply.'

Emily opened the classy envelope he handed her and read it.

'Well,' she said, '*Well!* Talk of the devil!'

'Who's it from, Emily?' asked Ben.

'Mr Paul Hartz,' she said. 'He wants to have a talk with me.'

'When?' said Toulson grimly.

'Now,' said Emily. 'And he insists that I go alone.'

'That is out of the question,' said Van Hale.

Toulson agreed. 'Absolutely. You can't go, Miss Strauss. The man is totally untrustworthy.'

'I've no intention of trusting him,' said Emily coolly, 'and I promise I'll be on my guard.'

'What's your answer, Miss Strauss?' said Johnny, still hovering in the doorway.

'The gentleman who's waiting, does he have a cab?'

'He's got a private carriage.'

'Tell him I'll be out in five minutes.'

71

Hartz Castle

Emily's ride from the Auditorium Annex on Michigan to Paul Hartz's famous residence on Prairie Avenue took ten minutes.

Her companion was a spare, tall man in his thirties with a hard face and cropped hair in the Prussian manner, who introduced himself as Lukas. His black pants and frock coat were more a uniform than a suit of clothes. If he had been at a funeral he would not have been out of place. In downtown Chicago, at the beginning of a weekend of festivities, with the city so vibrant and colorful and bent on enjoying itself, his long face, mean eyes and sober appearance meant he was only one thing, a Meister; and Emily knew it.

What surprised her as their somber carriage turned on to Prairie Avenue at 18th was that Paul Hartz should allow himself to be so openly associated with such a man. But, she guessed, his intention was to intimidate her which meant, she told herself, that in some way and quite unwittingly, she really must have intimidated him. Or at least got under his skin.

Prairie Avenue, once one of Chicago's finest residential streets, had an air of faded glory. Emily did not know whose mansions were whose but she knew that many of the great commercial luminaries of Chicago – Marshall Field, George Pullman, Philip Armour and Paul Hartz – had built opulent homes here through the seventies and eighties, some in the ugly and over-ornate Second Empire style, others in what might be called Bulky Utilitarian.

But by now anybody who was anybody in Chicago, including Hans Darke, had long since moved north to Astor Street to escape the stench of the Stock Yards. Except for Paul Hartz that is. Maybe he was just obstinate.

The first thing that Emily noticed as she climbed out of the carriage – her cheerless friend not offering to assist her – was the rumble and rush of a passing train along the nearby Lakeshore tracks, steam rising in the air and specks of soot falling from it.

'Must play havoc with the residents' washing,' she said to lighten things a bit.

'This way,' said her companion without expression.

Hartz's house was big, ugly and too ornate.

The porch alone would have housed several families from the Near West Side.

But after she had got past the front entrance, the huge ill-lit foyer and the gloomy corridor, Hartz was charm itself, as he had been at Hans Darke's party the day before, when they had been briefly introduced. But there was no disguising the coldness in his gray eyes now.

He did not, as Toulson had warned, dwell on niceties once their greetings were over and Emily's inquiry after Christiane Darke's health was politely ignored.

'I understand you work for Mr Pulitzer, Miss Strauss?'

She agreed she did.

'He's a friend of mine.'

She looked noncommittal.

'My firm has many clients who advertise in the New York *World*.'

'That's very astute of them, Mr Hartz. It's a widely read, well regarded daily, committed to the democratic principles of truth, justice and liberty.'

'There is no need to be arch with me, young lady.'

'And there is no need to patronize me or take me for a fool, Mr Hartz,' Emily replied. 'If you have something to say, say it; if not, please be kind enough to give my best wishes to your daughter when you next see her and I shall be glad to take my leave of you. Your carriage back to Michigan Avenue would be welcome; I have no wish to chance my luck at this time of evening walking through the Levee. I did it once and that was enough.'

His eyes hardened even more, but the smile remained rooted on his face, for the time being.

'I thought you could do with some help with your story.'

'Which one? I'm working on several.'

'The one about Anna Zemeckis.'

'Fire away.'

'How much is Mr Pulitzer paying you?'

'Rather more than even you could afford, Mr Hartz.'

This brought a skeptical smile to his face.

'Try me.'

Emily got up.

'Do you mind if I move around as we talk? I generally do when I'm thinking, so maybe while I consider what you've just suggested I should do the same.'

'Feel free,' said Hartz smoothly, relaxing a little and thinking he had his fish on the hook, 'I guess it's more generous than most.'

'Your study or your offer?'

Hartz shrugged complacently.

'Coffee, Miss Strauss?' he said, reaching for a bellpull behind him. 'Or something stronger? Most journalists I know, and I know a lot, take liquor after six.'

Emily considered this and, frankly, was tempted. But that's not what she said.

'I'm not planning to stay long enough for a drink, Mr Hartz.'

His eyes hardened again.

'Tell me, sir, who's the lady with you in this photograph? No, don't trouble to get up; I'll bring it to you.'

She picked up a silver-framed photograph and placed it right in front of Hartz on his desk, right on top of the papers he was looking at.

His eyes narrowed.

He did not like women who took the initiative.

He did not like being wrong-footed.

'It's a personal picture, Miss Strauss, of the kind civilized people are sensitive enough not to ask about. The lady's dead.'

'But the gentleman is not. That's Mr Darke, is it not?'

He nodded.

'And the lady is his wife, I guess?'

Hartz glowered.

On the face of it the little photograph, taken in one of the family residences no doubt, was harmless. Only thing was Mrs Darke's eyes were on a younger Paul Hartz, and his had a proprietorial look, while Hans Darke stood alongside them looking disgruntled.

Like Hartz now.

'Hans Darke was never an especially sociable man. He did not deserve the wife he had. But let's cut to the chase shall we? Name your price, Miss Strauss – to leave Chicago today and write up some harmless story about women at the Fair. I reckon you could do that standing on your head.'

'You did a financial deal with Mr Darke a few years later, did you not?'

'I did, and it benefited us both greatly. Not that it's any of your business.'

'Mr Hartz, I have no price, because I'm not selling. But if I were, I'd have to ask you – and you won't mind if I quote your own words in the matter – what price do you put on truth?'

Hartz's smile finally vanished.

'Miss Strauss, you're beginning to bore me,' he said. 'So, here's how I see it. I would imagine Mr Pulitzer is expecting you to file your story in time for the edition on the 30th, the day the Fair closes.'

'He is and I will.'

'Really? But what's the value of your story, and your job, if you file it a day late?'

Emily did not reply. She was thinking hard and her

heart was beginning to beat faster. Suddenly it seemed a long way to the front door.

'I'll tell you,' said Paul Hartz, rising. 'Not a lot. Nothing in fact. Worse than nothing because I happen to know Mr Pulitzer has no time for failure and no time for losers, however good their excuses may be. Am I right?'

'I guess you are, Mr Hartz.'

Hartz reached for the bellpull.

A door at the far end of the library opened behind her but Emily did not turn to look that way as she did not want to seem weak. Her heart thumped hard. There was a mean look in Hartz's eyes that rooted her to the spot.

'So here's the deal, Miss Strauss. You go away and write a nice, safe little story which one of my associates will help you with and for which you'll get handsomely paid in addition to the pittance Pulitzer plans for you, or you're going on a nice little vacation right now which will not be over until well past your deadline, by which time Mr Pulitzer will not be interested in hearing your excuses because he will have fired you.'

Emily managed a smile, but it was a strained one. Hartz obviously meant what he said.

'Tell me, Mr Hartz,' she said as coolly as she could, 'what is it in my story about Anna Zemeckis that worries you? Is it that I might find her alive and she'll tell me things people like you don't want me to know? Like the corrupt management at Dunning whose Board you're Chairman of? Or is it simpler than that – you and everyone else who operate as boosters for this great city don't want a bad word said about it, even though everyone knows that during the Fair crime rates have soared and people have gone missing, even from the best-lit and best-located of sidewalks. People like your good but late lamented friend Jenkin Lloyd Rhys, for example?'

'Miss Strauss . . .' began Hartz, angry now.

He glanced across the room and nodded.

Emily ignored the steps of the approaching man behind her and stepped right up to the edge of Hartz's desk.

'Or is it that the nasty, dirty business your son-in-law is running out of the Union Stock Yard might destroy Darke Hartz & Company's market value and in turn irrevocably damage the Old America Association, if I were to expose the fact that the OAA uses the profits from that business to fund illegal activities?'

'That's enough, Miss Strauss, I think,' the man behind her said, taking her arm.

'And don't *you* touch me,' she said, turning angrily.

She looked up and found herself staring into the eyes of Gunther Darke.

That made her angry.

'Mr Darke. How nice. May I congratulate you on your excellent lecture this morning,' she said graciously, brazening out Gunther's stare. 'I found it extraordinarily . . . revealing.'

He smiled.

'Don't mind my father-in-law, Miss Strauss, he's not used to women like you. He doesn't know how to handle them.'

'And you do?'

Darke came nearer.

She could sense the animal in him, the presence, the power.

'If we had time,' he said, his voice softer, his gaze

glittering and seeming to penetrate her anger and fear to something deeper that began to feel that it could easily slide out of control, 'there's a nice place down south I'd enjoy showing you. But, you've only got a few days, it seems.'

'I'm not going anywhere,' said Emily.

'Precisely,' said Gunther, taking her arm and pulling her nearer, 'except out of this city. You're out of your depth, Miss Strauss, and your meddling must stop.'

Somewhere in the distance Emily heard a doorbell ring.

She heard it grow more insistent.

She heard the rumble of voices, male and rising.

She heard a sudden thump.

Gunther let her go and turned toward the door into the hall through which Emily had first come in.

Steps approached it.

It opened.

'I'm sorry,' said Rorton Van Hale, 'but your butler has had an accident. I've come to collect Miss Strauss.'

He surveyed the room.

Gunther Darke stood there looking charming.

Paul Hartz was sitting at his desk, smiling a patrician smile.

Emily Strauss was standing in the middle of the room, her cheeks flushed.

Rorton Van Hale held a revolver in his hand.

'Our friend was just leaving,' said Gunther Darke.

'Indeed,' said Hartz rising and extending a hand to her.

She took it.

'You would do well to remember all that has been said and consider the consequences very carefully if you do not,' he said icily.

'Oh, but I'm sure she will,' said Gunther.

Emily turned and looked at him. His eyes had a menace that almost soiled the air between them.

As Van Hale ushered Emily toward the door, she turned back one last time with a smile.

'Oh, Mr Hartz, forgive me, I almost forgot to ask . . .'

'What?' asked Hartz acidly.

'Whether you would care to comment on the latest information I have about Miss Zemeckis?'

'Which is what precisely, Miss Strauss?' interposed Gunther Darke, swiftly moving forward.

'Why, that she's carrying your child, Mr Darke. I'm sure Mr Hartz would be the first to congratulate you.'

Darke looked furious but the look Paul Hartz gave his son-in-law was something else: it was positively murderous.

'Have a nice evening, gentlemen,' said Emily.

72

Day's End

CHICAGO Friday October 27, 1893   8.30 PM

Out on the Lakeshore, Anna Zemeckis sat contentedly with Mr Crazy by a roaring fire of driftwood and half-spent coal which sent sparks flying upwards.

She was now well fed on rabbit stew, potatoes and carrots and various wild herbs, with more hunks of fresh bread. Her dress and stockings, hung out as near the fire as she dared, steamed gently in the night.

Mr Crazy, who liked producing pieces of paper, suddenly produced another, this one very official looking.

Anna scanned it and look puzzled.

'It's some kind of land claim,' she said.

Mr Crazy beamed.

The light played bright on his beard, his cheeks and his eyes. He looked more like Saint Nicholas than ever and Anna, dressed cosily in her scarlet Mr Munsing union suit, its color all the richer for the firelight, looked like Santa's assistant.

She beamed too.

'What land does it lay claim to?'

Mr Crazy waved his arms about proprietarily and said, 'Why this very piece of extensive real estate you're sitting in. By squatter's rights. I've lived here long enough and there's not a man, jack or woman in Chicago can deny it. I'm just biding my time and then I shall claim my rights.'

'When will that be?'

A cloud settled on Mr Crazy's face.

'Been asking myself that same question for a very long time. I came here in '71, a broken man. Before that I had had my share of real estate. I wasn't rich but I was getting richer and I had a home and a good woman and a child. Then . . .'

He shook his head and poked the fire. Sparks rose into the air.

'See that?'

He pointed to a tiny speck on a piece of wood that burned with an exquisite blue-green flame, a tiny jewel of color.

'What is it, Mr Crazy?'

'That's a piece of ship's timber and it's the copper nails that shoot out little flames like that while they melt. Well, I've had copper nails in my brain since '71, but one by one they've all been burned away and it's made me whole again.'

'Has the last one gone?'

'Yes, I think it has.'

'So then . . . ?'

'So nothing,' he growled. 'Why am I still here? Is that what you want to know?'

'Yes,' she said.

The stars shone bright above their head.

The lighthouse was winking, as its reflector turned round and round, sending its routine flash of red and then yellow.

Trains rumbled and creaked out near the park, beyond which was a wall of black, pierced by gaslights blinking in the city to the west.

In front of them the waves of Lake Michigan lapped softly; a ship's red and green navigation lights bobbed on the horizon.

'Because I'm scared of leaving,' said Mr Crazy, 'even though I know my time here is up. Can't run from life forever.'

'What are you scared of?'

'Don't rightly know. But I know what I need.'

'What's that?'

'Something to give me back my courage. I planned it all long ago,' he said. 'Look, I'll show you.'

He went into his cabin and walked back brandishing a carpetbag.

'This bag, Anna, contains all the things I need for my future. I have the papers to prove it, right here.'

He sat down, putting the bag on the ground beside him.

'Talking of which, that document you stole and so carefully preserved does prove something, quite a lot, in fact. For one thing it proves what everybody's guessed long since about places like Dunning – that their treatment of patients breaks all codes of professional conduct and a few laws as well. Not to mention that it seems to me that your Dr Eels is conducting experiments he shouldn't be on human beings.'

'Oh,' said Anna.

'And another thing. Dr Eels mentions the little matter of how his experiment is being funded, which is very helpful to those of us concerned with truth and justice.'

'You mean who's paying for it?'

'Yes. It seems that it's the Old America Association that's putting up the cash and that touches me to the very quick.'

'Why so?'

'Because I just happen to be one of its original members, courtesy of my lifetime dues paid back in 1868 when it was founded with honorable intentions, in the true spirit of Republicanism. But in the last few years those values have been lost sight of, thanks to Mr Paul Hartz and his like.'

'What are you going to do?'

'Don't rightly know. I'd attend tomorrow's 25th National Convention in the Auditorium Theater if I thought they'd let me in. That'd ruffle a few feathers. Anyone who can disrupt a meeting chaired by Mayor Carter Harrison by democratic means – and believe me, I've done *that* a few times – ought to be able to make his point at a meeting run by a smooth-talking Eastcoaster like Mr Paul Hartz.'

Mr Crazy sat and pondered this for a while.

Anna's eyes began to close.

'Just remembered something,' said her companion. 'It's important.'

'I was almost asleep.'

'Not yet, I've one last thing to show you.'

'What?'

He produced a storm lantern and lit it. Then another.

'Take one of these and follow me.'

He led Anna along a track inland behind his cabin. They dropped into a hollow where the horizon disappeared altogether and came to what looked like an opening into the earthy bank itself.

In this eerie spot Anna could make out by the light of the lantern a crudely made wooden opening, though it was disguised as a pile of old lumber. Mr Crazy dragged it open and shone his lantern inside. It was a tiny space, the size of a coal hole, full of an assortment of wooden boxes and crates neatly stacked up on one another.

'My archive,' he said. 'Every subject under the sun classified and filed away under Mr Dewey's system.'

'May I?' she said.

Anna looked about her incredulously.

'There must be thousands of documents and pieces of paper here,' she said. 'How did you come by them?'

'They've been dumped. Make interesting reading if you have the time, which I have. Helps me keep an eye on City Hall and its business dealings.'

'Be hard to find anything here, Mr Crazy, if you didn't know about Mr Dewey and his system.'

'Too right. Now, where shall we file your document?'

He opened a couple of boxes, considered the matter, and finally placed it in a folder marked 'Miscellaneous'.

'Why?' she said.

'Harder to find should anyone come prying.'

'You said no-one will.'

'I did but I could be wrong. I hope I am. But it sounds like your pursuers are persistent. You should be all right for a couple of days out here. Then we must get you safely out of Chicago. But first you must rest. Meanwhile . . .'

He filed the papers she had taken from Dunning. Then Mr Crazy took Anna back to his cabin and left her by the door.

'There's your bed, Anna. It's clean and dry. And there's a warm shawl you can wrap around you in the morning. Sleep well.'

'But where will you go?

'I shall spend the night in my winter residence. Oh, and by the way, if you should hear splashing in the morning that's me, taking my ablutions in Lake Michigan. So I'd be obliged if you'd get the coffee brewing. Goodnight.'

Back at the Auditorium Annex, to which an exhausted Emily was safely escorted by Rorton Van Hale, Ben was waiting anxiously. But they had no sooner settled down to talk than a bellhop came over with a message. Mr English was at the reception desk asking for Emily.

John English, now crumpled and dusty after his day's exertions, explained that after leaving Emily on the wharf he had spent some more time looking around. He had been obliged to return home for supper with his mother, but after seeing her to bed at her usual early hour he had slipped out again, back to the wharf for one last look for Anna.

'I walked around a bit . . .'

'Alone? In the dark?'

'Didn't bother me, Miss Strauss, it's Anna I'm thinking of. I reckon there's only one place she would have ended up and that's why I had to come.'

He produced a Rand McNally map of downtown Chicago, pointing at the Lakeshore that ran parallel to Michigan Avenue where they now were.

'Out there, beyond Lake Park,' he explained, 'is a very large area of garbage dumps onto which almost everything spewing out of Chicago is likely to get unloaded by barges coming down the river from the wharves where we were yesterday.'

'The City Council has plans to reclaim it and make it part of the park eventually, though big business would like to cover it all with real estate. But meanwhile it's garbage. I'm pretty sure that's where Anna's barge ended up and I'm equally certain she's got enough sense to hide out there overnight.'

'But if you've worked that out then I reckon Mr Hartz, Mr Darke and their Meisters have done the same.'

'Yes, but searching by night is futile out there. The ground can be treacherous in parts and there's too many places to hide.'

Emily looked at the map. 'Where's the best access?'

'Only been there once myself to do some fishing, but I got out there from beyond the Illinois Central Depot on 12th. The only other place is to the north where the Chicago River flows out into the Lake. And you'd need to get there by boat.'

'Well, 12th is just down Michigan from here,' said Emily. So I reckon we head out first thing and start looking beyond Illinois Central. At dawn.'

'Don't we need backup?' said Ben.

'We don't have any, even if we wanted it,' replied Emily. 'Toulson and Van Hale have got their own investigation to deal with and it's coming to a head. I'm willing to take the risk, if you two are. John? Ben?'

Both men nodded. Then, suddenly, John's face registered a momentary sense of panic.

'But what about . . . '

'Your mother?' said Emily tartly. 'I'm sure Mrs English will survive a night by herself.'

Half an hour later John installed himself in Ben's already cramped bedroom, curling up on the cold linoleum wrapped in a blanket.

In her own room Emily was restless and for once did not fall asleep easily. She was thinking of Anna but also of her story and telegraphing it to the *World* offices in New York by Sunday night. She wondered how she was going to start it and came up with the perfect introduction until, the words slipping from her mind, she fell asleep.

Out on the Lakeshore, Mr Crazy sat in the dark as he had often done at day's end through the long years since his wife and child had died.

Ironically, he had always found comfort in a fire, even though it was fire that had destroyed his happiness. But now the time had come, he told himself, to finally come to terms with all that grief and loss and embrace the future.

He took one last look at the contents of his carpetbag and then closed it up.

'Yes, it's time, Mr Crazy,' he said aloud to the night and the stars. 'Tomorrow I'll do it.'

Then, as though in recognition of this momentous decision, somewhere in the distance, a church clock tolled midnight.

Tomorrow had come.

DAY TEN

Saturday October 28, 1893

73

Mist

When Anna Zemeckis woke early the following morning and poked her head out of the door of Mr Crazy's cabin to see what kind of day it was, she heard the distant sound of splashing, just as he had predicted. Not far in front of the cabin the man himself was standing facing east, as naked as the day he was born, up to his knees in the milky waters of Lake Michigan as the mist filled with the light of the rising sun rolled over him.

He looked like an older Adam, but not as old as his normal appearance – bearded, hatted and great-coated – would suggest. His body was bronzed, lean and strong.

The last time Anna had seen a naked man had been in circumstances of half-forgotten horror which now suddenly surfaced as, for the first time since it had happened, her bruised mind allowed her to remember again a few terrible moments of her first visit to the Union Stock Yard.

After making the special tour of the Darke Hartz killing floors arranged for her by Marion, Anna had been introduced to Mr Gunther Darke and invited down to one of the buildings at the far end of the yard for a small 'reception', where Marion had said she would meet her later. But inside, it was something altogether different; the place was virtually derelict. She had been taken to a room containing only a few dusty drapes, chairs and sofas, some randomly placed potted plants, and over in the corner, most incongruous of all, an enormous camera on a tripod.

'Where are the other guests?' she had asked incredulously.

'They will be joining us shortly. Let me offer you a drink meanwhile,' Gunther had murmured.

Anna had wanted to leave then and there but so awed was she by Gunther Darke, that she accepted a small glass of wine, something she only ever drank, and in small quantities, on high days and holidays.

The chloral hydrate that laced her drink took effect fast and feeling dizzy, Anna had got up, asking for Marion.

'I'll take you to her,' Gunther had said, still charming. He led her from the room, but his hand and arm were strong at her back and Anna, now fired by thoughts and feelings that were no longer her own, had become reckless, and went with him almost willingly. She had no idea that he might mean her harm, or even what the nature of that harm might be. Until, that is, Gunther had turned to her in the semi-darkness of the corridor and kissed her roughly.

Anna struggled and broke free, stumbling through a half-open set of doors into a large open space. It was one of the disused killing floors, where she saw something so extraordinary that it took several seconds for her befuddled mind to register what it was. Over on the far wall was a hog wheel, and attached to it by a chain was a half-naked woman. She was laughing as she flicked a pink, ostrich-feather fan back and forth across her bare breasts with her free hand. And then there had been a flash, and in that moment, Anna had seen a camera in a corner, just like the one in the other room.

Gunther Darke's strong hands now settled vice-like on her from behind and dragged her back into the corridor. As he did so she caught sight of something else: Marion Stoiber, naked but for black silk stockings held up by garters, lying on her back on a table used by butchers to dress fresh-killed meat. Her legs were splayed and there was a naked man climbing on top of her as another, nearer, watched.

Then another flash. And with the bright light of it still burning her eyes, Gunther Darke dragged Anna back into the room he had first taken her to, pushed her back onto the cheap, velvet-covered horsehair divan and raised her dress. He pulled aside her drawers, unbuttoned his fly and placed his whole weight on her. She felt what she thought at first was his fingers or his hand pushing up between her legs, harder and harder until, she crying out with the brief strange pain of it, he entered her.

As Darke moved on top of her and she moaned with the pain and discomfort, a dazed and dis-orientated Anna thought she saw a man come into the room. He walked over to the camera in the corner and shrouded his head in black cloth. As he did so, Gunther twisted her head in the camera's direction. Then there came that same flash and a smell of burning. And then the man was gone.

As the door closed, Gunther's grasp of Anna slackened; he shuddered and stayed inside her for a few moments, then finally pulled away.

It had happened almost before she knew it, as no doubt it had happened before to other gullible girls like her, here in this same room. She pulled her dress back over her. She felt sick and sore and dirty and violated. But worst of all, even in her drugged state, she felt it was her own fault.

'I want to go home,' she remembered saying.

'And so you shall,' said Gunther. 'Then, in a few days' time, you shall come back and we shall take some more pretty photographs of you, just like your friend Miss Stoiber. Otherwise, your father will receive a photograph of his daughter you would not wish him to see.'

He manhandled Anna back outside and put her in his carriage, ordering it to take her home, without saying another word.

Back on the North Side, Anna could hardly bear to look Mrs Markulis in the eye. She had said she was feeling ill and went straight to bed, refusing to answer all Liesel's anxious questions or accept offers of help. She lay hunched up on her bed and wept for hours. All she could think about was going home to her father and the look in his eyes if he ever saw that photograph.

The memory felt now less searing, almost faded, and although the strange sight of a naked Mr Crazy taking his morning bath had prompted it, Anna had had no sense of shock or disgust. For Mr Crazy, to her, was one of nature's own and she felt safe with him.

She put the coffee on and set some sausages to fry, then went and washed herself in Mr Crazy's makeshift bathroom at the rear of the cabin. Her dress was dry, her stockings too, but the morning was cold and she pulled the plaid shawl Mr Crazy had found for her tight around her as she joined him outside the cabin for breakfast.

'You look troubled,' he said.

'Yes, something terrible happened to me . . . It all came back just now . . . but I didn't want to remember until now.'

'It's about the baby, yes?'

'You know?'

'Don't have to tell me any more than that, Anna. I can guess. It's what some men do. It's why you're scared and why you're running. I know that much.'

'I have to protect my baby, Mr Crazy.'

'Yes, you must and I'll help you. But don't despair about the past or blame yourself. Things happen . . .'

Anna shivered and huddled closer to the fire.

'Yes, things happen . . .' Mr Crazy said again, getting up from his chair. 'But it's what we make of what happens that really matters. It's about taking responsibility.'

He was thinking now of himself.

'We put things off, refuse to deal with them,' he added slowly. 'Yes, indeed we do . . .'

For Mr Crazy the flight from reality of more than twenty-two years was finally coming to an end. And for Anna too, after seven long weary weeks of running and hiding, it was time finally to come to terms with what had happened.

Each of them now sat in silence in their own separate worlds, watching one of nature's eternal battles, that between the morning mist and the rising sun. But on this occasion the mist was winning and the new day was already darkening into damp grayness.

It was then that they heard the crunch of boots approaching across the ash.

74

Rounded Up

Emily, Ben and John English reached the south end of the Lakeshore just after eight.

But a thick mist made their progress slow. Only when it cleared a little could they spread out in a line from shore to rail track and move north. If they could have whistled or called out it might have helped but this, of course, might have attracted the attention of the very people they were trying to avoid.

It was Emily who first caught the aroma of coffee and something frying.

Then voices.

For the last few yards the ground was all crunchy ash and rustling paper and by the time they hit Mr Crazy's encampment right there on the shoreline he and Anna had heard them, had stood up, and were holding staves from a barrel as their pathetic defense.

'Anna!' called out John English in relief.

As for Emily, such was the strange anticlimax of the moment, that all she could think to do was stretch out a hand and say, 'Boy, am I happy to see you! Emily Strauss, New York *World*.'

She introduced Ben and explained the story she was working on and how he was going to do sketches to illustrate it – he had already started. But more important right now was to get Anna to safety. There were others out looking for her too.

'Yes, the Meisters,' said Anna, 'but I hoped they didn't work out which way I went.'

'Now listen,' said Emily, 'there are two Pinkerton men who have been helping us. We need to get you to them. They'll help us get you safely out of Chicago and home to New York . . .'

But it was too little too late.

Mr Crazy suddenly raised a finger to his lips and they all fell silent.

'Voices,' he whispered, 'men's by the sound of it. Coming from that way . . .'

He pointed to the north.

'How far?' said Emily.

'Two, three hundred yards at most.'

'One thing, Mr Crazy,' said Emily, 'whatever happens, one of us needs to get to Mr Toulson and tell him what's happened.

'If we set up a diversion, can you slip away?'

'Where shall I find your Mr Toulson?'

'He and his colleague Rorton Van Hale will be at the OAA Convention this morning . . . Auditorium Theatre, ten o'clock. But . . .'

Mr Crazy nodded. Then he gathered them around himself and warned, 'We're going to git fast. Keep close, there's boggy ground round here. Don't deviate from the route I take . . . Anna, you first behind me and then you, Ben. Then Miss Strauss and finally Anna's beau.'

John flushed, Anna smiled.

'Let's move,' said Mr Crazy.

They were as good as running when they heard a guttural shout and then another.

John, turning, glimpsed a man running behind him.

*

405

'Straight ahead,' cried Mr Crazy, 'over there and through that gap in the fence, it'll take you to the Lakeshore rail track!'

Mr Crazy signalled to John to go on ahead of him.

John did as he was told, hurrying the others past as he held open the gate. When he looked again the old man had disappeared into the mist. The only people he could see were the Meisters running straight for them.

They turned for the tracks but saw at once that, having got through one obstacle, they now faced a very different one.

It was a line of boxcars stretching right in front of them, a locomotive just visible on the left-hand side. The boxcars loomed high in the mist, the more so because they were all painted black. On their sides in big white letters were the words *DARKE HARTZ & COMPANY*.

As they approached them figures emerged through the gap between each wagon.

'The Meisters,' murmured John. 'May God help us all.'

One man now stood apart from these, in front of the train and faced them. He was massive and wore the same curled bowler as his men. His cravat was the only color in the whole grim scene. It was the color of blood.

'Good morning, ladies and gentlemen,' he said quietly, 'I would be most grateful if you would come without a fuss.'

'Who are you?' said Emily, her voice shrill and anxious.

'That is of no importance,' said Dodek Krol, nodding at the other Meisters who had now come up behind from the Lakeshore. The black-coated men moved swiftly and silently and surrounded the group. Resistance was futile and Ben's single attempt was felled with a blow that knocked him out cold. John too was overpowered after a brief struggle.

Emily and Anna, meanwhile, had been grabbed firmly by the arms, though Emily did not stop protesting until they put a hand over her mouth.

'You watch out for this lady!' she yelled 'She's with child.'

'Put them in a boxcar and stay with them,' commanded Krol icily.

The men did so, heaving the still unconscious Ben in bodily, and throwing his camera in after him.

'Where are you taking us?' demanded Emily.

'Union Stock Yard,' growled one of the Meisters.

Ben came round. He was shivering.

'It's cold,' he said.

'That's because it's refrigerated,' said Krol from the track. 'Now get that train out of here and them along with it.'

The car door was slid shut.

There was a whistle, a burst of steam and the locomotive moved off.

Krol, however, remained standing by the side of the track. He looked angry, very angry.

If he had known the Zemeckis girl was pregnant he would never have been party to hunting her down.

'I shouldn't have handed her over,' he muttered.

He stood a while longer, thinking.

Then, his mind apparently made up, and looking a lot happier than he had for two days, he set off to do some hunting on his own account.

75
Mr Crazy No More

From his place of hiding, Mr Crazy watched the Darke Hartz boxcars roll away in the distance and the big man leave before turning back to his cabin.

He walked round the outside, running his hand down the door frame and then along the lopsided windows that he had picked up long ago when they had come bobbing up on the shoreline nearby.

But now it was time to say goodbye. He picked up his carpetbag which had been thrown out with a heap of other things from inside his cabin when the Meisters had earlier paused briefly at the campsite to search.

He opened it up and surveyed the contents. He seemed well pleased.

Then he looked at his pocket watch and said, 'One hour. Just enough time.'

He boiled some water, got his shaving soap and razor, and then found a pair of large scissors. In his makeshift bathroom behind the cabin he squinted into the broken mirror, took hold of the beard he had been growing since 1871 and, without a moment's hesitation, cut it off in large handfuls. Then, nice and slow, he shaved the rest of it right back, sharpening his razor on the strop as he did so.

'Look like a plucked turkey,' he said, surveying himself in the mirror, before he took comb and scissors to his unruly hair and cut that short and neat too.

Then he went into his cabin and pulled out a small battered suitcase pushed far back under his wooden truckle bed.

'Time to cast off the old . . . and put on the, er, old,' he said with a chuckle as he opened the case and surveyed its contents. He took out a clean set of white combinations, a pair of black woolen socks, a neatly folded, starched white shirt and stiff collar, and put them on. Then he put on a pair of old but neatly polished boots. Behind him, from a peg on the door, he took down a dark gentleman's suit. He put on the pants, which still fitted his lean frame, leaving the jacket, which was cut in a style that had long since gone out of fashion, lying on the bed.

Outside the cabin, he once more sat down and checked the contents of his carpetbag. It contained several documents, all in good order but one. This was folded and stained and looked like it had been thrown out with the garbage. And indeed it had, only ten days before. Someone had received it in the post and discarded it and Mr Crazy was very much obliged to them.

It was the two-day Agenda for the 25th National Convention of the Old America Association.

'Ten o'clock, Auditorium Theater,' he read. 'I reckon they never thought *I'd* show up again.'

He went back to his file and produced another document.

It was the OAA's Constitution and Rules of Procedure. Mr Crazy skimmed it.

'There's not many men man alive who know it better than I do,' he told himself, 'seeing as I was on the committee that wrote it.'

409

Then he stood up, glanced at his pocket watch yet again and looked over the wasteland toward the tower of the Auditorium Theater.

He considered which way to get there.

'The scenic route,' he finally decided.

Taking one last look around his campsite, he went back inside and added the finishing touches to his outfit, carefully knotting a fine blue silk tie and adding a gold pin and pulling his old, much-loved and well-brushed derby down over his neatly cut hair.

Finally, he took his jacket from the bed and as he did so looked at the name written in permanent black ink on a white tab on the inside pocket.

Isaiah Steele.

It had been sewn on, neat and square, by his wife all those years back when he first bought it.

'She never did like my middle name,' he muttered to himself, 'and nor did I. That's why she left it out.'

Just as he was about to go, Mr Crazy saw his old greatcoat lying in a heap on the floor where the Meisters had thrown it.

He picked it up and hung it back lovingly on the hook behind the door.

'Mr Crazy no more,' he muttered, closing the door softly behind him.

As he picked up his carpetbag of papers by the door, Isaiah Steele saw that the mist was clearing and the sun was shining through on to the Lake at last. He stood and contemplated that tranquil scene as he had done so many times over during the last twenty-two years.

Then, after a great, deep satisfying intake of breath to enjoy the morning air, he set off downtown, a man transformed.

76

Democracy

The eagerly awaited 25th National Convention of the Old America Association had effectively started six days previously, with the advance meeting of the Audit Committee on Sunday, October 22nd. In the absence of President Jenkin Lloyd Rhys, and then the grim announcement of the discovery of his corpse, Paul Hartz, as Senior Vice-President, had taken over as Acting President with Ambrose F. Norman, one of his close colleagues, as Convention Chairman.

The venue for the two-day Convention was the imposing Auditorium Theater on Michigan Avenue and Congress, now the most famous and spectacular venue of its kind in all the United States.

By quarter-past nine the foyer was jam-packed with delegates. It was the business day when the OAA's officers were to be elected and re-elected, including the all-important position of president, to replace the late Mr Rhys and the four vice-presidents, who were traditionally unopposed. One of those standing for a VP position was Gunther Darke.

These last elections, the key ones, were to start at quarter to twelve, which is when Gerald Toulson, and his client, Hans Darke, as Emily had rightly guessed him to be, who was a member of the OAA, arrived. They sat at the back. Rorton Van Hale was somewhere in the main body of the hall.

Darke was thoroughly bored with these kind of OAA meetings, but he had been prevailed upon by Toulson to attend, in the hope that something significant or revealing might happen which would help the investigation. Toulson knew Gunther Darke would be present and wanted to keep an eye on him.

Paul Hartz, having taken the chair for the first half of the morning session, had now handed it back to Convention Chairman, Ambrose Norman.

'We now come to the election of our four vice-presidents and that of the president himself . . .' Norman began. 'Since all these gentlemen are very well known to us I will ask their proposers to keep their remarks brief – after all, it is the Vice-Presidents we wish to hear. Since each is unopposed we will proceed after each nomination to a vote by acclamation . . .'

The Convention Committee had organized matters so that Gunther Darke, though not the most senior member standing, should speak last. He was known to be a rousing speaker and it was hoped this would appeal to the younger members.

Toulson settled back ready to be bored and he was not disappointed until the shout of acclamation confirming the third Vice-President's election died away and the Chairman invited Mr Gunther Darke's proposer to speak. There was a buzz of excitement. Darke's reputation as the coming man preceded him and most people expected that if he kept his nose clean for a couple of years then he would, as his father-in-law intended, succeed to the presidency of the OAA, a perfect place from which to launch his career into national Republican politics.

Norman began with the customary overblown introduction of Darke's proposer.

'He is a young member, a highly skilled professional and a delegate from this year's host city, Chicago!' he declaimed.

This provoked a partisan cheer from Chicagoan and Illinois delegates as well as many locals there as observers. 'Yet he is new to this great city. Please, therefore, give a warm welcome to Dr Morgan Eels, who I am happy to say will in three days' time assume the important role of Medical Superintendent of Cook County Insane Asylum.'

Eels rose to loud applause, fresh from the triumph of his lecture at Dunning five evenings previously. He outlined Gunther Darke meteoric career in business and his suitability for high office and commended Mr Darke's generous funding of his valuable research at Dunning. He presented his case with the strange, focused zeal that audiences found at once compelling and repulsive and sat down on time.

Gunther, having been seconded, then rose to loud applause and made the kind of brief, inspirational speech such occasions demand. He reiterated his belief that immigration into the United States should now be more rigorously controlled, thanked his proposer, to whose medical work he said he was fully committed and, finally, to the expectant audience's delight, he thanked his father-in-law, seated to his left, whom he wished every success for the future.

The audience liked what they heard, clapped and stamped and began making their shouted acclamation in favor of Gunther's election even before Ambrose Norman had formally proceeded to it.

Throughout the proceedings Toulson observed that Hans Darke sat stony-faced. He expressed no emotion at all even when Gunther's name was mentioned or when his popularity with delegates was clearly demonstrated. Toulson decided he looked weary and resigned, as if the old world in which he felt comfortable had given way to the new and he did not like it very much.

'Let's go,' Hans Darke said impulsively as Norman moved proceedings toward the vote by acclamation. 'Watching Gunther's election is bad enough, but Paul's going to be President now as well . . . ! Let's get the hell out of here.'

They rose from their seats and were about to move along the row and out to the aisle when a commanding voice that resonated throughout the hall, called out, 'Mr Chairman, point of order!'

Darke, out of courtesy to those around him, sat down again, as did Toulson.

The audience, anxious now to get to the election of the president, first groaned and then shouted to the Chair not to allow any points at this juncture.

There were always one or two time-wasters who interrupted proceedings on such occasions but Norman was a practiced hand at dealing with them.

'I think, sir,' he said, 'that there can be no point to make, not until we have completed the vote on Mr Darke's election.'

'I disagree,' said the booming voice from the floor, 'and in any case all points of order must be heard at the moment they are raised, for how else are we, the delegates, to control the chair?'

This bold statement raised some appreciative cheers and many members, unable to see the speaker, half rose from their seats to get a better view. They sat down quickly. The speaker was dressed in old-fashioned clothes and looked, as they feared, like an old-timer whose day was over but who still liked the sound of his own voice.

414

'Sit down!' several delegates shouted.

Ambrose Norman, unable to make the speaker sit, glanced at Hartz for guidance. Hartz shrugged and nodded, upon which Norman, with a studied resignation that won the audience's approval, responded, 'You are absolutely right, sir, and I stand corrected. Make your point.'

'Thank you,' responded the speaker from the floor. 'I believe I am right in saying, Mr Chairman, that with respect to the election of vice-presidents, once they have spoken, it is the right of delegates to speak in opposition to their nomination. *Am* I right?'

Ambrose Norman frowned.

He was a past master at running meetings; he knew the rules inside out and he knew the speaker was right, but he understood at once the implication of what he said. He had no doubt that Gunther Darke's election would be ratified but he did not wish things to slow down or end on a sour note.

'You are right, sir, but that rule applies only when there is a rival candidate. In this case, where an election is unopposed, the matter is a formality and it does not serve any useful purpose to impede the business of the day.'

'Hear, hear!' came the cry from all over the floor and more shouts of, 'Sit down!'

The speaker was unperturbed and stayed firmly on his feet.

'Mr Chairman, that may be the common practice but it isn't the rule. The fact is that, though Mr Darke is unopposed, we do, through our right to abstain, have the means not to elect him. And I, for one, would like to explain, briefly, why I intend to abstain in this particular case.'

Norman decided the time had come to be categorical.

'Well, sir, the chair has final discretion. No doubt Mr Darke will listen to anything you have to say to him after the meeting is over. Meanwhile, I must ask you to sit down.'

'You may have final discretion, Mr Chairman, but not on this point you don't . . .'

'You have had your say, sir,' interrupted Norman very firmly, 'but now we really must proceed to a vote . . .'

'Mr Chairman, sir,' the voice from the floor now boomed out like an Old Testament prophet, 'you do not have that right and I have here, in the form of the OAA's constitution, the paper to prove it!'

It was at this moment that Hans Darke, who was sitting so far back he had been unable to see the speaker, stood up and took a good look at him.

'Well, I'm damned!' he said out loud, 'If it isn't Mr Isaiah Steele, come back from the dead!'

Hans Darke now called out in a voice every bit as loud as Isaiah's, 'Mr Chairman, point of order!'

Another loud groan reverberated around the auditorium, until the delegates, turning to see who was conspiring to slow things up still more saw that it was none other than Hans Darke. They fell silent immediately.

Darke was very well known in Chicago and throughout the state of Illinois, not least because he was a man of considerable dignity and few words, who only spoke when he had something worth saying.

The spectacle of one Darke rising on a point of order concerning another in the form of his youngest son, not to mention his detested business partner being on the platform as prospective president, sent a wave of excited chatter through the audience.

'Mr Chairman, since it was I who chaired the committee that originally drafted the Constitution of the OAA, I think I may speak with some authority. Since Mr Isaiah Steele, the speaker who has raised the point, served on that same committee and like me is a Founding Member of the OAA, I think he does so too. Believe me, sir, he has the right to speak and under the rules you must let him.'

Ambrose Norman glanced again at Hartz who simply looked furious. Gunther looked as incandescent as one of the modern electric lights that lit the hall above their heads.

'In that case, the gentleman may have two minutes,' said Norman dismissively, 'and please do us the courtesy of stating your name and delegation.'

'I'm with the Chicago Lakeshore delegation, total membership one – myself. Isaiah Steele is my name but there are some in the room who'll know me better as Mr Crazy, the man with the papers to prove things.'

This was indeed the case and Mr Crazy's announcement caused a sudden buzz right through the hall.

Hans Darke laughed and whispered to Toulson, 'Gunther and Paul are in for a bumpy ride. You don't have to worry about the health of democracy when Mr Crazy is on his feet.'

'I won't take long,' said Mr Crazy, 'and I hope when I've finished saying what I have to say that this Convention will abstain from electing Mr Gunther Darke as a vice-president.'

'Mr Chairman, sir, I have three questions, well four as a matter of fact, but the last one has nothing to do with Mr Darke. Let's start with Mr Darke's proposer, Dr Eels, whose work he said just now he supports.'

Mr Crazy paused, waiting for Gunther Darke's acknowledgment that he *had* indeed said that.

Gunther was forced to affirm he had with a nod of his head.

'Is Mr Darke aware, I wonder, that Dr Eels is conducting dangerous brain experiments on helpless patients at the Dunning Insane Asylum? I have the papers to prove it!'

This provoked stunned silence before a shocked Dr Eels immediately rose to his feet.

'I have the floor, sir,' thundered Isaiah Steele, 'and you've had your turn.'

Eels sat down, ashen-faced.

'Let's turn to another matter, the moral probity of Mr Gunther Darke, who we were about to elect as one of our vice-presidents. Far be it for me to question another man's morals. None of us is guiltless on that score. But when a man stands for public office he should expect some public scrutiny. Question Number Two: Are the members of the Audit Committee of which Darke is a member aware that the funds which finance certain of the OAA's activities under the heading of 'Anonymous Donations', in fact come from illegal activities of a profane and Godless nature?'

Again he paused and again there was stunned silence.

Various senior members of the OAA on the stage shifted in their seats uncomfortably. Hartz had ceased looking patrician. He looked like a man who would kill if he could.

'Ladies and gentlemen,' continued Mr Crazy, raising his carpetbag in the air, 'what do you think that I have here in this bag?'

'*The papers to prove it*!' thundered the audience, now relishing the spectacle.

'Now to my last question for Mr Darke and his friends up there on the platform. Maybe he noticed a sad little paragraph in today's *Tribune* announcing the death of a Miss Marion Stoiber, a stenographer and part-time model – for lewd photographs, I believe – who, yesterday afternoon at 2.15, inexplicably became caught in the machinery of the Ferris Wheel on the Midway Plaisance. Since Mr Darke's photograph was found inside this unfortunate lady's purse, may we take it that he has or soon will be contacting the Chicago Police Department to help them with their inquiries?'

'Have you the papers to prove it, Mr Crazy?' someone shouted.

'You bet I have,' roared Mr Crazy, pointing an accusatory finger at Gunther Darke and then, as it seemed, to all those on the platform.

The audience was on the point of uproar but Mr Crazy, with total command, stilled them once more and in a much quieter voice said, 'and finally, I have a very simple request. If there is a Mr Gerald Toulson present, would he please make himself known to me?'

With the gathered delegates now in total uproar, waving their order papers and shouting, Mr Crazy quietly gathered up his carpetbag and moved out into the aisle.

He felt a hand at his elbow.

'Name's Van Hale, I'm a Pinkerton man. I'll take you to Mr Toulson. There's going to be trouble and some of it will be directed your way.'

Van Hale ushered Mr Crazy up through the crowd toward the back of the auditorium, where Toulson and Hans Darke were already waiting.

Meanwhile, Ambrose Norman, having conferred

with the vice-presidential nominees, was trying to restore order.

'Fellow delegates, fellow *delegates* . . . I have an announcement. Mr Gunther Darke has withdrawn his nomination for vice-president and . . . gentlemen . . .'

As the uproar got worse, Van Hale and Mr Crazy made their way to join Toulson. Mr Crazy did not waste words.

'Mr Toulson, they've taken Anna Zemeckis and her beau along with Miss Strauss and that other gentleman . . .

'Who?'

'The Meisters.'

'Where to?'

'The Union Stock Yard.'

'When?'

'Nine o'clock this morning, from the Lakeshore.'

Toulson didn't need to hear any more, for as Mr Crazy spoke he noticed Gunther Darke leaving the platform in a hurry.

He turned to Hans Darke.

'We need to talk,' said Toulson urgently. 'It looks to me like our investigation into Chicago's pornography trade is reaching a climax. Can you get this gentleman away somewhere safe . . . ?'

Darke nodded grimly.

'I'll take him to my house and wait for you there.'

'We'll need backup at the Stock Yard and . . .'

Hans Darke nodded. 'My son Wolfgang is there right now and I'll call him and tell him to help you in any way he can when you arrive. And please . . . try to keep my sons apart. There's no love lost between them and there'll be even less after what's come out today.'

They left the building as quickly as they could, pushing through the crowds of shocked delegates.

Up on the stage, Paul Hartz's normal equanimity had deserted him completely. There had been a brief heated argument with Gunther before he had left for the Stock Yard and now Hartz was trying to sort out the procedural mess he was left with.

He turned to an aide: 'I want to talk with Dodek Krol,' he said. 'Find him.'

Which was not difficult since Mr Krol was waiting, ever watchful, in the wings.

Their conversation was brief and murderous.

'It's time for that final commission, I think,' said Krol.

'You'll deal with him?'

'Yes,' said Krol. He didn't tell me Miss Zemeckis was with child but nor did you.'

'I didn't know,' said Hartz.

For once, to his eternal credit, Paul Hartz looked concerned about someone else and said two words which rarely pass a politician's lips: 'I'm sorry.'

'So will he be,' said Krol.

As Krol left, Hartz sought out the one still and silent figure left sitting in the auditorium – Dr Morgan Eels. He was pale and frightened and he had reason to be.

'Eels, you're through,' said Hartz pitilessly. 'Through with the OAA and through with the Insane Asylum. If you're not out of Dunning and this city within twenty-four hours I'll file proceedings against you myself.'

'But, sir, I . . .'

'But nothing, Eels. You're finished.'

'But Mr Hartz, we've made a great medical discovery . . .'

Hartz shook his head.

'Dr Eels, it is my intention that not a single medical institution in all of America will ever give you a position again.'

Eels's mouth opened but no words came out. He was overcome by fear and rage, humiliation and despair. As he turned away into the crowd he looked a nearly broken man, yet still he made one last attempt to curry favor.

'Mr Hartz, sir . . . I . . .'

'Get out of my sight,' roared Hartz.

Moments later Paul Hartz was his familiar, smooth, calculating self again as he dealt with the clamoring pressmen who now surrounded him. He was aware that what had happened was personally damaging, as well as boding ill for the value of Darke Hartz stock, if he did not take control of the situation quickly.

His public dismissal of Eels had been part of his strategy, and now, gathering the pressmen about him he announced that he was indebted to that great Chicagoan Mr Isaiah Steele for his courageous intervention in the proceedings, both himself personally and the OAA having been as badly duped by Eels as everybody else.

'But what about your son-in-law, Gunther Darke, Mr Hartz! Isn't he implicated as well?'

Hartz affected both shock and surprise.

'I am not aware of any actual proof being found to show that that is the case, gentlemen. No . . . Dr Eels is the man you should be gunning for, not Gunther Darke, who so far as I am concerned is as hard-working and civic-minded a Chicagoan as you'll ever find. I won't entertain a word said against him until I have seen the evidence with my own eyes. Meanwhile, if any of you gentlemen should write anything libelous, trust me, you will be hearing from my lawyers as well as his.'

He smiled, but his eyes were cold.

'But what about the presidency of the OAA? Are you still standing, Mr Hartz?'

'Certainly,' he said coolly. 'In any case, I am Acting President. Who better to clean up the OAA than me? Eh?'

'Would you care to comment on the death of Mr Jenkin Lloyd Rhys?'

'Sure,' said Hartz, 'he was a very great man. I'll be leading the mourners from the OAA when they bury him in New York.'

'It's a bad day for the OAA, isn't it, sir?'

Hartz looked his most magisterial and contrite.

'Yes, it is,' he said disarmingly. 'But the way I see it is that what's happened here makes it a great day for democracy and we have Mr Steele to thank for that. Now, if you don't mind, gentlemen, I have work to do . . .'

77

Covert

CHICAGO Saturday October 28, 1893　　　　1.09 PM

Toulson and Van Hale approached the Union Stock Yard from the south, through a little-used workers' entrance at Halsted and 47th, to avoid the danger of being seen. After Mr Crazy's unexpected intervention at the OAA meeting and Gunther's hasty exit they were certain that Gunther and the Meisters he controlled would be expecting visitors.

From here they made their way to Packer's Avenue, where a broad, stocky figure emerged from a doorway.

Van Hale went for his revolver but Toulson stayed his hand.

'It's alright, it's Wolfgang Darke.'

They shook hands as Wolfgang pulled them into the shadows. 'My father telephoned, he said you might need backup. Gunther's men have been going in and out of the old Whetton building for the last half hour and Gunther himself arrived in a hurry about ten minutes ago. He'll know I'm here because he will have seen my carriage and he can hear the Darke Hartz hog wheel . . .'

He cocked his head to one side.

Rumpety thump rumpety thump rumpety . . .

'Hear it?'

They nodded.

'That'll stop in less than an hour, at 2 p.m. sharp, and Gunther will be waiting for it to do so because he'll know that my men and I will be leaving pretty soon after, say within twenty minutes. He'll see my workers walk back down to the main gate to make their way home.

'There's a couple of boys get left to hose down the killing floor. They're good lads and will do what I tell them. I'll send them off in my carriage to keep them out of harm's way and to make Gunther think I've gone too.

'There's no love lost between my men and Gunther's. He tends to employ low types but he has a small coterie of skilled ones who are Meisters – but of the worst kind. Most have been in trouble with the law and are tough, violent types so be careful. Many of my own men have suffered intimidation and bullying at their hands so there's not a man among them who wouldn't welcome a chance to stand his ground against Gunther's men and see them gone from the Yard.'

He paused to be sure they understood. Both men nodded grimly.

Van Hale took out his gun. Wolfgang seemed unimpressed.

'These men use a knife in preference to a gun and they're highly skilled in its use, not just with meat. Some are very effective fighters and one or two of them pride themselves on throwing knives to deadly effect.'

'We'll see about that!' said Van Hale.

'Gunther won't do anything till the yard is clear. It'll take a good fifteen minutes after you see my men leave the yard for them to get back in, unseen, in ones and twos and report back here, so try and do nothing before then: say around 2.45.'

'Understood,' said Toulson. He was getting more impressed with Wolfgang by the moment.

'I've put one of my men on watch in a warehouse overlooking the Whetton building to which I have access. Now, follow me and I'll show you a way of getting up to the northwest side of the Yard without being seen.'

With Wolfgang in front they proceeded cautiously down alleys, around the sides of unused buildings and then over causeways that he had known since he was a boy. They were heading for the part of the Yard bounded by Bubbly Creek. Only when the vista ahead opened up, as buildings gave way to railway tracks, did Wolfgang slow.

'They have a lookout just around the corner of this warehouse,' he whispered, 'so we'll use a side entrance. My man's hidden on the top floor.'

They crept in, catching sight of Gunther's man through a window at the far end of a corridor. He was a typical Meister: clean-shaven, stolid and well built, dark-suited and wearing the familiar bowler. Fortunately, he was looking the wrong way.

Five floors up they found Wolfgang's man keeping low at a window overlooking the Whetton Building across the railway lines, the same building Toulson and Ben had visited the day before.

The man stood up: he was stocky, gray-haired, with a lined face and clear blue eyes.

'Alfred's worked for my father from the first day he arrived in Chicago,' said Wolfgang. 'This is Mr Toulson, Alfred. He's the man in charge of the investigation.'

Toulson shook his hand.

'Alfred Spohr,' he said formally, his German accent still quite strong. 'I show you . . . but not too near the windows, please, or they see your movement.'

The room they were in covered virtually the whole of the fifth floor of the building and gave them views right round the Stock Yard.

It was the north part they were interested in. Beyond the main Whetton building was a network of rail tracks, a few curving away northward, but the bulk of them entering the yard from the east. Most of them circled round the back of the Whetton building and then disappeared on southward. But a couple of tracks effectively turned the Whetton building into an island, turning back and passing immediately beneath the warehouse they were in.

They could see innumerable storehouses, repair

shops, small reservoirs and coal tips. Beyond the more distant lines to the west and north was the South Fork of the Chicago River, and over to the east the sluggish gray channel of water that was Bubbly Creek.

'What's been going on?' asked Toulson.

'There's six men plus Mr Gunther in the main building,' said Spohr, 'and three lookouts, one below us here.'

'We saw him,' said Toulson.

'So you will not be able to get from this warehouse across the lines to the Whetton Building without being seen. Yes?'

They nodded.

'Four of these men are senior Meisters well known to us. Bad types. I taught butchery to several of them and there's not one I'd want my mother to meet. A new generation. Different values. Godless, nasty fellows. Two more of the men are in that storehouse . . .'

Spohr pointed out a low building on the west side of the site. It was small and single-storied, of dirty yellow brick and its windows were barred. There appeared to be only one door.

'What's going on in there?'

'I saw them manhandle four people inside; two men and two women. Their hands were tied. One of the women was shouting and struggling a lot.'

'Emily Strauss,' said Toulson without expression. 'And the other?'

'She didn't seem well, they were dragging her and she didn't struggle.'

'And two men? Young?'

Spohr nodded.

'Well, at least we know where they are,' murmured Van Hale.

'Anything else been happening?' asked Toulson.

'They've been shunting trains about, sir,' continued Spohr. The Darke Hartz one with the refrigerated cars that's standing north of the Whetton building was loaded with meat much earlier this morning. It should have left the Yard by now. Instead it's been shunted up alongside the Whetton building. But it ain't for meat, that's for sure.'

'How do you know?'

'The killing floors this end of the Yard aren't in use. They'll be loading something else.'

'Where's the driver?'

'He's in his locomotive below us now, the train with the two hoppers.'

'Is he known to you?'

'He is. He does what they tell him, gets well paid and keeps shtum.'

'What normally goes into the hoppers?'

Spohr shrugged, 'Coal mainly.'

'I must go,' said Wolfgang Darke. 'For the moment you're on your own, gentlemen. Whatever you do, don't move off before my men have had time to get back into the Yard unseen. Not before a quarter to three.'

Toulson and Van Hale nodded.

'What happens if that train takes off?' asked Toulson. 'Can your people stop it?'

'Depends which route it takes. Might be difficult. I'll see if one of my men knows what track it will be using.'

'Let's hope it doesn't come to that,' said Toulson. 'Meanwhile . . .'

He dug into a pocket and produced a silver whistle. 'When we're ready this end, Mr Darke, or if we need you, I'll use this. It's simple, but effective. So run like hell – in our direction. Do *you* carry a revolver?'

Wolfgang pulled aside his jacket and pointed to a leather sheath on his belt.

'As I said before, butchers prefer knives.' He indicated his own with a grim smile. 'Spohr, I want you back with me before two.'

Then he turned and was gone.

'A good man,' murmured Van Hale, as the three of them settled down to watch the Whetton building.

'You can rely on Mr Wolfgang as you can on his father Mr Hans,' said Spohr. 'But the blood went bad with Mr Gunther.'

78

Prisoners

CHICAGO Saturday October 28, 1893   1.34 PM

Emily Strauss was cold and hungry and did not appreciate being made to sit on a dirty, unswept floor. Her hands and feet were still tied. The windows of the room they were in were barred and the panes broken, the walls covered in a whitewash that had long since begun to peel and flake.

Anna and John were sitting shoulder-to-shoulder against the wall opposite, talking in low voices, Anna having told Emily as much of her story as she could remember. Ben lay on the ground, still in a dazed state. His head throbbed from being knocked out and Emily had persuaded him to try to rest. He moaned now and then and she had been worrying a great deal about him until, to her surprise, when she glanced in his direction, she noticed his eyes were open and that he winked at her.

He was, it seemed, now playacting. The Meisters had taken his camera from him when they'd loaded them in the boxcar and one of them on a chair near Emily was examining it. The other now stood guarding the entrance to the storehouse, watching and waiting, occasionally checking the revolver at his hip.

They both had refused to respond to Emily's constant barrage of complaints and questions, remaining as stiff and silent mannequins. Except they were a sight more intimidating than anything that ever stood in the window of Marshall Field.

'When are you going to let us go?' Emily called out again, out of sheer boredom. She expected no response.

But, as if in reply, there came a gruff shout from the yard outside and the Meister near it opened the door.

Emily strained to listen and was just able to hear what was said.

'Get the three of 'em ready to move. The hog wheel's just stopped and the moment the Darke Hartz workers are clear of the site we're finishing loading and getting out of here. The Latvian girl stays, orders of Mr Darke. You'll get instructions about her later.'

Emily looked at Anna, hoping she had not heard. Then at Ben, who obviously had. He winked and then moaned again. If he never made it as a photographer maybe he would as an actor.

79

Proof Positive

The moment Gerald Toulson heard the hog wheel stop he and Van Hale readied themselves for action. Spohr had already left to rejoin Wolfgang's party.

'Wolfgang's men are leaving,' said Van Hale from the other side of the room, which had a better vantage point from which to see the Darke Hartz building.

The men made their way to Exchange Avenue in a group, turning left and heading for the main gate. Spohr was among them and they were laughing and talking loudly. Minutes later a carriage went past, the curtains drawn so nobody could see in.

Shortly afterward, the Whetton building turned into a hive of disciplined activity. Doors opened and Gunther's men emerged from different directions. The doors of the eight refrigerated boxcars were slid open. Inside were sides of dressed hogs hanging in neat rows from a central running rail. And there were crates on the floor too, filled, presumably, with dressed meat and ice.

Toulson and Van Hale watched as three Meisters came and went with what looked like parcels wrapped in black oilcloth. Then Gunther Darke himself emerged from the Whetton building.

He was stripped down to his shirtsleeves, youthful and muscular, he stood a good four inches taller than the men around him. Even from such a distance he commanded attention.

'Well, well, well . . .' murmured Toulson. 'I think we can guess what Mr Darke and his men are loading on to the train, all nicely protected against the cold and damp.'

'Pornographic pictures,' said Van Hale.

'Exactly,' said Toulson. 'The last place anyone would look for them.'

The loading continued.

'Their entire stock by the look of things.'

He watched closely as the Meisters put the parcels onto the floor of the boxcars and then climbed in, out of sight, moving the parcels to either end of the cars. Then came what sounded like knocking and banging and crates being moved around inside.

'False panels,' said Toulson. It was a statement not a question. 'And they're positioning the crates of dressed meat inside as cover.

'Proof positive?' observed his friend, pulling back from the window.

'Not quite,' responded Toulson. 'We need to be sure what's inside those parcels. We need to see it with our own eyes. But yes, looks like we were right: Gunther Darke's meat distribution business is a cover for his very profitable pornography trade. It offers a perfect distribution network across the United States, which avoids the US Postal Service and Mr Comstock's all-seeing eye.'

The two men looked triumphant.

But not for long.

'Look!' said Toulson, 'Something's happening by the storehouse. They're being moved . . .'

Below them, they saw Emily, John and a beat-up looking Ben, their hands tied, suddenly being hustled out of the storehouse straight toward one of the box-cars. They were unceremoniously pushed inside. Ben, so unsteady on his feet, was practically thrown in.

One of the Meisters then jumped up inside with them, and closed the doors, leaving his colleague to guard the outside of the car.

'But where's the Zemeckis girl?' said Van Hale, as the storehouse door was closed again – from the inside.

'That means she's still in there and they've separated her from the others,' murmured Toulson. 'Not good, not good at all. We're going to have to try to get her out, but . . .'

Van Hale moved across the room to another vantage point.

'They've finished loading the train. They're beginning to close the doors . . .'

'It has no engine or driver yet,' said Toulson, indicating the two hoppers immediately below them, 'they've got work to do.'

He pointed below the building they were in, to which Gunther's men had now shifted their attention. They began wheeling trolleys over to it containing photographic equipment, bottles of chemicals, box after box of glass plates, and all the things that Toulson and the others had seen the day before.

They did not waste time, throwing the equipment into the hoppers hurriedly and not worrying if it got damaged. Once this job was done the locomotive moved off and the hoppers were shunted round the tracks in a circle and coupled to the rear of the line of Darke Hartz cars. That done, the locomotive was uncoupled again and began its circuitous route back to the front of the Darke Hartz boxcars.

'We're going to have to do something fast if we're

going to get Miss Strauss and her friends off that train before it moves out,' said Van Hale. 'We can't just sit here and watch the evidence and three good people disappear to God knows where . . .'

The two men looked at each other.

They had been in worse situations but rarely one that needed such urgent action against such overwhelming odds.

'I hope Mr Darke is paying good money,' said Van Hale laconically.

'*Which* Mr Darke?' said Toulson, taking out his revolver.

'Hans Darke, our employer, on whose behalf it looks as though I'm about to get killed.'

They took the stairs down to the ground floor two at a time, emerging at the entrance as the engine approached their building once more on its route to the front of the train.

'Get on!' commanded Toulson.

'Wha . . . ?'

Van Hale felt himself shoved toward the engine's foot plate as it passed by, the driver in full view but with his head leaning out the window on the other side as the locomotive took a sharp curve to the left.

'Get on for Chrissake,' hissed Toulson.

Van Hale jumped on the footplate, unseen by the driver and shielded by the bulk of the engine from the men over by the Whetton Building.

'And you . . . ?' he called urgently back at Toulson.

'The Zemeckis girl. Got to get her. Create a diversion in a few minutes . . .

Van Hale mouthed an ironic 'Thanks!', moved into the cabin and, keeping low, stuck a revolver in the small of the driver's back.

'Just keep on going nice and steady,' he said.

Toulson retreated back into the Whetton building fast, knowing that with the locomotive gone he could easily be seen by anyone on the other side of the tracks.

He found another way out on the far side, opposite a store of some kind. Darting across to it and round the bottom end of the building, he crept back toward the tracks and the open space they had been watching.

The storehouse was much nearer now, no more than fifty yards to his left. Straight ahead, past the back of the Whetton Building, was the boxcar into which Emily and the others had been manhandled. It was no more than a hundred yards ahead of Toulson. Beyond it was Bubbly Creek.

Nearer, to his left across the tracks, a couple of men stood smoking outside the Whetton Building. If he made a dash for the storehouse he would be in full view of them, so he waited, hoping that Van Hale would be able to create a diversion.

It did not work out that way. There came a sudden grinding of wheels on rail tracks, the sound of a locomotive being coupled to a car and before Toulson knew it the train across the tracks jolted and began moving forward.

As it did so he heard the unmistakable sound of a pistol shot; and after that a shout, a curse and then the sounds of a struggle.

The two Meisters at the rear of the Whetton Building drew their knives and looked about them, as uncertain as Toulson was as to where the sounds were coming from.

'What the hell was that?' said one of the men.

Toulson drew out his gun and waited.

He had no idea himself. But one thing was for certain: from behind the Whetton building the long line of freight cars was now moving out and taking the evidence and the hostages away.

80

Old Friends

If Hans Darke had been able to chose who in the whole world he would like to break to him the extraordinary and alarming news that he was going to be a grandfather and that the mother was a girl he had never met who was on the run, it would have been his old friend Isaiah Steele, whom all of Chicago knew now only as Mr Crazy.

The two went back a long way.

In the late 1850s, Steele had been a junior partner in a firm of lawyers specializing in real estate that prepared the conveyancing documents on Darke's first property.

They got on well and shared some times together when Darke could get away from butchery and Steele from the burgeoning world of Chicagoan real estate. Their common dream was not to make money, though both wanted that, but to be part of the adventure that was turning Chicago into the greatest new city in America, maybe in the world.

Then, on the evening of October 8th, 1871, the tolling of the Courthouse bell in the city center had warned that a serious fire had broken out. Steele was out of town looking at real estate in Kankakee. By the time was able to make his way back to Chicago the city was all but destroyed and his home, on the Near West Side, as well as his wife and child had all been lost in the flames like hundreds of others.

The first friend he turned to was Hans Darke, whose home on the North Side was beyond the conflagration, and stayed with him for three weeks, a man in grief.

Then, one day, he walked out the front door with just the small suitcase which was his only possession and began living the vagrant life that transformed him into Mr Crazy. He returned to Darke's house one last time to leave a package of documents for him. They were accompanied by a short letter begging Hans to agree to accept the enclosed Power of Attorney over Steele's affairs, along with the titles not only to the property he had lost, and the sites it occupied, but other blocks of real estate that Darke never even knew Steele had acquired. In addition were instructions about funds in an East Coast bank and the request that Darke 'at my expense, acquire additional real estate as herein indicated. Sell nothing except to buy more and better, for I believe in this city. It will grow again. If I never come back, then you will find among these papers an assignment of all my estate for you to execute in some charitable way for the good of women and children who may need the help I was unable to give my own, for which I pray God forgive me, for I never can myself.'

Later Hans came to hear of Chicago's best-loved eccentric. Inevitably, their paths occasionally crossed downtown, but the man who was now Mr Crazy never acknowledged the one person he trusted most in the world and Hans Darke, respecting his wish, pretended he did not know him either.

Mr Crazy never found it in his heart to leave the city he loved so much permanently. So when, as Isaiah Steele, he rose to speak at the OAA Convention, wearing the same suit of clothes Hans Darke had seen him last walk out of his door in, no-one was more delighted than he. His old friend had returned at last from his self-imposed exile and had resumed his true identity.

Now, seated comfortably in Hans Darke's new house on Astor Street, a glass of lemonade in each of their hands, for both were teetotal, and beaming at each other from the pleasures of rediscovered friendship, Hans said, 'Isaiah, you are a very rich man.'

'You mean *we* are rich men, for the firm of Darke Hartz is one of the biggest in the world.'

'And your real estate holdings are among the largest in Chicago.'

'That's as maybe,' said Isaiah, 'but we can talk of that later and how you must be compensated . . .'

Hans shook his head vigorously.

Isaiah nodded his head just as vigorously.

They both laughed and then Isaiah turned serious.

'Now listen, I've something important to tell you, but first . . .'

Hans Darke edged closer in his chair.

'. . . you must tell me about your two sons, Gunther and Wolfgang.'

And so Hans Darke did, from beginning to end, talking as he had not been able to do with anyone since his wife had died in 1880. The worst he had to say, and the thing which gave him most pain, was the hurt Gunther had done to Christiane Hartz, as she had then been, and by association to his own brother, Wolfgang.

'Two biblical brothers come to mind,' said Isaiah Steele, when Darke's tale was done.'

'They do, they do,' Hans said, shaking his head. 'But now . . . what was the important thing you have to say.'

Isaiah looked him straight in the eye.

'There's no other way of telling you but straight: Hans, you are to be a grandfather, and . . .'

Darke leapt to his feet in a state of shock and astonishment.

Then he sat down and stared at his friend in disbelief.

'But . . . who's the mother? In fact who's the father!? I know Christiane's not pregnant and Wolfgang does not play that kind of game with women . . .'

He stood up again. 'Are you sure?'

'I'm sure.'

'And I suppose you're going to tell me you've the papers to prove it?'

'In a manner of speaking Hans, yes. But this is no laughing matter and the girl's in some considerable danger.'

'So, it's Gunther?' said Hans Darke in a resigned voice.

'Yes. Now listen . . .'

Hans Darke was scarcely able to believe what he heard. His face registering first shock and then extreme distress, he paused in silence for a moment, then stood up and moved toward the door, 'I must go to the Yard at once.'

Isaiah got up and barred his way.

'No, Hans. I haven't spent all these years out on the Lakeshore without thinking about a lot of things and getting them right in my mind. You're about to retire, and, in a manner of speaking, so am I. You have to let go of things and trust a new generation to sort things out without the help of us old men. We did it, and they can too.

'Your two sons must resolve things between themselves, today over in the Yard, which is as it should be. Anna Zemeckis, who has carried your grandchild these four months through every difficulty and danger imaginable, and a lot more you'll never know, will continue to do so until that child is born. She's a fine young woman and she's not going to let her child, her father or you down. I don't know which of your sons is Cain and which is Abel but I have a pretty good idea and if my memory serves, and it's a while since I read Genesis, one survived and one didn't.

'Never did much like the way that story ended but that was God's decision, not man's. We'd better start praying that the outcome is a different one this time but I don't think matters will be improved by you heading off for the Yard in your carriage.

'Anna's found a few friends this last week or two, including, so far as I can judge, Mr Toulson, who packs a stronger punch and shoots a lot more accurately than you probably do these days. So sit tight and let's hope it's the right folks come back from the Yard through your front door.'

'But I can't just sit here. I want to *do* something.'

'Sure, you can do something. Use that new fangled gadget you so proudly showed me a while back. Send a telegraph to Mr Zemeckis in New York.'

'But what can I tell him?'

440

'That his daughter's been found and she's all right.'

'But we don't know if she is.'

'*He* doesn't know that, does he? Give him some hope and keep on praying.'

'Well, I suppose . . . I *could* . . .'

'And another thing,' said Isaiah, putting down his tumbler of lemonade with a sudden look of feigned distaste. 'How long have you been teetotal?'

'Since my wife died, thirteen years ago.'

'Well, I haven't touched a drop since the Fire. Reckon it's time for something stronger, just for medicinal purposes, to steady the nerves. Agreed?'

A slow grin lighted Hans Darke's face.

'Agreed.'

81

Attack

CHICAGO Saturday October 28, 1893   2.39 PM

Emily Strauss had never hurt anyone in a premeditated way before. Now, with her hands tied behind her back and certain she was about to be killed, she intended to have a go at the Meister who had pushed them into the boxcar and had climbed in after them.

After what felt like a long time the car had suddenly jolted back and forth, a sure sign the locomotive was being coupled up at the front of the train in preparation for departure. She reckoned if they were going to make a bid for freedom this was the moment, before the train gathered speed and they were taken out of Chicago and away from any hope of help.

So did Ben and John. The first winked at her, the other nodded.

The Meister had ordered them to keep quiet, fearing noise would attract unwanted attention.

'If you don't let us go,' Emily snarled at him suddenly, 'I'm going to scream so loud this car will fall apart.'

He was the taciturn kind of man with shiny jowls and humorless eyes who does not like women who talk. Even less women who threaten.

He got up, pulled his knife and headed her way.

He kept clear of John but not Ben, who he must have believed was still groggy, but who now stuck a boot hard into his shin and toppled him. The Meister grunted in pain and fell on his knees in front of Emily.

She didn't hesitate, lunging forward to head-butt his nose so hard that it crunched and broke and blood flowed copiously.

As the Meister grunted in anger and pain and lunged forward at Emily with his knife, John heaved himself upright and kicked him hard on the side of the head.

The Meister's knife went flying as he slewed over on his side, but his right hand went instinctively for the gun under his jacket. Cursing and roaring like a wounded animal, he pulled his gun clear and aimed wildly in John's direction, half-blinded as he was by his own blood and disorientated by the pain.

John kicked out at him hard again.

The gun went off and there was a scream of pain and rage. The Meister had literally shot himself in the foot.

Taking advantage of this, Emily rammed her heel in his face. John threw himself across the man's legs, as Ben, managing to rise into a standing position despite his tied hands, stamped hard on the Meister's privates.

There was a brief agonized squeal and then sudden silence as the man rolled onto his side, lost hold of his gun, one hand on his nose and the other between his legs.

Then there came a sudden shout outside the car from the side they had got in. A Meister, hearing the struggle and the gunshot, was trying to open the door.

The movement of the train made that hard. It suddenly jerked forward. John and Ben, having struggled to their feet, were tipped off balance and went flying, the Meister outside cursed.

The train continued to move forward, confirming Emily's earlier fear that it would soon leave the Yard. She struggled to grab the Meister's knife from the floor – not easy with hands tied behind your back.

She got a brief hold of it but, covered in the Meister's blood, it slipped from her grasp.

Suddenly there was a thump at the door on the other side of the car. It slammed open with a crash, light flooded in and with it came a large man brandishing a gun.

It was Rorton Van Hale.

He took one look at the chaotic scene, heaved the now groaning Meister out of the way, grabbed the knife and cut each of them free,

'Out!' he said as the door on the other side was finally hauled open and another Meister peered in. 'Now!'

Van Hale as good as hurled Emily, Ben and John out onto the track, firing at the Meister climbing in on the other side, and jumping out after them.

'Run for Chrissake – no, *that* way!' he shouted as he hustled them in the opposite direction from that of the rapidly accelerating train. For this would soon leave them exposed right at the front of the Whetton Building where Gunther's men had been standing.

If Van Hale sounded angry it was because things had not gone to plan.

At first the driver had done what he was told. He took his locomotive up-line of the cars and paused while the points were switched by one of the Meisters and the locomotive was coupled to the front car. But as the coupling began things went wrong. The train jerked forward and Van Hale lost his footing, giving the driver time to grab a coal shovel and swing it at his leg, knocking Van Hale to the floor, as he shouted for help to the Meister below.

Van Hale reached up and pulled the driver to the floor and as they both struggled they tumbled out of the moving train onto the track. Meanwhile, the Meister on the track had jumped up into the cabin on the other side and now found himself in charge of the moving train, desperately trying to make sense of the controls.

With the driver lying unconscious by the side of the track, Van Hale watched in alarm as the train began to run out of control.

In a last desperate attempt to get the three captives off the train he had raced along the track, found the right boxcar from the shouting going on inside, jumped up and managed to wrestle the door open.

But now, as the hoppers that had been coupled on at the end of the train rattled past, Emily, Van Hale, Ben and John were exposed to view, and found

444

themselves looking at the drawn pistols of two Meisters.

'Drop your gun,' said one of them curtly to Van Hale.

'Hey, now . . .' began Emily, stepping forward. But Van Hale pulled her back.

He slowly lowered his gun.

'I said *drop* it,' repeated the Meister, as he and his companion closed in.

Which Van Hale might have done had not two shots rung out and the Meister swung round and fallen, a bullet in his shoulder.

It was Toulson. 'Drop your weapons,' he roared at the Meisters, 'you're surrounded.' He fired another shot, this one zinging past the second Meister's ear and uncomfortably close to Van Hale, as he and the others dived to the ground seeking whatever cover the track could give them.

Then came shouts from the other side of the Whetton Building as the other Meisters woke up to what was happening. Toulson fired a fourth shot, sounded his whistle and shouted out another warning.

The wounded Meister rose onto all fours, cursing, as his companion fired a couple of wild shots at Van Hale's group.

'Run across the tracks toward Mr Toulson over by that warehouse,' Van Hale urged his three companions. You'll get cover from us both. Make it fast . . .'

'But what about Anna?' Emily said.

'I'll go for her the moment I see you're safe. Now *run*!'

Toulson waved an arm from the shadows to indicate exactly where they should head for and the three raced across the open tracks, Emily lifting her skirts to give her more freedom. It was no more than seventy yards but by the time they had crossed and were within reach of the protection of the warehouse shots were already being fired at them from the Whetton Building.

As they dived past Toulson into cover more shots whined past, one of them striking the building just above Toulson's head, sending brick dust and mortar flying. 'Anna . . .' gasped Emily, getting up and making to run back out to the storehouse which was no more than fifty yards to their left.

Toulson held her fast. 'No. Van Hale'll go for her.'

'You remember the layout of this place?' Toulson asked Ben urgently.

He nodded.

'Right. You three go down between these buildings to the Darke Hartz offices. Find somewhere there to hide. Wolfgang Darke's got reinforcements on the way. We'll find you later.'

'But Anna . . . we can't leave her . . .' said Emily desperately.

They heard more shouts and running feet. The Meisters were getting nearer.

'There's nothing we can do, Emily,' shouted Ben, 'not against Meisters with guns. Leave it to Van Hale. Come on!'

'We'll find Anna and get her to safety . . .' said Toulson reassuringly, 'but, meanwhile, you must get as far away from the Whetton Building as possible . . .'

With one last look toward the storehouse, the door of which was still ominously shut, Emily turned to Ben and John.

'Let's go,' she said grimly as they headed off at a run to the sound of ricocheting bullets and breaking glass.

Meanwhile, Toulson could see that Gunther Darke had regrouped his men and in only a matter of minutes the Meisters would cut off any hope of them freeing Anna from the storehouse.

The two men had been in this kind of situation before and had a routine. Toulson signaled to Van Hale who was lying prone between the rail tracks, as he reloaded his revolver and then fired a series of shots at the Whetton Building.

This was Van Hale's cue to get up and race for the storehouse. A shot hit the ground at his feet. Its sharper, heavier sound left Toulson in no doubt that it came from a Winchester '92.

He watched as Van Hale reached the door of the storehouse, shot the lock off and crashed the door open, pressing up against the wall outside.

A Meister appeared and as he did so Van Hale jumped him and disappeared inside.

Thwump!

Another heavy shot from a Winchester went by.

Toulson heard a shout and a woman scream. Then another shot and breaking glass. But no sign of either Van Hale or the girl. Not good.

He didn't hesitate. He made a fast exit from his cover and headed straight for the storehouse. A bullet fizzed through the right arm of his jacket as he dived into a strange, airy silence.

A Meister lay dead on the floor.

Van Hale was lying there motionless too.

The single window was open. Toulson ran to it. There was no sign of Anna Zemeckis.

He knelt down by Van Hale. Something had hit him in the face – the chair upended on the floor perhaps – and he was now coming round.

There was no way Toulson was going to leave Van Hale where he was.

'Wake up for Chrissake,' he growled.

Van Hale rolled on his side groaning.

Toulson kicked him in the butt. 'Wake up, I said.'

He went to the door and fired a couple more shots, just to show that the storehouse was still defended. Then he took out his silver whistle and blew it hard several times. Then he blew it again.

82

Hog Wheel

CHICAGO Saturday October 28, 1893   3.10 PM

Emily, Ben and John reached the Darke Hartz buildings undetected. They all had terrible misgivings about leaving Anna helpless in the storeroom, especially John, but without weapons there was nothing they could do to help Toulson and Van Hale free her.

They found an open door and slipped into the empty offices. Going on ahead of the others, Ben found a recess under some stairs near a doorway, from where they could make a hasty exit if necessary.

Emily frowned as they huddled in together.

'If you think I'm going to sit here waiting while Anna could easily get killed and the two Pinkertons are badly in need of support, you can think again, Ben Latham. I want to see what's going on. We've got to try and help them.'

John was looking pale and troubled. 'I should never have left Anna, I . . .'

'Come on,' said Emily 'we have to find help. Follow me . . .'

The two men obediently followed her down corridors till they reached the main foyer of the Darke Hartz offices and went to the front door. They slid the bolt and cautiously peered outside.

The position gave them a view right across the stock pens, acre on acre of them. There were no people about and no livestock either. But at the far end of the site they saw a puff of steam and heard the distant *chiff-chuff* of an engine. Closer-to, from the direction of the Whetton Building, they heard sporadic firing.

'It seems safe enough,' said Emily, stepping out into the open before anyone could stop her.

A shot zinged above her head and hit the door jamb.

She retreated fast back into the foyer and shut the door. They saw a figure up at a window at the top of the water tower. Gunther had put a man up there too.

'We'll try another way,' said Emily, refusing to capitulate.

'Emily . . .' began Ben helplessly.

Marching ahead, she led the others back the way they had come and out into the alleyway they had arrived at earlier.

'*Emily . . .*'

It was too late.

Ben heard a soft, 'Oh!' as he and John emerged into the alley.

Emily was not alone.

Gunther Darke was standing there, Winchester in hand, with several of his men brandishing weapons behind him.

Smoldering with cold anger, he looked down at Emily.

'I'm afraid you don't know the Yard as well as I do, Miss Strauss. There's no way out for you.'

Emily glanced around, her eyes now wide with alarm.

'And it's no good looking for your Pinkerton friends either. My men have them pinned down and they will soon be dead.'

'Where's Anna? What have you done with her?'

'She has been disposed of,' he replied indifferently. Then, turning away, he said to his men, 'Take them to the killing floor.'

John Olsen cried out and lunged at Gunther Darke. 'If you've killed her . . .'

One of the Meisters stepped forward and expertly grabbed John in an arm lock.

'It's your own skin you should be worrying about. Take them *now*,' Darke said sharply, 'while I have a last look around Darke Hartz to which, I fancy, I will not be returning after tonight.'

It was only then that Emily noticed they were not the only ones the Meisters now had captive. They had hold of one of their own too, his face beaten and his eyes terrified.

'I know him,' whispered John English. 'He's one of the Meisters who chased after Anna up by the wharves.'

The Meisters pushed them on.

Somewhere nearby they heard the sudden *thumpety thump* of an engine. It was the hog wheel starting up once more.

The Darke Hartz killing floor was much larger than the disused one in the Whetton Building that had been an improvised set for the taking of pornographic photographs.

This was a massive hangar of a space, rectangular in shape, with an open cobbled floor covering two thirds of its length and vast sliding doors at either end. These opened onto the same kind of alleyway Emily and the others had escaped down, along which ran rail tracks.

The remaining third of the killing floor was occupied for much of its length by a raised metal gantry on which were set a succession of vats, machinery and dressing tables. Before these, rising from the floor itself to the roof above, from which murky light filtered down through filthy glass, was Wheel No. 3 – famed as the largest in America.

The monstrous assemblage of wood and metal, which rose massively above the butchers who worked it, was turning now, slowly and ponderously, to the deafening clanking and clattering of the eight huge chains that hung loose from its edges. The three, now tightly pinioned by Meisters on either side of them, were frog-marched toward the wheel until, stopping only a few yards from it, they were ordered to sit on the cobbles.

All three resisted the command, until one of the Meisters grabbed John and pistol-whipped him to the ground.

They sat there watching the wheel turn. The chains clanked and the cobbles grew colder and more uncomfortable. Finally, Gunther Darke appeared.

He had removed his jacket and had put on a freshly laundered, full-length white apron and butcher's studded boots. His shirtsleeves were rolled up.

With a knife in a sheath at his waist he looked in his element. He seemed to dwarf the other Meisters and the wheel itself, though it rose so high above him.

Emily could not take her eyes off him. Despite her anxiety for Anna, for all of them, she was now gripped by a combination of fascination and fear. Where ordinary workmen were daily enslaved by the wheel, Gunther Darke was its triumphant, demonic master. His eyes glittered black and shiny.

'Bring the woman here,' he said.

One of the Meisters heaved Emily protesting to her feet and took her to Darke.

He calmly glanced at the pocket watch he pulled from beneath his apron.

'Time is limited, gentlemen, and for us butchers, time is money. Isn't that so, Miss Strauss?'

He stepped closer to Emily.

'I believe,' he said, 'we have not had the pleasure of a visit from you to see the workings of the hog wheel?'

'Let us go, Mr Darke,' said Emily simply, 'you can gain nothing by keeping us here or hurting us.'

'Oh but I can, Miss Strauss. I shall gain a great deal of *pleasure*.'

He pulled Emily closer to him, his face no more than six inches from hers. Then he wrenched her head toward the hog wheel. Raising his knife in his right hand Darke seemed about to slit Emily's throat. Behind her Ben shouted, 'No!'

Emily's heart was thumping painfully in her chest. But she tried not to betray her fear.

'You're a cool one, Miss Strauss. If all journalists had your mettle we would have a better and truer press in this country . . . A pity, you might have been a credit to your profession.'

He took the knife from her throat, pointed it at one

of the chains hanging from the wheel and traced its path in the air as it went round.

'I thought you might like a closer look at how it works . . .'

Emily tried to move her head but Gunther's grip was far too strong.

'Though, of course, having attended my lecture, you have the general idea.'

The wheel turning before Emily was terrifyingly large. Its roaring, grating sound seemed to magnify everything Gunther said into a thousand dark voices, as he continued to talk in his menacing way. He was as mesmerizing now as he had been in the lecture hall.

'Let's start with those chains,' he said. 'Take a good look at them, and the coupling at the bottom to which we attach the hog's hind quarter . . .'

His hand tightened painfully around her jaw, forcing her to look only at the wheel.

Take a really good look . . .

'. . . it is the most efficient killing machine of beast – or man come to that – ever invented,' whispered Gunther Darke in Emily's ear, 'don't you think?'

His grip slackened slightly.

Emily was able to look around more freely, though he still held the knife dangerously near her throat.

Having been both horrified and transfixed by Gunther Darke's lecture, she hated what the wheel was used for as much as she hated and despised the man who oversaw it.

The Darke Hartz killing floor was a vast cathedral of death and the hog wheel its vertical, ever-moving obscene altar. Here a blood sacrifice was made, of terrified living creatures, day in, day out for money. The floor danced to the wheel's eternal dreadful tune.

The overseers, the master butchers, the stickers, the dressers and the hogs themselves played out their lives in a cacophony of shouts, clashing metal, the scrape of studded boots on bloody stone and the terrified squeals of the animals themselves about to die.

Here, the animals passed from hell into an unrecognizable eternity in just a few minutes. Their bodies journeyed through a forest of knives wielded by dozens of men who reduced them to nice, neat joints of meat, all trimmed and dressed and packed for market in boxes at the end of the killing floor, ready to be loaded straight into the Darke Hartz boxcars.

'You find it fascinating, do you not?' purred Gunther Darke.

If Emily had been able to speak she would not have denied it. The sheer brute force and ruthlessness of it was what had brought wealth to Chicago. Emily knew the statistics better than most and that during the World's Fair of 1893 the Yard's daily, bloody drama had become the most popular tourist attraction of them all.

'Well then,' Darke continued, his voice softer still but touched now with a more sadistic menace, 'I'm sure your readers would like to think – they'll never actually know, of course, because you'll never file the story – that their lady journalist actually sees what she writes about with her own eyes. Don't you?'

He stepped back and pushed Emily roughly into the arms of a Meister. The charm had all gone and she knew she was looking into the face of the real Gunther Darke – cruel, cold, implacable.

He nodded at the Meisters to bring forward the one who was held captive.

454

'You know you've failed me . . .' he said, prodding the man toward the hog wheel with his knife.

The man's face was bloodied, his eyes dull and hopeless.

He nodded.

'And you know the punishment . . .'

'*Noo* . . .' the man began, as Gunther kicked his legs from under him. The Meister's head cracked against the moving wheel and then onto the cobbles as Gunther grabbed the next moving chain, attaching the Meister's leg to it and let him go. For a brief moment the man somehow struggled upright and for a moment more he tried to resist the relentless power of the wheel, but then he was dragged off his feet screaming and struggling.

His head crashed back onto the stone floor again, the chain tightened on his leg as he was hoisted upside down off the ground. As his free leg caught on a metal obstruction and was forced back under him, the wheel juddering briefly at the momentary obstruction, he screamed again, an animal sound now, and his leg broke with a sickening crack.

'*O mein liebe Gott!*' he cried in final, useless appeal as Gunther Darke, stepping forward and with the skill and speed of the master butcher, stuck the knife in the Meister's neck and with a flick of his wrist slit his throat.

Gunther stepped swiftly back, to avoid the sudden spurting flow of blood as the wheel continued to turn and the man, threshing and gurgling as he choked on his own blood, was lifted above their heads and carried into the gantry above the killing floor, his broken body twisting obscenely in the air.

Emily stared in horror; John went white and half-fainted; Ben's head slumped to his chest, unwilling to see more.

'Well then,' said Gunther Darke with a cold smile, his formerly pristine apron now splashed with blood and the wheel turning and clanking behind him, 'you wanted to see a spectacle, Miss Strauss, so let's do it again. Him next!'

Gunther pointed at Ben Latham.

As he did so there came a sudden rippling crackle of thunder overhead, followed by a *bang!* that reverberated right across the killing floor. Moments later, as the Meister dragged Ben toward Gunther Darke and the hog wheel and its chains, a hundred thousand drummers seemed to be pounding on the iron roof overhead as the heavens opened and rain began to fall.

83

Bunker

CHICAGO Saturday October 28, 1893   3.39 PM

The thunderous rain woke Anna Zemeckis and the first thing she did was put her hands to her distended belly to see if her baby was all right.

She felt carefully, both hands gentle and wide, fingers sensitive to the slightest movement. She sensed a flutter inside and then, to one side of her womb the unmistakable shift of shape as the baby moved inside her.

'Thank God,' she whispered.

*

Her escape from the storeroom had been sudden and violent, only made possible by the man who came and disabled the Meister guarding her. After she clambered out of the window and fell to the ground she lay low a short while. Then she had got up and run in the opposite direction, using the wall of the storehouse as cover from the men shooting at it.

She could not run fast for a spasm of pain in her womb had told her the baby was in distress. So, seeing a coal bunker by a track, she kept as low as she could and crawled behind it to rest. Ahead were more tracks and sheds and an embankment she guessed was the Chicago River. To her left the acres and acres of buildings which she knew were the meatpackers' offices and killing floors.

NELSON, MORRIS, ARMOUR, SWIFT.

Huge white letters on smoke-blackened walls.

The only name she could not see was Darke Hartz. It was obscured by the other buildings.

But to her right, on the rail tracks, she could see that dreadful name painted white on black on the side of every boxcar of a freight train.

That way too, as she dared to peer further round the bunker she was using as cover, lay Bubbly Creek. It was where she had run that terrible night, stumbling and terrified. That way, she never wanted to go again.

Anna looked to her left once more for a way to go. She was surprised at how far she had managed to run but saw something that made her realize at once she had to stay where she was.

Back by the bigger buildings rose the water tower, all two hundred feet of it. At its very top, on the observation platform, stood a Meister with a shot gun. He was not looking her way but toward where the Darke, Hartz building must be.

He fired a shot and she saw the flash.

Knowing that the moment she left her cover she would be seen, Anna decided to stay where she was. The bunker was about four feet high and covered on top to keep the coal dry. There was a wooden hatch on one side that had to be lifted for men to shovel the coal out. She heaved it up with difficulty and propped it open with a stick.

Then she crawled inside, shifted the coal about to give herself space and hunkered down. Here fatigue caught up with her and she closed her eyes.

A brief respite of restless, troubled sleep followed, but now the violent storm woke Anna and rain was finding its way through the cracks in the roof of the bunker and dripping onto her.

She had no idea how much time had passed but the light had faded and the murk and rain of the fall afternoon made it difficult to see very far.

She got up, keeping low, and turned to her left, away from Bubbly Creek, toward the buildings she had seen earlier. Somewhere there would be a place to hide that offered safer and dryer protection than a coal bunker.

Her head down, and shivering now as her clothes once more became sodden, Anna Zemeckis headed off into the rain in search of refuge.

84

Guns and Knives

The moment the Meister dragged him to his feet and began hauling Ben toward Gunther Darke and the hog wheel, he started to struggle, as did Emily and John in his defense. But they were no match at all for their captors. These were men with brute strength, used to the dying struggles of hogs and steers. Mere humans were no problem.

'No . . .' grunted Ben, '*no* . . .' but his voice was a whisper, barely audible against the thunderous rain above and the grinding hog wheel below: '*Noooo . . . !*'

Gunther towered over him, knife in hand. He bent down and grabbed Ben's right ankle and pulled. Ben went flying backwards as Emily, reaching forward, managed to block his fall.

'No . . . !' she screamed.

A Meister put both arms around her and pulled her back. Knocking Ben to the ground, Gunther dragged him bodily toward the wheel.

Ben struggled, kicking out with his other foot, snatching at a handrail and trying to hold on to it.

But with the wheel turning only inches from his other hand, Gunther yanked Ben free and grabbed a chain.

'Oh, yes,' he said, his eyes triumphant.

The noise grew louder still, as the whole of the

459

killing floor reverberated to the chunter and chatter and banging of the hog wheel.

Then Gunther suddenly stopped. His eyes widened as, looking beyond his terrified captives and the Meisters holding them, he saw something they had not. Surprise, and then bewilderment flashed across his face. He let go of the chain in one hand and Ben's leg in the other.

As Ben scrabbled away Emily turned and looked. At the far end of the killing floor the sliding doors were opening, their sound having been masked by the noise of the wheel. As they did so, the fading light beyond filled with steam, revealing, as it dispersed, the front of a big, black, shiny locomotive, its wheels squealing as it ground to a halt. The door of a boxcar rolled back and a man jumped out.

Another followed close behind, and both raised their guns.

It was Toulson and Van Hale. Then, from the lengthening shadows behind the locomotive, came the sound of boots on cobbles, as they were joined by Wolfgang Darke and his men, knives drawn.

A single shot rang out.

Emily looked back at Gunther. The bewilderment on his face was replaced by shock as his knife clattered to the ground and his hand went to his right shoulder, where a widening patch of blood showed through his shirt.

A second shot and the shoulder seemed almost to burst open and Gunther was spun round and back, straight into the still-turning wheel. Instinctively, he grabbed a chain with his left hand and let the wheel raise him up to the gantry above, a trick he had learned as a boy.

The Meisters were thrown into utter confusion by

the sight of their leader so unexpectedly shot and wounded. Faced by the advance of an overwhelming number of their own kind and the sight of two Pinkertons with guns picking them off from the vantage point of the boxcar, they ducked and pulled back, leaving Emily and John to dive for cover dragging Ben with them.

Pulling out their knives and what guns they had, the Meisters retreated to the door behind them to escape and regroup. But it did not open.

From up on the gantry Gunther crouched and watched, clutching his shoulder but not flinching as Toulson aimed another shot at him which hit a girder above his head.

'You may get my men, Mr Toulson,' he roared down at them, 'you may even get me, but you will never beat the Meisters. They will strike you down sooner or later and anyone else who stands in their way. You too, Miss Strauss, and all those you try to protect!'

Van Hale fired again at the gantry. But Gunther ducked back behind a girder, and then disappeared behind the machinery.

But he was not alone up there. From behind a girder high up in the gantry another man was watching from the shadows and awaiting his opportunity: Dodek Krol.

Knowing the Darke Hartz killing floor as well as Gunther he followed the wounded man soundlessly to a metal stairway down from the gantry and out of a far exit into the gloom.

The rattle and rumble of the hog wheel faded behind them, overtaken now by the rush of rain in the storm drains outside.

Dodek had an idea where Gunther was headed – the only remaining place of refuge in the Stock Yard

– a fire-damaged warehouse on its western side alongside an obscure reach of the Chicago River. It was a place the Meisters sometimes used for certain of their meetings, especially punishments.

He guessed Gunther would wait for night – and probably for the rain to stop too. Gunther had long since made contingencies against this day and Dodek, once his right hand man, was the one person who knew them all.

Satisfied he knew where to find Gunther later he made his way quickly out of the Yard. He had a few final arrangements to make before returning to fulfil his commission from Paul Hartz. Then he would be free. Free of Darke and Hartz and of Chicago too. It was a city that had grown too small for him.

Back on the killing floor the trapped Meisters made a last stand. It was boldly done but, now leaderless and faced by much larger numbers and the weapons of Toulson and Van Hale, there was no hope for them.

Two with guns fell dead before the Pinkertons' bullets, a third was wounded and lost the use of his knife hand. Sensing they were weakening, Wolfgang and his men moved in ruthlessly.

The final confrontation was one between men with knives, a fight in which Toulson and Van Hale took no part. It was the culmination of years of antipathy between rival butchers, trained men with knives who do not hesitate and go for the kill. In the ensuing close-hand knife fight, another of Gunther's men was killed and two more badly wounded defending a third who, himself wounded, managed to escape.

The outcome might have been far worse had not Alfred Spohr, who took no direct part in the fighting, finally stepped in with Wolfgang and ordered his men to stop. The remaining Meisters threw down their knives.

'Shut the wheel down,' Wolfgang shouted, as he moved forward to help deal with the wounded on both sides.

The machinery ground to a juddering halt and suddenly there was an eerie silence – except for the rain drumming on the roof and on the cobbles outside.

'Which one of them was that?' demanded Toulson, pointing in the direction of the Meister who had got away.

'Lukas,' said Spohr, 'a bad lot. He's in Mr Hartz's employment these days.'

'A Meister?'

'I should say so. One of their best.'

'We'll catch him later. He's wounded and can't get far. Gunther's the one we must get to first.'

John English was among the wounded, still weak from the battering he had received in the boxcar and having sustained a knife wound in the arm as well from a Meister in the mêlée. Ben was badly shaken but not otherwise harmed.

Emily, meanwhile, was frustrated and angry. Anna was still missing and now Gunther Darke had made his escape.

'Why aren't you and Mr Van Hale going after him?' she challenged Toulson. 'You can't let him get away. He might know where Anna is . . .'

Toulson did his best to calm her.

'The only person here with any chance of finding Gunther Darke is his brother because he knows the Yard better than any man. But right now he wants to see his men get medical attention and that the Darke Hartz premises are secured.'

'But what about Anna?'

Van Hale stepped forward, 'It's all right, Miss Strauss, she's probably safe somewhere. I helped her get out of the window in the storehouse and told her to run and hide – somewhere away from the Darke Hartz building, out beyond the coal tips and lumber yards near Bubbly Creek. She'll stay there till things have died down.'

'But we must find her, we can't leave her there alone in the dark. I'll go and look for her myself,' said Emily.

Toulson shook his head.

'No, you won't. For one thing Gunther Darke's out there somewhere too; for another it's already getting dark and the Yard is no place for you to get lost in. We've alerted the police and you'll wait until they get here. Then we'll mount a search for Anna and a manhunt for Darke.'

'When you do I'm coming too,' said Emily.

'I've no doubt you will,' said Toulson. 'But for now you must wait for the police.'

While they did so, Wolfgang and Alfred Spohr explained to Emily what had happened.

They had heard Toulson's first whistle, but it came too soon, and his men hadn't yet re-grouped. Then the train had appeared which Spohr recognized as the one the Meisters had been loading. Fortunately, when it started running out of control Wolfgang's men had managed to switch it to a track that ran harmlessly in circles right round the yard. One of them had jumped aboard and taken control of the runaway locomotive from the terrified Meister attempting to stop it.

Wolfgang had then decided that the quickest and

safest way to get his men up to the Whetton Building was to use the same train, picking up Toulson and Van Hale en route.

Later, after the police had arrived, the dead and injured were removed to the nearest hospital, John English among them but under protest.

Emily refused point blank to be evacuated from the scene. With Toulson, Wolfgang and other armed men setting off in search of Gunther Darke, she and Ben insisted on accompanying Van Hale and a few more of Wolfgang's men in search of Anna. The rain was still falling, heavy and persistent now, and the light was so bad and visibility so poor that by five they had given up calling Anna's name as they searched the northwest corner of the Yard near Bubbly Creek.

'God, it stinks,' said Ben.

Emily stood staring at the fetid channel below them. All she could see was an occasional ripple of light in the gloom and the dull patter of rain hitting water.

'It's filling up,' she said, as she peered back across the gloomy rail tracks to the Yard behind them.

'Where are you, Anna, where have you gone to this time?'

They lingered a while longer at the Creek until Van Hale called a halt to the search and from the direction of Darke Hartz a whistle was heard.

'Well, I guess our search is over for now,' Van Hale said to Toulson wearily.

'No, we mustn't stop,' said Emily urgently, 'we mustn't give up trying.'

Van Hale and Wolfgang's men drew round them in a circle, their hats dripping with rain, their clothes and their boots sodden.

'Unless you can read her mind, Miss Strauss,' said Van Hale, 'we're going to have to wait until morning. It's just too dangerous with the light fading.'

Wolfgang appeared in the gloom. 'I have spoken to my father on the telephone,' he said, 'He is most concerned about Miss Zemeckis. Mr Steele informed him of her condition and he begs us to do what we can. It was all I could do to stop him coming to the Yard himself.'

'He's right, we should keep on looking,' interjected Emily forcefully. 'If she's gone to ground we should be able to find her . . .'

Toulson shook his head.

'No. You're deadbeat and no use in a search, least of all at night. Some of Mr Darke's men, who know the Yard back to front, have offered to assist police reinforcements with a further search when they get here. You must leave it to them.'

'But . . .'

'No, Miss Strauss.' It was Van Hale who interrupted her this time. 'You've no chance of finding her.'

Emily was forced finally to concede, and with Ben reluctantly accepted the carriage provided by Wolfgang Darke and the offer of a meal and a change of clothes at Hans Darke's house. But she continued protesting, poking her head from the carriage window to call out to Toulson one last time.

'I'll come back . . . just as soon as I can.'

'Yes, Miss Strauss,' he sighed wearily. 'I know you will.'

85
Search

A short while later a cab turned off Halsted for the short run down to the Union Stock Yard entrance.

Dodek Krol had come back. This time he was carrying a bag. It contained a great deal of money and a few things he needed for a night or two.

The rest of his worldly goods, and they didn't count for much, he had now sent on to New York.

'You're sure you don't want me to wait, sir?' said the driver, who had brought him straight from the Nord Chicago Turnverein where he had cleared out his office and locked up for the last time. 'You'll never find a cab out here again at this time of day, let alone later. It ain't a safe place to be, when it gets dark.'

Dodek shook his head and the cab turned round and left. He took off his bowler and let the rain fall on his bare head and stream down his face and bull neck as he listened to the roar of the water in the storm drains flowing out toward Bubbly Creek behind him.

He didn't move, he just stood in the rain and looked at the Main Gate, knowing that this was the last time he was going to go through it.

The first time had been twenty years before when he was young and had been one of thousands of immigrants arriving for work from Back of the

Yards. He had come, alone, to Chicago from his home town in Pennsylvania to work as a hog sticker with Darke Hartz & Company. He was alone again now and finished here. Time to move on and start again.

In all those years he had wept only once and that was because of what the rain had done. Four years before, in May 1889, he had arrived at the Yard to find his workmates crowded over the newspaper. There had been a terrible flood the day before when a dam had burst on the Stonycreek River in Pennsylvania and had flooded Johnstown, wiping out almost its entire population of two thousand people.

Krol had wept because Johnstown was where he had been born and raised in a poor immigrant community. It was where his five brothers and three sisters, his parents and twenty other members of his extended Polish family had lived. And died.

A man never forgets something like Stonycreek. Dodek retreated inside himself and over the years channelled his anger and his desire for revenge into honing his own body, his strength and his dexterity with the knife. He became one of the most skilled master butchers in the Stock Yard, one of its leading Meisters, and, to only a select handful of people who hired his services, a paid killer. One day he would have his revenge for Johnstown, but meanwhile he bided his time.

Then, in October 1893, it had finally come, when Paul Hartz had offered him the commission to kill OAA President Jenkin Lloyd Rhys, the engineer who had been largely held responsible for the disaster.

As for his other commissions, Krol didn't always say yes. He needed to know why he was killing a man and to feel the reason was just.

Which is why he had said no the first time that Paul Hartz had asked him to kill Gunther Darke.

Darke in fact had trained him and had promoted him from the killing floor to his distribution business; Darke had made Krol a Meister. The fact that Paul Hartz wanted revenge on his son-in-law for betraying his daughter Christiane and making her life miserable was not, in Krol's book, reason enough to kill him.

But from that time on, Dodek had held Gunther in contempt. He didn't like men who were cruel to their wives. A man should count himself lucky to have found one.

'Give me a better reason and I might do it,' he said to Hartz and that's how matters had lain for a long while. As a killer for hire, Dodek might have done it had Hartz been man enough to tell him that the real reason he wanted Gunther out of the way was so that he could gain control of the company. But he never did admit that.

Then things changed. Gunther began bringing money into the OAA's coffers with his covert trade in *poses plastiques*, cleverly using Darke Hartz's own refrigerated boxcars across the US rail network to avoid police and postal scrutiny. So for a while Hartz had relented, seeing Gunther as useful to his own ends and the greater good of the OAA.

But that morning at the OAA Convention things had changed yet again. The intervention of that old fool Steele had destroyed Gunther Darke's reputation and his chances of election as a vice-president. It threatened Hartz's political career too and put him in a weak position.

Krol's brief conversation with Paul Hartz at the Convention after Steele had denounced Gunther was all it had taken to tip the balance for him to finally agree to kill Darke. What Hartz did not know was that Krol's true reason for agreeing was because Gunther had tricked him into going after a vulnerable and pregnant woman, Anna Zemeckis.

Now, as he stood in the rain at the Stock Yard gate, Krol felt sure that fate decreed the time was right.

The rain convinced him. For Krol knew from his years at the Yard that it was just a matter of time after the first heavy rains of fall before the storm drains across the Yard that get clogged with refuse through the hot summer months start singing a sweet song as they busily discharge their contents into Bubbly Creek and make it flow again, like the stream it once was, which offered a fitting way of disposing of a man like Gunther Darke.

Now it was just a matter of completing this final commission.

Krol went to the Main Gate and roused the sleeping guard inside, whose eyes widened with apprehension when he saw who it was. There wasn't a man in the Yard who was not afraid of Krol.

'Mr Krol!' he bleated, 'You come to help?'

'I guess I have.'

'Not many of the police are here yet. They asked for reinforcements but there's flash floods on 30th and 32nd, the men can't get through.'

'I know,' said Krol. 'Just been through 'em and it's getting worse.'

'It's Gunther Darke they're after, sir. They're sayin' he . . .'

'What are they doing now?' Krol cut in impatiently.

'Searchin'. They started at the Darke Hartz buildings but now they've moved the operation to the Exchange Building. I reckon they need men like you who know the Yard.'

'I got a bag that's getting wet,' said Krol. 'I'll leave it here till I'm done. All right?'

'Safe with me.'

'Better be,' said Krol.

He passed on through to Exchange Avenue and made the short walk to the Exchange Building . . . Its lights were on. Krol could also see groups of men checking out the stockpens, the lights of their storm lanterns bobbing about to east and south.

He looked up into the rain. They had no chance at all of finding Darke in this weather. He wouldn't risk coming out of hiding with so many people about. He'd stay where he was until the searchers gave up for the night.

An officer from Harrison Police Station, whom Krol knew well, was now masterminding the search. He found him in the Exchange Building poring over a large-scale map of the site.

'Pretty hopeless, eh?' said Krol.

'Pretty much. But we gotta try. After what he's done Darke'll be desperate. We want to apprehend him before he does worse. There's a girl missing too.'

'What girl?'

The officer spat.

'Called Anna Zemeckis. Got out of Dunning. Wanted for attacking and injuring one of the attendants up there who happens to be the wife of one of our officers.'

Krol looked indifferent.

'She won't stand much chance then, if she's found!'

'Not by the time our people have finished with her. No sir.'

'What's she got to do with Darke?'

'Nothin' so far as I know.'

'Then what's she doing at the Yard?'

'Search me. Orders are if we see her to take her in.'

'Show me what ground you've covered.'

The officer obliged. He waved a hand over the northwest part of the site, right where Krol knew Gunther would be holed up.

'Started there where he was last seen and now we've moved to the nearer buildings and pens. But if this rain continues I'm calling it off until morning.'

'Mind if I look about?'

'Better not by yourself, Mr Krol, you might get mistaken for Darke and get shot.'

'I don't think so. I know what I'm doing.'

'You be careful then,' said the officer. 'There's two Pinkertons on the site as well, just to confuse the issue. In the employ of Hans and Wolfgang Darke.'

But Krol had already slipped out the door.

Anna Zemeckis, meanwhile, had no sooner found a dry, warm boiler house to hide in after leaving the coal bunker, than she heard the men approaching, hollering and shining their lanterns in the dark. They didn't sound friendly, not like the man who had shoved her out of the window and who had promised help would come.

As their lights got nearer she could see the men were searching buildings like the one she was in. There was nothing for it but to run – yet again. But she emerged into the twilight having no idea now where she was headed. One thing at least she knew: darkness and secret places were her only friends.

She shivered as she crept on between buildings, feeling safer outside than in, trying to get her bearings.

Then, quite suddenly, the rain stopped. She looked up at the sky, obscured till now, and saw racing clouds lit by a rising moon. Opposite the building she now found herself standing by, she saw open space and then a rail track between buildings, and there, on the horizon, like an apparition rising up among the clouds, something bright and lit up and beautiful.

'The Fair,' she whispered, 'the World's Fair . . .'

Stillness, no rain, nor any wind: just ambient light in the darkening sky, and a far off place, a dream she knew now she could never reach.

She turned to seek shelter near the building, away from the light and found herself staring up at a man.

'I . . .'

Her voice stopped dead as he reached a hand straight for her throat and pushed her violently backwards.

It was Gunther Darke.

'You,' he said as she choked, '*you* . . .'

And Anna Zemeckis, her womb tightening once more, felt the world spin round as she slumped down in a near faint, her hands scrabbling at an arm, a chest, legs and feet.

'*You*,' he said again, looking down at her on the ground with such hate it was like a knife in her heart. Then he hit her one way and then another and then a third time.

The next thing she knew Anna was being hauled back upright, then half-carried, half-pushed back the way she had come.

She screamed for help but the moment she did so, Gunther stopped, let her drop back to the ground and hit her hard in the face.

'Do that again and it'll be the end for your baby,' he said, raising a fist to her stomach.

It was then that Anna saw his right arm was limp and the shirt he was wearing was dark with what must be blood.

He hauled her up again with his good arm and shoved her forward.

'Where are you taking me?'

Gunther grunted, his face set with pain and the strain of holding her tight with his one good arm, his breathing heavy.

He too was an animal in pain, an animal at bay, seeking sanctuary.

But he was angry as well, angry beyond measure, and his anger was directed at Anna.

'Please . . . don't . . .'

'Don't talk,' he snarled. If he could have struck her with his good hand he would have done so.

Anna could sense his growing weakness beyond the anger and the strength it gave him. She knew she must do what he said and hope he would weaken enough for her to break free.

'Where are we going?' she whispered.

Gunther grunted again, forcing his body against hers as he prodded her across the rail tracks.

She looked to her right and saw the distant illuminations of the Fair more clearly; closer to were the approaching lights of the search parties and the silhouettes of buildings. She now knew where she was. She had been here before.

A new fear raced through her.

'*Where are we going?*'

'Bubbly Creek,' he said, his grip tightening, his face set and determined.

Something in those words gave Anna the strength to turn on Gunther in one last desperate attempt to free herself. She pushed her fists into his face, trying to stab at his eyes and scratch him.

It had no effect, as Gunther turned and, half-laughing, taunted her.

'One more time . . . just one more time.'

His hand tightened on her arm.

Anna began to shake and cry; she could do no more.

'Yes,' he said softly, 'that's better now, we're nearly there. Yes . . .'

Then he stopped dead in his tracks and let her go as a voice called out to him from the gloom ahead.

'Good evening, Mr Darke.'

Anna recognized the man but struggled to remember his name.

'Hello, Anna,' he said.

It was the man who ran the Nord Chicago Turnverein. Mr Krol. Dodek Krol.

'Let her go, Gunther,' said Krol as the injured man made a final grab at Anna.

Gunther pulled back and Krol stepped swiftly forward and pulled Anna toward him.

'You'd better run for it,' he said softly, eyes on Gunther, 'because those men with lights will have heard your scream and they'll soon come this way. But don't go near them. They're police and they mean to harm you.'

He pushed Anna behind him and she stumbled off into the dark.

'Why are you here, Dodek?' said Gunther.

'I've come for you.'

Gunther seemed unsurprised. He hardly reacted at all.

'A commission?'

Krol nodded.

'Who?'

Krol said nothing.

'My father-in-law,' said Gunther matter-of-factly. He stepped sideways, circling Dodek.

475

'Well then, Mr Krol, you're going to have to take me, aren't you, and that won't be easy, will it?'

He pulled his jacket aside and revealed a sheath knife as his eyes glittered.

Then he said again, '*Will it,* Dodek?'

86
Final Commission

CHICAGO Saturday October 28, 1893   5.17 PM

Anna Zemeckis did not look back.

She ran on into the gathering darkness, her mind confused, her body exhausted. Instinct alone was driving her now, that and the knowledge that she could not go back the way she had come or risk asking for help from the searchers. All she could do was run on with the sound of drains rushing with storm water all around her.

A man shouted suddenly in the distance, jogging a frightening memory. She had heard shouts like that before and with them had come laughter, mocking and cruel.

Anna Zemeckis knew exactly what she was running toward, but even so, when she got there, she was taken by surprise. The ground suddenly dropped away, causing her to lose her balance and crash forward on all fours.

She found herself staring into a black void from which came the heavy sound of running water and the odor of decay. Behind her loomed bobbing lights and more shouts.

She groped along the soggy, filthy ground ahead of her until it fell finally away and she knew she was at the edge of Bubbly Creek.

The shouts were louder, the bobbing lights nearer.

Anna knew what she must do if she was not to be caught.

She turned round on all fours and eased herself backwards until she felt the bank of the Creek drop away under her knees. Very cautiously she lowered herself down until her feet were in cold mud and water. She could feel the water's flow at her dress and legs, fierce now after the storm.

She pushed herself further out and down into the water until her whole body was below the edge of the embankment. The deeper she got the more the Creek surged around her, pulling at her body to loosen the precarious grip of her hands and fingers on the bank that was now above her.

The cold water made her gasp as it reached her chest and then her neck.

She hung there, knowing she could never climb back to safety. She didn't have the strength. She began to shiver with cold and fear. She had done her best but it had finally not been enough.

Her father . . . Gunther . . . John . . . so much pain, so much distress. Now there was no hope left, nothing for her or her unborn child. Nothing but a life no longer worth living. If they caught her they would punish her and send her back to Dunning and never let her free; if her baby lived it would be taken from her forever.

In final despair she let her body slide out into the water. Its flow began to take her as she let go of the last hold she had on land and on life.

'I'm sorry,' she whispered as the current took her.

The last thing she saw as she succumbed to its flow was the lowering sky and racing storm clouds above, lit up by the hundred thousand electric lights of the World's Fair beyond her to the east.

Dodek Krol stared into Gunther's face.

Each was waiting for the other to move but it was Gunther who felt his strength draining away from him. There was a time he might have beaten Dodek Krol but now . . .

He moved suddenly and fast, diving to his right to protect his damaged shoulder and to give himself time to pull his knife.

Dodek struck hard at him but missed as Gunther fell sideways.

Gunther hit the ground and rolled, feeling the stab of violent pain as his weight went on to his wounded shoulder. He fought through it, and a moment later he was up again, knife in hand, ready to strike.

Dodek eyed him coolly, his own knife still in its sheath. His senses were alert to a thousand things, animal-like. The men to his left, across the tracks, lights flickering in his peripheral vision; the sound of water in the drains around them, and behind him, in the direction the Zemeckis girl had run, the sound of the Creek, as loud as he had ever known it.

He sensed another thing too, he almost smelt it: Gunther Darke was weakening, his knife shaking in his hand, his stance unstable.

So Dodek did not draw his blade because he knew that two knives are always more dangerous than one. The one he was facing he could deal with.

When he made his move it was sudden and brutal. As Gunther made a lunge forward, he swept his knife hand to one side with his left arm and grabbed

478

Gunther's shot-up shoulder and arm in his huge hand and began to squeeze.

Gunther dropped his knife and grunted in agony.

Krol's great hand squeezed tighter still.

What little fight was left in Gunther Darke evaporated. Moaning, his left hand waving ineffectually, he sank to his knees.

Krol leaned over him and whispered, 'You should not have asked me to go after that girl. She is innocent.'

With one huge blow he sent Gunther sprawling, then looked round in the direction of the Exchange Building to see if the searchers were any nearer. They were.

Bending down, Dodek heaved the now unconscious body in a fireman's lift across his shoulders. Darke was a big man but Krol did not grunt or stagger as he carried him away toward Bubbly Creek.

Yes, there are good times and bad times to dump a body in Bubbly Creek, as locals call the South Fork of the Chicago River . . .

Spring and fall are best because the stench is not so bad and there's a flow of sorts, especially after heavy rain, ensuring that the evidence of your crime is carried away, out of sight and out of mind.

You hope.

But hope is for amateurs who leave things to chance. Dodek Krol was never one to do that. He carried Gunther Darke to the edge of Bubbly Creek and set him, groaning and only half conscious now, at its dark edge, his back to the water that ran along out of sight below them. Then, holding him with his left hand, Krol used his right to pull out his knife once more.

The light was not good but a man like Krol, trained to kill steers and hogs, knew exactly where to find Gunther's heart.

But the man he was about to kill was trained too.

Weak though he was and in terrible pain, raw animal instinct flooded back into Gunther as he came to from Krol's blow, infusing him with the will to live when all reason and all hope for it had gone.

He saw Krol's blade flash and, beyond him, the searchers approaching as they crossed the last of the tracks before Bubbly Creek, their lights bright now and their faces easy to make out.

'Hey! *You!!*' one of them shouted.

As Dodek turned in the direction of the shouts, Gunther found strength and speed enough to grab his wrist and twist. The knife slipped from Dodek's grasp. Gunther did not relax his grip. He did something Dodek could not have expected. He simply toppled backwards, pulling his former friend with him into the foul, black water.

It was so cold that the shock of it brought Gunther back to full consciousness. As he surfaced, gasping for air and kicking furiously to stay afloat, with his one good hand he reached for a second small knife he kept concealed in his belt.

Dodek didn't see it coming, but felt a sudden stab of pain in his side. Instinctively he smashed his elbow in his opponent's throat. Gunther screamed and choked.

Lights flickered in the air above them both, slightly upstream.

'*Anyone there!?*'

Dodek knew he was badly hurt. Taking a deep breath, he summoned his formidable strength and forced Gunther's head under the water and dragged him down.

Gunther's knife sank to the bed of Bubbly Creek as his hand scrabbled at Dodek's chest. Then he finally went limp . . .

'There's nothing down here!!' called out someone from the water's edge.

The lights receded as Gunther's body surfaced briefly, his face contorted, his limp hand and arm caught by the flow, seeming to give a grotesque final wave.

Dodek let the current take him. He waited a while until he was sure the men had gone, and then clawed his way up onto the bank.

Over the years he had undertaken many commissions, but none of his victims had ever before managed to wound him. He scowled in the dark, knowing he needed attention fast.

Hauling himself upright he staggered away from the Creek until he had crossed the rail tracks. The stock pens lay ahead of him. Beyond them the lights at the main entrance seemed suddenly a lifetime away.

'. . . but I'm going to make it,' Dodek muttered, 'I'm not going to die like a stuck pig in the Union Stock Yard.'

87

Last Chance

CHICAGO Saturday October 28, 1893   5.18 PM

Hans Darke paced restlessly up and down the lobby of his house on Astor Street awaiting further news of the search and the return of Wolfgang and the others from the Yard. He was in considerable distress.

He had felt momentary relief to know that Wolfgang was safe and Toulson, Miss Strauss and the others as well. But as soon as he heard what had happened to Gunther a profound sadness overtook him. It came with knowing that his son's downfall, that had seemed so inevitable for so many years, had finally come. Even though he had cut himself off from him years back it didn't lessen the pain.

But his greatest distress came when Hans had a second call from the officer in charge of the search at the Yard saying that Anna Zemeckis, mother-to-be of his first grandchild, had gone missing during a gunfight. The floods weren't helping the search for her.

'What floods?' demanded Hans. 'It's dry as a bone up here.'

As if in answer, the line went dead.

When finally a third call came through Hans grabbed the phone.

'Mr Darke?'

'Yes.'

'Mr *Hans* Darke.'

'Yes, yes, what is it, man?'

It was the officer in charge of the search at the Union Stock Yard again.

The line was bad and Hans could hardly hear.

Isaiah Steele took over and listened. Finally he put down the phone.

'There's floods on the South Side. Wolfgang's probably delayed because of them.'

Hans opened his front door.

'Looks like the rainstorm's moving up here,' he said, scowling as he saw the racing clouds above and heard the first rumbles of thunder.

He closed the door and continued pacing about, wrestling with emotions he had never dealt with before. He was a man for whom his work had been his life and he knew that if he had been a father in any proper sense of the word it was a bad one: too busy to care; too strict to give ground to boys who needed it; too focused on all the wrong things to notice those that really mattered.

The only two women he had ever known well and was easy with, had been his wife and, more lately, his niece Elfrieda.

It was she who came to him now, shooing Isaiah Steele away as being less than useful in a situation like this.

'Men!' she muttered.

'This is my fault,' said Hans, 'all of it, from beginning to end. I helped make Gunther what he is and now there's a poor girl out there, a poor, lost girl . . .'

Elfrieda was doing her best to comfort him when a knock came at the door and a sodden Wolfgang, Emily and Ben finally arrived. They told him immediately all that had happened. After that, for a time they sat in silence, because there seemed nothing more to say.

Wolfgang and Hans sat together in a corner, quiet and stony-faced, in shock about Gunther and his possible fate; Ben sat with Isaiah, relating how he had come so close to death that afternoon.

But Emily could not sit still. She refused Elfrieda's offers of refreshment and a change of clothes and was pacing about as restlessly as Hans had been.

'I shouldn't have left, but Mr Toulson persuaded me it was for the best. I should have stayed at the Yard. That's where she is and where my story is too. And it won't reach its conclusion until I find her.'

Hans finally got her to sit down, anxious for the slightest scrap of news or information about Anna.

'No one will find her tonight. Not in the Yard, not in all Chicago, not unless they know where to look. She . . . she . . .'

'What is it, Miss Strauss?' asked Hans in alarm.

Emily had turned pale, her eyes wide.

'I think I . . .'

'What is it?' said Wolfgang.

'Something Mr Van Hale said, just as we were leaving.'

'*What?*'

Ben and Wolfgang came over.

'He said I wouldn't find her once night fell "*unless I could read her mind*". Well, I think I can . . . She's tired and she's scared and she's pregnant and she can't trust anyone, least of all men, and she's nowhere left to turn. She . . . I think . . . Have you a telephone, Mr Darke?' she said urgently.

He nodded.

'Right in my office.'

'Can you put in a call to Hull House on the West Side?'

'I guess so . . .'

'I mean *now*, Mr Darke.'

Wolfgang took over.

'Who do you want to speak to?' he said when he finally got through.

'Katharine Hubbard.'

Wolfgang repeated the name into the receiver.

After a couple of minutes she was on the line.

'Katharine, this is Emily Strauss, New York *World*. You remember?'

'I remember. What can I do for you?'

'Listen. You got flooding over your way?'

'Yes.'

'Bad enough to stop you going out with a carriage?'

'Depends what for.'

'Someone who needs help.'

'You only have to say.'

'Right, this is what I want you to do . . . No wait, just a moment. Wolfgang, can you get a carriage ready and your best driver? And tell Elfrieda I need her. And close the door as you go, I don't want to raise anybody's hopes, least of all your father's. Oh yes, and a map of the South Side. I need one.'

Five minutes later Emily Strauss was outside the Darke house and climbing into a carriage alone.

'Won't you say where you're going?' said Wolfgang, following after her.

'The South Side.'

'You need someone with you, Emily,' said Ben.

'No, Ben. A man is the last person I or Anna Zemeckis needs right now,' said Emma tartly. 'Drive on!'

'Where to, miss?' asked Hans's coachman.

Emily named a street.

'Never heard of it.'

'Can you get me to 31st?'

'I reckon.'

'Then hurry. This map'll take us from there.'

'Where on earth is she heading?' said Hans, overwhelmed by the speed of events.

'Don't worry. She knows what she's doing,' said Isaiah Steele.

Ten minutes after, there was a ring at the door.

It was Paul Hartz.

He did not look his usual confident self as he was shown into the drawing room. Without greeting Hans Darke, he took one look at the assembled gathering and insisted they speak in private.

'I would rather we have witnesses, Paul,' responded Hans coldly . . . 'Isaiah, Mr Latham, please follow us.'

The four went into his study where a file lay on Hans's desk.

It contained a simple document, which Isaiah Steele had drawn up that afternoon in anticipation of this very moment, and in the hope that Wolfgang, Anna and the others would return safely from the Stock Yard.

Isaiah Steele had been extremely surprised that Hans had asked him to draft the document – or that he had even *thought* to do so in the first place.'

'It does not seem quite the appropriate time, Hans,' he had said.

But Darke had shaken his head.

'I have not built up my company into one of the four largest meatpackers in the world,' he had said, 'without knowing when to make the most of an opportunity. Against Paul Hartz they come but once and briefly.

'Fifteen years ago when I needed money to expand my business he helped me, but he also made a fool of me as bankers and financial men often do of their hardworking but less sophisticated commercial clients. He tricked me into giving him effective control of the company I had built, using Gunther and his own daughter as the vehicle, by encouraging Gunther to steal Christiane from Wolfgang. Had today gone differently at the OAA meeting and had he not been exposed by Isaiah, he would have pushed Wolfgang and myself out.'

'Yes, but Hans . . .'

'But now, suddenly he is weak and vulnerable,' Hans continued, 'and this is the moment to make him an offer which, while preserving his tattered honor, will give me back what I should never have given away.'

Isaiah had drawn up a simple document that transferred a controlling stake in Darke Hartz back to Hans and Wolfgang. He took that document out now and placed it before Paul Hartz who read it with the greatest distaste.

'It gives you too much for too little,' he said.

'It gives me what I believe to be fair and leaves you with a holding that, were you to dispose of it, would give you a very handsome profit indeed. Take it or leave it. I shall not negotiate.'

'But I have no guarantee that you will keep your side of the bargain.'

Hans Darke glowered.

'You have the best guarantee in the world, Paul, if only you knew it. You have my word before witnesses. Now, shake hands on it and sign and I will never mention this matter again. From now on Wolfgang runs the company.'

A beaten man – so far as politicians are ever beaten while their hands are still on at least some of the levers of power – Hartz shook his partner's hand.

Then he turned without a further word.

It was Hans who opened the door for him, closing it behind him without a farewell, even before Paul Hartz had reached the sidewalk.

So he did not see, and nor did anyone else, the man who was waiting in Hartz's carriage for him, a man wearing a black bowler and a frock coat. Blood was seeping through the heavy bandage on his right hand.

'A satisfactory outcome, sir?' said Lukas.

'Not entirely,' said Hartz, 'there's something I want you to do.'

'Sir?'

As the carriage headed off south down Astor Street to on its way to Prairie Avenue Hartz pulled a green file from his briefcase.

'Tell me, Lukas, what chance has Gunther Darke of surviving this night?'

'None, sir. If the police don't get him, we will.'

'As a matter of fact . . .'

'Sir?

There was a mean, calculating glint in Hartz's eye.

'Who would you say is in charge of the Chicago Meisters now?'

'Depends. Needs to be sorted. All the while Mr Krol . . .'

'Supposing I told you that Mr Krol will be leaving Chicago tonight after he has completed a final commission.'

'For Mr Darke?'

'For me,' said Hartz.

'A final commission?' said Lukas heavily, wincing with the throbbing pain from his wound.

'That's right.'

'Well then, I would say that the next in line is myself,' said Lukas.

'Then you'll need this.'

Hartz handed him the green file.

'A new commission?'

'Yes, and an urgent one.'

Lukas eyed the file but did not open it.

'There is the matter of my men who were apprehended at the Stock Yard tonight. They face stiff sentences.'

Hartz's eyes narrowed. 'I daresay that my lawyers will convince the court that there were mitigating circumstances.'

Lukas smiled.

'In that case, Mr Hartz, we understand each other perfectly. So, this commission . . . ?'

He opened the file. There was another inside it on which was written a name.

'Anna Zemeckis,' said Lukas without expression.

'I have to cover my back. There is always the possibility that unlike Mr Gunther Darke she *will* survive. She seems to have a capacity for it. If she does, then Mr Hans Darke will spare no expense getting her out of Chicago as soon as is humanly possible.'

Lukas thought for a moment.

'We have colleagues in that city,' he said simply.

'Then I would be obliged if you would ask them to pay Miss Zemeckis a visit, sooner than later.'

'It shall be done.'

88

Flow

CHICAGO Saturday October 28, 1893   5.50 PM

Emily made faster progress than she had expected.

The driver, who had made the run to the South Side a thousand times on Darke Hartz business, knew every twist and turn even if their final destination was one he had never been to before.

They stopped at 31st and consulted the map.

'Are you sure you want to go there, miss? It's a bad neighborhood and no place for ladies.'

'I don't give a damn about that,' said Emily, 'and anyway I'm no lady, so just get me there!'

The streets, rock hard throughout summer, were now awash with water and the carriage jerked and bobbed about sending spray everywhere. There was no-one much about on the sidewalks but the saloons were heaving, it being a Saturday, and snatches of music and song came to them from behind closed windows.

'Folk celebrating the end of the Fair,' said the driver.

They turned into a small street, dark and mean, with few lights showing.

'Make a right,' called out Emily, poring over her map.

The next street was no better than a slum.

'Make a left and then a right again . . .'

The carriage slowed, negotiating piles of trash and potholes.

'Not good!' exclaimed the driver, slowing still more and having trouble controlling the horses.

They finally pulled into a street where only a single light showed with a row of houses down one side of it.

'This must be Benson Street,' called out Emily.

'Don't see no sign,' said the driver dubiously.

'Can you see another carriage?'

'I can.'

'Make for it and stop.'

The driver drove on cautiously, the houses to their right, and stopped.

Emily got out.

There was a bad smell in the air. Peering between the ramshackle wooden houses and beyond the railing at the top of the embankment, Emily saw what she was looking for.

'Bubbly Creek,' she whispered. She couldn't see it in the darkness below, but she could hear its roar and smell its stinking water.

On the far side of the Creek loomed the dark mass of the Armour Glue Factory. The air was so pungent and heavy that Emily nearly retched.

Then a figure loomed out of the darkness beyond the other carriage. Emily's driver eased back his jacket revealing a revolver. Mr Darke had said to take no chances.

'It's all right,' said Emily quietly. 'And keep that out of sight, it won't help anyone.'

The advancing figure was a woman.

'Katharine Hubbard?' she called out. 'Is that you?' The two women embraced.

'Glad to see you, Emily. I've brought the things you suggested and two lanterns . . .'

'Could you see anything in the Creek?'

Katharine shook her head.

'Nothing, I walked the whole length of the street from the bridge at one end to the conduit at the other. But two pairs of eyes will be better than one.'

They fetched the lanterns from Katharine's carriage and the drivers lit them, both offering to help.

Emily thanked them but shook her head.

'Best not,' she said. 'We're looking for a girl whose been running from men for weeks and the sight of a couple more calling out her name will send her running again. If you're needed we'll call you.'

The houses were mostly unlit, or those that were had their blinds and curtains tight shut, revealing only a sliver of light.

'There were lights on when I arrived,' said Katharine, 'but people in these neighborhoods shy away from any sign of trouble. They probably heard my carriage, took one peek and decided I was the police or up to no good.'

'Right,' said Emily, 'let's try looking again, nice and slow, from the conduit right up to the bridge. But take care not to alarm Anna if she's down there. She'll be jumpy. We don't want to scare her.'

They peered down at the racing water calling Anna's name. But the light from their lanterns didn't reach very far and they could see little more than the muddy bank on the nearside, let alone the surface of the water.

'What makes you think she's here?' asked Katharine.

'It's no more than a hunch.'

'Why on earth would she deliberately get into Bubbly Creek here, on Benson Street of all places?'

'She wouldn't. If she got in anywhere it was up at the Yard.'

'But that's half a mile away. In this weather, with the Creek running at full spate, she wouldn't stand a chance.'

'She made it before. I'm reckoning that if she felt that the Creek was her last place of refuge this is where she'd fetch up. Right here where she was found before. But she may be too cold and weak now, and maybe we're too late . . .'

Emily leaned over toward the Creek again, holding her lantern. Then she gave the lantern to Kate and peered into the gloom below.

'It's so hard to see,' she muttered irritably. 'I have to get closer.'

There was an air of grim determination about

Emily now as she took off her cloak and handed it to Katharine, along with her purse.

'Emily Strauss, I am not letting you . . .'

'A bit of cold and wet's not going to hurt me.'

Kate pointed at the racing water below and said, 'One slip and you'll get carried away.'

'And where would it take me if it did?'

'Into the Chicago River. The Creek joins it about a hundred and fifty yards from here. Can't you hear the roar?'

They listened.

It was loud and angry.

'I think it runs down into a chute in the final stretch, like a waterfall. You'd end up in the river and you'd end up dead. Please, Emily, don't . . .'

But Emily was already hoisting up her skirts. She climbed over the railing, which wobbled precariously, and clambered down on the far side, lowering herself into the darkness.

'My, it's cold!' she said, 'But I have a foothold. Of sorts.'

One of her hands reached up into the light.

'Give me the lantern.'

Katharine placed it carefully into her hands so that it did not gutter and go out.

'Oohh!'

'What is it?'

'I slipped. The current's very strong.'

'Is there anywhere to walk along the Creek's edge?'

There was silence for a moment or two.

'There's mud and worse,' said Emily eventually, 'and a ledge of sorts, but it's very, very slippery. Oh!'

'*Emily!*'

A hand appeared on the wall at the foot of the railings and Emily's face showed.

'I'm going upstream to the conduit and if there's nothing there I'll come back down to the bridge where the railings are lower and I can get back out more easily. Okay?'

'Emily, please . . .'

But Emily had disappeared into the darkness below again and all Katharine Hubbard could do was follow on the street above and try to keep sight of her lantern.

Emily was half in water and half out, her left hand on the embankment for balance, her feet in mud, her skirts swept and dragged at by the flow of the water. She held the lantern in her right hand.

'Anna!' she called softly, '*Anna!*'

She waded on, the water feeling colder by the minute and the Creek, its banks getting higher as she went, seeming ever darker.

'Anna?'

Nothing.

The ledge narrowed and soon she was wading in the water up to her waist, her skirts a hindrance, the stream deep and faster on the right-hand side. At one point she made the mistake of letting her right hand drop and the bottom of the lantern caught the water which nearly ripped it out of her hand.

No woman, no man, could survive in this, she told herself.

At last, already very cold and tired, she reached the entrance to the tunnel which carried the flow from under buildings upstream. It was six feet high and had once had wire across it, to stop people going in when the water was low. Most of this had broken and swung up against the wall on the side where Emily was. She used it to pull herself the last few feet and then, placing the lantern on mud and flotsam to one side of the flow, she climbed inside.

The place roared with the sound of water but it was big enough for her to nearly stand upright, the roof curving above her head.

'Anna!' she shouted, as loud as she could against the Creek's roar. She moved ahead for ten yards or so before she decided it was folly to go further. If Anna was still alive, and now she had to face facts and believe she probably wasn't, she would have got out of this place fast.

Reluctantly, Emily turned back, the water rushing past her with such force that she lost her footing again, fell and was propelled back the way she had come.

Only by grabbing onto the broken fence again was she able to right herself, her lantern nearly going out in the tumble.

She stopped, caught her breath and took stock.

A sense of the serious danger she was in suddenly hit her but she was determined to carry on the search.

'Now for the other . . . W . . . W . . . way,' she muttered aloud, her teeth chattering with cold and fear.

Something wet and slimy brushed across her face and she started back. It was some kind of material caught in the fence. She raised her lantern and saw at once that it was a woman's plaid shawl.

'Oh, Anna,' she whispered.

It was the same shawl she had been wearing earlier that day.

With a gathering sense of urgency, Emily splashed back down the way she had come, holding on as best she could to the bank, shining the lantern and calling out every which way until she reached the point where she had left Katharine. She felt a surge of renewed energy.

'I'm going on down to the bridge,' she called up.

'Please!' said Katharine.

'Follow me down . . . by the time I get there one of the drivers may have to haul me out.

The next section of the Creek was wider and safer but it was a whole lot muddier and Emily lost first one boot and then another. Mud and slime slurped between her toes. Her hands touched fetid matter and garbage that she could not identify.

But still she pushed on, with a fierce, angry energy. She blamed herself for what had happened. She should never have left the Yard in the first place.

She reached the bridge where, she still hoped, Anna might be taking shelter. But she was nowhere to be seen under the arch, the logical last place to hide. Nothing.

Emily knew now she was too late.

Nobody could survive Bubbly Creek

They all said it.

Anna Zemeckis had survived it once but not a second time.

'I'm sorry, Anna,' Emily whispered in the raging, racing, bitter dark, 'I tried, I tried but . . .'

The she saw that there was a barbed wire fence of sorts across the conduit which took the flow of Bubbly Creek into the river. All sorts of flotsam had got caught in it just as in the conduit she'd been in upriver. And there was something over there, bobbing up and down in the water. It could be, *it could be*.

'Anna!' she shouted again, her voice lost in the dark roar about her, as she struggled to keep hold of the slimy wall, her hands numb with the cold and making her fumble and slip.

'Emily!'

Katharine's voice rang out in the distance, up on the bridge. 'Are you all right?'

Emily was now nearly at the barbed wire fence and the thing that she had seen was still moving feebly in the flow. What was it? An arm, . . . or something?

Then Emily, slipping and sliding the final yard or two, got close enough to see – and screamed.

She found herself staring in disbelief and shock into the white eyes, gaping mouth and snout of a huge hog, rotten and stinking with death, water flowing right into it and around it, the 'arm' she had seen no more than a front quarter, its hind quarters trapped in the wire.

She turned away shocked and exhausted, knowing she had to get back upstream out of the Creek soon or she never would at all. She looked again at the hog and then beyond it across the river. She could see a ship's lights and the silhouette of what must be a grain elevator. To its left were the rounded mounds of coal heaps and a jumble of shapes that was probably lumber.

The river itself was a wide, steady flow of water. Powerful, deep, dark and remorseless. A river of life that had now become a place of death and nightmares.

'Anna!' she called a final time, but her voice held no hope now, 'Anna!'

'Emily! I can't see you. Where are you?' called out Katharine anxiously from above.

Emily turned back toward Katharine's voice and the safety of the bridge.

'Emily!'

'I'm coming!' she shouted back, angry with herself, with Chicago and with everything, '. . . but it isn't exactly easy!'

'Be careful!'

Emily was dead beat but she knew if she was to win her battle to get back to the bridge she was going have to win by brute force.

She grabbed whatever she could by way of hand-holds, and, putting her shoulder to the racing water, inched her way forward until she finally made it back to the nearside of the bridge.

Above she could just make out Kate's lantern.

'I'm coming back up the other side!' she shouted. 'I can't get to it from here.'

Emily tried to heave herself back up onto the ledge inside the low bridge, but the water was high and she didn't have the strength.

She pulled back to see if there was another way, her eyes looking up past the arch and then across to the far side where it dropped back down into shadow.

It was then, as Emily clung on seeking a way back to safety, that she saw Anna Zemeckis, caught in the lee of the bridge, just out of reach of the creek's violent flow. Right where Emily had passed by before. She was huddled down, half in the water and half out of it, looking no more than a bundle of rags.

'Anna?'

The water rushed between them, great raging surges of it, '*Anna!?*'

The sodden rags moved and somewhere within them eyes opened, white in the gloom, and stared across the water at her.

'*Anna! Don't move!*'

Emily threw aside her lantern, using both hands now to feel her way along the arch of the bridge until she found a handhold. She glowered at the water, and then, with a pull and a rush, she heaved herself across to the little haven Anna had found.

It was a tiny jumble of mud and flotsam. Behind it rose an unyielding brick wall. In front, the water rushed and sucked.

What Emily saw before her now was something she surely would never forget. A woman who was hardly more than a girl, so cold and exhausted that she was shaking all over. Only one thing was steady and that was her right hand which clung on to the pile of flotsam.

'I wanted to die,' whispered Anna, 'to drown in the Creek, as I should have done in the first place. But I couldn't do it. I couldn't because I knew my baby was alive.'

Emily reached out to her.

'It's all right Anna, it's over. You're safe now. I'm taking you home.'

After Emily and Katharine and the two drivers had hauled Anna out of the Creek, Katharine helped the two women get dry in her carriage and put on the change of clothes Emily had asked her to bring from Hull House. Then she gave them food and something to drink.

'She must come to Hull House, straight away. And see our doctor. We'll take care of her,' insisted Katharine. 'She's in no fit state to go further.'

Emily shook her head.

'No, Katharine, she can't stay in Chicago, because she's still in danger. And she needs protection. The authorities are after her and probably the Meisters too. I'm taking her back to Mr Darke's house on Astor Street.'

'But Emily . . .'

Anna opened her eyes and stared at them. Her face was blue and puffy from the beating Gunther had given her and her eyes bloodshot.

'Please . . . I want to see John. Where is he . . . ?'

'It's okay, Anna, he's safe,' Emily reassured her, then turned to Katharine.

'Please call Hans and Wolfgang Darke the moment you get back to Hull House. Tell them what's happened and that I need to get Anna on the first available train to New York. Tell Ben to have Johnny Leppard bring my luggage from the Auditorium Annex. Emily Strauss and the *World* are taking Anna home. Back to her father.'

Soon after, Katharine Hubbard's carriage went one way into the night and Emily's the other, leaving the Creek behind them for good.

A short while later, a body, flopping its way down Bubbly Creek, was carried past Benson Street before being briefly caught in a back-swirl of water on the far side of the bridge.

Then, the water surging once more, the body was lifted and carried on down toward the Conduit where the water hurled it against the dead and bloated hog already entangled in the wire there, which it embraced obscenely.

From there, man and hog together, looking pretty much the same in the dark, shot off into the anonymous expanse of the Chicago River.

89

À Bientôt

When Hans Darke received the call from Katharine Hubbard of Hull House that Anna and Emily were safe and on their way back to Astor Street his relief knew no bounds.

He and Wolfgang at once organized a doctor to come and check that Anna was fit to travel, sent for Emily's luggage and booked places on an express train leaving Dearborn for New York at 7.30 p.m. that night.

As he waited for Anna's arrival, the relief Hans felt fled and he became anxious, pacing the room once more.

'What do I *say* to her?' he asked Isaiah over and over again.

'I should think she'll be as nervous as you are,' his friend replied, 'but very tired as well. She has been through a great deal. She is the innocent party. And all you can do is try to be accepting, welcome her and make her feel she is safe.'

'Yes, but . . . *Elfrieda*! I need you!'

'Leave Miss Zemeckis to me when she arrives, uncle,' Elfrieda said. 'She will need to rest and change and I dare say Miss Strauss will as well. Miss Hubbard says they have both been through a great deal.'

To add to the atmosphere of uneasy excitement, John English now turned up in a cab from Cook

County Hospital, his face cut and bandaged but otherwise recovered.

The two apparitions that finally entered the door of Hans Darke's splendid home on Astor Street could not have been more incongruous with the elegant surroundings. Dressed in a motley assortment of clothes, their hair a mess and their faces streaked with the grime and filth of Bubbly Creek, one looked exhausted and the other as if she had been in a prizefight.

The doctor immediately checked Anna over and reassured her that all was well with the baby, after which Elfrieda took them in to see Hans Darke.

Emily and Anna entered the drawing room where the others sat waiting for them, Hans Darke immediately rising from his seat, mute and staring at the bruised and battered girl.

'Mr Darke . . . this is . . . Miss Zemeckis . . .' said Emily, her voice soft. For once she found herself unable to think of anything else to say.

Hans remained rooted to the spot, lost for words. All he could do was stare with a mixture of shock and pity at the exhausted, disheveled girl in front of him.

It was Anna herself who broke the ice.

'I am very sorry,' she said quietly, 'for all the trouble I have caused you, Mr Darke. But I am glad to be here and glad to see you here too, Mr Crazy, and I . . . I . . .'

Emily was ready now to move to Anna's side, for she seemed about to break down. But she did not.

Instead, she turned back to face Hans Darke and said, '. . . but I am sorry, sir, to meet you in these . . . circumstances. Please do not think that . . . that . . .'

'What?' said Hans Darke, instinctively leaning forward, his voice no more than a whisper. It seemed to him that he had never in his life heard a young woman say anything so painful and difficult with such grace and he cursed himself for a lifetime of not knowing how to be himself where emotions were concerned.

Sensing his confusion, Anna continued, '. . . No, please. You don't have to say anything. And do not think that I expect anything of you except, please, some food, and a glass of water and a little time to rest and . . . and then . . .'

She stood before him, he one of Chicago's richest citizens, she one of its poorest, and she was asking nothing of him but his compassion and a glass of water.

After so many long years of reserve, of ruthless self-discipline, of never saying more to anyone than what was necessary, or doing anything that was not to his own commercial advantage, something suddenly gave way right in the center of Hans Darke's heart. It opened up new feelings that took him into a different world that was frightening and strange.

He did something that felt like the hardest thing he had ever done in his life: he crossed the few feet between himself and the brave, hurt, frightened girl before him, and took her in his strong arms and said, 'You are more welcome to my house than you will ever know. Welcome, Anna, welcome.'

And it was *his* voice that broke.

Not long after, Toulson and Van Hale arrived.

Toulson was relieved when Hans informed him that he had arranged berths for the two women out of Dearborn at 7.30 that night.

'I'm very glad to hear it, Mr Darke,' he said.

'Whatever Paul Hartz may have signed, and wherever Gunther may now be, I don't think the Meisters will let Anna or Miss Strauss be and it is impossible for the two of us to protect them here . . .'

'In any event,' added Emily, 'I have to get a story to the *World* that I haven't even written yet. I shall have to write it on the train and file it by telegraph at the first station with a Western Union en route.'

'I'll be traveling with Emily part of the way,' Ben explained, 'to work on the illustrations for her story and then get back to Chicago for the closing of the Fair. I'll have to get off at Fort Wayne which we should reach around 10.30, to file Emily's story there before catching the last train passing in the other direction, back to Chicago.'

Emily added, 'We'll need a drawing of Anna tied up in the storehouse and . . .'

Ben produced his sketchbook from his pocket.

'Don't worry, Emily, already done it,' he said matter of factly.

'But your hands were tied behind your back!'

Ben gave her the wry look of an old pro.

'This is journalism, Miss Strauss, not scientific truth. I did these sketches while you were down at the Creek searching for Anna. And Wolfgang went back to the Yard and retrieved my camera too, from the storehouse.'

Emily looked at the drawing of Anna.

'You've captured her likeness perfectly, and even how tired and helpless she looked.'

'That's what I *do*,' he said.

'Let's see the others,' said Emily.

She flicked through Ben's sketchbook. There were dozens of them, some no more than thumbnails, others a whole page of the book.

She stared at them in amazement.

'But these are just as I imagined I would write about it . . .'

'Yes, I know. It's my job. But they'll only use a couple at most, so prepare yourself for disappointment.'

There came a ring at the door. It was Johnny Leppard, in his uniform, just in time with Emily's luggage.

'The housekeeper packed it, Miss Strauss. And I demoted myself to bellhop again so I could be sure to come and say goodbye.'

Emily tipped Johnny generously and thanked him for all he had done. For no good reason she knew she would miss him.

'And Mr Ritz, Johnny, did he come up trumps?'

'Of course he did. I persuaded him that he needed my services at the Savoy, London.'

'And why would that be?'

'Told him guests from England at the Auditorium Annex appreciate an English voice among the staff. Makes 'em feel at home.'

Emily laughed.

'And Americans at the Savoy would do likewise? Namely yours?'

Johnny nodded.

'And he bought it?'

'He did, Miss Strauss.'

'And is he paying your fare?'

'Course miss. "Don't give me a tip, sir," I said, "just give me the fare."'

'When are you going.'

'Soon as the Fair's over. All the hotels'll be shedding staff fast. Got to be ahead of the game. You look me up if ever you're in London, won't you?'

'I will,' Emily said.

'Meanwhile, I'll get on with improving my French.'

'Au revoir, then' said Emily.

'À bientôt,' Johnny replied.

'What's that mean?'

'See you soon and I hope I do, miss. I hope I do.'

The train for New York left Dearborn promptly at 7.30 that evening and none of the group were sorry, for now, to see the last of Chicago.

John English saw them off. He wanted to travel with them but common sense prevailed.

'Let me talk to my father,' said Anna. 'It would be too much for him right now . . . And you should talk to your mother and Mr McIlvanie. And we shall write and see what we shall see. And then . . . after the baby . . .'

She could not bring herself yet to be more explicit. 'You will feel very differently toward me, I expect,' she said matter of factly.

'No, Anna,' said John very firmly, 'I won't. And yes, I shall write, but Anna . . .'

'What?'

'I am not going to lose you again.'

As the train pulled out of Dearborn Station into the night it hit thunderous rain: rain that hammered on the roof and slanted down the windows in streaks and rivulets and which caught the light outside, especially when, twenty minutes later, it passed the bright electric lights of Jackson Park and the World's Fair.

'Last time,' said Anna.

But Emily was looking the other way, toward the Union Stock Yard. No lights there, just darkness. And beyond, between the glimmers of sheet

506

lightning, the lurid glimpses of chimneys and drifting smoke.

Then the rain fell heavier still.

'Rain. Good, cleansing rain,' said Emily with a sense of satisfaction, '. . . to wash away the dark heart of Chicago.'

90

Fort Wayne

CHICAGO Saturday October 28, 1893   10.30 PM

Half an hour out of Chicago, after a short doze, Anna Zemeckis at last began to talk and open up. It was as if, with the city behind her, she now felt free to tell Emily all she had been through: to re-live it in order to then try to forget it.

For an hour or more Emily listened and wrote and listened some more, but she still had not got to the heart of Anna's story.

Finally, she interrupted her gently, saying, 'Anna, there's something I need to ask you and there isn't much time . . .'

'Then you must ask me the things you need,' said Anna.

'There's one thing you haven't talked about . . .'

'What?'

'How did you end up in Bubbly Creek?'

Anna hesitated a while and looked out of the window at the passing night. Finally, she said in a low voice, 'I don't want to talk about it because it's the worst part of all . . . and it was my own fault.'

'So what happened?'

Anna sighed wearily and said, 'I should have taken Marion's advice and stayed away from Gunther and the Stock Yard. She *warned* me. But I went back to try and confront him . . .'

She put her hand to her belly.

'I was desperate; I couldn't believe he wouldn't help. Most of all I couldn't believe he really wanted his child never to be born. Day after I day I hid away in Marion's little room. One day . . .'

'The 18th October?'

'It was a Wednesday, I think, yes . . .'

'Ten days ago.'

'Is that all? Yes, about then. Well, Marion was at work so I knew she couldn't stop me. On the spur of the moment, I got on the Elevated and from there walked to the Union Stock Yard. I felt sick and sad. I don't know what was in my mind but I just needed to talk to him, whatever he had done to me. I just . . . didn't want to be alone.'

'At first they wouldn't let me into his office but I began to shout and he came out. He was furious. He led me away, where no-one could see, and he slapped me hard.

'"How dare you come here and cause a scene," he shouted. "How dare you!"

'Then he grabbed my arm . . . He was holding it so tight and he forced me along and I was scared, really scared.'

'He took me back to the killing floor where I had been forced to wear those garments and have photographs taken and I thought he was . . . I thought I was going to be made to do things . . . like those other women . . . like Marion Stoiber. I begged him to let me go but when Gunther was angry he was like a demon.'

'He said nothing, but dragged me up to the hog

wheel where I had seen a girl . . . chained up . . . the afternoon he violated me, when . . .'

She looked down at her belly.

'He said, "Is this what you want? To be chained to the hog wheel? I will if you don't stop screaming . . ."

'But I did scream.

'He hit me again, in the face this time and then dragged me up some stairs. Bump! Bump! Bump! It hurt so much! And then, suddenly, he opened a door and threw me into a room and locked me in. It smelt horrible and it was dark and I banged into things and knocked over liquids and bottles of powder and I was so frightened and the smell made me want to vomit.

'I don't know how long I was in there, but eventually I heard voices and the door opened and two men were there. Two butchers. They came into the room and I knew what they wanted and what they were going to do. I had seen them before with the girls all dressed up in their corsets and stockings.

'I ran round the room crashing into things and throwing everything I could at them, as they laughed and made grabs at me. It was all a game to them. Then I found the door and ran down the dark corridor. But it was night by then and I had no idea in which direction to go.

'I ran and ran with the men behind me and then went tumbling down some stairs. There was another door, but as I wrenched it open I fell straight out onto rail tracks – bang!

'I got up and ran right across the tracks, stumbling, hitting things, getting caught in the wire of a fence, and then the wooden palings of another fence. The men followed, laughing. They were enjoying the chase. They knew they could catch me if they wanted to.

'I was so confused I didn't know where I was. It was dark and there was the smell of smoke and the stink, such an awful stink, and suddenly I was falling straight down, and down, which seemed to go on forever until I hit what felt like water but wasn't. It felt all filthy and slimy and I tried to wade through it but my skirts dragged me down and suddenly I was sinking.

'I came up once and heard them and I knew I mustn't make a sound and I didn't. But I hurt everywhere – inside and out – and I was cold. I didn't know I was in Bubbly Creek. Then I blacked out.

'That was the last thing I knew until it was light and they fished me out and threw cold water in my face.'

Anna looked at Emily and then said very quietly, 'Is that what you wanted to know?'

Emily said, 'Yes, Anna, thank you. Now rest. You must get some sleep. For the baby's sake.'

Toulson, Van Hale and Ben had all listened to Anna's story in silence as well, but not one of them had said a word.

Emily helped Anna to her berth, gave her one of her own clean nightdresses and made sure she was comfortable.

'I'm so tired,' she said, closing her eyes.

'I know,' said Emily. 'Sleep now, and tomorrow you shall see your father again.'

Three hours out of Chicago, Ben Latham got off the train at Fort Wayne. It was half-past ten.

He did so carrying Emily's dramatic story of how the *World* had rescued Anna Zemeckis, one of its reader's own, and had brought her safely back home to her loving grief-stricken father in New York, rescuing her from a fate worse than death at the hands of the evil merchants of filth in Chicago, America's most dangerous frontier city . . .

. . . or words to that effect, because, as Ben had said, by the time the *World*'s editors and headline writers had finished with it, that's how it would read.

Ben's job at Fort Wayne was to get the story telegraphed ahead of Emily to New York so she could go straight to the *World* on her arrival the following evening in the certain knowledge that she had met her deadline – and met it in good time.

He had left three pocket sketchbooks with her on the train and some worked up illustrations of a kind he knew his editors would want. Being drawn from life, they were sharp and evocative and he was confident they would serve Emily's story – and his own reputation – well.

He then gave Emily one more thing. It was a piece of folded paper.

'Open it, Emily.'

It was a series of thumbnail sketches of a woman in some of the locations they had been to.

'Why, Ben, it's me! But I never noticed . . .'

'That's the secret, capturing the subject when they don't know you're watching,' he said, with his usual grin. 'A souvenir.'

Emily looked at the sketches; in some she was laughing, in some frowning, in some peering at things, in some just standing clutching her notebook and looking like a journalist with skyscrapers rising all around her. There was the Ferris Wheel, the Stock Yard and the Auditorium Annex. It seemed she had been all over Chicago.

'Thank you, Ben,' she said, folding the page back up carefully again before she slipped it in her purse.

They were both dog-tired but elated. They had done a good job and they had done it well.

Fort Wayne's Western Union office offered a twenty-four hour service, seeing as it was one of the busiest stations in the Midwest and that the train had a scheduled stop of half an hour before continuing its journey. Ben raced off hoping he could get Emily's copy sent by an operator in time for him to run back and reassure her it was on its way.

'It's a sure-fire winner,' he said as he got off the train.

'Really?' said Emily. 'You really think so . . .?'

'Yes. I *know* so. I know a great story when I see it. They'll *love* it.'

'Are you sure?' said Emily, beset but sudden and uncharacteristic doubts.

'Absolutely,' said Ben. 'I'll be as quick as I can so you know it's been sent. Stay right there!'

'Don't worry,' said Emily, 'wild horses wouldn't get me off this train.'

The Western Union was seconds away across the concourse of the depot but when Ben got there he found a line of people waiting and the telegraph operators were all busy.

Come on, come on . . . Ben urged them under his breath, looking back to see if Emily's train was still there.

It was.

When he finally reached the desk, the operator eyed his sheets of scrawled handwriting and said, ironically, 'Is this it? *All* of it?'

Ben nodded.

'Well . . . I don't know,' said the man, shaking his head.

Ben smiled his most charming smile.

'It's for the New York *World*,' he said.

'Don't care if it's for the moon, makes no difference to me.'

'How long will it take?'

'Long enough.'

'I've got someone on a train to say goodbye to.'

Ben put down several dollar bills, more than he needed to. The clerk softened a bit.

'Just so you know I'm coming back,' said Ben. 'Give me five minutes.'

'You can take longer than that . . .' said the clerk, picking up the bills. 'If it's a girl, take longer still!'

Ben raced back onto the concourse and then stopped dead in his tracks. Something was odd. The Depot seemed strangely busy for late on a Saturday night. Come to think of it, the Western Union had been busy too.

There were people standing around in huddles doing nothing much but staring; there was a newsboy at the Depot entrance shouting excitedly but Ben couldn't hear what he was saying; over by the refreshment stand a man was talking and gesticulating to a group of people crowded around him. There was, Ben suddenly realized, a deathly chill right round the place and it wasn't the weather.

'What's happened?' he said, grabbing someone.

'He's dead,' the man said, 'he's been shot.'

'Who's been shot?'

'Harrison, he's dead. Happened this evening.'

'What, Benjamin Harrison? The former president?'

'No, *Carter* Harrison.'

Ben couldn't take it in. The world whirled around him and his face was a blank.

'Mayor Carter Henry Harrison,' said the man emphatically.

'Of *Chicago*?' said Ben, still incredulous.

'Shot at eight this evening, right on his doorstep.'

'Shot!'

'It's terrible, terrible . . .'

Ben turned and walked back toward Emily's train in a daze. Even when he saw it beginning to pull out he hardly had the strength to run.

Mayor Carter Henry Harrison, the best known Mayor in America, host of the World's Fair . . . *shot just hours before the Grand Closing Ceremony*.

He began running, trying to catch the departing train, desperate to tell Emily so that . . . so that . . .

'Ben!'

He saw her hanging out of a window, waving and grinning.

'Did you send it?' he heard her shout.

She didn't know.

If she did she wouldn't be laughing.

'Did you?' she shouted again.

'Yes!' he mouthed, nodding his head in case she couldn't hear, '*Yes* . . .'

But the train was moving too fast and now, even had he been able to, Ben would not have told her the truth, not then, not there, the implications were too cruel.

As Emily's train rattled out of Fort Wayne Depot she sank back in her seat, confident in the knowledge that her story had been safely telegraphed to the *World* and would be published in Monday's paper.

But Ben knew otherwise. He knew it wouldn't be, couldn't be published, not now.

For Emily Strauss's first big story and a hundred others would be killed. The sensational and wholly unexpected assassination of Mayor Carter Henry Harrison of Chicago would take over the newspapers for days to come.

It would surely be the biggest story of the decade and, on a newspaper like the *World*, which made its reputation and its money by publishing only the very latest, hottest news, whatever that might be, Ben Latham knew that the story of Anna Zemeckis would die a death as surely as if it had never been.

Emily, meanwhile, slept the night right through in blissful ignorance of the assassination of Harrison and its implications for her story.

It was only when she awoke the next morning, as the train pulled in further up the Pennsylvania Railroad, that she heard the newsboys shouting 'Harrison dead!' and 'Chicago already in Mourning' and 'World's Fair Closing Ceremony Celebrations Cancelled', and she realized what had happened. The train was already abuzz with the news circulated by the guards and from passengers who had been awake earlier and picked up newspapers along
the line.

Emily asked to look at someone's paper and read the basic facts:

The previous evening, a twenty-five-year-old Chicagoan newspaper distributor called Eugene Prendergast had knocked on the door at Harrison's house on South Ashland Avenue and asked to see the Mayor personally. The sixty-two-year-old Harrison, an affable, open-hearted man, had given standing instructions that if callers came and he was available he was to be informed.

Having just had dinner with two of his children he went out personally to greet the caller and ask his business. In response to which Prendergast had produced a .38-caliber revolver and fired three shots into Harrison at point blank range. The mayor fell to the ground and the assassin stepped forward and fired a fourth shot into his upper body.

Hearing the shots, the mayor's coachman came running but arrived too late to stop Prendergast, who, after firing a final shot, escaped. Less than an hour later he got off a streetcar near Desplaines Police Station and calmly walked in and gave himself up.

The motive was as yet unknown but already the morning papers were calling Prendergast a 'lunatic' and 'mad'.

For hours and hours people on the train could talk of nothing else, unable to believe the story or even accept it. For no mayor in Chicago's short history had ever been more respected and more loved than Harrison – a familiar figure to Fairgoers and citizens alike, many of whom, including Emily only three days before, had seen him on his white horse in the streets downtown – a habit that had made him popular with all.

It was not long before Emily realized that her story was in jeopardy. If the morning papers at each station along the line were giving Harrison's assassination increasingly blanket coverage she knew well enough that her story about Anna Zemeckis would now seem an irrelevance and be as good as dead.

So she sat in a daze, torn between sorrow for Harrison and Chicago and dismay at her own ill-fortune, unable to do anything but listen to those around her declaring their own shock, telling their stories of the Mayor and his many good works in their city, and watch men, as well as women, openly weeping.

It was a somber train and a shocked and disconsolate Emily Strauss that finally arrived at Jersey City at ten minutes past eight that evening.

It took them a little while to spot Janis Zemeckis standing waiting for them. He was not alone. By his side stood a figure very familiar to and much-loved by Anna – Mrs Kopecky, their Czech tenant, who had been with them so many years. Janis had brought her along for moral support because among the many mixed emotions he felt the most powerful was simple fear.

So he stood there waiting, a small, shrunken man in a situation he did not understand, who had grieved for the loss of his daughter who had been miraculously found again.

'Papa,' said Anna as she approached him, and her eyes were fearful too, '*Papa . . .*'

But Janis did not move. He looked at Anna and at her rounded belly and at her tired face and he looked so sad and uncertain of himself that he bent his head because it was all too much to comprehend.

'Anna!' cried Mrs Kopecky, moving forward and embracing her. 'Anna my dear! You look so exhausted! Come now,' she added, whispering in Anna's ear, 'embrace your father and he will be all right.'

So Anna reached out and held her father, and there on the bustling concourse, Janis Zemeckis shook and cried in his daughter's gentle, loving arms.

Someone had listened. Someone had brought his daughter back to him.

DAY ELEVEN

Sunday October 29, 1893

91
Lion's Den

As soon as she could, and after she had said her goodbyes to Anna and Janis Zemeckis, leaving them in the care of Toulson and Van Hale, a deflated Emily Strauss took a cab to the *World*'s offices on Park Row. It was the most miserable and unhappy ride she had ever taken.

She got out, paid a fare she knew now she could ill-afford and approached the entrance of the tall, lit-up building.

The doorman blocked her entry.

'Sorry, Miss, not this late, unless you've business here.'

Emily produced her visiting card and her press pass.

He looked at it and peered at her and then said grudgingly, 'Didn't recognize you Miss, er, Strauss,' and ushered her in.

She decided the best thing to do was to put a brave face on things and try to see Mr Hadham, the City Editor, himself. Perhaps after all they might use her story somewhere deep inside the paper – they surely couldn't fill it all with Harrison.

She took the elevator up to the editorial offices on the eleventh floor and marched boldly along, ignoring the curious glances she knew a woman always got in a male preserve.

But at the entrance to the great room which was the City Office she was stopped again, this time by two youths, hall boys by the look of them.

'Yer not comin' in,' said the taller and gawkier of the two.

'I'm Emily Strauss,' she said as forcefully as she could.

'Don't matter if you're the Queen of Sheba,' said the other youth laconically, shooting a mouthful of tobacco juice into a spittoon at her feet. 'Women not allowed'.

A dozen images shot through Emily's mind of the men she had encountered in Chicago in the last ten days. It seemed to her that, compared to them, these boys, and that's all they really were, were nothing; and that she had nothing to lose.

She reached forward, took hold of the taller youth's upper arm, leaned all her weight into him, raised her right leg a little, curled it around the back of his and gave his chest a sharp push with her right shoulder.

He went flying backwards through the door and collapsed on the floor, a look of shocked surprise on his face.

She might have expected that a body crashing into a room at no small speed might attract a modicum of attention from those inside.

But it did not.

Never in her life had Emily seen a room as chaotic, as noisy and purely energetic as the *World*'s city office now was. It wasn't always like this on a Sunday, of course. But today was different. The Harrison assassination had ensured that the place was humming, even at this late hour. The great bank of desks were all lit up, and hunched over them, men typing, men writing, men shouting 'Coppee!' at the top of their voices and holding aloft pieces of paper for the copy boys to fetch and rush over to the raised podium at which four men sat, in a fug of cigar smoke, Charles Hadham, City Editor of the *World* among them.

Emily stepped over the boy she had sent sprawling on the floor and entered this lion's den and headed straight for Hadham.

'Sir!' she shouted above the din, aware that others were looking up from their work straight at her.

'Mr Hadham!' she cried again.

He looked up at her and stared.

Perhaps she hoped he would leap to his feet in welcome recognition but he did not.

'I'm busy,' he said.

'I filed a story.'

'Half the world has filed a story. Come back later.'

'But . . .'

'Miss Strauss, we've a paper to get out and you shouldn't be here.'

'But my story, it's important.'

'Go and wait somewhere then, preferably where I can't see you. Now, go!'

Emily went, but she didn't leave. Instead she turned and looked at the great office once more. She was damned if she was going to budge until Hadham had told her what he'd done with her story. She looked around for a seat. There was only one, in a far corner of the vast, smoky room, at a small, unoccupied desk. She sidled along the back wall to it, took off her cloak, sat down and watched.

It was, she realized, probably the last time she would ever be in such a purely male preserve and she wanted to take it in, to remember it, because this was what she had dreamed of breaking into for so long.

Except it wasn't hers, it was theirs, and she was no part of it.

But as she sat and watched Emily began to make sense of the chaos and to understand the pattern of the place and its rhythm. The more she did the more it excited her.

The hub of things was not quite as she imagined. The City Editor and his colleagues might sit up on their 'throne', but they weren't the *real* men in charge. No, the hub of this whole enterprise, as she quickly observed, was a little man with a pale, wizened face and eyeshade who sat under a light at a table in front of, but lower down from the editors. It was to this man that all the copy produced in that huge great room came and went in a never-ending backward and forward flow, between editors, journalists and others whose role she did not fully understand, all of it carried by the copy boys who ran around continually, stopping only sometimes to scent the air and see where next they were needed, like so many rabbits running and hopping round the maddest, busiest, smokiest warren in the world.

Gradually it dawned on Emily that all these people were working to one song and one song only: that of the assassination of Carter Henry Harrison.

As the editors read, compared, consulted, argued and made decisions, each piece of copy was passed down to the wizened man beneath them whom Emily now recognized as the man Ben had introduced her to as Mack the Senior Story Editor. He was the very hub of the great machine that was the New York *World*.

'Coppee!' came the shout and another sheet was

on its way to Mack. 'Coppee!' and another arm was raised across the room. But she was not part of it.

Unable to bear it any more Emily decided to leave. She looked around a final time, so she might remember it. On the walls all around her the same notices were pinned up at regular intervals. They were exhortations from Mr Pulitzer himself to his journalists: *Accuracy! Accuracy! Accuracy!* was one. *Who? What? Where? When? How?* was another. *The facts!* was a third.

'No! No!' she suddenly heard a man roar above the cacophony that was the City Office.

She looked up.

It was Charles Hadham, his cool exterior quite shattered.

He looked furious and he was holding some copy in his hand.

'For God's sake this is one of the most sensational stories of the age and you give me *this!*' he shouted at some hapless journalist who had just sent the copy.

'I want color! *Color!* Isn't there anyone in this office who has ever been to Chicago!?'

Suddenly Emily remembered something Johnny Leppard had said, about seizing his opportunity with Mr Ritz.

Opportunity. That's what it was all about.

Johnny knew when to seize it – he knew how to *make* things happen – and so must she. They were, as she had told herself, two of a kind.

Emily looked around for some paper, pulled the typewriter nearer and put the paper in the roller. She stared at it, and stared at it, and remembered those shocked Chicagoans on the train: their grief, their regret and their stories. She remembered Wabash and she remembered Mr Crazy; she remembered State and the Chicago River and Hull House and the Fair and the Union Stock Yard and the people and the buildings and the smoke and the smell – all the life and color that was Chicago.

And then she began to write.

When, not that long after, she reached the end of the page she ripped it out of the machine and held it high in the air and yelled as loud as she possibly could, 'Coppee!'

If for a moment that great office paused and fell silent it was because it heard a woman's voice.

'Coppee!' Emily yelled again and a boy came running.

'Who to miss?' he asked, astonishment in his eyes.

'Mr Hadham,' she said.

The boy glanced at the page.

'Needs a catch-line, miss. They all have that.'

She took the page back, thought for an instant, and wrote in the top right-hand corner the single word *Color*. She was about to give it back to the boy when she thought again.

She crossed the catch-line out and put another: *Strauss* followed by a slash and the figure *1*. The 1 showed that there was more.

They wanted color? They would get color! Chicago was inside of her and she wanted to let it come pouring out.

She grabbed a second sheet, typed *Strauss/2* and began typing once more, so fast and furious, that the room faded away and she was back on the streets of the city she had just left and among its people.

'Miss Strauss?'

She looked up. It was the same boy as before.

'Mr Hadham wants to see you.'

She got up, pulled the second piece of copy from her machine, and walked down the room aware, as ever, of men watching. She walked as tall as she could and as she did she saw that Mr Hadham was conferring with Mack and they were reading her copy.

'Got any more?' said Arthur Hadham.

She handed him the second sheet.

He grabbed it, scanned it, handed it to Mack who did the same and then a third man had a look. The three conferred.

'I want a page,' said Hadham finally.

'You've got two pages there, sir,' she said.

He exploded.

'I'm surrounded by idiots tonight and not just those of the male gender! A page for God's sake! Get on with it.'

She retreated, dazed, not sure what he meant.

Mack detached himself from the others and followed her. He looked kindly.

'That's his way of saying he likes it. He wants to fill a whole page.'

'A page?' she said in astonishment.

'Seems so.'

'But I filed another . . .'

'We know what you filed, Miss Strauss. Don't think about that right now, just do what he wants – color and more color. I have to send a man over to illustrate what you're doing . . .'

'I have illustrations already, sir.'

'Mack, call me Mack. You've *got* illustrations? Show me.'

Emily dug in her purse and produced the sketch-books Ben Latham had given her.

Mack took one look and said, 'This is Ben Latham's work.'

'He was with me. Mr Hadham *sent* him.'

'Right, I'm sending you one of our best picture men. He'll select the ones to use, and you'll write your copy to them so far as you can.'

'How much is a page?'

'A lot and you ain't got much time. Understand?' She nodded.

'Then get on with it!'

An hour or so later Emily noticed that the room had grown quiet around her. Looking up she saw that she was almost the only one writing now.

Mack was still editing her copy as fast as he got it and then giving it to waiting boys to race off with through a door.

Then he came over and said, 'Seems we have no image of you on file. Don't suppose you've got anything?'

She dug into her purse and pulled out the page of drawings that Ben had done of her as a souvenir and unfolded it.

'Latham's a genius,' said Mack. 'I'll send it over to Mr Hadham for his approval.'

'Hey, Mack,' Emily called after him. 'Be sure I get it back.'

When she finished her final sentence Emily didn't have to shout 'coppee' this time because the room was silent and waiting for her.

Hadham himself read the last sheet.

He made a small adjustment of some kind and handed the page down to Mack, who marked it up and gave it to a boy who raced out of the room. Hadham looked in her direction. He half-smiled, half-nodded and then he turned away to other things.

Emily got up not knowing where to go or what to do.

Mack called out, 'There's a waiting room down the corridor where you can freshen up, Miss Strauss. But you don't leave the building and that's an order.'

'Who from?' she said, because she could have done with some fresh air.

'Mr Pulitzer,' said Mack.

DAY TWELVE

Monday October 30, 1893

92

En Route

The waiting room Emily found herself in wasn't much of a place to actually rest in. It was sparsely furnished, with only a wooden bench and a couple of chairs to sit on. The fire in the grate had not been lit and she was cold and tired.

She took off her boots, and laid her cloak over herself for warmth as she tried to get comfortable on the bench and rest.

She was asleep in a moment, her unconscious mind a place of a thousand restive dreams.

She woke at dawn, the New York sky visible through the slats in the sides of the blind which, she was sure, she had not pulled down herself. She drifted back and forth into consciousness, aware each time of something new about the room. It was now pleasantly warm, the fire had been lit and crackled and glowed. Over to her left, there were two feet wearing shiny boots, just in her peripheral vision. When, finally, she craned round to look, she saw that the feet belonged to Gerald Toulson and that on his lap, plain to see, was a revolver.

Emily sat up in some alarm.

'Relax,' he said, 'you're safe.'

'Well I know that, Mr Toulson, but . . .'

He got up and went to the door.

'She's awake. Bring some towels and hot water and then some coffee . . .'

A boy went running. Toulson left the room while Emily washed and tidied herself. Then he returned to share a mug of coffee with her.

He looked serious.

'There was an attempt last night on the life of Anna Zemeckis . . .'

Emily gasped and got up at once.

'It's all right, she's fine. She's safe.'

'What happened?'

'The Meisters have a network across the major cities of America, including New York. We knew that, of course, but we saw no reason to alarm Miss Zemeckis and yourself unduly.'

'What *happened*?'

'Two Meisters came, probably under orders from Chicago. They were dealt with . . .'

Toulson paused for a moment and then added, 'We felt it prudent to evacuate the Zemeckises from the country at once, in the company of several Pinkertons.'

'Where to?'

'You don't need to know.'

'Manitoba,' said Emily after a moment's thought. 'Her Aunt Inga's place.'

'You're too clever for your own good.'

'You're not the first to say that. But she's safe . . . ?'

Toulson nodded.

'Now listen. That means you're not safe either, or you won't be if ever the *World* publishes that story you wrote, and especially not if it mentions the Meisters.'

'Well of course it does.'

'A couple of Pinkertons and I are going to accompany you everywhere until you can be taken to a place of safety . . . But for now we're just going to take you up to the 26th floor.'

'What's up there?'

'Mr Pulitzer's penthouse office. He's come to New York overnight from Bar Harbor, in his yacht. He wants to see you the moment you wake.'

'But . . . when's Anna leaving New York for Canada?'

Toulson glanced at his pocket watch.

'In about thirty minutes.'

'Where from?'

'Grand Central.'

'Well, let's get going,' said Emily.

Toulson frowned.

'No way are you going to see Miss Zemeckis off, Miss Strauss . . .'

'We had a deal, Mr Toulson. I help you with your investigation, which I did; you help me with mine. I'm not going to report the final act in Anna Zemeckis's story second hand. I want to see her heading off into a safe and happy future with my own eyes . . .'

Emily was up and off down the corridor with her cloak on before Toulson could argue further. She bumped into Alfred Butes, Pulitzer's secretary, on the way. He was looking anxious.

'The old man's waiting to have his breakfast with you and he doesn't like that.'

'So he didn't fire you, Mr Butes?'

'Oh, but he did, Miss Strauss. Twice. But . . . he reappointed me. That's his way. Now, please, you need to hurry.'

'He'll have to wait a while longer, I'm afraid. I haven't quite finished my story . . . I'll be right back.'

'Which story?' said a bewildered Butes as Emily, followed by Toulson, followed by two Pinkertons, made her way to the elevator.

They reached Grand Central with only minutes to spare, Toulson waving Emily past the heavy security he had arranged for Anna and leading her to a carriage at the far end of the train Anna was leaving on.

'Inside,' said Toulson, 'this is best done discreetly, and you better be quick because I just heard a whistle blow.'

Emily rushed to find Anna's carriage, embraced a surprised Mr Zemeckis and then Anna.

'I just wanted to say . . .'

They embraced again.

'. . . good luck,' said Emily. 'To you all, baby included!'

A whistle sounded again and the train shunted slightly one way and then the other.

'*Miss Strauss*,' called out Toulson.

'Got to go,' she said. '*Must* go.'

'Miss Strauss!' said a quieter voice.

It seemed the whole world wanted to talk to her, but this time it was just Mr Zemeckis. He was holding out something for Emily to take.

'I couldn't sleep last night, not one minute. So many things in my mind, so many things to get used to. And my daughter Anna back home. And then . . . so many things. So I do what I do best to find peace of mind. Please, take it.'

He thrust a package into her hands.

Emily did not need to unwrap the paper to know what it contained.

She knew it from its wonderful aroma and the good friendly feel of it. It was a loaf of bread.

'I make it for the journey,' he said, 'it is what I do best.'

Emily could find no more words to stay. Having said one last goodbye, she stood with Toulson at her side as the train eased slowly away, Anna and her father waving at the window.

'Better get back to Mr Pulitzer,' he said.

'Do you really need so many men to guard men?'

''Fraid so.'

Outside Grand Central, Emily climbed back into her cab, sat down and took one last look out of the window.

The concourse was a mass of people, men and women going off to their offices at the start of a new working week.

'There's a hundred thousand stories out there, all waiting to be told,' she mused.

As Toulson climbed in after her and one of the other Pinkertons took up a position on the sidewalk, Emily could not help noticing a man in the crowd. Massive and broad shouldered, he stood there staring at her.

He seemed like a great solid rock in the middle of a rushing river.

He smiled slightly and raised his bowler to her.

'Who's that?' she said to Toulson.

Toulson leaned past Emily and peered out.

'Who?' he said grimly. 'Where?'

'*There!*' said Emily, pointing.

But it was too late.

All they caught was the fleeting glimpse of the curled bowler of Dodek Krol as it was swallowed up by the early morning crowds of New York.

Back at the *World* building they took a special elevator, the Pinkertons stationing themselves outside Mr Pulitzer's office when they arrived.

'I'm not likely to get shot in Mr Pulitzer's office,' Emily complained. '*He* is.'

'We'll wait outside,' conceded Toulson.

The door was opened by Pulitzer's secretary.

'He's in a vile mood, Miss Strauss. You may have lost everything.'

As Butes ushered Emily into the great man's presence, he got up and moved in her direction.

'Miss Strauss?'

'Good morning, Mr Pulitzer . . .'

'You've kept me waiting.'

'I'm sorry, Mr Pulitzer, but I . . .'

A delicious aroma overtook her.

'. . . I have a gift for you. For us all, in fact.'

'What is it?' growled Pulitzer.

She put Janis Zemeckis's bread that she was still carrying into his hands.

'It's a present from one your readers, sir. His way of saying thanks.'

'What reader?'

'Mr Zemeckis.'

Pulitzer raised the bread in its wrapping to his face and smelled it. A smile actually broke out across this face.

'That's good,' he said.

Then he scowled and said, 'But it makes me more hungry still. Butes, fetch Mr Warren.'

Moments later a tall, rounded, mustachioed man of sixty or so appeared.

'Miss Strauss, this is Mr Mike Warren, Chief Crime Correspondent of the *World*. Mr Warren, you've already heard tell of Miss Strauss.'

'Indeed I have.'

They shook hands.

'Now,' said Pulitzer impatiently, 'can we *please* have breakfast.'

They ate in silence, the way Pulitzer liked it, except for one brief exchange.

'You seem hungry, Miss Strauss.'

'I am, sir, very.'

'Mr Butes tells me I get irritable when I'm hungry. Are you the same?'

'Yes,' said Emily, 'I am.'

She took her third piece of toast.

'Good bread,' said Pulitzer.

'Very,' said Emily Strauss.

Later, over coffee, Joseph Pulitzer came to the point.

'I have had Butes read your story about Miss Zemeckis to me, Miss Strauss. It's that about which I need to talk to you.'

'Did you like it?'

Pulitzer sighed. 'Miss Strauss, it is not fitting for a journalist to ask an editor if he likes a story. In any case liking doesn't come into it. Editors are interested in what's publishable and what sells newspapers, not in what they like.'

'Oh.'

'But yes, I did, very much. Though of course we cannot print it.'

'The Harrison assassination?'

'That's part of it. I'll let Mr Warren explain.'

'We've been working undercover on the Meisters for several months, Miss Strauss,' said Warren, 'and one of our reporters has been killed in the process. They are dangerous men in a very dangerous organization and pornography is not their only trade. You said enough in the story you filed – the extraordinary story if I may say so – to suggest that you met these men face to face . . . Tell us more.'

Emily did so, as succinctly as she could.

'So there's a lot you left out?'

She nodded.

'Did she say yes, Butes?' said Pulitzer.

'She did, sir.'

'Humph! Please speak rather than nod, Miss Strauss.'

'Sorry, Mr Pulitzer.'

'But you have chapter and verse?' said Warren.

'I have.'

'Do you realize you are the first reporter ever to witness a Meister slaying and come out of it alive?'

'I did not. I was just doing my job and I needed to get Miss Zemeckis out of there. I didn't have a good story without her.'

'Well you certainly got your story,' said Warren, 'and although of course the final decision will be Mr Pulitzer's here and Mr Hadham's, I think I can say we would very much like to incorporate your sterling work in the series we'll be running in a few weeks time.'

Emily frowned.

'So I won't get my name on it?'

Pulitzer sighed and look irritable.

'It's the story that counts,' he growled.

'That's not what Nellie Bly would say,' replied Emily.

'No, it isn't,' he said. 'You've got me there.'

'Actually, Miss Strauss, it would be dangerous to have your name on the story,' said Warren. 'You are aware, of course, that an attempt was made already on Miss Zemeckis's life?'

'Yes,' said Emily somberly.

'So we're going to run the series anonymously.'

'But the Meisters know it was me. Otherwise you wouldn't have Pinkertons following me around. What is liberty worth if you can't put your name to truth?'

Pulitzer smiled and leaned back.

'Ever the idealist. What did I tell you Butes? I knew that's what she'd say.'

Then Pulitzer was serious once more.

'You give us only one choice, Miss Strauss. We run the story – or that part of it that you have written – and it carries your name. But if we do so, we get you somewhere safe until the fuss dies down.'

'And when were you thinking of spiriting me away to somewhere I don't want to go?' asked Emily. 'And for how long?'

'Today,' drawled Pulitzer. 'And for as long as it takes.'

'Where to?' said Emily.

'London,' he replied. 'It's the capital city of the British Isles.'

'I know, Mr Pulitzer.'

Emily's heart was thumping as she framed her next question.

'What shall I do there until I can come back?'

'Work, Miss Strauss, there's nothing like it.'

'Who for?'

'The *World*. Probably undercover for a time, for your own protection, reporting directly to our News Editor who handles all the foreign correspondents. As for myself, Mr Butes seems to like you. He lets you in when he shouldn't. He'll be your point of contact with to me.'

'As a member of staff?' Emily held her breath as she asked.

'How else do you think we can keep an eye on you? We protect our own.'

Emily sat in silence not knowing what to say.

'Miss Strauss, I liked your story very much,' said Pulitzer after a pause. 'But please, never tell anyone I said as much, for they'll think the old man's slipping. Now, you must be on your way.'

'But how am I to get to England?'

Pulitzer got up, stretched and went unerringly to the window that overlooked Brooklyn.

'Show her, Butes.'

Arthur Butes ushered Emily to the window and pointed a finger at New York harbour in the distance below: 'From over there,' he said

'But where exactly, Mr Butes?'

Butes pointed and said, 'See that steamer down there with the two big black funnels with the white bands on them and the nice fluttering pennant with a red star on it?'

'Yes.'

'It's a ship of the Red Star Line . . .'

'. . . and it sails for Southampton in two hours time,' said Pulitzer. 'Butes has your ticket and is sorting out the necessary documentation and whatever else you need.'

'Thank you, but may I ask, Mr Pulitzer, how much am I to be paid?' said Emily.

'Too much,' said Pulitzer, 'far too much, Miss Strauss. Good morning and good luck.'

Three hours later, having retrieved her luggage from the left luggage depot where she had deposited it, Emily was on the quayside saying goodbye to Gerald Toulson and Arthur Butes.

'Oh dear, I have nothing decent to wear, she

542

remarked ruefully, as she saw her trunk carried on board. 'Nothing but the few things I took to Chicago. And none of them are smart enough for a steamer like this.'

'Don't worry, Emily,' said Toulson warmly, 'your natural charm will more than make up for it en route.'

'Miss Strauss, there's one last thing,' said Butes, as Emily turned to go. 'Mr Pulitzer asked me to give you this.'

In his outstretched hand was that morning's edition of the New York *World*.

'Take a look . . . page five.'

Emily found the page.

It was her piece on Chicago, containing all the 'color' she had so rapidly produced on demand in the *World* offices the previous evening, accompanied by several of Ben Latham's illustrations.

In pride of place, right in the center of the page, was Ben's sketch of Emily standing on State Street and looking up at the Chicago skyline with the caption, 'A Special Feature by Our Own Correspondent'.

And there, on a separate line below it, was the name 'Emily Strauss'.

AFTERMATH

Anna Zemeckis arrived at Lac du Bonnet in Manitoba, Canada, four days after Rorton Van Hale and three Pinkertons, hired by Hans Darke, had got her safely out of New York, along with her father, on the night of October 29th, 1893.

She stayed initially with her Aunt Inga and encouraged her father to return to New York. Within a month of his return that November, Janis's bakery was up and running once more and within six months, he had recovered the losses that had resulted from his journeys to Chicago in search of Anna.

John Olsen English, with the encouragement and approval of Chicago's Deputy Chief Librarian Mr McIlvanie, journeyed to Canada six weeks later and proposed to Anna. After some initial resistance from Janis Zemeckis, who had his doubts about Chicagoan men, they were married in the December of 1893, the snow already thick on the ground.

Their first child was born three months later, on March 25th, 1894, and baptised in April that year as Tomas Janis English. He had four godparents: from Chicago came Mr Tomas Steffens, locomotive driver; Mr Wolfgang Darke, meatpacker; and Mr Hans Darke, gentleman; and from New York, Mrs Klara Kopecky who travelled with her good friend, the baby's grandfather, Mr Janis Zemeckis. The Englishes went on to have three more children in quick succession.

Gunther Darke's body was recovered from the Chicago River three days after he died and formally identified by Wolfgang. An inquest gave the cause of death as being the result of a combination of injuries, including gunshot wounds and drowning. Gerald Toulson gave evidence regarding the circumstances preceding his disappearance. But Darke's killer was never found and the case was closed. He was buried in Graceland Cemetery in a plot acquired for the family by Hans Darke.

Some months after the death of Gunther Darke, Wolfgang and Christiane were married quietly in Chicago. They soon had a much-loved son of their own and later a daughter.

Dr Morgan Eels left Chicago on the night of October 29th, along with Nurse Lutyens. They moved to Europe. Mr Mould, later Dr Mould, stayed on at Dunning for several years before moving back East to work in various state hospitals in Washington. It is not known whether or not either he or Dr Eels ever further developed their discovery of a means of frontal lobe surgery as a 'cure' for insanity.

It *is* known, however, that American neurologist Walter Freeman, in collaboration with neurosurgeon James Watts, developed a very similar procedure, carrying out their first operation in 1936 at the hospital of George Washington University in Washington. In 1946 they announced their refinement of a new procedure, which they called 'transorbital lobotomy', half a century after Dr Morgan Eels had discovered it by accident.

Lobotomy had a brief and terrifying popularity in America through the early 1950s, after which it rapidly lost credence and was replaced by drug therapy.

From 1904, when he reached the age of ten, Gunther and Anna's son, Tomas English, along with his siblings, vacationed in Chicago as guests of Hans Darke. Tomas was a good-looking, hard-working boy and no secret was made of his origins. Perhaps his genes, combined with having grown up on a farm with livestock, gave him a natural aptitude for stock-breeding and the meat-trade and, in 1910, at the age of sixteen, he joined Darke Hartz & Company as a trainee, on the same footing as every young apprentice. Wolfgang drove him hard, as he himself had been driven hard by his father. Tomas English became a master at his trade. Later, in 1926, he was made a director of the company, to Hans Darke's great pleasure. Hans died in 1928 and was buried at the Graceland Cemetery, not far from arguably the greatest of his contemporaries in the meat packing trade, Philip Armour, and in sight of his son Gunther's memorial.

Mr Isaiah Steele settled his claim for squatter's rights on the Lakeshore out of court for a very substantial sum, most of which he donated to various Chicago charities. He lived quietly on the North Side, remaining to the end of his life a close friend of Mr Hans Darke. Right up until the early 1920s, the two could often be seen taking their daily constitutional in Lincoln Park, where they would sit on a park bench, happily arguing the hours away together.

Joseph Pulitzer, the greatest newspaper magnate of his generation and, with William Randolph Hearst, of the nineteenth century, died aboard his yacht *Liberty* off the coast of South Carolina in 1911, having established the very first school of journalism – at Columbia University in New York State – and gifting the Pulitzer Prize for Literature in his will.

Chatwold, his home at Bar Harbor, was demolished in 1946, but the *World* offices survived until 1955, before they too were razed.

Most of the Chicago of 1893 is now long gone. The extraordinary White City, largely constructed of wood and plaster of Paris, did not long outlive the Fair itself due to vandalism and several fires. Only the Field Museum, one of the major, permanent structures specially constructed for the Fair, remains standing today. The Lakeshore of Mr Crazy's time was eventually reclaimed and, as a testament to Chicago's liking for open spaces, preserved in perpetuity for the use of its citizens and visitors. It is now Grant Park and those who wonder where Mr Crazy conducted his naked early morning ablutions could do no worse than stand and look into the foam and spray of the grand and imposing Buckingham Fountain, accessible along Congress Parkway, which was built very near the spot where Mr Crazy had his much-loved Lakeshore cabin.

At midnight on Friday, July 30, 1971, the Union Stock Yard finally closed, but its glory days had long since passed and many of its buildings were by then lying derelict. The site was razed and is now a characterless industrial park. Visitors to the Sears Tower can still make out, beyond the city on the South Side, the dark and now largely barren footprint where the six-hundred acre site once was.

The Masonic Temple and Woman's Temple, once great cathedrals of the new age of the Chicago school of architecture, were both razed after only a relatively short existence – the Woman's Temple in 1926 and the Masonic Temple in 1939. However, enough of 1893 Chicago remains for an imaginative visitor to walk around its streets and get a sense still of the dynamic of the place when it was a thrusting new city. The Auditorium Theatre and its associated hotel is still there; Dearborn Station with its familiar clock tower – now minus the mansard roof; and the familiar great emporiums of Marshall Field, Carson Pirie Scott and several others from that era also survive and thrive.

But four great landmarks, three more or less dead and one gloriously alive, tell of those times like nothing else. The Main Gate of the Union Stock Yard remains standing, as a reminder of the thousands of immigrant laborers who worked there, and the millions of cattle and hogs who ended their days on its killing floor.

The rail tracks on which Toulson and Van Hale observed the Darke Hartz boxcars from one of Gustavus Swift's buildings are still there as well, but Bubbly Creek, whose precise extent shifted through time, can only be intermittently traced. A few remaining feet, where it once emptied its filthy contents into the South Fork of the Chicago River in sight and smelling distance of the tenements of the immigrant poor, are still just visible.

Most of the original lunatic asylum at Dunning has long since been demolished, although part of the original site is still in use as a residential home for those in need of special care. In the small memorial garden at Dunning there is a plaque commemorating the lives of the institution's many thousands of forgotten inmates. But much of the remaining site remains derelict and overgrown behind a high wire fence.

But one landmark is still as alive today as it was back in 1893, and without it Chicago simply would not be the wonderful Chicago it was and still is: the

Elevated Railway. It is far more extensive now than in Emily Strauss's time, but that part of it which rumbles, rattles and races southward down Wabash was already open in 1893 and a ride on it round the Loop – as downtown Chicago is now known – is as unforgettable now as it was then.

. . . As for Mr Crazy's seemingly outrageous claims, he was proved right on all three counts. The World's Fair did end in disaster: on the night of January 8, 1894, fire broke out and destroyed several buildings, a conflagration watched by fifty thousand people. Later that year, Illinois State was the scene of one of the most bitter and violent conflicts in US history – the Pullman Strike, which lasted from May to July – during which all but two of the remaining Fair buildings were torched. Mr Crazy was right too about the 'tunnels', which everyone in our story assumed were a figment of his imagination. A whole series of service tunnels were constructed from the late nineteenth century under most of the streets in the Loop. Many of them are still there today.

Acknowledgements

First, we have an enduring debt to Chicago itself. From its earliest days Chicago has had a grand sense of its own history, expressed in 1856 with the formation of the fabulous Chicago Historical Society. Now known as the Chicago History Museum, its book and newspaper collection and its visual archives and facilities have been a great help and a continual inspiration, as too its indispensable *Encyclopedia of Chicago*. But there are other highly impressive institutions in Chicago available to researchers, including the Frank Washington Library, the Newberry Library, the Ryerson Art Library of the Fine Art Institute, and the Hull House Museum. The staff of all these institutions have been unfailingly courteous, enthusiastic and erudite.

Chicago city boasts an exceptionally rich bibliography. There are far too many great books that inspired and guided us in the writing of this book to name here, but a selection of what we feel are the best and most entertaining sources on the history of the city, as well as Chicago novels of the period, can be found at our heroine's website www.emilystrauss.com.

Numerous individuals helped along the way with expert advice and information. Dave Joens of the Illinois State Archives put us in touch with the Chicago Area Archivists Online; Robert Andresen of the Chicago Greeter Service took us on a guided tour of Graceland Cemetery; Liora Cobin gave us a special private tour of the Frances Willard House at Evanston; Amy Slagell and Carolyn DeSwarte Gifford at North Western University kindly gave us advance sight of their collection of Frances Willard's speeches, *Let Something Good Be Said*; Bob Storozuk, President of the Milwaukee Road Historical Association, offered absolutely invaluable help and advice about the US railroads; and John LaPine offered his unique brand of good conversation, coffee and the congenial surroundings of Printers Row Fine & Rare Books. Innumerable Chicago taxi drivers took us on what seemed to them bizarre searches for now nearly non-existent places such as Bubbly Creek.

But it is to the city that we are most indebted and we would like to thank the numberless and nameless people of Chicago who stopped and chatted with us on street corners, in cafes, on the El, sheltering from the rain and gave us their unique perspectives and points of view, mostly sane but occasionally wonderfully insane. Mr Crazy, you're still out there and we love you!

Finally, back in the UK, we were lucky to have the unrivalled facilities of the Rothermere American Institute and the Bodleian Library on our doorstep. We would also like to thank Mike Ware for his expertise and advice concerning nineteenth-century photography and its techniques. Finally, our special thanks to Paul Sidey, our commissioning editor at Hutchinson, who first saw the potential of the project and gave it his continuing support, to his production colleagues at Random House and to Kate Elton at Arrow, who took charge of this paperback edition.

William Horwood and Helen Rappaport,
Oxford, UK, September 2007

If you have enjoyed *City of Dark Hearts* and would like to pass on your comments then please email info@jamesconan.com or write to James Conan c/o:

Hutchinson
The Random House Group Limited
20 Vauxhall Bridge Road
London SW1V 2SA

Read on for further information and an interview with the authors.

Interview: William Horwood & Helen Rappaport on Scott Pack's 'My Big Mouth' blog, March 19, 2007

William Horwood is the author of *Skallagrigg* and the popular *Duncton Wood* series, as well as the more recent volume of memoirs *The Boy With No Shoes*. Helen Rappaport started her career as an actress before turning historian with books on Stalin and women social reformers. Her latest non-fiction book is *No Place For Ladies: The Untold Story Of Women In The Crimean War*.

William and Helen have co-authored a new novel *City of Dark Hearts* which I mentioned a short while ago on this blog. They kindly consented to be interviewed for this site, the results of which are below. They, rather courageously I think, agreed to answer most questions separately and without consulting the other, a technique which has thrown up some enlightening responses.

Welcome to the blog, and thank you for agreeing to answer a few questions. Perhaps I should start by asking how the two of you got together to write this book?

W: We met on-line nearly three years ago and since couples benefit from a shared activity if they haven't got kids together, writing a book seemed a good idea. We put a few suggestions to Bill Hamilton of AM Heath and it went from there.

H: After meeting and discovering we were both writers, I guess, in the first flush of lurve, we naturally thought it would be wonderful to do something creative together. Oh yes, why not write a book we thought. Hmm . . . little did we know all the pitfalls, stresses and strains we were letting ourselves in for. But we optimistically went ahead with our first venture – a Russian mail-order bride/mafia type thriller, which would draw on William's talent as novelist and mine as a historian with a specialism in

Russia. Soon after we'd written some sample material we were pre-empted by a big TV series and decided to abandon the idea. As researcher, I then went in search of new ideas and came up with something around late nineteenth-century American newspaper girls . . .

Had either of you read each other's work before embarking upon this project?
W: Er, no, not being into Women Social Reformers or Joseph Stalin. I had done something better though – breathe the same dusty-but-scented air as Helen at the Bodleian Library where, for fifteen years, we had both been using the Lower Reading Room, possibly even the same seat.
H: Well, having read *Watership Down* I was vaguely aware of the Duncton books but to be honest, I'd never read any of William's work, though as soon as we did meet I read the proof copy of *Boy With No Shoes* and absolutely loved it. Not only that, but it struck a very personal chord for me. William and I both grew up in Kent, William by the sea, me by the Medway Estuary, in the 1950s and had the additional common bond of having suffered bullying – William at home, me at school.

And why choose Chicago during the 1890s as your setting?
W: Combination of things . . . Helen was interested in American stunt girls of the 1890s (i.e. early female journalists) while I, as an economic geographer by training, have always been interested in Chicago's extraordinary growth in the second half of the nineteenth century; and, as a novelist, in the human stories that the dynamics of rapid urban change throws up. When we discovered how the whole world visited Chicago for the 1893 World's Fair (27 million people to be precise) and that crime rates went through the roof

as a result it seemed logical to bring 'Helen's' stunt girl to 'my' Chicago and the novel was born.

H: As soon as we had settled on the central premise of a feisty young American newspaper girl in pursuit of a story, we then agreed that the best plan would be to tie each book (hopefully there will be a whole series of Emily Strauss stories) to a specific historical event, ranging from the 1890s to possibly as far as World War I. As soon as I started looking for dates and events Chicago 1893 shouted at me and William agreed. And once we started looking at the bibliography and fabulous visual material we were hooked. Here was a wonderful dynamic city during the Progressive Era, with a richer tale even than the well worn gangster stories located there in the 20s and 30s.

Could you tell us a little bit about the book to whet our appetite?

W and H: A nice innocent New York girl, Anna Zemeckis, goes missing in Chicago during the 1893 World's Fair. After evidence emerges she's dead, her father writes in despair to Joseph Pulitzer's New York *World* warning other parents not to let their daughters go near Chicago. Feisty wannabe girl reporter Emily Strauss spots the potential in the story and persuades Pulitzer to send her to investigate. When she discovers Anna's still alive, Emily sets out to find her and bring her home. Suddenly the social, economic and urban maelstrom that is Chicago becomes a very dangerous place indeed as the 'dark hearts' of Chicago target both women and set out to kill them . . .

How did the writing process work? Who did what?

W: Well, it certainly worked: after the initial six months of development to contract stage the book took less than a year to deliver. I wrote the first draft in batches and Helen edited, commented, added, and sent them back. Morning, noon and night we argued and debated each twist and turn, our separate egos having to yield to the remorseless logic of the other's critique. Bit by slow bit it became easier as we found the voice we wanted, which was different from either of our own. Not unlike putting two (superb, of course) single malt whiskies together to produce a (wonderful, of course) commercial blend. Towards the end I was writing the draft much faster and more loosely and Helen editing with much more freedom and confidence. Who did what? We both did bits of everything with me starting the process and Helen finishing it.

H: Initially we read and talked a lot about Emily, the plot and some of the major characters. William went away and drafted some early chapters, most of which got binned because the story line and the emphasis morphed very rapidly. Having discussed the overall idea with our agent Bill Hamilton, we then worked up a first 16,000-word chunk. Fundamentally, I collect and compile the research material, bibliography etc. and feed stuff to William – though he reads independently as well around the particular things that interest him. We endlessly discuss the research material and refine the remit of the research. Meanwhile, William writes a draft and passes chunks over to me which I edit, cut, expand and rewrite and then hand back. I was pretty timid at first but as we picked up the pace and got into a working method I became more and more ruthless and intervened far more in the text. After initial passes by each of us the material would go back and forth several more times till we were happy with the end product. But the revisions and refinements were never-ending. Even after delivering the book to Random we then decided the denouement wasn't strong enough and went and re-wrote the last ten chapters.

Did that process lead to any clashes of personality or style?

W: The personality clashes were monumental, Helen being one of the most unreasonable and irritating people I have ever met . . . and me being the same to her. Seriously, there was a six-week bust-up two months into the writing but somehow we kept talking – and suddenly the characters, like those in Pirandello's *Six Characters In Search Of An Author*, positively demanded we got back together and told their story.

H: Of course. Many, some very intense and fraught. We were on a very steep learning curve – not just getting to know each other, within a relationship – which added another sometimes difficult dimension to the writing process – but also we were finding our way in terms of maximizing on our individual talents within the book and learning to live with and accept each other's often infuriating idiosyncrasies – personal, emotional and stylistic. There are hundreds of examples e.g. William would get demented at my use of 'And' at the beginning of a sentence and my tendency to what he called 'girly' turns of phrase; I, meanwhile, would ruthlessly cut some of his overly emotional, three-hanky stuff and veto any gratuitous use of violence.

Who had the final say?

W: I think I did. Someone had to have it. You can't decide creative things by committee. But the question is hypothetical because it rarely if ever happened that way.

H: Actually, I think any differences were always ultimately resolved by a democratic decision – albeit arrived at sometimes after rows and stompings off and days of disgruntlement with each other. I do not think that William, even though he is a very strong-willed alpha male, ever totally imposed his will over me – though he frequently tried! This is because I was equally stubborn in my views and my passions. The only way we could get the book right in the end was by means of endless discussion, heated debate and negotiation between two people with often very different and strongly held points of view.

What was the highlight of writing this book for you?
W: The realisation that a writer's life does not always have to be a solitary and largely unsupported grind – a thought that occurred to me on our first wonderful trip together to Chicago.
H: Undoubtedly it was learning a whole new way of working with narrative. It has taught me as a historian to be far more 'visual' in my writing, to move away from a slavish devotion to fact and a style of rather 'academic' writing and set my creative mind free in finding newer, more imaginative ways with historical narrative. I am certain it will have a huge influence on my approach to my next history project (currently out to publishers for consideration). Working with William has freed me up as a historical writer and shown me that you can write about real things in a far more lyrical way to engage the reader.

And William, did you learn anything from working with a writing partner?
W: Lots, but not what others might expect. Being ex-Fleet street I had long since stopped being temperamental about my words. Most of us improve with being edited. Helen taught me better research techniques and that I occasionally write not only badly, but real-life drivel. I – or rather we together – learnt that plotting a thriller is a very different thing from writing fantasy or history and intellectually very challenging.

Now that your novel is about to hit the shelves, what are your future plans?

W: We're working on the next Emily Strauss novel together. It has already been sold to Hutchinson . . . Separately I'm working on a major new fantasy series.

H: I feel I have a lot of catching up to do, having come to writing relatively late. I spent far too long as an out-of-work actress and regret that, even though I was at least working as a translator in the theatre from time to time. There certainly will be another Emily Strauss novel with William, as well as my own history title, as No 2 is already contracted. But these first two were a financial gamble for us because we felt so passionate about the project that we were prepared to accept an unfashionably low advance. Now, if these first two take off and establish a following then if we are to agree to do more it will only be if we get what a modern Emily Strauss would call 'adequate compensation'. That said, collaborating offers a refreshing break from the normal isolation of writing and we particularly enjoy going to places and doing the research trips together. But William has a lot more novels in his head and I have history books in mine too. Ideally we would like to keep the collaboration going, whilst simultaneously continuing with our own very different projects – but somewhere in between, first and foremost, we need a long holiday in the sun.

And finally, if you could recommend one book each for readers of this blog to add to their libraries, what would they be?

W: I prefer to name two, one fiction and one non-fiction. My fiction is Patrick White's *Tree Of Man*; my non-fiction Edmund Gosse's *Father And Son*. Both are classics of their kind which I read at the right time for my own development as a person and writer. They changed my life.

H: Only one is impossible – it means choosing between fiction and non-fiction, but if I really have to come down to one book that others might have overlooked then it is A. J. A. Symons's *The Quest For Corvo*, a ground-breaking literary biography-cum-quest-cum-detective story that in 1934 turned conventional biography on its head. It's a compulsive read. Frederick Rolfe, aka Baron Corvo, was the most elusive of subjects and the miracle of this book is how Symons got to the real man and the real story by the most fascinating and gripping of circuitous routes. A brilliant but forgotten classic. Something for the Friday Project? As for fiction – it has to be George Eliot's *Middlemarch* – a massive, compelling work of genius, nothing less.

Article from the *Oxford Times*, 15 March 2007

Writers join forces
by Mary Zacaroli

What happens when two writers find romance – after they already have eight children and three grand-children between them? William Horwood and Helen Rappaport met online through Dating Direct nearly three years ago. Within two months of their first meeting over tea and scones at the Old Parsonage in Oxford, they knew things were serious, that they wanted to propagate. From such fertile beginnings, *City of Dark Hearts* was born.

A historical thriller set in Chicago during the 1893 World Fair, the action takes place over 11 days. Young, ambitious reporter Emily Strauss tricks her way into newspaper magnate Joseph Pulitzer's office and per-suades him to send her on an assignment: to find out what happened to a young Latvian woman, Anna Zemeckis, whose body has allegedly been found in Chicago. Only, Anna is not dead. Pulled beaten and bloodied from the horrendously polluted Bubbly Creek, she's been carted off to the local insane asylum, where she's in great danger of being lobotomised.

Literary it ain't, but *Dark Hearts* is such fun to read, with two feisty female leads and a punchy, gutsy story that makes magnificent use of its brutal, corrupt, grandiose backdrop. Rooted in extensive research, sometimes it's difficult to assess where the lines of fact and fiction blur.

'The historical context, the central events are correct and the details are correct, but the characters are fiction, apart from one or two key characters,' William explained. Even so, all the characters are born of research. Emily, for example, is a composite of three female reporters from that time.

William has written 16 novels, including the *Duncton Wood* series, several sequels to Kenneth Grahame's *The Wind in the Willows* and – most recently – a fictionalised memoir, *The Boy with No Shoes*. Meanwhile, Helen is a 19th-century historian and expert on the black Crimean nurse Mary Seacole. She has just published an account of women in the Crimean War, *No Place For Ladies*. So, given their very different areas of expertise, how did the novel come about?

William said: 'With a mutual need to do something together, rather than a book idea.' She added: 'Initially, we thought of doing a contemporary Russian project. There would have been an element of my Russian knowledge, with William's knowledge of London's Fleet Street.' But that idea had been pre-empted, so they took a list of six more to their agent, who liked best the idea of a historical thriller set in Chicago. Two research trips later, they had the plot and characters in place and over the next nine months the book was brought to term.

Helen is in her late fifties, William a little older. He said: 'It's the maturity that comes from two older people and life experience that made it possible for us to write the book.'

She said: 'Assimilated knowledge, too. There's a huge amount in both of us that's come through into the book without us probably being able to realise it.' They do that a lot; finish each other's sentences. So how did they actually write the book?

At the time, William lived above Helen in a flat on Woodstock Road, although he's since bought a house nearby. He wrote the first draft and after completing a few thousand words would email it for comment to Helen. 'At the beginning, I was a bit timid about cutting and rewriting William's sacred prose,' Helen said.

He cut in: 'She thought I was a genius and then realised I wasn't.' However, as the book moved on and the story developed a momentum, she became more confident and the writing more collaborative.

They both feel that working together, as well as being enormous fun, has strengthened their own writing. 'It's taught me to look differently at how I write history and to have a greater sense of narrative,' Helen said. Meanwhile, William thinks he writes much tighter than before and his research skills are much improved.

There were clashes. 'I would get on to William about violence and he would go on about my repeated use of the word And at the beginning of sentences.' Interestingly, it was Helen who cut the sentiment. He said: 'It's a deeply dispiriting thing to sit weeping over your typewriter and half an hour later to have a hardnosed modern woman slash the very things that have made you weep.'

Both are looking forward to their slot at the Oxford

Literary Festival. He said: 'Readers have paid money to come and see us, so we intend to move them, shake them, change them, make them excited. It's going to be illustrated, dynamic, highly interactive.'

'We want to get away from this ridiculous mystique that writers are some kind of royalty,' Helen said. 'Our primary purpose is as communicators.' So don't expect Queen Helen or King William to take the stage on Thursday. Instead, there will be two mature entertainers keen to explain the pain and ecstasy of birthing a book together.

THEY TOLD IT LIKE IT IS

The Real American Newspaperwomen
Who Inspired a Novel
by William Horwood and Helen Rappaport

In July 1888 Chicago was rocked by a series of extraordinary undercover reports about the abuses of the cheap labour system in the city's overcrowded sweatshops.

Published in the *Chicago Times* under headlines such as 'A POOR GIRL WHO WORKED FROM JANUARY TO JULY TO MAKE $15.00' and 'NO REST FOR THE WEARY AND WRETCHED CHILDREN THIS SIDE OF THE GRAVE', the articles set a new standard for socially concerned investigative reporting.

What was new was that they were written by a woman who got her stories the hard way – working undercover in the garment trade. Her reporting shocked with its trenchant condemnation of American values.

'The birthright of an American girl may be a glorious attribute on the deck of a transatlantic steamship or the floor of a London ball-room,' she wrote later, 'but it is not worth the flop of a brass farthing in the cloak factories of Chicago.'

Nelson pulled no punches, combining interviews with downtrodden female workers, quotes from bullying and cheating employers, and graphic descriptions of the degrading conditions in which garments sold in classy downtown stores for high prices were being made by girls as young as eleven – often just around the corner:

> Here in a crowded room, with low ceiling and dingy walls, poorly ventilated and insufficiently lighted sit between eighty and a hundred and fifty young girls surrounded from Monday morning until Saturday evening by the ceaseless chatter of the sewing machines in an atmosphere so thick it can be cut with a knife. There is the smell of dye . . . and the still more offensive odor from 'English Plaids' . . . Clouds of lint from the textiles in hand cover everything and are constantly inhaled by the sewers . . . then too there is the rancid smell of machine oil, the overpowering exhalations from so many perspiring and unkempt persons and an occasional whiff from the six or seven toilet closets . . .

The author of these pieces was Helen Cusack, a young journalist writing under the pseudonym of Nell Nelson. We came across her work during our research on Chicago for a subject – and a possible heroine – for a historical thriller we planned to set during the 1893 World's Fair.

Nelson's stories were a revelation in subject and style and our novel's title, *City of Dark Hearts*, like the story itelf, owes much to the pioneering, hard-hitting reportage women like her were for the first time delivering to America's rapidly growing but still male-dominated newspapers.

The world had seen nothing like this young, feisty generation of 'free American girls'. Abandoning homes in Midwestern towns, often desperate to escape controlling parents, backward-looking communities and the traditional expectations for women of marriage, motherhood and domesticity, they shared a unique, Frontier spirit of adventure.

Elizabeth Jordan, one of the best known, describes in her biography the subterfuge needed to start in journalism. Like our heroine, Emily Strauss, she knew exactly what she wanted:

> I left home for what was on the surface a holiday in Canada and the East . . . but I was growing restless and uneasy. Progress, to me, meant only one thing – New York and a place on the New York *World's* staff. The next move I decided was to be made by me not my father . . . I went straight from the train to the *World* building and asked for the editor. I didn't even know his name.

Elizabeth 'Pink' Cochrane from Pittsburgh had done the same in 1887, rising to fame under the pseudonym Nellie Bly. Her first job on the *Pittsburg Dispatch* had soon bored her. So one day, her head full of ideals, she upped and headed for the big city, leaving a scribbled note on her desk:

> 'I am off for New York. Look out for me.'

The Manhattan that greeted would-be newspaper girls like Bly and Jordan was an exciting place, a world of endless opportunity. Park Row, and the two blocks south to Ann Street in Lower Manhattan, where all the New York dailies were located, was their Mecca. Here, Bly talked herself into a job on Joseph Pulitzer's New

York *World* and within months had become a household name.

Her sensational reports published under the banner *Ten Days in a Mad-House* graphically described to horrified readers how she had feigned mental illness in order to have herself admitted to New York's notorious Blackwell Island insane asylum. Here she witnessed at first hand the often brutal way in which women – many of them impoverished, semi-literate immigrants – were being committed to insane asylums. Women such as Mrs. Louise Schanz, a German whose English was too poor for her to explain herself:

> Here was a woman taken without her own consent from the free world to an asylum and there given no chance to prove her sanity. Confined most probably for life behind asylum bars, without even being told in her language the why and wherefore. Compare this with a criminal, who is given every chance to prove his innocence. Who would not rather be a murderer and take the chance for life than be declared insane, without hope of escape?

In similar fashion, determined to do 'straight reporting' rather than the usual kind of tepid women's stories assigned her, Elizabeth Jordan won her reputation at the *World* with her story 'The Death of Number Nine', the tale of a sick baby carried three miles through the New York streets one night in its mother's arms only for the poor mother to discover at Bellevue Public Hospital that the child was dead.

> She had no money for her car fare. She had no money to bury the baby. She was forced to leave him in the City Morgue, as Number Nine, to be buried in Potter's Field . . . I went to the morgue and found the tiny pine box in which Number Nine, who had never known comfort or

proper care in his little life, lay in peace at last, waiting to be carted away in the morning. I was determined that he should have proper burial. On the cover of that box I wrote in chalk: *Hold this baby till instructions are received from the New York* World.

The exploits of Bly, Jordan and Nelson quickly inspired dozens more eager, young would-be 'Stunt Girls', as they became known. They would do anything in pursuit of a story. They laboured undercover as rag-pickers, cigarette-makers, book-binders and box-factory workers. They worked as laundresses and flower sellers; posed as chorus girls, serving maids, artists' models, beggars, lunatics, Salvation Army girls and prostitutes.

They went up in balloons, risked attacks of the bends going down into the caissons of the newly constructed Brooklyn Bridge, rode on elephants and went into the lion's cage at the circus. They ventured alone into the backwoods to report on moonshiners and even camped out in haunted houses watching for ghosts.

Some subjected themselves to mesmerists. Others even sought 'treatment' at the rough hands of back-street abortionists in an attempt to expose their rackets. One young girl reporter, arriving for her first day on a Utah newspaper, volunteered to report on an execution, the paper's male reporter being too dead drunk to handle the story. In the all-out war to win precious scoops they regularly put their lives at risk. The competition between them became so fierce that one cynical newspaperman alleged they would even 'sell their honour for a column of newspaper matter'.

But Nellie Bly set standards that few could follow. In early 1890 she capped her madhouse story with one of most glamorous newspaper stunts of all time, beating Phileas Fogg's fictional voyage created by

Jules Verne in *Around the World in 80 Days*. She completed the journey in seventy-two days, filing exciting reports every step of the way.

During the vicious newspaper wars sparked by the rise of the American 'yellow press' of the 1890s, Bly found herself up against an equally determined rival in Winifred Black (aka Annie Laurie), the star reporter of William Randolph Hearst's San Francisco *Examiner*.

Black's biggest coup came when she disguised herself as a boy to investigate conditions in the city of Galveston, Texas, closed down after a freak hurricane in 1900 had killed 7,000 people there. The presses soon rolled, bannering the portentous tones of Black's lead story: 'Corpse-Laden Waters Lit by Funeral Pyres: Winifred Black Crosses the Dismal Bay of Death to the Desolate City of Disaster'. The kind of headline guaranteed to sell thousands of extra copies of Hearst newspapers.

But the life of an American newspaper girl was a short one: disillusion and burn-out set in quickly for many. The long hours, exhaustion and danger to which they constantly exposed themselves took a heavy toll. Personal relationships and marriages rarely survived the strain, or were simply rejected – a pragmatic choice on the part of many of these ambitious young women who from the outset had consciously rejected the domestic sphere.

Black's two marriages failed and the light went out of Nellie Bly's reporting the day she married in 1895 and became embroiled in her husband's business ventures. Nell Nelson briefly enjoyed a reporting career in New York until the early 1890s, but her star rose and fell all too soon. Although her articles about the Chicago sweatshops were published in book form in 1888 as *The White Slave Girls of Chicago – By One of Them*, this powerful and provocative piece of early investigative journalism today is virtually unobtainable.

We would like to think that the work of Nelson and her long-forgotten contemporaries has a new lease of life in the character of Emily Strauss. Their vivid reporting gave colour to the backdrop of *City of Dark Hearts* while Emily herself has inherited their steely determination. She will live on to chase other stories guided by Nellie Bly's own mantra: 'Determine Right. Decide Fast. Apply energy. Act with Conviction. Fight to the Finish. Accept the Consequences. Move on.'

It's only fitting that Joseph Pulitzer, the man who gave Nellie Bly her first big break, should have given his name to one of the greatest prizes in journalism.

© William Horwood and Helen Rappaport
26 March 2007